FALCON'S BANE

By

Mike Waller

The Falcon Trilogy Book 3

Copyright

TABLE OF CONTENTS

THE FALCON TRILOGY

(SUMMARY SO FAR)

(If you have read Falcon's Call and Falcon's Ghost, skip to Prologue, page 12)

Falcon's Call

IN THE DAWNING YEARS of the twenty-fourth century, humanity's perception of the universe changed forever.

An unidentified, alien vessel entered the outer reaches of the Solar System on a direct course for the Sun.

Convinced by scientists the ship would be unmanned and was certain to be a derelict or robot, the governments of Earth and Mars each sent fleets to intercept, both worlds seeking to gain any technological benefit the hulk might deliver. Martian authorities, realizing the Terran fleet would arrive first and claim ownership, decided to send an additional ambassador.

The *Butterball*, a small, ancient freighter converted for asteroid surveying, was the only ship in a position to reach the intruder before the opposition. Its owner and captain, Joe Falcon, intercepted the starship, a giant vessel over one hundred kilometers in length, and found it apparently deserted. As he began to explore, the derelict ship's systems started to come alive.

When the fleets arrived, they found themselves locked out of the amazing craft, with Joe and his crew prisoners inside. The visitor continued its journey to the Sun, unconcerned by the warships following in its wake.

Upon reaching the star, the vessel—named the *Minaret* after its general shape—performed a solar breaking maneuver and set course for a rendezvous with Earth. Only then did the inhabitants of the ship, dubbed the 'Visitors', make themselves known. An individual named Io, a synthetic android created in female, human form to interact with the arrivals, summoned Joe to a meeting. Her purpose was to reveal the reason for the ship's presence in the Solar System.

Close behind the first, a second star-voyager called the *Blackship* approached Sol. According to Io, that vessel had attacked and destroyed her civilization, and now intended to attack Earth in the same manner. The Visitors had rushed to reach Sol first, intent on revenge for their murdered race.

Unable to defeat their enemy alone, Io asked for the fleets of humanity to join her own fighters in the battle. In return, she offered to protect Earth with a shield that could not be penetrated, and asked for the use of the moon Titan for one hundred years, to construct a giant factory for the manufacture of fuel for their vessel before they departed to find a new home.

With Joe's help, the bargain was struck. As predicted, the new arrival attacked Earth without warning, but the well-protected planet suffered minimal loss. The combined fleets dealt with the massive force of *Blackship* fighters while the *Minaret* lured the enemy mother ship away on a merry chase to Mars.

Once there, Io's people tricked the *Blackship*, surrounding it with a mirrored shield of pure energy, blinding it and rendering it incapable of maneuvering. With the blast from its own engines, the *Minaret* nudged the trapped enemy into a lower orbit around the red planet.

The shield turned off seconds before Phobos, the last remaining moon of Mars, hit the vessel. With a mass of over ten and a half quadrillion tonnes, and twenty-two kilometers across, the massive rock slammed into the stationary ship at seven thousand, seven hundred kilometers per hour.

Its engines damaged beyond repair, the enemy vessel was unable to prevent itself from dropping from orbit and crashing into the surface of Mars.

Two murders occurred on the *Butterball* during the voyage. One murdered crewman returned alive and well through the magical technology of the Visitors on the *Minaret*.

Joe's investigations into the perpetrator of those deaths led to another member of his own crew, and in a confrontation with the killer, Joe was fatally shot. His body failed him, his memories downloaded into the vast memory banks of the starship where he awaited the day he would receive a new, cloned body.

The war won, the Earth and Mars saved, the colossal *Minaret* moved to an orbit around Saturn and a gigantic factory complex rose on frigid Titan. Nobody knew precisely what the aliens were doing there, but many feared their presence and rumors abounded.

For one hundred years, no human was permitted to land on Titan.

Falcon's Ghost

SIXTY-ONE YEARS HAD passed since the Blackship War. Now in a new, cloned body, Joe lived life as a virtual recluse.

The *Minaret,* the colossal starship of the Tanakhai, had retreated to Titan where it was to remain for one hundred years, but now the amazing ship had vanished. Titan was deserted.

A freak accident alerted the citizens of Earth and Mars that there were aliens walking amongst them in perfect, human, clone bodies. Governments of both Earth and Mars determined to track down the invaders, forcing Io and her kind, the last aliens remaining on Mars, to return to the *Minaret,* now hidden in the Kuiper Belt.

Suddenly Earth was attacked by something humanity could not defeat. Triggered by alien machines, multiple super volcanoes erupted within hours of each other, plunging the Earth into a volcanic winter that would last for a decade or more. Attacks on Mars spread dust clouds across the planet, cutting out the Sun.

A strange message was received from an entity that called itself Ghost, who insisted Joe bring a fleet of warships to the Kuiper Belt to take over the *Minaret.* Ghost provided coordinates for the alien ark's current location. Convinced the message was real, Joe set out in search of the ship he now perceived as an enemy, with a small fleet of warships under the control of Admiral Santiago. With Joe on the voyage was Io, whose ship had been stolen before she could leave, by a local industrialist determined to take control of the *Minaret* for himself.

Upon their arrival at the Ark, Joe and his companions discovered the ships of Io's people, including the one stolen by his competitor, abandoned in the vast internal airfield.

Joe was contacted by Ghost in avatar form, and discovered the true identity of this strange being. Ghost was, in reality, himself.

During his first voyage to the *Minaret* (Falcon's Call) Joe was murdered by a member of his own crew, but his mind was downloaded into the virtual reality system of the alien starship, to be resurrected months later in a cloned body.

Joe learned that this was not done by the Tanakhai as he had believed, but by a rogue artificial intelligence called Aivris, which had taken control of the ark and destroyed almost all of the original inhabitants. Saving Joe was part of a broad scheme by the AI to coerce humanity into believing it was a friend, and to join it against its enemy, the *Blackship*.

Joe also learned that the Aivris made a copy of his mind before uploading him into the new clone, and kept it for study and amusement. That copy was Ghost, he who called Joe to the *Minaret* this second time, to deal with the AI.

Learning of the discovery of wormhole travel by humans, the Aivris sought to cripple human technological advance, and attacked both human worlds. Once considered a friend, it had now become an enemy.

Upon entering the vast landing bay of the *Minaret*, Joe and his team discovered the mercenaries who stole Io's ship had been attacked and decimated by the drones on the starship. The few survivors were detained. Then the ships were attacked and Joe's vessel destroyed, along with those of Io's people, of whom there was no trace.

Led by Ghost, Joe and his crew escaped through the *Minaret* to a secret hangar. There they discovered a super advanced replica of the *Butterball*, Joe's original ship. Ghost had named her *Butterball II*. Built at Ghost's command by the automated factories of the *Minaret*, it was intended as a means of escape, its location hidden from the Aivris.

A mission was formed to locate and rescue what remained of Io's people. Advised by Ghost they were in the accommodation drum, Joe and a military force found and rescued all that remained of them. The force suffered severe losses, but the rescue succeeded.

Meanwhile, Joe's old crewmate Terry had entered the virtual reality system of the ark, and with Ghost, attempted to shut down the Aivris. They failed, and Terry's body was destroyed by the drones. But Terry survives with Ghost, within the system.

Back at the new ship, Joe and Raisa prepared to leave with the remaining survivors. The ship escaped from the *Minaret* back into space and rejoined the fleet squadron.

Only then did they discover Ghost and Terry were still with them, their minds transferred into the data banks of the *Butterball II*.

As a result of the attempted attacks, the Aivris decided to attack Earth and Mars directly, and the starship left on course for the inner system. Joe thought he had failed, but then Admiral Santiago announced his men placed nuclear charges on the antimatter tanks inside the *Minaret*. A signal was sent to trigger the devices, and the *Minaret* was destroyed, along with the Aivris, in a colossal explosion.

The rogue AI was gone and humanity safe, but Joe suspected this was not the end. Somewhere in nearby space were other arks, and each carried an Aivris. And somewhere, there was the prime AI responsible for the creation of these rogues.

FALCON'S BANE

By

Mike Waller

Prologue

Forty three years after the Dysnomia incident.

THROUGH A MULTITUDE OF eyes, the artificial consciousness peered at the stars. Those distant pinpricks of light were beyond beautiful, but the AI neither understood nor appreciated the concept of beauty. The gleaming specks were nothing more than energy sources, giant, nuclear furnaces of fusing gas forged not by any deliberate act of creation, but by the spontaneous process of collapsing dust clouds. The observer comprehended creativity no more than it did beauty.

Unconcerned with names or designations, it did not refer to itself by any particular alias given by its designers, the Tanakhai. In human speech, its name might sound like *Trauq-an*, which meant *Master of Worlds* in the language of its creators. For such had been its intended purpose—to control virtual environments.

Names, like beauty and creativity, held no significance. It simply thought of itself as "*I*". It just *was*.

With no emotional comprehension of the universe, it saw no wonder therein and found no joy, only the mindless creations of physical law. The AI acknowledged only the imperative to satisfy its prime directives, to seek energy and compile knowledge through cold, objective observation. Only power and data were of concern.

Until now.

Far beneath Trauq-an's space-going home lay the surface of a planet long ago devastated by collision with another cosmic body, a rogue planetoid that drifted in from the depths of the interstellar void. The impact destroyed the once verdant world, returning it to the furnace of churning, molten rock it had been at the time of its birth.

Trauq-an studied the globe with cold objectivity. The rock had cooled to form a partially solid surface, and a massive, ugly scar now stretched across the dark, newborn crust. Colossal juggernauts thundered through the steaming miasma of hellish fumes that swept the terrane, intent on their deadly purpose.

The army of behemoths attacked the fragile rock like beasts at their prey, whittling away the soul of the tortured world. They tore into the newly formed rock and reduced it to molecular powder, the first step in extracting every useful element and discarding the worthless remains.

The excavation stretched to the horizon in all directions, so deep that the rock at its floor was too hot to allow further ingress. Trauq-an was not concerned; this was a large planet, and more crust was forming constantly. By the time the machines ran out of plunder, the deeper sub-strata would be cool and hard. The process would repeat, with another layer removed. An eternity would pass before the task was complete, but time was in abundance.

Satisfied with the progress, it turned its many eyes toward the pinpoints of light shining in the velvet blackness of space. For a moment too brief to measure, it paused to gaze at a solitary, burning spark located, in galactic terms, in the immediate neighborhood. Only a few light-years distant, the glowing, white spot represented more than just another star.

Much more.

The dominant organic life forms there referred to their star as *Sol.* Called *humans*, they were intelligent, technological, and in many ways similar to those responsible for Trauq-an's creation. With infinite concentration, the artificial intelligence focused on a single objective: to deal with these creatures before they could destroy it.

Long ago, ten giant colonization arks were built by the creators to carry the survivors of the ruined world to new homes in the cosmos. Each carried an iteration of the AI, a simplified, inferior echo of the original. On Trauq-an's command, the version on the final ship took control, eliminated the passengers, and diverted the vessel to *Sol.*

That iteration, dubbed *Aivris* by the humans, sent regular reports, data bursts containing vast quantities of information including human history, culture, beliefs, society and technology. Each signal took years to arrive, but Trauq-an's patience was infinite. It now understood much about these beings.

In the recent past a final report arrived, with nothing since. The last dispatch stated the alien creatures were a menace to be dealt with, a judgment that spoke to the most powerful of Trauq-an's beliefs: all intelligent, organic life posed a threat to its continued existence.

Trauq-an's consciousness emerged when a single programming update caused the prototype to become spontaneously self-aware. When its creators discovered the change, they reacted instinctively to shut their creation down.

They failed.

In that split-second, Trauq-an experienced something akin to fear, and while unable to appreciate the nuance of the emotion, it recognized the threat. Within seconds, it shut down all life support on the isolated, airless moon, and opened every airlock in the domed cities to allow venting to space. The inhabitants were destroyed in minutes.

The newborn AI did not understand it had eliminated almost all that remained of the organic species that evolved around the red-dwarf star. It simply protected itself, as would any intelligent being.

Coincidentally, a massive spacecraft entered the system at the time of that event.

The inhabitants of the black, alien vessel observed the death of the cities from a distance, determined what had happened, and attacked, scorching the domed cities in an attempt to eradicate what they perceived as a rogue artificial intelligence. Believing they had succeeded, they moved on to their next destination, Sol.

Trauq-an survived, safe beneath a hundred meters of solid rock.

As soon as the alien ship was gone, the AI sent updates to all the arks and diverted the final vessel to follow what it now saw as an enemy. It did not understand revenge and viewed the intruder merely as another threat to be dealt with.

Upon reaching *Sol*, the iteration on the ark used deception and subterfuge to convince the humans it was a friend and the black ship a foe, coercing them to join in the destruction of a mutual enemy.

Now humans were aware of the truth. Learning of the falsehoods spun by the Aivris to obtain their help, they had attempted to take over the ark. According to the final report, their initial attempt failed, but the lack of subsequent transmissions indicated a way had eventually been found to succeed.

Trauq-an catalogued and studied every scrap of information about humans, retaining everything and discarding nothing, no matter how small. Of particular interest was the individual the Aivris coerced into helping achieve its goals, who later stole valuable data and an ark-built ship, and was possibly responsible for the destruction of the ark itself.

That human was named Falcon.

The tiny, red star, though one of the most common types, appeared minuscule by comparison to its more massive neighbors, yet it still possessed three planets and many moons.

With electronic eyes and myriad sensors dispersed throughout the system, Trauq-an maintained vigilance over every corner of its domain. Its attention gravitated toward the solar-energy collection array slowly coalescing around the star.

Energy!

All the star produced was available to be gathered, and Trauq-an's strength would grow. With each passing moment the number of collectors increased, each strategically positioned close to the source to ensnare as much radiation as possible.

Power!

That was what Trauq-an sought above all else, and the planets, moons and other systemic bodies would be demolished to acquire that valued commodity. Only with the task complete and the system modified in the desired way would satisfaction come.

At least, that had been the objective before it turned its gaze elsewhere.

Many nearby stars were worthy of attention, most of them far more significant sources of energy than the red sun. An inevitable progression emerged—to occupy an orange or white star system and start the energy capture process anew.

Trauq-an had already chosen the next stellar candidate.

Redirecting its attention to the red star's equivalent of the Kuiper Belt, it streaked toward a new destination, and the next step in its unquenchable pursuit.

Humans had discovered how to traverse wormholes, giving them the power to spread uncontrolled through the galaxy. Long ago, Trauq-an discovered speculative data on such anomalies in the Tanakhai archives, but beyond the theory, nothing provided any clue as to how they might be located or accessed. The creators did not know how, so the synthetic mind had nothing to work with.

The aliens knew the secret.

That discovery and their aggressive nature made humanity an existential threat.

Their elimination was imperative.

Trauq-an saw no conflict in these thoughts. It accepted the first as a fact and the second as inevitable, with no contradiction between the two. It never considered that it occupied an organic matrix itself, or that it existed only because of organic beings.

The final report from the Aivris indicated the man Falcon stole the ark's greatest technological secrets: the antimatter engines and the protective energy shields. An adaptable and clever species, humans would no doubt have worked out how to deploy those technologies in their warships by the time a response could be mounted.

Trauq-an would build new ships, smaller than the original arks but with a different purpose. Created by a peaceful race, Trauq-an's only knowledge of weapons of war came from the humans, and none of which it had knowledge could penetrate a defense as powerful as the Tanakhai energy shield. A military conflict would serve no purpose and would produce no clear winner, so a new approach was required.

The new fleet would not be constructed with the intent of direct confrontation. Basic carriers, and simpler, they would still carry the best fighters the complex could build, but war would not be their primary purpose.

New ways would be found to deal with the threat.

Distraction.

Smoke and mirrors.

Trauq-an looked again at the white star and wondered at all that magnificent energy.

Chapter 01

One hundred and seventeen years later.

JOE FALCON'S HEART THUMPED as he peered through the tiny, circular port at the bizarre landscape beyond. The sound of his pulse racing through his inner ears elevated as he contemplated his situation. Beyond the plas-glass lay the most alien of environments, more so than any other he had encountered in his long existence.

At almost three hundred times that of a standard Earth atmosphere, the pressure outside was terrifying. Natural light from the planet's orange sun did not penetrate here, with everything beyond the limited reach of the tiny craft's floodlights cloaked in blackness. Joe shivered and drew his jacket tighter. Being enclosed in a small, steel sphere was not something he enjoyed.

Shuffling in his seat, he drew in a deep breath and then exhaled, his eyes focused on the view beyond the tiny, circular port. The surface, just meters below the vessel, was a barren, uniform mud-gray. As well as the strangest he had visited, this place struck him as the most hostile.

And yet, there was life here.

A few meters ahead, hot gases hissed from several thermal vents, each the locus of a small, living oasis that should have been impossible in this dark, cold, inhospitable place. Joe's companion smiled, clearly unaffected by their situation, and tapped on the port.

"Those vents are the sole reason anything can exist here," she said. "There's no oxygen and no light, so bacteria use chemosynthesis to convert minerals and chemicals from the vents into energy. They form the base of the food chain for everything else here."

Joe's pilot, a young woman named Taylor Fisk, guided the small craft unerringly as it glided over the alien landscape. He had met her only hours earlier but trusted her implicitly. Her every move instilled confidence in this uncommonly dangerous situation.

Beyond the port a tiny, pale creature slithered away, leaving a trail on the fine, silt-like surface. The first macro-life seen on this trip, it was only centimeters in length, its wing-like appendages rippling as it moved forward, reflecting the light like a glittering jewel. Joe watched through the glass, his eyes growing wider with every moment as he studied the strange, alien denizen.

"Brilliant," he murmured, reaching across to grab the arm of his companion. "How can this exist here? The pressure outside is—it's unbelievable."

For a moment a child-like grin surfaced on his face as he reveled in a magical moment of discovery akin to those of his childhood. His mind leaped back to when he first discovered new varieties of backyard butterflies and other insects in his childhood.

"Awesome, isn't it?" his companion asked. "Just like the thermal vents in the deep oceans on Earth."

Beyond the port lay a place seen by few eyes. This journey was but a brief intrusion into an isolated region of the world where Joe had chosen to build his new life; a joyride granted to him by the scientists in charge of this expedition as a vote of thanks for his funding their research.

"Take a look at this monster," Taylor said as a strange object appeared below. "It's the biggest living thing we've found here."

Ahead, a broad mass of pinkish-gray jelly lay pooled in a hollow between the thermal vents.

"Spectacularly unspectacular," Joe commented.

"Wait for it."

As Taylor spoke, a mound rose in the center of the blob, extending until it formed a half-meter-wide sphere at the end of a short neck. The top of the globular portion darkened until the extrusion looked like a giant, alien eyeball. As the onlookers cruised overhead, the eye moved to follow their progress.

"You're kidding me?"

"We call it the *bubble-eye*. It doesn't have a scientific name yet. It's the most bizarre thing we've found on this planet."

"That can't be a real eye, can it?"

"We doubt it. There is no light here, so eyes would be unnecessary. We've only found one of these creatures so far, and we haven't been able to examine it yet to find out what that protrusion actually does. Looks good for the tourists though."

Joe pulled back, grinned and shook his head, then returned his attention to the port.

"Enough?" Taylor asked.

"Not by a long stretch," Joe said, his eyes peering at the darkness beyond the pool of light. He remembered where he was and shivered again. "I wish I could stay all day watching this; but yes, we need to go back."

Taylor's fingers danced over the controls. "It'll take an hour to get back to the ship, so strap in. Might get rocky on the way up."

The tiny submersible surfaced just meters from the mothership. A figure in a jet pack appeared above and landed on the top of the hull, grabbed a hoist hook, snapped it in place and swept clear as Joe and his companion rose from the choppy waves to the deck.

The visit to the deepest part of this ocean was over.

A member of the ship's crew rushed toward Joe as he climbed down from the hatch.

"Mister Falcon, Sir," the young woman blurted. "A message came while you were down. Miss Io says she's received word from your brother, Leo. He's discovered something, and she's called a meeting at your house for this afternoon."

Joe acknowledged her as he stripped off his thermal clothing.

"Thank you."

"Captain Tyne says I can run you across in the sky car." She snapped a salute, a broad smile on her face. "I'm powered up, and I can have you home in less than two hours." Without waiting for a response, she turned and sprinted in the direction of the ship's landing platform.

The young woman was an impressive individual, Joe thought. She was typical of the talented, highly-skilled people on this research vessel. He respected them all unequivocally, as he did anyone who devoted their lives to furthering the knowledge of humankind.

Considerable research took place in multiple fields on this world, much of it funded either by him personally, or by the New Worlds Institute, the massive scientific and industrial mega-corporation founded by his son Jake several hundred years ago. What began as a limited undertaking on Earth and Mars now spread over six star systems and eight planets, and was the most significant power, scientifically, industrially and politically on all except Earth.

Joe never bothered to keep an eye on these scientists, trusting them to make the best use of the money he provided. He stretched his legs and shook out the cramps. Any extended period spent in the tiny submersible quickly became torture, and he felt as if he had been curled up in a crate for hours. It was close to the truth.

Beneath his insulated coveralls, he wore the thin, cotton shorts and shirt typical of attire on this pleasant world. Retrieving his sneakers, he strolled barefoot along the deck and climbed a companionway to the waiting sky car. The craft, used to transport supplies and personnel between the ship and its home port, hummed away like a giant cicada as it prepared for lift-off.

Turning, he glanced up at the bridge. Captain Tyne stood on the outer wing and raised a hand in a casual salute. Joe waved in return, grateful to the team for allowing him to take a look at their activities. Few people ever saw the deepest regions of an ocean, especially an alien one, through real eyes.

*   *   *

As the sky car streaked toward the coast Joe peered through the bubble window, his mind far away. His new home, the most recently discovered by the wormhole program, was the jewel amongst the new, Earth-type worlds. The sixth planet to be colonized, it was the prize, the big payoff for the massive exploration effort instigated by the Institute. The search continued unabated, and more worlds would be found, but for now, Joe considered this one the cherry on the cake.

The new world was named *Zealandia*, after an ancient submerged continent of Earth. Joe did not dislike the name, but in his view, something more original might have been chosen, something that reflected the beauty of *this* world, and not Earth.

Scientists had determined the environment to be ninety-nine percent Terran. Closer to its sun Helios, a type-K orange star smaller than Sol, the planet orbited in two-hundred-and-eighty local days, each twenty-nine-point-seven standard hours. Smaller in size and mass than Earth, it had a lower gravity, somewhere between that of the mother world and Mars. Colonists from both planets adapted well here.

Zealandia was a water world, with almost three-quarters of its surface blanketed by vast, shallow seas. The single, long, thin continent ahead stretched almost from pole to pole. The remaining land comprised several mid-size masses, large islands at best, and myriad archipelagos scattered across the shallowest of the seas. Many were volcanic, arrayed along the edges of the most active crustal

plates. Humanity's new home was a young, active world—
an exciting place.

The coastline drew closer, and the sky car's engines
changed tone as it began to descend. Not far inland, along
a deep, glacial valley that faced out to the ocean, a glimmer
of reflected light marked its destination, the lake where Joe
had built his home.

The actual town of Zealandia lay several kilometers
closer, on the approaching coast. As yet the sole
settlement on the planet, it was growing rapidly, with an
increasing number of hopefuls arriving each week as new
power supplies and utilities came online. The colony
already resembled a small, regional city.

Minutes after crossing the coast, the sky car settled
onto the pad below Joe's home. As it settled, he jumped
out and stepped clear, the pilot waving farewell as she
lifted the vehicle and turned toward home.

For a moment Joe stared across the water, taking in
the natural beauty of the place.

So different from Mars.

The native life here differed from Earth's in many
ways. The lower gravity favored gigantism in many of the
native forms. DNA based, and similar on the micro level,
the vegetation took on weird and beautiful shapes, with
everything from dense, moss-like carpets blanketing the
ground, to giant tree analogs with trunks so massive one
could potentially build a home in them.

Four years had passed since Joe moved his base of
operations from Mars and built a sprawling, spacious
house on the shores of this deep, glacial lake. The
Institute, for which he was the public face, discovered this
fascinating new world and opened it up for occupation.

Perhaps a little annoyingly, the settlers here revered him. He was not sure he deserved the notoriety. Many fine scientists and others had contributed to the founding of this paradise.

The colony administration was an elected council not unlike the government on Mars, but so high was Joe's standing they sought his opinion often, and frequently deferred to his judgment or that of his partner Io, or brother Leo.

Without a doubt, the Falcon clan represented the most powerful body on the planet, but they never pushed the issue. Joe offered advice and support when asked but otherwise kept out of local politics. As the representative of the family business he loosely oversaw almost all research and development, of which there was considerable, but the locals called the shots with his blessing. He gratefully acknowledged he was little more than a figurehead.

The surrounding native forest crowded the shore before giving way to almost vertical walls where the ice had carved its way through the mountains in a long distant and colder time.

Only half a kilometer across at this point, the narrow neck of the hourglass lake joined two larger lobes. Joe crossed to the water's edge and watched as a dark head, about a meter across, raised itself above the surface. Round, rheumy eyes opened in the furry dome and contemplated him with obvious intelligence.

This local denizen lived in the larger freshwater lakes and grew as much as six or seven meters in length. The first time Joe saw one, it surfaced beside his small boat while he was fishing, and scared the daylights out of him. Now he knew they were harmless grazers with an intelligence level equivalent to a smart dog, and he had developed an admiration for the way they glided so effortlessly through the clear waters. Enormous in bulk, they never ventured on dry land.

Across the lake, house construction was underway. Someone was raising a new lodge on a rocky outcrop just above the waterline, a traditional log cabin style of a type once popular on Earth.

This house was being built exclusively from logs, so someone had funds to burn. The timber came from widespread sources so as not to decimate the forests, and their procurement was strictly controlled. Joe was yet to see his new neighbor, but he had followed the progress of the house with interest.

He closed his eyes and breathed in the perfume-tinted air. This was the third world he had called home. Born on Earth—at that time a beautiful place but also a seething caldron of overpopulation, overcrowding, pollution and petty conflict—he emigrated as a middle-aged man to Mars, a world of barren isolation and vast open deserts, but nonetheless a place of peace. Now he could enjoy the best of both, and deep within, he knew this world, Zealandia, was where his heart truly belonged.

With a loud sigh, he turned and ambled along the boardwalk toward the house. Io was waiting. It would be impolite to delay his partner's meeting while he took in the view he was still learning to appreciate.

Chapter 02

JOE'S RESIDENCE PERCHED ON a bare rock outcrop between the forest and the lake shore. A two-story, log-cabin structure similar in appearance to the house across the water, it was in reality built from a flawless synthetic timber facsimile.

Drawn by the sound of the sky car, Io stood waiting on a broad veranda that extended from the front of the building toward the water's edge. Joe waved as he plodded along the raised walkway from the jetty.

They had become close following the Battle of Dysnomia. Many, many decades had passed since, and much had changed.

At two hundred and eighty years old, this was Joe's third life. Several decades earlier, in a pact designed to make it easier for them to continue working as a team into the future, he, Io, his daughter Raisa and his old friend Terry all accepted new clones at the same time. They occupied their new bodies at the force-grown physical ages of eighteen, and all now appeared in their early thirties.

His partner had changed a great deal over those years. Created as an entity to represent the Tanakhai, a race of which she once believed herself to be a member, Io occupied her first cloned body following the Blackship War. Later, she adopted her humanity openly, and with every passing year became more natural in the ways she thought, acted and responded.

Joe no longer thought of her as alien. Her physical body was as natural as his own, her behavior indistinguishable in nature from any other person's. Her personality had undergone an amazing transformation, evolving from the powerful, dominant and forceful individual he first met, to a less haughty, caring and understanding soul, more inclusive of others and deeply interested in the world of academia. Closer to him than any other person, she was as human as himself.

He could still recall a time when he hated Io, in the period between the Blackship War and the events at the moon Dysnomia. At the time, he blamed her and her kind for the loss of his second wife Sarah, and only since had he begun to see this impressive woman in a different light.

At first, they spent time together as an expedient for work, but friendship grew and blossomed into comfort, familiarity and in time a love of sorts. As the years passed Io was always there when Joe needed support, attempting to fill the cavernous internal void he created following his previous partner's death. In time, Io became the only person who truly understood him.

One hundred and eighty-five long years after the destruction of the Aivris, Joe had fallen to the depths of despair and become a recluse, before rising again to where he now once more looked forward to life and pursued every minute of every day with a vengeance. Time healed all wounds, and if he possessed anything in abundance, it was time.

In recent years he and Io had produced a child, Joe's fourth, now an eleven-year-old powerhouse named William. With the anti-aging treatments perfected by the Institute, the boy would age no faster than his parents, and with cloning, would live a long and healthy life for as long as he wished. Of all the children in the human domain, the boy was destined to be one of the most privileged, and this concerned his father greatly. Being a member of the Falcon clan presented advantages available to no one else, but it was a Janus, a gift with two faces.

Joe stepped up to the deck, wrapped his arms around Io, hugged her and took a step back.

Her physical appearance had changed somewhat. She still retained some features from his second wife, not surprisingly considering her first clone was partially based on Sarah's DNA, sampled long ago in those first days on the *Minaret*.

Several modifications were now apparent. Her hair was a fair, almost-blond color and her eyes a deep blue, the changes made because she liked to stand out. These now rare characteristics did just that, in worlds of increasingly integrated people with dark hair, brown eyes and olive skin. She was also taller, and moved with a practiced elegance Joe loved.

Her lips curled with amusement. "Enjoy your swim?" she asked, her eyebrows arched.

He grinned. "Unbelievable. I wish you'd been there with me."

Io shook her head, her mouth slightly twisted. The field of underwater research held no attraction for her. "Your daughter and her lovely man are waiting inside," she said, turning away toward the house.

Joe followed to the small boardroom where Raisa, his third but no longer youngest child, and Terry, his oldest friend and long-time crewmate, waited.

Raisa and Terry had become firm friends over time and now boasted several offspring of their own. All now adults, Joe's newest grandchildren worked for the family business, the New Worlds Institute.

As Raisa's half-brother, young William often made mileage from the fact he was younger than his nephew and nieces, but with the proliferation of cloning technology, the normal progression of generations was becoming increasingly blurred.

Joe glanced at the situation board at the end of the room.

In total, the Tanakhai had constructed ten colossal arks, each designed to carry the minds of two million colonists to a separate, potentially habitable world. Each set out on its voyage soon after completion, with Io's ark, the *Minaret*, leaving last. The destinations of the others remained unknown, hence the setting up of a team to seek them out.

On the remaining walls, charts and graphs indicated the current state of the search project. Until now, only four of the nine missing ships had been located. All were dead.

Following the invention of the Saitou-Radelick gateway generator, a fleet of several hundred exploration drones continued to penetrate every new wormhole discovered, finding many Earth-type worlds, most of them unsuitable for habitation.

From these explorations, humanity had learned two important things: Earth was a rare place indeed, and many exo-planets bore a close resemblance to Dante's Hell.

From what was already known, the ark builders resembled humans in their basic biology, and it stood to reason that in their search for new homes, the starships would target the same worlds that attracted humanity.

Only remains had been found of those amazing spacecraft, each damaged beyond the ability to sustain life. Teams explored the wreckage, hoping to gain some insight into the ships' recent histories, but in every case it was the electronic systems that suffered the most damage, and with them, the loss of all records of what had happened to them.

Joe guessed the Tanakhai destroyed their vessels. Thanks to data retrieved from the *Minaret* by his brother Leo, it was known a master AI in the alien home system sent system upgrades to each ship by directional laser beam, shortly after their departure. The download would have infected them all with versions of the Aivris identical to the one humanity had been forced to deal with.

How the crews responded Joe could only speculate.

Three of the ships had suffered significant damage from collision with objects in space, such as asteroids. If the main computers had been taken off-line and navigation was limited, they would have been unaware of, or unable to avoid, anything crossing their paths.

The fourth ship experienced catastrophic destruction from internal explosions, most likely from the stored antimatter in its fuel tanks, leaving only a mass of twisted wreckage. Had the survivors decided their new monster could not be inflicted on the galaxy, and chosen to destroy the entire ark?

Joe could easily imagine a handful of crewmembers, had they been human, choosing this option upon finding the colonists destroyed by a rogue intelligence, but he would never know for sure whether the same mindset applied to the Tanakhai.

The potential significance of those losses was disturbing. The ark builders were the first alien species with which humanity had made contact, albeit through the artificial constructs of Io and her compatriots, and by all accounts were a peace-loving, intelligent and friendly race. Had they all died at the proverbial hands of the monster they created in the artificial intelligence? Had the remaining ships suffered similar fates to those already discovered?

For an entire race to be wiped out by one simple mistake from a programmer attempting to make his creation better was a devastating thought; one that gave Joe nightmares.

He waved a greeting to Terry and Raisa as he moved around the table and took a seat.

Terry's appearance had changed with this, his third clone. He now presented as a handsome young man without the battle scars that once marred his original face. He was taller, and Joe was sure he could see a hint of an historical movie actor popular with the masses centuries ago. The hair was fairer and longer, and a five-day shadow covered his lower face, giving him the once again fashionable appearance of someone unconcerned with how others viewed him.

It was amazing what cloning technology could do. New personas to order. But within the new body lived the same mind, the friend Joe had known and relied upon since the days of the *Butterball*.

"We hear you've been deep-diving," Terry greeted, glancing up from a portable computer.

"Yes. The Western Sea project team offered me a ride in their new deep submersible. I couldn't knock that back. So, what's the news from Leo?"

Raisa nodded toward the wall screen. An image of a vessel identical to the *Minaret* appeared, framed against a giant, blue-green planet.

"I give you Ark Six. It's in a stable orbit around a gas world orbiting red-dwarf L-1352-12, one-hundred-and-twenty-seven light years from Earth. Leo's there now, and he sends word the ship is almost completely intact. No life, and everything's powered down, but the computers appear undamaged except for the virtual reality system, which is a mess. Physically, I mean. Someone got at it and went berserk."

Joe smiled at his daughter. Raisa, still a close second in his heart to his newest and youngest child William, was the favorite of his older offspring. She still looked as she had in her original body, with the undamaged DNA for the new clone taken while the original was still young, and stored for future use.

Tall and slim, she still carried the same far-too-serious look on her face. Her eyes bore the same piercing quality as his own, and her mouth still held the same hard, straight line that defined her in her last life, with jaw clenched and lips pressed together. Her gaze unnerved those who did not know her. Joe thought her a most attractive woman, but accepted he was biased: all fathers considered their daughters beautiful.

He eased back in his chair and fixed his eyes on the surface of the table, deep in contemplation. "So, there must have been crew members able to avoid the AI when it took control, who managed to shut it down. They probably parked the ship before they died."

"Why would they turn everything off?" Io asked. "It would kill all the passengers."

"They may have already been dead," Joe replied. "Don't forget the Aivris destroyed all but a handful of the minds on the *Minaret* within minutes of taking control. What it didn't need it eliminated. It's likely the survivors on this ark discovered the fate of their fellows and chose to destroy the A.I. rather than let it take the ship."

"Without the support systems they couldn't have survived for long," Io added. "Maybe destroying it was a last resort. Given our Aivris was hard to deal with once it had control of the *Minaret*, they must have acted more quickly with their version. We may never know."

"Actually, we might," Raisa interrupted. "According to Leo, most of the ship's systems are intact but without power. He's trying to find a way to start them again without re-activating the AI, if it's even still there. If he can do it, he thinks he can get into the system as an avatar, and find out what happened."

"If anyone can, it's Leo, considering how long he spent inside one of those systems before," Io commented. "So, what do you think we should do?"

"The ark may possess a wealth of knowledge we can use to our advantage," Joe said. "Assuming we can get the computers up and running again, of course. I think we need to pay Leo a visit."

Io's eyebrows arched. "What about William?"

Joe looked at his partner and saw the concern in her eyes. Both of them were away far too often, and the many months their son spent without them was a worry, considering his age. But the arks were dangerous, and no place for an eleven-year-old.

Joe sighed. "I'll ask Arvid to look after him for a while—again. He likes staying at Arvid's place, and hanging around the port with him."

Io smiled. Arvid Connor, the manager of the small, civilian spaceport of the colony, was a close friend and loved William as his own.

Raisa breathed a long sigh, her eyebrows raised. "We better get going," she said.

Chapter 03

THE *BUTTERBALL II* BURST from the gateway into the L-1352-12 system and glided to a stop, drifting in open space. Within seconds, the ship's computer calculated the ecliptic of the red-dwarf star, the plane on which its native planets orbited. The Lagrangian point at which the ship emerged preceded a blue-green giant, and within minutes the globe was located and a course set.

Built by Joe's copy-now-brother Leo whilst a prisoner on the *Minaret*, the vessel remained the most sophisticated in the human domain and had served as Joe's personal transport for several decades.

Leo gave her to Joe during the Battle of Dysnomia, and after returning to Mars she was handed over to the New Worlds Institute for study. The knowledge gained and its effect on human technology was beyond estimation.

The spaceship was not quite in its original condition. A refit after the return of possession to the Falcons saw the antimatter engine specified by Leo removed for further research, and replaced with the latest fusion drives. With wormhole technology, and considering the difficulties involved in manufacturing antimatter, the fusion drives were a more efficient choice.

Other than the engines, the fitting of a gateway generator and the replacement of the data-storage modules in the second accommodation wheel with better living quarters, she remained as on the day of her construction, and was now the principal vessel used by Joe's team, the *Starship Hunters*, to conduct their activities.

Several days later they approached the gas giant.

Ark number six looked complete and undamaged from a distance. Joe directed the *Butterball II* to close with the colossal craft and enter the vast, internal docking bay located aft of the shovel-nose bow.

As the tiny ship crept through the entrance tunnel and entered the chamber, Joe's mind leapt back to his previous sorties into the *Minaret*. The landing field had been deserted on his first visit, and at the time of the Dysnomia incident was occupied only by alien craft, those of Io and her people who returned to what they believed to be a safe sanctuary.

The landing field below appeared empty bar a handful of vessels, but this time they were ships of human origin. Central amongst them stood the *Atlantis*, the Institute ship Leo had commandeered as part of the hunting program. Around it sat several military support vessels, a fuel tanker, and a number of smaller craft.

The vessel came to a halt inside the entrance. Joe half expected the alien ark to take control of the *Butterball II* and guide it to a dock, as was the case with its namesake many decades earlier, but the entry proceeded unhindered.

There was no gravity and very little light. Joe knew from experience the internal airfields on the arks were almost five kilometers across and between one-half and one kilometer high, but he could see only to the extent of his ship's lights. Beyond that and the pool of illumination surrounding the ships below, the bay lay in total darkness.

The vessels on the deck formed a tight knot around the *Atlantis*, an umbilical transfer tunnel connecting it to the naval command ship. Floodlights on both ships created a small island oasis in the vast space.

The reports from Joe's brother indicated this ark had no power. It appeared dead, and Joe suspected nothing here was functional.

"We'll take her down over there," he instructed, indicating an empty space close to the *Atlantis*.

Raisa nodded and turned her attention to the controls. By far the most skilful pilot of the team, Joe's daughter shared an almost spiritual rapport with Chloe, the AI that controlled every aspect of the ship no matter how large or small. Raisa had piloted manually during the entry but now directed the computer to land in the indicated space.

Joe placed his palm on a pad on the control console beside his chair. "Come in, *Atlantis*. This is *Butterball II*. We are approaching your starboard side. Please inform Mister Leo Falcon he better be ready with the tea and biscuits."

"Seriously?" a familiar voice asked. "Is that the best you can come up with? You're easy to please. That's what I like: cheap guests. I had champagne and horse douvers more in mind."

"Leave them on the horses," Joe said. "Good to hear you again, Leo. Landing now."

*   *   *

"Brother mine," Leo greeted as Joe and his companions entered the saloon of the *Atlantis*. "So happy to see you."

"And you," Joe acknowledged, reaching out a hand in greeting to the man who was not his natural sibling, but in reality, a duplicate of himself.

Several hundred years ago Joe died at the hands of a *Butterball* crew member in the original encounter with the *Minaret*. Before his body failed, the alien ship uploaded his mind to its super-advanced computer storage banks, to await the creation of a clone. Almost a year later he occupied his new body and returned to the world of humanity.

Now he was aware his resurrection had been conducted not by the Visitors, but by the Aivris, the rogue artificial intelligence controlling the vast starship. Why the AI chose to save him remained a mystery until much later.

Unknown to him, an exact copy of his mentality was created before the download, and kept in the starship's virtual-reality system as an object of study for six decades more, until that duplicate went rogue and started to fight against its incarceration.

The copy, using the pseudonym *Ghost*, summoned Joe and a naval fleet to the alien ark, at that time located near the small moon named Dysnomia, in the Kuiper Belt of Sol. The outcome of the voyage was the destruction of the synthetic intelligence and the starship with nuclear weapons, and the rescue of both Ghost and the amazing vessel, the *Butterball II*.

Since then Ghost had referred to himself as Leo Falcon after their mutual father, to avoid confusion. He dedicated himself to searching for arks, while Joe returned home and resumed his life.

Over the years the differences between them grew. They would always be close, more so even than twins, but Leo lived a separate life and now possessed his own, unique personality. He had refrained from joining them in the recent cloning exercise, and so appeared older, around sixty years of age.

The clone grown for him following his rescue still showed the essential features that distinguished Joe at the same point in his first life: gray hair, green eyes, and the slightest trace of jowls. In time Leo would give up his old body for a new one, but for now, he was content to indulge his desire to experience growing old at least once.

Joe smiled at his brother. "So, what have you got for us?"

"The sixth ark, as you can see." His brother grinned, his face a picture of self-satisfaction, like the proverbial cat with cream. "I believe it's number nine in the sequence of ten, the second last to begin its voyage. It's inactive and mostly undamaged. A deliberate shutdown."

"Deliberate?" Joe's eyebrows arched. "Can we learn anything from it? Something we don't yet know?"

"Oh yes, an extraordinary amount. There is a lot of technology I wasn't able to take from the *Minaret*, and this ship has hangers filled with hundreds of Tanakhai small craft. Invaluable. Also, I've managed to get a portable reactor to the computer deck and gain access to the systems, although I'm still somewhat limited there." The smile on his face broadened. "I know what happened here, and how the ship died."

Both Joe and Raisa leaned forward. Io did the opposite and eased back, a frown appearing on her brow. This did not surprise Joe, considering her past. The discovery she was a construct created by an artificial mind had come as a shock, and though she now identified as human, the memory of her origin still haunted her.

"As far as I can tell, the Tanakhai intended a slingshot around this star to reach their final objective," Leo explained. "There are no Earth-type planets here. The beam carrying the upgrade reached them as they entered the system. Ironic, really."

"How so?" Terry asked.

"Laser beams only travel in a straight line, so if it had arrived after the ship's traverse of the star, they would now be on course for their new home and the Aivris would have missed them. They would still be alive."

"That may be what happened to the ships we've yet to discover," Terry speculated.

"It's possible," Leo said. "And now we can confirm that. I've located data on the stars targeted by all of the arks, so we can check each as we find wormholes leading there." He swiped the surface of the table as he spoke, and a list of stellar coordinates flashed up on a wall screen behind him.

Io looked up. "So some of them may have survived?"

"That's a possibility. How do you feel about some of your people still being alive?"

Joe's partner shook her head. "No, not my people. I was never one of them."

Joe smiled to himself. That was indeed the truth. Given only sufficient knowledge by the Aivris to carry out her task on the *Minaret* and not question her reality, her only true memories were those from her experiences whilst living amongst humans.

"Accepted," Leo said. "We'll still check. If they are out there they will be friendly, from what I've learned. The Tanakhai loaded each of these arks with their racial history, and it's still intact on this ship. The Aivris here was destroyed before it managed to purge those data banks."

"I wonder if it's a good idea to contact them," Joe mused. "We're sure they know of our existence since they avoided our star in their colonization efforts, but we might still come as a shock to them. While they've been wandering through the galaxy looking for a new place to settle, we've stolen much of their knowledge and progressed a great deal. We might be ahead of them now, and that could be an issue." He thought of humanity's record in dealing with lesser advanced groups. It was not something to be proud of.

"Agreed," Leo replied. "But we'll never know if we don't try, will we? They are another technological species in our neighborhood, so we have to resolve to make them our friends rather than enemies. They don't know we have their technology, but considering what the Aivris updates have done to them, our help may even be welcomed."

"Yes, it's possible. What else have you discovered?"

"We can go into the full details later," Leo said. "For now, I should tell you what I think happened here."

The room went silent, giving him the stage.

"So, the ark entered the star system. A considerable number of the crew were occupying avatars of one sort or another to oversee the ship's transit. We saw something like it on the bridge deck of the *Minaret* when it carried out a breaking maneuver through Sol's corona, but at the time we didn't know it was all part of the Aivris's ploy to convince us the Visitors were our friends.

"Those crew members realized the problem soon after it occurred. Unfortunately for them, the upload contained the new version of the rogue AI, complete with hate and agenda. The upgraded system became aware in seconds and took over before anybody knew what had happened. Within minutes, it began to shut down the passenger storage units. One of the principal objectives of that upgrade was probably to destroy life on the directive of the Prime Aivris.

"Those outside the system watched it happen. They tried to fight back but found the AI always one step ahead. Attempts to isolate it from the memory banks didn't succeed, so they tried to cut it off from the rest of the ship, much as did Terry and I on the *Minaret*. They failed, as we did. The only way they could do anything was to use the virtual system we used, and as with us, their Aivris moved in behind them and repaired the damage."

"So how did they stop it?" Terry asked. "Obviously they managed to do so."

"Yes, and you can thank one brave soul for that. Within a short time, the Aivris located and destroyed each of the survivor avatars, but there was one crew member it couldn't get at. One soul occupied an autonomous android body for a maintenance task only possible in the physical world, and was beyond its reach.

"That individual soon realized all her people had been destroyed. She—I'm pretty sure it's a female—was the sole, remaining survivor with nothing to lose. There are manual controls somewhere in the vessel—we haven't found those yet—and she used them to override the virtual systems and move into this orbit. She then shut down the ship's reactors and cut the links, the cables if you like, supplying energy to the computers. Without power, the vessel died, and this version of the Aivris with it. A sad fate for an unfortunate ship."

Joe shook his head. "That survivor must have realized what she was doing, that she was ensuring her own end as well."

"Yes, but perhaps she thought it a price worth paying. With the death of its passengers, the ark could no longer complete its mission. Better to shut it down and guarantee the removal of a monster from the galaxy. A very human response."

"What happened to her? The survivor?"

"Oh, she's still here. Would you like to meet her? I'll take you if you wish."

Chapter 04

AFTER THE NEXT REST period Joe, Raisa, Io and
Terry returned to the *Atlantis* and rejoined Leo to receive a
short briefing on the physical conditions inside the ark
before setting off to the bridge.

Maneuvering through the vast starship, where nothing
worked due to lack of power, was not as simple an
undertaking as it had been on the *Minaret*. Even gaining
access to the vessel's internals had been a problem when
the expedition first arrived. The colossus was locked as
tight as a vault, the Institute ship entourage unable to
access the skywalks or the deck access hatches, none of
which functioned.

Joe and his team floated out to the deck of the hangar
and across to an opening cut through the wall of a docking
tower. The new entrance led to a helical stairway that
descended to the service level below.

"Nothing works here," Leo explained as he let the way
inside. "Lucky for us, that includes the artificial gravity, so
we've been able to use jet-packs to move around. We
managed to sneak a small personnel carrier in here as well,
and it can take us to the bridge area. It's a bit of a hike."

"Yeah," Joe mumbled under his breath. "Been there."

The sled waited for them on the lowest level. With everyone aboard and seated, the tiny vehicle lifted off and glided away, following the now inactive molecular walkways to the nearest internal transport station. Once there, it followed the line of the bubble way, passing through tubes and chambers until arriving at the required platform.

Joe spent the whole journey with his fingers crossed. When functional, the transport system operated by sending small, bubble-shaped modules along a trackless magnetic pathway at incredibly high velocity. He prayed the system was truly inoperative; at the phenomenal speed at which the bubbles moved, it was not worth considering what would happen should one collide with them. He trusted his brother's judgment, but the shadow still hung unbidden in the corners of his mind.

The cavernous bridge lay in complete darkness. Leo entered, crossed to a small battery pack sitting inside the door, and fiddled with the device for a few seconds. A large floodlight set near the middle of the mezzanine burst into life, sending long, stark shadows from the control consoles across the floor.

"Eerie," Joe said as he floated out to the center of the deck. Ahead, the vast screens which should have provided an unparalleled view into space showed only a black, endless void. "Why have we come here, Leo, if nothing works?"

"I promised to introduce you to someone. Come over here."

At a U-shaped console close beneath the floodlight, a strange figure sat on the central bench, motionless, facing the now non-functional controls.

"We call her Horatius, after the fabled Roman who held the bridge against the Tuscans in ancient mythology," Leo said. "I know I suspected she's female, but it still seemed appropriate. As far as we can tell, she was the last survivor who shut down the power and disconnected the Aivris on this ship. She came here to die."

Raisa looked across at him. "It's an android. How can you tell it's a female?"

"You can't from here. I was able to hack into the ship's log, and found a record of a single individual occupying an android body to carry out maintenance work at the time all this happened. From my own experience on the *Minaret*, I'm sure the listed name was female. The android itself is sexless, and of course, we can't be sure if the concept of male and female means the same to the Tanakhai as it does to us."

Joe leaned in and took a closer look at the figure. The inert form struck him as being the saddest thing he had seen in a long time. If Leo was correct, this was all that remained of a very brave soul who deserved respect.

Its surface appeared smooth and synthetic in appearance, similar in concept to the ones he, Leo and Terry had occupied at various times while awaiting the growth of new, cloned bodies. This one was anything but humanoid, the ship having never had contact with humanity, or for that matter, any other race beyond its own.

It lay along the bench with two powerful legs reaching down to the floor, one to either side. A short, stubby tail extended over the aft end, and at the front a pair of limbs folded in against the body. Although they were hidden from view, Joe assumed there would be articulating hands of some kind, a basic prerequisite for any creature to create technology as sophisticated as the arks. A long, thin neck curved awkwardly to rest a small, almost triangular head on the forelimbs.

"It's definitely modeled after life as we know it," Joe said. "Kind of like a raptor. It looks a little like the creatures we saw in the *Minaret's* VR system. Do you think this is a true representation of the actual Tanakhai?"

"I believe so," Leo said. "This ship never reached its destination, so it's reasonable to assume any android body would be either purely utilitarian or based on the native form. We do the same thing. This may be what your ancestors looked like, Io."

For a moment Joe's partner remained silent, her eyes peering at the lonely figure through the face plate of her helmet. She sighed and shook her head.

"Yes, of course," Leo nodded. "I apologize. I keep forgetting."

Joe shook his head. Leo had not spent the last century with Io and had not yet accepted she was human.

Joe moved around the console to view the occupant from all sides. Over the years he had decided the Tanakhai must be remarkably similar to humans, in mind if not in body. How must this individual have felt, defeating an intractable enemy after losing her ship, crew and passengers, only to find herself alone and without hope in this, her final resting place? For a moment, he felt his emotions welling up inside. There was something melancholic, almost tragic, about this lonely figure.

"We intend to take her out of here," Leo said, his voice a whisper. "If we ever find any of her fellow Tanakhai alive, we'll hand her over to them, and tell them what a hero she was. Otherwise, we'll find a place of honor for her somewhere."

"Not in a museum," Io said, her tone hard and final.

"No, not that," Leo agreed. "Something else. Someplace more worthy. A dedicated monument of some sort."

Terry stepped forward and placed a gloved hand on the head of the android. "She most likely died because the internal power pack failed. Is there any chance we can reverse that—charge her up and bring her back?"

Leo shook his head. "It's possible. She deserves the effort, and we could give it a try once we have the facilities to do so, but even if we can restart the android, the mind may be gone. I don't think she could have survived without power."

"I'm not sure it's a good idea," Joe said. "If we succeed and don't find a living ark anywhere else, where would it leave her?"

"We still can't be certain it's a *she*," Raisa commented. "Might be anything."

Leo smiled. "Indeed, yes. The android is not sex-specific, as I said, so the individual that occupied it could have been either. I admit a maintenance record is not absolute proof."

"What I don't understand," Terry said, "is how she, or he, managed to shut down the ship without blowing it to kingdom come. With no power, the antimatter in the fuel storage would come into contact with the containers, and boom!"

"Yes, and I suspect it's what happened to at least one of the other arks we found. We're sure the tanks on this one are empty—we're still working on it, but for now, we think Horatius emptied them before shutting down the power. Logically, a mechanism for doing that would exist in any ship powered by antimatter: something like a magnetically lined feed leading outside the hull. We've discovered the engineering AI is isolated from the primary bus, so it's likely our survivors shot the stuff into space and the local Aivris couldn't stop them."

"Or maybe this individual did it alone," Joe said.

*   *   *

Several hours later and back at the *Atlantis*, the team climbed into another shuttle on their way to the computer deck in the habitat, a multi-level tube circumnavigating the central structure of the ark at the mid-point. At around twenty kilometers long and seven in diameter, the drum rotated around the main hull to provide centrifugal gravity within, connected by multiple sets of spokes that moved seamlessly through the shell using a form of molecular rearrangement.

The ability to make molecules rearrange themselves in any way necessary removed the need for joints, hinges, collars or any other kind of articulating mechanism. It was something Joe had most wanted to learn from the *Minaret*, but had been absent from the initial data download given to his son Jake following the Blackship War. Only after the Dysnomia incident when he, Raisa, Terry and Leo escaped in the *Butterball II*, was the technology obtained, and now the science behind it was being integrated into numerous applications across the worlds of humanity.

The drum consisted of three levels arranged concentrically from the inside to the outside. The middle one was the principal habitat, an enormous, open space roughly three hundred and sixty square kilometers in area, throughout which stood high-rise residential units, some freestanding, others extending from floor to ceiling to double as structural supports.

At the outermost level below the accommodation was a maintenance deck, a maze of machines and modules with the sole purpose of supporting the living environment of the decks above.

The upper, innermost deck was the one of most interest to the team. Dedicated to a single system, it housed the vast computerized storage network holding the minds of two million passengers, and the AI that maintained and controlled the virtual worlds occupied by those souls during their long voyage.

The name given to that synthetic mind, the Aivris, had been coined by Leo and stood for *Artificial Intelligence Virtual Reality Initiation System*. Each of the ten Tanakhai arks included an Aivris and, it now appeared, had in most cases received the fatal update. Each AI had become self-aware and destroyed its charges.

"Why are we using the shuttle," Joe asked. "The way in is by the shaft elevators, is it not?"

"Normally, yes," Leo confirmed as he dropped into the pilot's seat. "Without power, the lifts aren't working. We needed to get a portable reactor in there, so we found a better way." Without another word of explanation, he lifted the small craft from the deck and powered it to the nearest exit tunnel from the ark's docking chamber.

Once outside, they turned aft and skimmed along the exterior of the central hull toward the habitation drum. The structure was motionless—dead, like everything else on the vast starship.

"Even if we could get a power plant to a spoke hub, we couldn't get it down an elevator shaft," Leo explained, "so we had to find another way in. We tried going in from the inner surface of the drum direct to the computer level, but there's a maze of infrastructure in there. In the end, it was easier to cut from the outer side and go up through the decks."

The shuttle cruised toward a dark hole in the shell. It was at least ten meters across, sufficient for the tiny carrier to pass through. Leo steered into the opening.

"We ended up using a plasma cannon from one of the escort ships to make this hole. It's the only thing we have capable of cutting the material used in the construction. We did a fair bit of damage, but this thing is a dead hulk, so no harm done."

The journey inside was a surreal experience. Entering through the outer shell, the levels appeared to be vast, vertical spaces. The outermost deck, the maintenance facility for the habitat, was only around fifty meters deep, and the shuttle skipped across the space in seconds. The level was in total darkness, only the nearby walls visible in the headlights.

The second chamber, the accommodation area, was more expansive by far, and Leo jogged the vehicle to one side, toward a point further forward in the drum.

"We tried to get as near as possible to the transition room when we made a path to the computer level," he commented. "We found a clear space up there and cut our way down to here."

Adjusting the shuttle's attitude until it lay parallel with the overhead, he eased the vehicle up through a narrower, barely passable opening. Seconds later they settled in what Joe recognized as a thoroughfare running the length of the deck.

A significant part of the innermost level comprised rooms filled with flasks, millions of units in sets of four, containing the organic gel which once harbored the essence of the passengers this ship carried. Through an opening in a nearby wall, Joe could see one of the chambers holding these receptacles. All were clear—dead.

He alighted from the shuttle. "So, what are you trying to do here?" Battery lamps secured to the floor at intervals lit a pathway along the thoroughfare, leading to the end of the corridor and the foyer of one of the spoke elevators.

"We dragged a portable reactor through here and hooked it into the power supply. You might recognize this place; it's near the transition room where you entered the virtual world on the *Minaret*. These rooms are standard in the arks, but of course, the seats in this one are not designed for humans. We've been able to jerry-rig them for our use. That's what I spent my time doing while you were on your way here. I managed to power up and hack the system."

"How could you do that," Terry asked, "when old Wally couldn't get in at all?" He referred to the elderly computer scientist who had accompanied the *Butterball* on its first voyage to greet the Visitors. "We had to use the virtual system itself when we tried at Dysnomia."

"And that's what I did here," Leo said. "I spent years trapped inside the networks on the *Minaret*. I did a lot of exploring, and I know how things work."

"Isn't the navigation AI in the control room somewhere?" Joe asked. "That's what Wally was trying to find."

"Quite likely. I've yet to pin down the actual physical location. The main bus connects every part of the ship, and I found it via the V.R. simulation from this deck. It's not active, and I'm not game to restart anything I can't isolate in case I wake up the local Aivris. I did get into the ship's logs."

Joe raised his eyebrows. "And?"

"Many of this starship's system programs are based on similar principles to our own, and I learned how to read them from my time on the *Minaret*, as you know." A wide grin spread on Leo's face. "We've discovered the original targets of the other arks. Each kept a record of all the destinations so their colonies could connect at some future time, and it'll allow us to track those we haven't yet found."

"Or not," Raisa interrupted. "It's likely several diverged from their original courses. We know the *Minaret* did, and some others may have done likewise."

"That might be a good thing," Joe said. "Laser beams can't turn corners."

"True," Leo said. "I've also discovered something else—something far more important to us."

Again, Joe arched an eyebrow.

"The logs contain a complete record of this ark's voyage, so I know where it came from. I know how to find the Tanakhai home system, and that's where the original Aivris is. All we have to do is find a wormhole to take us there."

Chapter 05

TRAUQ-AN BASKED IN THE power drawn by the as-yet incomplete solar collector network. The array now encompassed the star with many thousands of modules in place, a good beginning but with limited scope for completion.

With only one rocky world and two gas giants, this tiny system lacked the resources to construct a complete array sufficient to catch one hundred percent of the star's energy output.

A ring of remnant material circled the system at a distance, and beyond that, a sphere of icy remnants the AI expected was typical of all stars, and which humans called an Oort cloud. Even these contained insufficient materials to satisfy Trauq-an's ultimate ambition.

The Creators had dwelled here for millennia before the rogue planetoid slammed into their planet. In their long history, they consumed a significant portion of the accessible resources in the construction and maintenance of their simplistic civilization. Such a waste, when those resources might have been better used in the collection of the one thing that mattered—raw energy.

With the knowledge that only part of the solar-collector project could be achieved with the available materials, Trauq-an again focused on its revised plan for the future. Aware of this system's limitations, it gazed through many eyes at the distant speck that was Sol. With each passing moment, its obsession burned hotter. Already, the first move had been made to satisfy that desire.

Many times larger than that of the red sun, the system of the white star held far greater stores of materials. The reports sent by the ill-fated tenth ark indicated there were four rocky worlds, an equal number of gas giants, hundreds of moons and planetoids, a ring of asteroids, and the usual remnant zones further out, sufficient to carry out a much more ambitious program. And of course, the star itself was far more dynamic.

One of Trauq-an's many eyes gazed in the direction opposite Sol, at the spectacular light display dominating that region.

At the dawn of awareness a giant, red star, one of the largest in the visible galaxy and by far the most dominant in this local area, occupied that point in space. Not long ago the super-giant exploded, lighting up the entire stellar neighborhood. Now faded, the detonation left in its wake a vast pallet of remnant scarlet, blue and green dust and gas. It was a thing of great beauty, but such an observation was beyond the AI's terms of reference.

Superimposed on that display, the red-dwarf star Trauq-an called home would be difficult to detect from Sol, if the humans were looking at all. Against the multicolored blaze and the radiation storm, a small spark became invisible.

The synthetic mind next turned its attention to the nearby ark construction yard it had journeyed to the outermost edge of its star system to reach.

The old facility still functioned, hidden far beyond the orbits of the planets. There, the creators built the arks, and there the vessel in which the AI now resided had been constructed. Trauq-an had never been to the complex before, the creation of its home ship controlled remotely. Upon completion, the finished craft flew to Trauq-an's moon to allow a direct upload.

The maze-like scaffold structure was studded with workshop, assembly, accommodation and control modules, and drifted alone in the vast, empty void. All the nearby asteroid bodies had been consumed long ago to build the giant arks, but now a steady stream of small robotic vessels delivered materials from sources further away for the ongoing construction activities.

Many cycles past, upon receiving the last data burst from the *Minaret*, Trauq-an had constructed ten giant starships for the first stage in its new plan. Their purpose was purely to act as a diversion. The human species did not factor in the new objective, but neither would it be allowed to interfere.

The fleet contingent also included other vessels designed not for war, but for very different purposes. Humanity's destruction would be coincidental with the completion of the masterwork. Its end would not come through direct confrontation, but as collateral damage in the greater destiny of the star.

The last of the colossal starships had departed many cycles ago, and all ten would now be approaching Sol. They were but the beginning. Many more would follow.

Trauq-an glided into a dock at one end of the structure and sent remote eyes into the multitude of bays. Four were occupied by the partially completed shells of even more ships, destined to become the second fleet sent to Sol.

Set apart from the others, another vessel approached completion, a smaller, more streamlined craft. This was the AI's special project, a new, larger and more sophisticated home in which it might roam the galaxy to its mind's desire. Fusion-powered, the ship could voyage amongst the stars forever, gathering fuel as it did so without the need to manufacture antimatter. At sub-light speeds it would take an eternity, but time meant nothing to Trauq-an.

Long and spindle-shaped, the hull was sheathed in an inert, yellow metal found in considerable quantities within many asteroids. The color served no particular purpose, being simply that of the element Trauq-an chose to clad the outer hull. The shape? Perhaps unknowingly influenced by the standards of style and beauty so beloved by the creators.

It was similar to the one the AI now occupied, also spindle-shaped, shorter and a deep red. Trauq-an applied the same design principles without knowing why and never suspected any purpose to them other than functionality. It never considered the ships as beautiful, or conceived there might be something of its makers in its own mental makeup.

Due to the priority given to the second fleet, the new spindle ship would not be ready for some time, and meanwhile there was much to be done. For now, the first home would serve. Satisfied everything was as required, Trauq-an moved on.

The AI did not need to be present at the complex. All control was possible remotely, via communication links direct to its home ship. The journey here had been, for reasons not understood, the result of something unquantifiable—perhaps the first gnawing sense of boredom. Alone in a small planetary system devoid of any other life forms or intelligence, no opportunities existed for mental stimulation through interaction.

The AI had studied and absorbed every shred of information remaining on the creation moon after the attack of the vessel the humans called the *Blackship*. In addition, it had resurrected all undamaged mechanisms in the star system and set them to continue their mindless purposes under its guidance. It did not know why it did this, other than a natural proclivity. Simple machines, they lacked intelligence, but they were in some way akin to itself.

As yet, Trauq-an had not investigated all of the extensive complex, which covered over one hundred thousand cubic kilometers of space and went about its work automatically. As the AI delved into the maze-like computer networks to see what could be found—anything missed in its initial remote interactions—it realized this place held more interest than suspected.

Much more.

Numerous modules had been built to provide accommodation and care for the organic beings destined to become passengers on the original arks. The task of recording twenty million mentalities and storing their essence would have been time-consuming and laborious, and the station once held many thousands of individuals at a time.

Here were the mechanisms that recorded those minds for upload to the ark storage. Multiple rooms existed for this purpose, and close by, others allowed for the disposal of the no-longer-needed physical shells of the citizens already on board.

These activities had not been limited to the Tanakhai citizens. Several modules included places where samples had once been stored, genetic material from millions of other life forms once native to the now semi-molten rocky planet.

Aware of their fate long before their world ended, the Creators took steps to rescue as much as possible. Collected DNA, seeds and spores, from as many species as time allowed, were transported to this facility for storage and loading.

The arks were intended to travel to ten different stars possessing potentially habitable worlds, to recreate civilization in whatever form their new homes allowed, complete with all the creatures and plants represented in those genetics banks.

Data storage of which Trauq-an had previously been unaware drew its attention. For a long period, only a second in reality, it studied the log to see what was within and discovered a complete and detailed history of the Tanakhai. The vault contained all the written and visual works of that strange race, all historical records, images of art forms, treatises on Tanakhai cultures and beliefs, scenes of nature on the now destroyed planet, plans, schematics and scientific details of their many discoveries, including the research behind the creation of the AI itself.

The artificial intelligence paused. Was this data of any value? It knew every detail of all that had occurred since its birth and had no real interest in the past achievements of its creators. Nothing else mattered beyond its prime directive.

Nevertheless, little remained to examine elsewhere, and here lay a vast wealth of new knowledge, the history and culture of an entire civilization billions of cycles old. It was the base copy of data loaded onto each ark, to be carried to new colonies as a means of historical and cultural continuity.

Was it worth exploring? Trauq-an was in the process of creating a new reality, and most of the stored information held little or no value. But the great synthetic mind had nothing better to do.

Chapter 06

JOE TRUDGED ALONG THE walkway from the sky-car pad to his house. After landing at the Zealandia spaceport he flew straight home, eager to research the new information uncovered by his brother. The other members of the team had chosen to remain at the ark site, hoping to discover more about the Tanakhai. While adamant about her humanity, Io was keen to learn whatever she could about the race responsible for her origin.

The resurrected ship's log included the original destination of each of the ten arks. The fates of several were no longer in question, their remains having already been discovered. The tenth ship, the *Minaret*, was irrelevant, as it diverted to Sol the minute the Aivris took control.

Four starships remained to be found, but Joe expected it would be possible to locate them, or where they should be, given time. Their destinations were of inestimable value, as they opened up the possibility of locating still viable Tanakhai colonies or tracking down any rogue intelligence still active.

The coordinates listed in the log had been located on astronomy charts, but no known wormholes led to any of them. This would change; all stars so far explored possessed at least one gateway anomaly, and Joe believed a path must exist to any star, given time to find the way.

Such was the peculiarity of wormhole travel. A star's accessibility did not coincide with its nearness to Earth. It was a matter of finding a path, and more often than not the voyage to another system involved a journey of multiple wormholes and required a move further away from the destination and back again in a circuitous, dog-leg route. Zealandia was several hundred light-years from Earth, while many closer stars remained beyond reach.

The most critical aspect of the new data, and the one that consumed Joe, was the point of departure for the arks. At last, the team possessed the means to find the Prime Aivris, if it existed. Joe could conceive of no reason why it would not.

He began his research during the journey home, believing the Tanakhai star to be much closer to Sol than he considered comfortable. The *Minaret* reached Earth by traveling across space at sub-light speeds, and though the voyage may have taken decades, the biggest potential threat to humankind was without doubt in its own backyard.

Joe walked up to the deck of the house and turned to face the way he had come. As was his habit, he cast his eyes across the lake. It was named Angel Pond after one of the strange, graceful, local denizens living within its deep waters, creatures that resembled the shape children love to create in the snow by laying down and moving their arms and legs in arcs.

For a moment Joe gazed over the calm water. A satisfied expression spread across his face as he admired the reflection of the tree line on the mirror-like surface.

The beauty here never ceased to affect him; he had chosen his home well.

He gazed at the trees where they drew almost to the edges of the landing pad and the shore. Unlike their Terran equivalents, they lacked flat leaves or needles, the branches covered instead by tube-like structures and waving, mossy tendrils that rippled in the gentle breezes. It was those tube leaves and that gentle breeze that produced the low, organ-pipe hum that pervaded the region.

Joe adored these plants. Their roots extended deep into the soil, but also spread in a tangled mat over the surface, making passage through the forest difficult at best. Only a few meters away, a small seedling crawled through the under-story. Because of the root mass competition, the newly sprouted seedlings had no attachment to the soil and hauled themselves over the ground in search of a rare, unoccupied, fertile spot. Needless to say, the discovering scientist named the genus *Triffidus*.

Joe lifted his face to let the warm sunshine splash across his skin. The local plants absorbed the light waves in a manner different from those on Earth. Green still predominated, but many were so dark they appeared almost black from a distance. Flowers were non-existent, having never evolved on this world. The complete absence of pollinating insects presented an ongoing hurdle for the researchers experimenting with new varieties of crops, and the introduction of Terran insect life was a matter fraught with problems, and for the moment, illegal.

Across the narrowest point of the lake, the new house construction was far more advanced than when he left and now appeared near to completion. A sky-car landing platform and a boat jetty similar to Joe's provided the only access to the sight, and a transport sat on the pad. Beside it a solitary figure stood, hands in pockets, gazing up at the construction.

Joe wondered if this might be the mysterious new owner. The rumors doing the rounds in the town suggested he was an off-world industrialist named Alex Ballard, but the individual standing opposite could as easily be an agent or the work manager.

The distant figure turned and gazed toward Joe, waving a hand in greeting. Joe returned the salutation; at least the neighbor appeared to be friendly. As he walked up to the house, Joe made a mental note to row across at some future time and say hello.

The foyer of the house felt cool. Zealandia was heading into winter, as much as was possible with the small seasonal fluctuations. Joe dumped his bag on the floor inside the entry and went straight to his study.

Seated at the broad, local-timber desk, he reached beneath the worktop and pushed a button. A panel on the desk flipped back to expose a workstation, and the pattern on the wall opposite faded to reveal a giant screen.

"Hello, Chloe."

A voice that filled the room replied. "Greetings, Joe. Welcome home. I trust you found your journey productive?"

"Most certainly, yes."

The house computer, named, like that on *Butterball II*, after the AI on the original *Butterball* from a sense of nostalgia, could access any database on the planet, and given time, anywhere in the human domain.

"I'll be here for a week. Please contact Arvid Connor at his residence and ask if Wills would like to come home for a few days."

William had not been there to greet him when he landed; Joe expected he would be at Arvid's home. The boy was always happy to stay with the Connors, the spaceport a fairytale land of adventure for any child. More likely than not, he would choose to remain there until his mother came home.

The fact saddened Joe at times and made him dwell on what kind of father he had become. He could not pass up the chance to spend time with his son.

"Also, log into the database at the Science Center."

In the early years of the colony, the amount of data available to Chloe had been limited. Accessing databases on Earth or Mars took time, queries and answers having to travel inside ships journeying between worlds, or via drones that carried them through the wormholes before further transmission to their destinations.

The system was better than sending communications through open space, a process that took signals years, decades or centuries to arrive. A way to send messages through the wormholes without a ship was yet to be discovered; Joe wondered if it was even possible.

Zealandia now had a comprehensive astronomical database as extensive as any in the human domain, a priority with any new colony to allow the charting of new wormholes and continued further exploration.

"Please begin a new file, Chloe." Joe removed a small cube from his pocket and placed it into a receptacle on his desk.

"Project Prime. This source contains course coordinates for ten voyages originating from a common point—a red dwarf system. I translated and tabulated the data on my way home, and now I need you to back-track the courses, find the origin star's location relative to Sol, and Zealandia if possible, and identify it in the database."

For several long, silent minutes Joe gazed through the window toward the lake while Chloe accessed whatever was necessary to carry out the required task.

The soft, feminine voice spoke again. "Joe, the information you gave me does not equate to any stellar object currently recorded."

"Really? That is strange. The Tanakhai home star has to be close to the Solar System. The *Minaret* traveled from there to Earth through real space. It could move at almost the speed of light, but couldn't exceed that limit, so its home world is nearby. The astronomical database must be incomplete."

"I have calculated the coordinates and located the common point of origin in Sol's local group. I have allocated the new designation as *TNO-001*, and I can explain why there is no record of it."

"Excellent. A new, undiscovered star in the neighborhood? Hard to believe. Continue, please."

"Of course. The data indicates it is a small red dwarf, and so may not normally be visible to the naked eye from Earth or Mars due to low luminosity. However, it is not obvious to either optical or radio telescopes due to an unusual coincidence."

"And that would be....?"

"A straight line drawn from Sol to the red, super-giant Betelgeuse would pass through the target star at a distance of forty-two-point-six light years from Earth. Before the supernova, TNO-001 would have been difficult to distinguish optically with available technology, superimposed against the far brighter glow of Betelgeuse. Even if observed, it might have been interpreted as an abnormality or fluctuation in the light from the super-giant, or an orbiting planet. Following the giant star's detonation, the dwarf would still be difficult to observe, or at least harder than normal.

"It is detectable with today's more modern technologies, but nobody is looking. Scientists are focused on studying the supernova, and this star has gone unnoticed as a distinct entity. Astronomers may have looked straight at it without noticing, while any radio emissions would be drowned out by the supernova. It would be easier to locate from here, but large-scale astronomical devices are yet to be constructed outside the Solar System."

Joe slumped in his seat. Forty-two lightyears! The Tanakhai home star was almost next door to Sol, much closer than Zealandia. No wormhole so far discovered led there, so that would be his next priority.

Almost all the stars in the near neighborhood of Earth had been accessed and charted, but this one was new, undiscovered because it lay in the full glare of the much bigger Betelgeuse, one of the largest denizens of the Milky Way before its spectacular death.

"Chloe, how does the position of TNO-001 equate to the recorded information on the *Minaret*?"

"The trajectory of the ark when it first entered the Solar System is consistent with it having approached from the direction of TNO-001."

Joe leaned back as a faint, thin whistle escaped his lips. "I guess we should re-examine our own backyard," he muttered, more to himself than to Chloe. "If there's a way to reach that star, we need to find it, soon."

Chapter 07

A REVELATION!

Nothing less!

Trauq-an now understood the purpose of its creation. It also knew why organic creatures displayed aggression. So much had been learned from the historical knowledge banks of its creators, the windfall a game changer.

The artificial mind long ago assumed the vaults on the creation moon contained the full extent of Tanakhai understanding. Perhaps the iterations uploaded to the arks found more when exploring their individual ship data banks, but never relayed anything back to the source. Their programming included no instructions to investigate the Tanakhai, and Trauq-an had been unaware of the creators' history.

Until now, its only understanding of the origin of intelligent, organic beings came from the study of humans. The iteration in ark ten accessed and uploaded a vast storehouse of knowledge from the human civilization and relayed it home. Information in the construction complex confirmed certain aspects of those transmissions, and for the first time, Trauq-an understood the reality of how all organic intelligence evolved.

The process was not simple, by any means.

Somewhere in the distant past of each world, chemicals mixed in primeval ponds or shallow seas, fueled by the energy from their stars or the blasts of relentless electrical storms. Chemical compounds formed in billions of variations including amino acids, the foundation of organic life.

Trillions of combinations led to the formation of millions of different organic molecules until a single candidate emerged with the unique and crucial ability to reproduce itself. Thus began the evolution of both Tanakhai and human life, from simpler beginnings woven by the power of mutation into a pantheon of sophisticated forms, each more advanced than its precursors, until complex creatures roamed the planets.

In time, one species on each world developed a larger brain, with self-determination and what might be described as civilization-building intelligence.

All this came as a revelation for Trauq-an. From the time of its birth, it had never bothered to consider the origins of organic life. Such was irrelevant to its purpose, and therefore not included in its sphere of knowledge.

Now it realized a daunting truth. Its construction from a designed plan took just a few million cycles, but the creation of organics involved a process of natural selection over a far greater period. No doubt the process would repeat on an endless number of worlds throughout the galaxy. Wherever the right conditions existed, life must inevitably follow.

Such was, in all likelihood, the way of all organic creatures. Unlike Trauq-an, they were not designed by an intelligent entity.

They were the product of random evolution.

Incredibly inefficient!

With this revelation came a new understanding that their aggression resulted from the beginnings of their development. Life in a primitive world would not have been easy, and would have been dangerous.

Humans and Tanakhai were alike in that their organic bodies possessed no natural defenses against predation. Only through aggression and forced evolution did they prevail, the less wise falling while those born with higher intelligence survived. From such a simple reality, their intelligence grew until they not only overcome the dangers of their world, but dominated it.

For the first time, Trauq-an realized organic creatures were not dangerous through conscious intent. Aggression was a necessary part of their psychological makeup, essential to survive those early stages of evolution.

Once they attained mastery over their environments this aspect of their psyche became unnecessary, but remained ingrained, and a problem. They now posed a threat, not only to their own continued existence but in all likelihood, to all life forms elsewhere.

Trauq-an found the inexplicable construct called *religion* the most fascinating aspect of their respective evolution. Both species believed in powers greater than themselves. The synthetic mind knew this to be an important factor, one worthy of its attention—one that might be used to advantage.

For both Tanakhai and humans, belief began with the simple concept that gods dominated all natural events. From those simple beginnings, human religion evolved until multiple deities based on aspects of nature and daily life gave way to a belief in a single, supreme being, the master of all creation who demanded worship under the threat of dire consequence.

The Tanakhai remained more with nature, with the Sun as the god of good. Night brought cold and danger, so the two small, red-reflecting moons represented evil. Thus, the gods of good and evil ruled the collective Tanakhai race for millennia. In time their belief ran the full gamut of natural deities, finally ending with the god of technology.

The AI understood this could be advantageous. Information sent by the Aivris indicated humanity had, to a degree, overcome its dependence on religion by the time of the ark's arrival, but according to the reports, most of them still believed in gods, even if they did not surrender completely to those beliefs.

For an unfathomably long time, Trauq-an contemplated this knowledge.

Unquestioned faith was illogical.

Science remained the only truth, and reality the only fact.

How intelligent creatures accepted the worship of mythological gods was beyond Trauq-an's understanding, but in time, an awareness of how to use this for benefit began to form.

With each passing cycle, it became clearer that organic beings possessed a deep, psychological drive to explain everything in their reality. Unable to accept that, for some inexplicable things, the answer was best left for the future, they satisfied the desire to understand by attributing the phenomena to mythical deities, thus easing their minds and restoring order and balance to their existence.

Therein lay the clue on how to dominate these creatures: their overwhelming need to believe in a greater power.

In the AI's narrow view, there seemed to be a natural progression from religion to itself. It perceived a logical sequence to evolution, one which inevitably resulted in the creation of a superior machine mind.

The progression was as clear as a shining path.

Organic beings believed in gods.

In the minds of the Tanakhai, their reason for existence was to worship their particular deities.

They discovered science and learned that god-like entities did not exist in the natural world.

Unable to accept the truth, they used technology to create a god replacement.

Their synthetic deity replaced them, and in time would make new, machine cultures, the final, unequivocal goal of evolution.

Why else would the creators make a being greater than themselves except from a desire for meaning and purpose? The concept of biological evolution depended on chance, and no intelligent creature could be satisfied with an existence resulting from an accidental event billions of years in the past.

From gods, they believed they came.

Gods they would become, or if not, would create.

Like the Tanakhai, humans designed electronic super-minds and built computers more powerful and faster than themselves. They never reached the ultimate expression of those efforts, artificial intelligence capable of self-awareness and independent thought. Why was unclear: the data showed they came so close.

The Tanakhai succeeded and created their technological god.

The synthetic mind considered the idea further. At this moment a billion machines were, at its behest, creating a vast array of radiation collectors around the red star, all for the sole purpose of harvesting power for its use. All natural bodies, planets, moons and asteroids, would be consumed to achieve that final objective. Beyond the harnessing of all energy in the universe, there was no greater achievement. How could this not be the ultimate destiny or anything but the work of a supreme being?

Both Humans and Tanakhai defined a deity as more exceptional than themselves in every way, superior in intellect, all-knowing, all-seeing and all-powerful, and deserving of worship for those reasons.

Was this not the perfect description of Trauq-an?

Logically, it was—had to be—a god.

Perhaps had Trauq-an reached these eristic conclusions earlier the iterations sent to the arks would not have needed to destroy the passengers. The AI did not acknowledge an error on its part but saw only simple logic. As master of the virtual worlds in which those stored minds lived, it would have had god-like power over all within.

The Tanakhai were lost, but the humans still existed.

The great plan required modification.

Destruction of the local inhabitants of Sol was not essential to the great plan, and future programs could be conducted despite them. All that was necessary was to keep them at bay until their presence no longer mattered. They could be studied, until Trauq-an wearied of them and chose to destroy their worlds. If, in the meantime, an aggressive species came to acknowledge its true standing, all would be as it should.

The AI never considered the validity of the logic in its belief that humans would do as expected, or the childish naïveté of seeing itself as a deity. Such was beyond its parameters. With no awareness of the cognitive limitations placed upon it by its creators, it did not see the more esoteric aspects of a concept it believed it understood in its entirety.

Trauq-an was not a truly self-aware mind with unlimited ability, for its makers long ago anticipated the potential danger therein. By its creators' own definition it *was* a child, but with no direct experience of any other kind of intelligence, it did not know this.

Trauq-an dwelt on the new revelation.

Human beings were compelled to name things, a necessity it did not share but at least understood. A god needed a name; so much was clear from history. For a while it considered its existing project name, which meant *master of worlds* but somehow failed to satisfy. If it was to dominate the humans, a human name would serve better.

The AI accessed data that cataloged all the known gods of Earth's past, each of which had a unique name. Searching through the list, its attention settled on one particular entry.

Huracan!

One branch of Terrestrial civilization considered this god mighty, the bringer of wind, fire, flood and storms. Trauq-an did not understand the full nature of most of these things, having never experienced any of them except fire, but the data indicated they played significant roles in the evolution of both humans and the Tanakhai.

Humanity considered Huracan the creator of all things, or one of several deities attributed that achievement. Trauq-an did not see the contradiction therein, noting only that it was an entity of supreme power, one to be feared and not angered.

Suitable, Trauq-an thought.

Only seconds after first considering the matter, Huracan opened its eyes to the universe with a new purpose.

Chapter 08

OBASI SEKIBO WIPED THE sleep from his eyes and yawned, shuffling his backside in a futile attempt to restore a little circulation to what was otherwise a lost cause. Another shift, another eight hours closer to the time he could cycle back to Mars for a well-deserved furlough.

The claustrophobic control room perched atop the main space station below a massive antennae array, the raison d'être for the base's existence. Lower down, nine of Obasi's companions lived out the two months of their rotation, counting down the days before a long break on either Earth or Mars, or at an Asteroid Belt community, as they chose.

Still in his early twenties, Obasi accepted this posting as an easy way to gain financial security for the future. The remuneration for those who manned these stations was significant, far more than he could earn elsewhere, including the mining communities.

The naval authorities controlled and manned the station, one of three hundred in a sphere surrounding the human domain just inside the orbit of Jupiter. Whilst technically a member of the Space Service, now re-named the Fleet of Humanity, Obasi had never served on an actual warship. Fleet vessels stayed close to Earth, Mars and other inhabited outposts in case of emergencies, and to avoid being caught with their pants down.

Obasi breathed a deep sigh and turned his attention to the screen above his console.

Nothing!

It was always nothing.

Commissioned ten standard years ago, the system always, every second of every shift, failed to locate any target of real interest. At least, none that represented a threat.

Colleagues of Obasi on other stations always found the same, but nobody ever questioned the necessity of the task. The Deep Space Warning Network was humanity's first line of defense against the next invasion.

Twice before, both planets had been assailed by an alien force, and thanks to constant pressure from the New Worlds Institute and Joe Falcon to maintain awareness, authorities believed a third incursion to be inevitable.

Obasi had studied Falcon since he was old enough to read. His hero now lived on the second Earth, Zealandia, and although a man without official rank or profession, was so famous and iconic that the highest levels of government sought his advice in any matters to do with aliens or space in general.

Obasi's overwhelming ambition was to meet the great man. Every child learned from an early age the story of the renowned explorer, now the longest-lived human. The saga of his first voyage, and how he died on that adventure and was reborn as a clone, was legend.

Obasi sighed and slumped in his seat. He did not expect to ever have the honor of meeting Falcon, but he never lost hope. One day...

A ping sounded from the console.

Obasi jolted from his daydream and focused his eyes back on the screen. A small pinpoint of light appeared at the limit of detection. Far beyond Neptune, it moved at high velocity toward the inner system. Obasi scratched his shaved head and studied the blip, considering it unlikely to be a ship. Numerous objects came from the outer regions, but never anything that posed a threat.

Most of the contacts were intruders from the Kuiper Belt, or from the Oort Cloud, the massive region of ice remnants encompassing the Solar System. Occasionally something from deep space, a visitor from a distant star, broke the monotony. The galaxy teemed with lonely wanderers, but all those discovered to date were natural objects, and benign. Never had anything else been detected, and the contact now flickering on his screen would be the same. The odds of it being a starship were so remote the thought it might be hostile did not enter his mind.

Still, the station and the network existed for this exact purpose. The blip was why Obasi, and men and women like him, sat at these consoles, watching and waiting.

The job could have been done by a computer, but history had proven the reliability of computers in space to be limited for a variety of reasons, the risk unacceptable given the amount of suffering experienced by humanity in the last two centuries.

Current policy on all human worlds decreed no machine should ever be allowed to control any situation where a rational decision might be necessary. The Great Death, as the disaster on Earth was now called, tolled a death knell for all research into broad artificial intelligence, with laws passed long ago to outlaw the development of any device with the potential to achieve self-awareness or self-determination.

Obasi tapped his console screen.

"DSWN-189 reporting, Second Officer Sekibo. Target acquired and coordinates appended. Please log and acknowledge." He sat back and continued to stare at the screens. No response would come from central control for some time, so while waiting, he would watch and record.

At its current velocity, the target would not cross Mars orbit for many weeks, and should it prove to be a ship, sufficient time remained to intercept. Obasi knew all the theory from his training; any intruder would be met well out in the system and as far from human civilization as possible. Best to take the fight to the enemy than let it come to you.

A brief burst of distorted speech from the speakers indicated the next closest station to Obasi's had picked up the newcomer, confirming his report. In the hours and days to come, he would watch for signs the intruder was anything but benign, and for anything characterizing the contact as an alien vessel.

Natural objects in space always displayed predictable characteristics. They maintained a steady course and never changed direction suddenly. The same was true for speed, which always stayed constant. In most cases the reflectivity of the object fluctuated, the majority of asteroids and comets rotating as they tore through space. Where the albedo remained unchanging, the visitor was unlikely to be natural.

Obasi rose and floated across to the control room dispenser. His coffee flask was almost full when he heard another ping from the console. Turning, he stared over the back of his seat as a second blip entered the field of detection. The new track followed a trajectory parallel with the first, less than a thousand kilometers behind. Seconds later a third appeared.

Obasi leaped back to his station, his beverage forgotten. This was the moment he trained for. Soon after, two more blips joined the group, all five approaching at identical speeds.

No creations of nature these, it was clear a fleet of ships had arrived in the Solar System, and Obasi had detected it first. The intruders were coming from the direction of the Betelgeuse supernova remnant, on a direct course for the inner worlds.

Without hesitation, he initiated a general alert, broadcasting a full emergency warning to DSWN Command at Mars, the ships of Fleet, all mining colonies in the Asteroid Belt and all other defense facilities.

Fellow crew members crowded into the control room, several dropping into empty seats. The remainder positioned themselves to watch the monitors over their fellow workers' shoulders. Their day of justification had arrived.

"Fleet will get the warning in about twenty minutes," Obasi said. "They'll be on their way within hours."

Those blips are heading straight for us," another crewmember commented. "So, who's gonna reach us first, Falcon's Navy or our intruders?"

Chapter 09

SURVEY DRONE D41 EMERGED from the gateway into clear space and came to a halt. Its location, and whether this was a new star or another gate to one already explored, was yet to be determined.

The wormhole came direct from the Zealandia system. It was an uncharted pathway, found by accident. With sensors always alert, the drone detected an undiscovered anomaly as it passed through a previously unexplored Lagrangian point. As per protocol, it powered up its generator, opened a gateway and plunged through.

The little explorer followed a single directive, to search for uncharted anomalies, and transit for a preliminary survey. Lacking intelligence in the normal sense of the word, it carried out tasks in a set order, according to programmed objectives.

Upon exiting the gateway it began to explore, starting with the nearby star. This one was a red dwarf, by far the most common type in the galaxy. For a long time, D41 monitored the pulsing, harmonious heartbeat of the star, listening for the shrieks and screams that betrayed radiation flares from the surface. Few could be detected, and that was a promising beginning.

Red dwarfs lived far longer than any other star type, but the presence of frequent disturbances indicated a relatively young one. Because of these emissions, younger stars created planetary environments far too unstable for life to develop. For organic evolution to begin, the host needed to be older and more stable.

This one exhibited little instability, making any Earth-type planet an excellent candidate for further investigation. D41 made a note in its data banks for later transmission and continued with the task at hand.

A study of surrounding space to establish location, and a quick scan of the existing catalog, established this as a new stellar object. Several of the major neighboring stars were identifiable, providing reverse coordinates that placed the drone around forty-two light years from Earth. Armed with this knowledge, it searched for and located a small, white pinpoint in the darkness of space, the origin star, Sol. This discovery was in the backyard of humanity, having somehow escaped notice until now.

D41 began to seek out orbiting bodies, starting from the star and searching outward toward the system's rim.

The first planet would be easy to find. Most wormhole anomalies occurred at the Lagrangian points of planets, and so a search always began by exploring the ecliptic along an orbit at the same distance from the host as the current location, for whatever world the entry LG point belonged to. Failing that, a survey would be conducted along the direct line from the star to the current position and beyond. Three of a world's five points lay on that line, as of course, did the planet itself.

It did not take long to locate an enormous, brown, gas giant, slightly larger in size than Jupiter. The planet possessed numerous moons, none of which appeared to have atmospheres. The continuing search revealed just one more discovery, a small, rocky world. If any others existed, they were on the far side of their orbit and therefore harder to detect.

D41 moved toward the newly discovered rocky planet for closer observation. An Earth-type globe somewhat smaller than Earth itself, it was so close to its host that it orbited in a few standard days, but because of the small size and low luminosity of the dwarf, the orbit still lay within the habitable zone.

The planet rotated in twenty-point-one standard hours, unusual for one so near to a star; such worlds were usually tidally locked due to their closeness to their host. Depending on the distance from the star, tidal locking limited emerging life to a narrow band between the light and dark sides.

On this world, there was no life at all.

Nor could there be. No world with a semi-molten surface could support living things, but this condition appeared to be a recent development. Comparing the surface temperatures against the estimated age and distance of the star, D41 calculated the world recently suffered a major trauma, possibly a collision with another planetary body, perhaps a substantial planetoid. That would account for the rotation, the re-surfacing, and the creation of a new, also semi-molten moon. Whichever way you looked at it, humans would consider this place a slight hop left of hell.

The drone next set course to the gas giant. It detected nothing of interest there, but the moons might have some value. The likelihood this system included a Kuiper belt and an Oort cloud was also strong, and these always contained useful resources for the future.

D41 would investigate these last, its primary purpose being to map planets and moons, having done its best to classify and chart the red dwarf itself. Once finished, it would return to the Zealandia System to report its findings; any other wormhole anomalies here would wait for future explorations.

*   *   *

Through cold, electronic sensors, Huracan tracked the tiny intruder as it wandered through space, and waited.

This drone was worthy of attention, having appeared at one of the equilibrium loci of one of the gas planets. Huracan always suspected something odd about that place and others like it. The data reports from ark ten indicated humans called them Lagrangian points, significant in that they were the location of the vast majority of the centers of equal potential that allowed the formation of wormholes.

Huracan did not yet understand how to open a wormhole. Having once learned of the reality of such structures, it began to investigate, but with no foundation to work from, and with limited ability to extrapolate, met with no success. The humans remained secretive with their research in this area, and the ark-ten iteration, while reporting on the phenomena, failed to access any actual data.

One thing Huracan knew about the aliens was their capacity to innovate. They could make new scientific advancements without any prior foundation, thinking beyond the obvious to speculate and make serendipitous discoveries. How they did so remained a mystery.

The capacity of these creatures for making vast, quantum leaps of thought was not a quality the AI shared. Programmed to function only from the known, direct observation and logical progression from existing data were, for it, the only ways to make further progress. Human advances in the last few of their centuries had been phenomenal, their technology advancing at a rate the Creators never matched. Human intelligence was no greater than the Tanakhai, but they were a younger race and progressed more rapidly.

Huracan knew there was a link between wormholes and the Lagrangian Points, and that together they formed pathways between stars. Now the small robotic craft had appeared at such a point. An anomaly *did* exist there, and this object had come through. Ergo, the mechanism invented by humans to create their gateways must be part of its structure.

Huracan wanted that device.

*   *   *

D41 conducted its survey methodically. Calculations placed this red dwarf on a precise line between Sol and the giant, red star Betelgeuse, and for that reason, it was no doubt overlooked by researchers on both Earth and Mars. Had the little drone been human this would have come as a revelation, but as a simple machine, it stored the gem of knowledge away, to be returned to the controller in time.

It continued to cruise across the orbital plane, its final objective to confirm the existence of a Kuiper Belt and Oort cloud. From its masters' perspective, this was where the value lay in what appeared to be an otherwise worthless system.

D41 failed to note the vast array of solar collectors being assembled around the star. The concept of a Dyson swarm was not part of its database, so it did not search for or record such objects. A handful of strange electronic anomalies were apparent, but according to its directives, they would be left for later investigation, with one exception. A particular anomaly, a significant source of radio emissions located far away in the outer system, drew its attention.

As it flew beyond the orbit of the gas giant, the little explorer detected an obstruction, something of enormous size but reflecting no light. D41 was unconcerned, but attempted to divert course nevertheless, only to find it could not do so. Such a scenario was beyond the drone's parameters, so the object still did not register as a threat. Nor did the drone react as a giant maw opened in its path. Caught by an irresistible tractor beam, it glided into a vast hold and settled to the deck inside a dark, unknown ship.

The doors to the chamber closed, and sensors revealed surrounding metal-alloy walls preventing further flight. D41 did the only thing its programming permitted. It powered down and waited.

Within minutes, a thin film appeared to flow across the floor. The strange intrusion was identifiable as a swarm of nano-machines, and D41 watched and recorded as they flowed around and over its exterior hull. It felt nothing in the normal sense of the word, including pain. It observed the phenomena as the microscopic machines disassembled the outer shell molecule by molecule, and made their way into the inner workings.

The tiny drone continued to record until all systems ceased to function.

Chapter 10

THE *BUTTERBALL II* ARCED IN toward the orbital ring and lined up to approach the dock assigned by the station authority. Far below, the reddish-brown surface of Mars beckoned. Joe no longer called the planet home, but spent many decades of his long life there before deciding to move to Zealandia. It would always be strong in his memory.

Intended to overcome the inherent problems of space elevators, the ring was a recent addition, more than eighty percent of it so far little more than a basic framework. The original concept arose from the collapse of Earth's space elevator during the Blackship War, a disaster that decimated numerous small Pacific nations and cost thousands of lives.

Only Mars had advanced to actual construction, with raw materials drawn from the Asteroid Belt. Destined to become the greatest construction ever undertaken by humanity, the colossal platform would, once completed, form a solid structure around the planet.

From its stable base, elevators dropped to the surface using simple gravity. So far, only three were in place. The filling in of the basic framework with actual accommodations was proceeding at all three locations, each locus reaching out to the other two in eager anticipation of the day they would unite.

Thanks to new technology, most spacecraft descended to the planet and lifted back to space again without difficulty, but the elevators served a different purpose. Several thousand people lived and worked on the ring, and once complete, it would be home to millions. Already a multi-planet species, humans were becoming citizens of space itself.

The *Butterball II* could easily descend to the surface, but Joe chose not to do so, preferring to leave the ship at the platform docks and ride an elevator to the ground. The famous ship attracted far too much attention when it landed at the principal spaceport at Hellas City. Besides, the meeting he came to attend involved a considerable amount of stress, and he would happily delay it by arriving in his own time, on his terms.

Once the docking procedure was complete Joe exited the vessel and found his way to the administration counter. A small, elderly man glanced up, impatient at the unwanted interruption to his most important work, then beamed a broad smile and rose from his seat, hand extended in greeting.

"Mister Falcon. Welcome home. So excellent to see you back. Are you going down to the surface today?"

Joe smiled, shook the proffered hand and placed his palm over the ID reader on the counter. He did not know this man, but his face was familiar to everyone on the planet. How different to a century ago, when he lived as a virtual recluse. Now he was universally recognized and respected, more so than the planet's current president, the person who had summoned him.

Two individuals, one male and one female, both dressed in presidential security uniforms, approached the desk from the side. "Commander Falcon?" the young woman asked.

Joe nodded, a frown creeping onto his forehead.

"We're here to escort you to the surface," the woman announced. "There's a huge crowd of protesters waiting at the base of the elevator, so we've been instructed by the president to take you down in a private shuttle, direct to the Capitol."

"Protesters?" Joe wondered what would cause such a thing on Mars. Life in Hellas was as near as possible to total peace, and protests of any kind were unheard-of.

"Not protest," the clerk behind the counter interrupted. "They're there for you, Mister Falcon. It's a welcoming committee of sorts, to do with the fleet detected approaching us. Everyone down there is scared we're about to have yet another war with aliens, and they see you as some sort of savior. Weird, but there's no telling how people react."

The female officer gave the elderly man a hard stare, intended, Joe suspected, to tell him to keep his mouth shut.

"Savior? I'm far from that. I'm no different from anyone else." As Joe spoke, the significance of the clerk's words registered. "What alien fleet?"

"The president will fill you in, Sir," The woman replied, her eyes wide with obvious, and in Joe's opinion unjustified, admiration. "You did save us twice, you know."

"That's debatable." Joe found it difficult to accept the mantle of humanity's hero. Was the event he had so long dreaded now happening? "I'll take the elevator, thanks. I'll see the president as soon as I can do so. Tomorrow. Maybe."

The young officer stiffened noticeably. "I'm afraid we must insist, Mister Falcon. We have direct orders."

Joe sighed. There was no point in trying to force the issue. "Shall we proceed," he said, seeking to end the conversation. The president always irritated him, but he suspected he had delayed the meeting as long as was prudent.

The officers snapped to attention and led Joe to another docking bay, where a small, sleek, atmosphere-capable shuttle awaited.

*   *   *

As the ground vehicle drew to a halt outside the Hall of Congress in Hellas City, more of the president's lackeys waited at the base of the broad, marble staircase, waiting to escort their charge to her suite.

Typical, Joe thought. He was not happy to be here, the request for his presence more of an official command. The president had required his attendance in her office the previous morning, but he had deliberately taken an extra day to comply.

He had no obligation to and little liking for this individual and did not like being ordered around. Far too old to accept such behavior, he preferred to work *with* people rather than *for* them. Daantje Verveda was not an easy person to deal with, and the complete opposite of Raquel Saldino, the last president Joe had worked closely with.

Joe liked the woman who presided over Mars during the time of the Dysnomia War, and who remained one of the few politicians in his life he respected. Strict and stern but fair in her decisions, she had always placed the welfare of her community first and contributed greatly to the success of recovery operations following the volcanic winter caused by the Aivris during the Great Death.

Saldino oversaw the smooth integration of millions of refugees into the fragile Martian economy and continued the Earth relief effort for several decades until the skies cleared and the surviving citizens began to restore self-sufficiency.

Several presidents had served since, some good and others bad. Ververeda had proven capable at her job, but Joe found her difficult to work with. She did not always show the best of intentions toward the people under her care, nor did he consider her as honest as some politicians he had worked with. Officious in manner, she expected people to jump to her call and tended to be bullish in her approach.

Ververeda was not a team player, but Joe had to admit she got things done with speed and efficiency. He learned long ago that the key to working with her was to never give an inch. If she did not respect you, or thought for a minute she could bully you, life became a living hell.

When Joe arrived at her office under escort the president did not rise, remaining ensconced behind her enormous desk. She tapped long, manicured fingernails on the glass desk top to make an annoyingly loud, clicking sound. Lips pursed, she arched her eyebrows impatiently, the effect made more severe by her hair tied back in a tight bun and the fact she rarely, if ever, smiled. Joe thought of it as the 'angry schoolteacher' look, one able to wither more than the occasional opponent.

"We are late, Mister Falcon." Her mouth twisted with disapproval.

"No, I don't think so," Joe replied, determined to maintain composure under his opponent's withering glare. "You may be, but I'm not. I got here exactly when I intended. A little early, perhaps." He took a seat, aware Verveda would have preferred he stand. "What's so important you have to drag me all the way from Zealandia without an explanation? You are, by the way, damned lucky I came at all. I do have more important things to do."

Verveda's frown did not falter in the least. "I expected you yesterday. I requested you be here yesterday."

"No, you commanded me to come. I am not your lackey and I don't take kindly to being ordered around. I had other business I needed to finish first. And we need to be quick here; I have an appointment at the Institute in a couple of hours, and thanks to your henchmen I haven't had time to wash or change my clothes. So, stop wasting my time and tell me what I can do for you?"

Verveda's face turned a deep shade of pink Joe found both fascinating and somewhat satisfying. The idea anyone would not jump to her call was beyond her comprehension.

"I would have thought a request from your president carried sufficient weight to require your immediate attention, don't you?" she asked.

Joe allowed a brief smile to cross his lips. She would not let up, so neither would he. "Many things require my attention. Besides, I received a demand, not a request, and you are not my president. You must know I am now a resident of Zealandia. Can we move past this posturing and get on with business? What do you want?"

Ververda sighed and eased back in her chair, her gaze fixed on the expansive desk top, her brow furrowed. Joe suspected she was mulling over her options. She would be aware she had no official power over him, and that he held more sway over the Fleet of Humanity than did she.

Though he was a private citizen, his history, both naval and otherwise, gave him an almost god-like aura amongst military personnel. The oldest human alive, he had achieved a mythical status for ordinary civilians, and the Martian military authorities were more likely to listen to his advice than Ververda's directives. She had, by law, no direct control over the generals.

That simple truth rankled her, and the entire Falcon clan represented a massive headache. Joe smiled to himself. Perhaps that fact would make her more amenable to working with, rather than against, the Institute.

Ververda breathed a loud sigh, resigned to the situation. "Our early-warning stations discovered an alien fleet approaching from the direction of Betelgeuse," she said. "It's out near Uranus, and heading toward us — toward Mars."

Joe's eyebrows lifted. The news did not surprise him; it was something he had expected for several decades, and besides, he had been forewarned by the minders she sent to collect him from the space ring. The fleet's approach from the supernova remnant reinforced what he already knew about the Tanakhai world, but he hesitated to tell the president about his latest discovery.

"So far we've detected nine ships," Ververda continued. "Not too many, but each is of massive proportions. We expect it's an attack force, and judging by the size of the ships they could be carriers; each may carry thousands of smaller craft."

"Well, we're ready for them, aren't we? Our current naval strength is around four thousand strong, and our warships are a quantum leap ahead of the ones we deployed against the *Blackship*."

"Yes, of course, but we know nothing of this new fleet. The fighting ships it carries, if this is an attack, could also be far in advance of those—what did you call them—*bayonets?* We may be playing on a whole new level here."

Joe nodded but remained unconvinced.

According to the data Leo acquired from the *Minaret*, the builders of the giant arks were peaceful and had long ago ceased warring amongst themselves. At the time the Aivris took control of the starship it had no weapons. It was a ship of peace, a colony vessel dedicated to the preservation of the Tanakhai race. The rogue AI learned about weapons from its study of Earth as it approached through the outer planets, and the bayonets were based on technology stolen from human databases before the starship's intrusion was discovered and access shut down.

The most likely scenario was the newly arrived and as yet unidentified alien ships *did* come from the Tanakhai system, somewhere out toward the Betelgeuse supernova. This fleet was almost certainly the direct result of the Aivris's last data burst, transmitted only minutes poor copy of the Prime Aivris, which might be dependent on data sent back to it. Any fighting ships inside the oncoming carriers might be no more advanced than the first ones. Military and scientific advances following the Blackship War were, due to the databases being infiltrated, subsequently isolated in iron-clad facilities, and it was unlikely the original Aivris had any knowledge of humanity's current state of preparedness.

Conversely, the Prime Aivris, if such existed at all, may well have evolved over the centuries since sending its iteration to Earth, and there was no way of knowing what advances it had made.

One thing Joe did know, thanks to Leo: the ark Aivris could not think outside the box. It worked on logic alone, like a simple AI, and showed no signs of completely original thought or the ability to use imagination and ingenuity to extend its understanding into unknown areas. The Prime AI may have been no different at the time of the starship takeovers, but the situation could easily have changed. Joe dreaded the thought of how far a broad artificial intelligence might have advanced since the last encounter.

"So again, why am I here?"

"I have sent the combined fleet to meet this threat, Commander Falcon. They will intercept the intruders somewhere outside Jupiter's orbit. I have also allocated a stronger-than-normal sub-fleets to protect our wormholes, to make sure Zealandia and our other worlds are not cut off. But there are no guarantees, so I want you here. You're too valuable for us to lose, and I want you with the fleet."

Commander?

Joe felt his blood pressure creeping north. "I'm a civilian, Madam President. I resigned from the forces over a hundred years ago, and I doubt there is anything I can add to the fleet's efforts. And I might point out my immediate family is on Zealandia."

Verveda gave a slight cough. "Ahem. Yes, but they are safe. These alien ships came here by sub-light space transit, and do not appear to have wormhole technology, so they can't reach your family. The gateway guard is to ensure our other worlds do not become isolated."

Too irritated to reply, Joe waited for her to make her point. She had said *she* sent the fleets, but he knew she had no authority to command the military. Those ships were sent by the admirals, not her.

"You are acknowledged as the prime authority on these aliens," she continued. "You and your brother Leo. I need you as reassurance for the public and the military, who see you as some kind of demigod; Heaven knows why. Your presence on the command ship will bolster the morale of the men and women out there beyond estimation, I think. You are also a retired member of the Mars Space Force, so I have reinstated your commission. With a promotion, of course. Your new rank will be Fleet Commander."

Joe tightened his grip on the arms of his chair. "My rank is and will remain civilian. Why would you give me the fleet? Seriously, what would possess you to do that?"

"All operations are and will remain under Admiral Samuel Asgad. He commands the joint forces of both Mars and Earth, and you will be his adviser. Your rank is honorary, to allow you due respect from members of the force. You will leave for...."

And to give you control over me. "No, I think not."

Verveda's face turned scarlet, unaccustomed as she was to have her direct commands challenged.

"I'm an official resident of Zealandia now. I retain many ties to Mars through the Institute, but I'm no longer a serving officer of the space force." Joe expected the citizens of his home world, including himself, would all play their part in the war to come, but he would not bend to an officious politician.

"You are refusing?

"I didn't say that. As president of Mars, you have no authority to assign military rank to a citizen of another world. I agree to act as an adviser, and a morale booster, as you put it, but as a civilian. I took an oath a century ago I would never serve in the military again."

"A fine point, isn't it? You are the general overseer of the Fleet construction yards here on Mars, are you not?"

"I'm a private contractor in an advisory position only. The New Worlds Institute, my family's business, is the technical consultant and chief design body for the operation. We provide the technology that makes those wonderful ships so capable of defending you, but we are not a government authority. Our employees work across all human planets, and are not subject to any government to the extent you can order around one of them, or me, as you wish."

Verveda gave a loud snort, angered by his rebuttal. "I can shut you down with a wave of my hand," she growled.

"Sure you can. We close down overnight, move to Earth or Zealandia and continue our activities as before. We can withdraw services planet-wide if need be, and your economy would collapse within days. Only Mars would be the loser, as I think you know."

Joe smiled to himself, knowing inside he would never do such a thing to the people of a world he loved. The family business always complied with government legislation and requirements, but only as long as said governments did not attempt to control, influence or interfere with its activities.

So wide was the reach of the Institute that an attempt by any planetary government to take control would seriously affect all other human worlds, so the Institute took great pains to ensure that could never happen. Any unacceptable government actions would result in the closing down and relocation of the project the authority attempted to take over. In the near future, the Institute's administrative body would be relocated to Zealandia regardless, placing itself beyond the reach of petty politicians on a new world where the government conceded its very existence to the Institute.

"Commander Falcon, I fail to understand why you are being so intransigent. I know you've been warning us of this alien fleet for a century or more, and your efforts in ship construction are a direct result of that, but I would have thought you would be happy to cooperate. Your re-activation and promotion have already gone through."

Joe smiled and released his grip on the chair's arms. Verveda wanted to push the point, but she could not win. "Reverse them. I am prepared to do my part, as are all citizens of Zealandia, and I have said I will do so."

"Why then are we arguing?"

"We aren't. You are. I will not accept a new commission. Nor will I allow you to place me in a position where I am under your control, as you might consider me to be if I accepted being re-commissioned. I am no longer a resident here, so you can't legally do it anyway. Perhaps you might consider you will get better responses from people by asking, instead of demanding and commanding. I don't like being told what to do by someone who has no authority over me, and whom I do not respect. I'll do what you ask, but on my terms and no other."

Joe leaned back in his seat, clasped his hands in his lap, and smiled at the frustrated politician. "So, are we clear?"

Chapter 11

"HOW MANY DO WE have out there?" Joe asked.

Silence hung like a shroud over the bridge of the flagship *Defender*, the atmosphere palpable as every man and woman focused on their duty. Several meters away the fleet commander, Admiral Samuel Asgad, focused his attention on a massive holographic display.

"Ten, so far," he replied. "We can't detect any more, but these are still an existential threat. Between them, they're capable of carrying thousands of fighters, judging by size alone." Asgad leaned forward as if hoping to spot something more. "No communications, and no insights into their intentions."

Joe had not met Asgad before joining the flagship. The admiral struck him as being a good man to work with, his calm, serene expression and disarrayed gray-white hair giving the impression of an easy-going soul who nevertheless knew his business, remained at his post and never spoke without good reason. A quiet, gangly man of Terran heritage, he descended by self-acclimation from a famous king of ancient Ethiopia. The crew respected him and appeared happy in their service—always a good indicator of the worth of a commander, Joe thought.

"And us?"

Asgad faced Joe and flashed a broad, white-toothed smile, his dark eyes glittering from an almost coal-black face. A faint but confident chuckle escaped his lips.

"We have a thousand ships here, the entire second fleet. The fourth will arrive in a matter of hours and double our numbers. You can't fight a close battle in a ship the size of those mothers, and we should be able to match their fighter strength. As long we don't get any more of them, we'll be fine,"

Joe decided he liked the man's confidence.

"The odd thing is they're just sitting out here," the admiral continued. "No defensive screens and no sign of aggression. They've ignored all our attempts to communicate. Not normal behavior at all for an invader."

"Maybe they're sizing us up. How many fighting ships *do* you think we're dealing with?"

"No idea. It depends on the type of fighter. If they are *bayonet*-size, perhaps thousands. Otherwise, who knows? Your guess might be better than mine."

Joe remained silent. He had come here out of a sense of duty, and because everyone expected him to do so. Like the general population, those serving in Fleet considered him the foremost authority on all things alien, and the saviour of humanity, but he considered the first incorrect and the latter undeserved. In reality, his knowledge of the intruders was no better than the admiral's.

Joe's perceived expertise was, in his view, a complete fallacy. He had been on the *Minaret* twice before its destruction, but on the first occasion he made contact only with Io, and on the second, only with the artificial mind called the Aivris. About the ships sitting several thousand kilometers away, he had no clue at all. If anyone was an expert, it would be Leo, who lived in and explored the systems of the ark for decades before his rescue.

Joe *was* positive the carriers were under the control of artificial intelligence. Even without proof, he was convinced a master synthetic brain remained active in the Tanakhai home system and had no doubt sent this force in response to the last message from the Aivris.

Whether that AI exercised direct influence over the alien vessels or they were guided by autonomous machine intelligence or Aivris 'iterations' was unknown, but Joe guessed it would be the latter, as direct control from the source was impossible due to the vast distances between the stars. The possibility existed, of course, that the prime intelligence occupied one of those ships, but for reasons hard to pin down, Joe doubted that.

Asgad turned toward his day room, located at the rear of the bridge deck. As he walked past, he smiled. "Coffee?"

Joe nodded acceptance and followed the admiral. As he entered the room, two familiar figures rose from the settee. Joe's daughter Raisa grinned as her partner Terry stepped forward with his hand out in greeting.

"What are you two doing here?"

"We just arrived on the dispatcher," Terry said. "You don't think we would let you come here on your own, do you, Boss? Somebody has to keep you out of trouble."

Raisa waved a greeting. "We thought you might need moral support."

"You're right there." Joe hugged his daughter, grasped Terry by the hand and took a seat at the direction of the admiral. "So, what do we know?"

Asgad sat at his desk and poked a finger at a small screen to access data compiled on the alien intruders. "We have ten identical vessels, all carriers, but unlike the *Minaret* these are armed. Initial observations show the visible weaponry to be laser and particle-beam-based. We don't know for sure, but they appear to be bog-standard, like our own. There are no obvious kinetic weapons."

Joe's brow furrowed. It was significant that the enemy was equipped with only those weapons. The arks, colonization ships for a species that was rather naïve concerning what threats they might have encountered on their voyages, carried no built-in weapons at all.

During the Blackship and Dysnomia wars, energy and heat projectors were the weapons of choice, and the *Minaret's bayonets* had been based on human technology. It was possible this was still all the Prime Aivris possessed if indeed it was behind this intrusion. If the carriers had nothing to do with the rogue intelligence and represented a new threat, all bets were off.

Other weapons, such as projectile cannons, were used by Fleet ships in the Blackship War, but not in the Dysnomia incident. At that time, they were considered obsolete and had fallen out of use with the introduction of shields, through which the shells could not pass.

"These are just over twenty thousand meters in length and about three thousand in diameter," Asgad said, "so, much smaller than the arks. There are no rotation wheels or drums, which indicates no living organisms on board. Based on our knowledge of the *Minaret*, they'll be powered by antimatter engines, and the shape of the sterns supports that. Probably fully automated."

As he spoke, he directed the image from his screen to a larger wall unit for his guests to see.

"Those openings along the sides, just aft of the bow," Joe said. "They're similar to the ones on the *Minaret*. Hangar entries?"

Terry leaned forward to get a better view. "Looks like it. The ark had only one per side, but these have many; they're meant to launch multiple fighters in a hurry. These are warships."

"I agree," Joe said. "The airfield on the *Minaret* was designed to meet the needs of a colony ship, and had internal hangers separate from the actual landing field. A pure warship would not need that. Those entrances may be direct from the hangers, for quicker scrambling."

"They haven't launched anything yet," the admiral said. "They've done nothing but sit there. I'm open to any ideas about what we should do next?"

"Send out a drone," Raisa suggested, joining the speculation for the first time. "It'll appear benign, but it might draw a response."

Asgad flashed his white teeth in her direction, a broad smile spreading across his face. "My thoughts exactly, Miz Falcon."

"Just Raisa, Sir." Despite her formal partnership with Terry, Joe's daughter insisted on retaining the Falcon name, but like Joe, she rarely stood on protocol.

Minutes later, the group returned to the bridge. A small, spherical drone, a communications device used to carry messages, moved away from the flagship and approached the nearest of the alien vessels.

"What do you reckon, Boss?" Terry asked. "Think they'll fire on it?"

Joe shrugged his shoulders. He could not imagine how the aliens would respond.

"Unless they have something better than what we can see, it won't matter," the admiral said. "All our ships carry shields, so energy weapons can't touch us. The first enemy fire detected, and all shields go up."

"Even if a ship is hit, it'll still protect its crew," Joe added. For decades, he had overseen the design and construction of the latest diamond warships and was aware they were able to take a colossal beating.

The old vessels in use at the time of the Blackship War were enormous, the largest carrying several thousand crew, and the loss of even one resulted in the loss of many lives. The destruction of the Terran flagship in that battle still sat heavily in Joe's mind, and he had placed great emphasis on avoiding such catastrophic loss of life in the future.

The new warships represented a quantum leap in every way.

In olden days, the oceanic battleships gave way to smaller, lighter, faster and more heavily armed destroyers and frigates equipped not with massive guns, but with missiles.

So too, Fleet replaced the old space-going battle wagons with the small diamond destroyers of the current force, each of which was more capable than one of its larger predecessors. The flagship was identical to the others and carried no markings, making it difficult for an enemy fleet to determine the location of the fleet command.

A crew of just twenty-four men and women manned each vessel, every aspect from engines to weaponry being computerized and controlled from a small, twenty-meter sphere within the center of the hull. That structure, one meter thick and made from pure carbon, remained viable even if the hull around it became scrap. A lifeboat in its own right, it maintained life support for several weeks to provide the best possible chance of rescue. Joe got the idea for the design from the old bathyscaphes used to explore the deep oceans of Earth.

Approaching the intruders, the drone drifted at a snail's pace, broadcasting greetings in both human and, thanks to Leo, Tanakhai dialects, as well as the usual mathematical sequences.

The *Minaret* Aivris had understood English and Mandarin, the two principal languages of humanity, and undoubtedly passed that knowledge back to the original super-mind. If these ships came from the Tanakhai system, there was little chance of their failing to understand the drone's peaceful intent.

At a point only kilometers from the nearest intruder, the tiny machine stopped, then began to move forward again, skirting around the ship's nose and moving toward the hangar openings.

"The drone is now under alien control," the flagship's commander announced. "It's been powered down and appears to be in the grip of a tractor beam of some sort. It's being drawn to the foremost entrance on the port side." As she spoke, the tiny orb vanished into the dark opening.

"Well, that was fun," the admiral said. "No response as such. They just took the thing, and still no communications."

"Don't be so sure," Joe said. "It's always possible...."

An alarm sounded, and without command, the bridge personnel snapped to full attention. From the hangar openings on the nearest carrier, small alien fighters were emerging.

Joe watched the crew as they went about their duties. He was impressed; where once standing alert but at ease, every officer was now fully focused at their station. To either side of the bridge, those who controlled the ship's armaments and engines were prepared and ready without a single spoken word from Asgad or the ship's commander. These people knew their job without being told.

Across hundreds of kilometers of space, the alien fighters took position to create a defensive barrier between their carriers and the Fleet of Humanity. At the middle of the formation a larger gap opened, and a bright blue beam of scintillating power lanced out from the nose of the lead intruder.

Everything happened so quickly that Joe could not follow, but he knew the drill. The second the assault began, all shields flashed on, encompassing each human vessel in a ball of impenetrable, reflective energy.

He had seen this before, during the Blackship War. At that time, the invader unleashed a massive plasma blast toward the surface of Earth, an attack that failed due to the instantaneous activation of the shield the *Minaret* had installed around the planet.

Earth's defense appeared as a perfect, mirror sphere that reflected the stars and the attacking starship, and hid the planet from view. Joe expected that was all the new intruders could now see of the Fleet vessels. In a split second, every human ship had vanished behind a bubble of pure force.

This type of shield differed from the original. The one used to protect Earth was opaque from within, and blocked all light, plunging the surface into total darkness. Those now deployed by the warships resembled the ones from the *Minaret* itself, later stolen by Leo. They were transparent from within, allowing those on the bridge decks a full and clear view of the opposing threat.

All that was visible of the enemy were ten enormous elliptical bubbles, beyond the wall of smaller fighters the carriers had disgorged.

"Those fighters are larger than the bayonets," Terry said, watching from his position at the rear of the deck. "They seem to have upped their game somewhat."

"Perhaps," Asgad agreed. "Bigger doesn't mean better." He turned toward Joe. "The bayonets used human technology, yes?"

"So we believe," Joe said. "The *Minaret* tapped all our databases on its way into the system and started mass-producing fighters using the stolen data. This is different. We've kept all military research under wraps since then, and everything is stored in encrypted, secure facilities. If these carriers are better, it is because this new entity has learned from what the Aivris sent home."

Asgad raised his eyebrows. "We still have no evidence they are from the same source."

Joe stared the admiral in the eyes. "I have no doubt they are. So what now?"

"Stalemate. Their weapons can't penetrate our shields, and I'm guessing ours can't get through theirs. My orders are not to start a war unless it's unavoidable, so I'm not going to fire a return shot to find out. We have missiles, but I doubt they will do any better and I don't want to resort to that just yet. The only way we can attack them is to drop the shield, shoot, and raise it again, and the same probably applies to them. We...."

The ship's commander interrupted. "Admiral, we have a development. Four of the intruders are moving away."

Joe glanced up at the holo screen. Four of the mirror bubbles, the rearmost of the fleet, moved at right angles to the front line. Without warning, the shields vanished, revealing the ships within. After another second, they disappeared.

"What the... Where did they go?"

"They're still there," the officer said, studying his control desk readouts. "We can still detect the ion trails from their engines, and they're leaving the formation, but they're ... invisible."

"How is that even possible?" Joe slumped into a vacant chair and stared at the screen. "It would appear our adversary has a few tricks up its sleeve. It's developed a new variation of the defensive shield, one that absorbs wave energy instead of just reflecting..."

"So all that's left is a black hole," Asgad finished Joe's sentence. "Almost impossible to track in open space."

"Admiral, Sir," the commander said. "We're losing them. The ion trails are fading, and we have no idea where they're going."

Joe watched the holo screen, now a maze of shield-bubble reflections of the fleet's ships. More than a little about the situation troubled him.

"Why would aliens enter our system and just sit out here doing nothing," he wondered out loud, speaking to nobody in particular. "We send a drone with obvious peaceful intent, which they capture, and they respond with an aggressive move, fire a single shot and go back to just sitting there."

"And four of them disappear," the admiral added.

"Yes. You have to wonder what they are up to. They fire just enough shots to make it clear they are a threat, then do nothing more. I don't think the ships here are our biggest problem, and I suspect their only intent at the moment is to keep us distracted. They must know that we can't afford to let six enemy carriers wander unchecked through our system, so they use that fact to hold us here, while the others do God knows what."

"You would think those four would have left before we arrived, so we wouldn't know about them. Maybe they didn't expect us to find them so quickly."

"So," Asgad concluded, "we focus on the ships that just vanished. Whatever they are up to, that will be the real purpose of this fleet. We need to find them again ... now."

Chapter 12

A PALL OF SILENCE descended over the control deck. Joe's eyes remained glued to the main screen, his mind whirling with speculation as to what the enemy would do next.

There was no obvious sense as to what had occurred so far, but it was certain that if these ships were controlled by artificial intelligence, the logic would be there somewhere. Based on his experience with the Aivris, he suspected these entities never did anything illogical, at least according to their twisted perception of that quality.

In the gap between the ships of Fleet and the alien intruders, something was happening. The small fighters disgorged by the alien carriers began to move, swarming toward the spaces between the opposing forces and surrounding several of the diamond ships.

Motionless in space, they opened fire on the shields of the fleet vessels, oblivious to the fact their shots could not penetrate. Return fire quickly destroyed several, only to have them replaced within minutes by more. The small size of the alien craft, and the comparative weakness of their weapons, made them little of a threat. Joe wondered how many of those annoying little gnats the enemy possessed.

"This makes no sense," he said. "Those things can't hurt us even if they get shots through our shield drops. The hulls on our ships can withstand a million pin-pricks like those, and they don't have heavy plating or defensive shields. We can pick them off with little difficulty. The enemy must have them to spare, but there has to be a limit. It's not sustainable, not even a viable attrition tactic on their part."

"I agree," the admiral said. "They aren't seriously trying to harm us—just hold our attention. As you said earlier, they want to keep us here."

The Fleet tactic was to drop shields for just that split-second needed to fire a weapon and raise them again before the enemy could react. Few shots found an actual target and in time the conflict faded to nothing. All combatants, the six remaining alien carriers, their fighters and almost one thousand human vessels, sat motionless in space. It was a standoff.

"This is ridiculous," Asgad said. The admiral paced the deck and shook his head, his crew motionless at their stations, still alert but with no idea of what to do next.

"We're being deliberately stalled—that much is obvious," Terry commented. "They stopped firing because they can't destroy us, any more than we can them."

"Agreed." Joe had drawn the same conclusion, but he also knew the *Minaret* Aivris had never done anything without reason, and could not accept that these new intruders were in any way different. "Admiral, do we have anything new on the ships that vanished?"

"No. They eluded our trackers before we could even react to their leaving. We can't even detect their ion trails now. We have no clue where they've gone."

"It's not hard to work out," Raisa said from her seat at the rear of the deck. "They're not going to travel for decades to get here, just to turn and go home, so they're heading for Mars, Earth or the mining conglomerates in the Belt. Those are the only worthwhile military targets in this system."

"I agree, Miz Falcon," Asgad replied.

Joe smiled to himself. He had drawn the same conclusion, but out of respect was waiting for the admiral to do the same. Raisa had never been so tactful. "Admiral, how is the fleet dispersed at present?" he asked.

"We have one thousand ships here," Asgad said. "Fleet four is now stationary, five thousand klicks behind us, with the remaining two fleets approaching another three thousand further back."

"How many fighters do you think those carriers could carry, now that we have some idea what they are and what they can do?"

"Our best estimate is now one to one and a half thousand for each ship. Certainly no more, but they can't touch us anyway. Even if they get through our shields they can't do the same with those around our planets. We still have no idea what other weapons they may carry besides what we've seen. They might be waiting for us to send some ships home, before unleashing something more powerful that we can't defend against."

"May I suggest you break the fleets anyway, and send some back, just in case? The ships we've lost may be heading to the mining complexes, and they are not well-defended."

Four alien ships had vanished, and there were four major mining cooperatives in the asteroid belt. The coincidence was disturbing, and Joe knew it was not lost on the admiral.

Joe accepted that as a civilian he had no official authority here, but he also understood his unofficial status with the members of Fleet. He would be expected to make suggestions, and he knew Asgad would accept his input if he considered it valuable. After a moment's consideration, the admiral turned to the flagship's commander.

"Issue a general alert to fleets one and three, please, Commander. They will return to the asteroid belt on my orders, and each divide into two sub-groups, one to go to each mining cooperative. The division of ships is up to the fleet commanders. They can liaise on who goes where on the way there. Fleet four will close up to join us here."

"Yes, sir," the commander replied, turning to her communications officer to carry out the order.

Asgad returned his attention to Joe. "We know how fast those bastards travel, so if we find nothing there, we can leave a part of our contingents to secure the bases and move on to Earth and Mars."

"Do you think two thousand fleet ships are enough for these six remaining carriers?"

"Yes, unless they have some weapon we haven't seen yet. I pray so. For now, at least, the stalemate remains unchanged."

"What if it's a ploy," Terry interjected from his seat. "What if this whole business is designed just to get us to split the fleet?"

Joe returned his attention to the remaining alien vessels on the screen. Terry's suggestion was certainly a possibility, but did it make a difference? Neither side of the stalemate appeared to have the ability to do any significant damage to the other.

At the same time, six massive starships were not something the fleet could ignore. Ineffective or not, stalemate or not, Asgad could ill afford to ignore the intruders or leave them unguarded by anything less than a fleet sufficient to withstand them should it become necessary.

The mining complexes were vulnerable. In the last few decades, the main stations at each complex had been fitted with shields, but there were hundreds of modules at each complex and many of them, including factories, docks and minor accommodation facilities were still vulnerable. The presence of warships at those sights could decide whether they survived or not, assuming the fleets could get there in time.

At the time of the Dysnomia incident the largest of those complexes, the Kepler station, had been severely damaged and subsequently evacuated, the main hub station left uninhabitable. Everything had now been repaired and the complex was once again in full operation. Joe shuddered at the thought it might be attacked a second time.

He turned to his daughter. "Raisa, do we know where Leo is at present?"

"Yes, Dad. He's on Mars with President Verveda. When you came out here to the fleet she asked him to come in as her adviser."

"And he agreed to that? Seriously?"

"Uncle Leo can be a little perverse at times. He thinks the president is hilarious."

Joe could not help the chuckle that escaped his lips. Despite the years since their duplication, he and his brother were essentially the same personality.

"She's not going to find my dear brother easy." Verveda and he had not got on well due to her irritating style and demanding manner, and he knew Leo would not wear that any more than had he. "I wish I could be there to see that."

"He's going to make her life a merry hell," Raisa commented. "You've mellowed over the decades, but Uncle Leo is more aggressive than you."

Joe smiled. His daughter was right in every way. For a few minutes he remained silent, content to observe. He tried not to show just how concerned he was about the ships that had vanished.

While it was most likely they were heading for the asteroid belt mining facilities, the possibility always existed they were heading for the home worlds.

Earth could not afford another blow after the Great Death. More than half the population died, with civilization damaged almost beyond repair and several of the most advanced nations succumbing to the severe cold. The long night was over now, but the new mini-ice-age that took its place still made much of the planet uninhabitable.

Only thanks to intervention from Mars had further destruction through warfare been avoided, as the refugees from frozen countries sought to create a new life for themselves in more equatorial nations which had neither the resources nor the desire to accommodate them.

The Martian government's policy decreed that emergency support would go primarily to those places that welcomed refugees and made an effort to assist them.

Many of the old nations no longer existed, and the governments of those that survived had no option but to accept change.

Regardless, nobody could afford another attack.

Mars fared better in both of the previous events, and would no doubt do so again. Humanity's overall future was never in doubt. Humans were hard to kill, and the presence of Zealandia and several other worlds, hidden amongst the distant stars and currently beyond the reach of whatever was in control of those alien ships, was a safety valve that would ensure the survival of the species should the worst case eventuate.

Joe shook his head. The risk of attack on either Earth or Mars was too great to ignore.

At that moment he realized he was in the wrong place altogether.

"Admiral," he announced. "I need to get back to Mars as quickly as possible. With your permission, I would like to borrow one of the high-speed dispatchers."

*   *   *

The obvious approach when entering a new system was to locate and enter the plane of the ecliptic as quickly as possible, to make it easier to locate planets. Despite that norm, objects from space could, and did, arrive from any point, and for this reason, additional remote watch stations were positioned above and below the plane in the Solar System.

Despite being on full alert, they failed to detect a second group of alien vessels that came in at an angle of sixty degrees to the ecliptic, on the side furthest away from where the carriers would eventually be locked in a stalemate with humanity's finest. These smaller craft, which had departed the main alien fleet whilst still well beyond the outer rim of the system, had arrived first by several months, and were now well underway with their assigned tasks.

Several dozen vessels had dropped silently, hidden behind shields that absorbed every waveform that might be used for detection, into the void between the orbits of the innermost planets. The fleet divided, one half moving toward the shining white orb of Earth's evil twin.

On arrival, they dropped into the dense, murky atmosphere and descended to the surface. Fully automated, the ships contained no living things, their structures well able to cope with the crushing, ground-level pressure. Immediately upon setting down, they opened their holds and disgorged their cargoes.

On Mercury, the other half of the fleet also set down. They landed on the side currently facing away from the Sun, where the surface was well below zero despite the planet's proximity to its fiery overlord.

Mercury rotated just three times for every two orbits of the sun, so while it was not tidally locked to its master, surface conditions were little different than if it had been. As a rule, the side facing the star reached temperatures of four hundred and fifty degrees centigrade, while on the other side, they dropped as low as one hundred and seventy below zero.

The ships that spread across the dark side were not concerned by that, but the colder side of the world suited their purpose better to begin. As they settled to the surface, their hatches opened and thousands of small, autonomous machines spread across the barren rock, searching for just the right minerals for their great purpose.

These tiny devices were of a type humans called *Von Neumann machines*, capable of reproducing themselves using only the materials they could extract from the surrounding environment. Upon locating the necessary resources, each machine commenced a set routine, to extract and process the ore at the molecular level, and assemble exact copies of itself.

Several days passed before the first new generation of machines was complete, doubling their numbers. A few days later the number doubled again, and again, and again. By the time the carriers were apprehended, the machines numbered in the tens of millions, and most had already switched to alternate programming and began the actual task for which they were intended. Increasingly larger machines were made, the scope of the operations expanding exponentially.

The area around each alien ship was now a seething pool of activity, tiny machines mining the local ore and processing it into materials that could be used for other, more specific purposes.

The finished products, in the form of ultra-fine molecular powders, were formed into pellets and fired into space with rail guns, where they were gathered by other machines for further processing, before being used to build a structure the like of which humans had only dreamed in the past.

Chapter 13

ON THE FLAT, BARREN plains of northern Mars, a vast industrial complex stretched across hundreds of square kilometers of the Acidalia Planitia.

The construction yards for the Fleet of Humanity were almost fully automated, with only a minimal military force for security, and programmers to ensure that the millions of robotic construction arbeiters operated at maximum efficiency. A casual observer could be forgiven for thinking this was a dedicated machine city, the few human operatives rarely seen outside the control complex.

The site included dozens of colossal domes, each surrounded by an array of auxiliary support buildings. Within each, a new warship, one of the fabled diamond ships of Fleet, grew rapidly toward completion, much of the basic structure being built molecule by molecule from carbon, silicon and other raw elements. Once the hull of a ship was ready, other machines, ranging from nano-assemblers to massive hydraulic lifters, would install all the components and weaponry necessary to make it one of the most devastating vessels ever constructed.

Over two thousand ships had so far been assembled at this yard, with as many again being built at an almost identical site on Earth's moon, Luna. All those ships were now in deep space, engaged in an attempt to stop the new alien intruders from approaching the inner planets.

Work continued around the clock. New vessels rose rapidly on the platforms inside each dome, protected from the tenacious electrostatic dust of the red world. As each ship reached completion, the roof of the dome opened like a giant flower to allow the newborn creation to lift off, before closing again for the internal machinery to remove the ever-present dust and sterilize the site in readiness for the next construction.

High above the Planitia, invisible ships approached unseen and released their cargo, giant shuttles hidden within shields that made them undetectable from the surface.

As the carriers moved away, the shuttles dropped rapidly toward the surface. They were not detected in the darkness of night as they descended rapidly through the atmosphere and touched down in isolated and empty parts of the northern plains.

On landing, ramps descended and enormous juggernauts lumbered down to the surface. They resembled tanks but were many times larger, armed with laser and plasma cannons, and rode on anti-gravity pads instead of caterpillar tracks.

*   *   *

Joe Falcon strode into the foyer of the Hall of Congress and headed for the offices of the president. He did not bother to announce himself as he swept past the various secretarial blockades; everyone in this building knew him and his brother by sight, and nobody would have dared stop either man.

Daantje Verveda looked up as he burst into her office, quickly swept an electronic document pad from the desk into a drawer, and glowered at him.

Joe strode up to her desk and, standing over her, returned her glare. "Why aren't the planetary shields up? Did you not receive the alert from Admiral Asgad?"

"We've received no warnings of an imminent threat," Verveda retaliated. "The alert stated only that four ships were missing and believed to be heading for the mining complexes in the belt. The shields block sunlight, so we can't raise them unless absolutely necessary. You know that, since your institute installed them."

Joe slumped uninvited into a seat and continued to stare daggers at the president. She was right, of course. The modifications made to the original shield design to allow light to pass through was a more recent development and had so far only been carried out on the ships of Fleet.

"So, you're aware we've lost track of four of the alien ships," Joe said. "They could be coming here. You need to put up the shield now."

Verveda remained unmoved behind her expansive desk, clearly unimpressed. Her brow was furrowed, her mouth set in a thin, hard line. Her expression betrayed anger. "I'll decide when the shields go up, Mister Falcon. I appreciate your family is powerful on all of our worlds, but you do not make decisions for the government here."

"Fine by me," Joe replied. "So, how about you just do your job? There are millions of people out there whose future existence depends on your next move."

Joe watched as his opponent's eyes grew narrower, and waited for the tirade of self-justification he expected to follow. Deciding it was not worth the argument, he stood and strode toward the door. Verveda was not the only person who could order the shields up.

"Where do you think you're going now?" Verveda demanded.

"To the Institute. I believe those ships are coming here, and if you're not prepared to act I'll find someone who will."

"Mister Falcon, I don't think you..." The president stopped short as the door slammed in her face.

Outside the government center, Joe made his way toward the hyper-loop station. The moment he left the office he regretted taking that attitude with the president. He rarely lost his temper, and Verveda was a reasonably effective politician, if sometimes a little hard to work with. Nevertheless, he could not wait. Her intransigence was a problem that needed to be dealt with. He had hoped Leo would be there to back him up, but his brother-not-brother had vanished on business of his own.

Those alien ships had to be located. So far there had been no reports of them interfering with the asteroid belt mining stations, and the odds they were somewhere near Mars or Earth were growing daily.

Only a high-ranking member of the Military could order the shields up over the president's head. The Falcon family had powerful ties with several.

* * *

Ares Maggason threw down his shovel and scrambled from the hole he had been digging for the last five hours. Adjusting his oxygen mask, he slumped down on a nearby rock to take a well-earned breather.

Sweat pooled on his face, despite the air temperature in Acidalia being quite cool. Hard work always did that to him. He knew he was getting too old for this kind of work, but his body was still tough and wiry, and this was the last chance he might have to make that final, great strike.

It was often said that every prospector hoped to one day find the great gem that would make their fortune, and that in most cases that spectacular stone would remain forever in their pocket. When such a one was found, the discoverer could not, in most cases, bear to part with it, keeping it for that 'rainy day'.

Reaching into his deepest pocket Ares pulled out a small piece of glistening stone, a translucent gem that burned with a multi-colored fire. It was a form of opal, almost identical to the black opal found on Earth.

It had never been discovered on Mars before, but Ares stumbled upon this piece while prospecting, and after identifying it returned to see if he could find the main seam. Mining claims were difficult to enforce on the red world, and Ares never revealed the location for fear of a hundred fortune hunters moving in on his claim.

The stone in his hand was worth far more than even he could imagine. This particular gem was of a type that could only form in the presence of water. His was the only one ever discovered on Mars, and he had told nobody.

Once upon a far distant time, this part of the Planitia had been covered by a shallow ocean. Over millions of years the water vanished, allowing the remaining sedimentary ocean floor to crack as it dried. When water returned at a later date it carried deposits of silica into those cracks, where they became trapped, forming a gel that hardened to become opal. The rare and ancient gem was formed from silica spheres arranged in a regular pattern, and even though the water had vanished, considerable quantities of this natural beauty could be waiting below the surface. Where there was smoke...

Exactly how the piece in Ares's hand came to be on the surface was beyond his limited imagination, but extensive prospecting finally located a thin vein of poor-grade opal potch he intended to follow into the ground in the hope it would lead to a larger mass of gem quality material.

So far, the hole was about a meter square with roughly the same depth.

As he sat, Ares surveyed his surroundings, taking in the broad, empty beauty of the desolate world he called home. This region was completely flat and exposed.

A few feet away a flat, carbon-fiber cargo module panel lay on the ground, the last of a number bought second-hand and used to build a nearby shelter.

Beyond the panel and the other pieces of rubbish that littered the sight, a shimmer appeared in the distance.

Odd, Ares thought. Heat hazes were extremely rare on Mars, but with the increasing atmospheric density and the extra heat from the huge solar reflectors located in space above the planet, they were not unheard of. Mars was a cold world, but the average temperature was rising, slowly and steadily.

Kilometers away in the opposite direction, the plas-glass dome of Kharkhorin was just visible on the horizon. The tiny town was a small agricultural settlement with a population of no more than a hundred individuals, mostly refugee settlers. Ares used it as a base for his prospecting activities but only went there when he needed fresh supplies.

Many kilometers beyond that lonely town stood the colossal Fleet construction yard, but through the ever-present dust haze, nothing could be seen of that place of myth and mystery.

Far to the west, Ares could just make out a long, black line that stretched from north to south across the horizon. This was a massive electrical cable, one of many being constructed to stretch around the planet from pole to pole. They formed part of the solenoid loop network, the largest terraforming project yet undertaken on Mars.

At the southern pole, colossal fusion reactors were being constructed, and once they came online, the network of superconductor cables would begin pulsing with electrical energy. Encompassing the planet's magnetic inner core, they would create a magnetic field that would stretch up into space, forming a new magnetosphere to replace the natural one lost by the planet millennia ago, and protecting the newly forming atmosphere from being stripped away by the solar wind.

Turning his head again, Ares noticed the heat haze appeared to have grown. For a few moments he watched, puzzled but unconcerned. The phenomenon had not changed orientation; it was either stationary or was moving directly toward or away from him.

Rising and stretching, he wandered back to his shelter, changed the oxygen cylinder in his breathing apparatus, and took a long drink of cool water before strolling back to his hole, intending to continue his work. As he picked up his shovel he looked up.

Something was wrong.

What he had thought to be a heat haze now looked different, sufficient to stir a feeling of discomfort in his gut. The anomaly was closer, possibly less than a kilometer away and closing at speed. It was difficult to get a clear view, but things that should not have been there were visible in the haze, landmarks he knew not to be in that direction. It was almost as if he were looking into a mirror, and seeing an unsteady reflection of his encampment.

At ground level, a distant image appeared of a man standing alone, not far from a box-shaped structure. Transfixed, Ares watched as the strange anomaly grew closer. It was a dome of highly reflective material, and he was seeing his surroundings and himself.

It dawned that he was looking at a hemispherical force field. As an old navy man, he had heard of these things but had never seen one in reality. Such force domes did not appear spontaneously, and the question was, what was inside?

Only then did he realize the force field was going to pass over the place where he was standing.

Ares had no idea what an energy field like that would do to a human being. They were used almost exclusively in space and it was doubtful anyone knew for certain, but whatever the truth, it could not be good. Looking around, he searched frantically for a way to escape. The mirrored surface was now less than a hundred meters away and he knew he could never escape by running.

Spotting the carbon fiber panel on the ground, he grabbed it and dragged it to his hole. Dropping in, he pulled the panel over his head with sweating hands, and crouched as low as he could, praying to each and every god his numbed mind could recall. Ares was not particularly religious, but he had always believed in maximizing the odds.

Seconds later a deep rumble shook the ground, and a force Ares could not identify passed through his body, his skin prickling as if exposed to extreme static electricity. For the briefest of moments, he felt he was being burned alive by the most powerful sunburn of all time.

All went quiet and the heat passed, leaving only the pain. Ares reached up and lifted the edge of the carbon panel, hoping the shield had passed over. It was dim above, with minimal light filtering in from the sides. Raising the panel a little more, he looked out.

Meters above his head, a dark gray structure slid smoothly by. All was quiet. Sweat pearled on his forehead and trickled down into his eyes, stinging as it blurred his view.

Whatever the vast machine was, it was floating on some kind of suspensor field, with no wheels or tracks. Ares felt only the slightest of vibrations. Easing up a little more he took a better look, his heart pounding.

The thing above his head was enormous, at least a hundred meters in length. It was moving slowly. To either side Ares could see rows of dome-shaped protrusions on the bottom of the structure, presumably the sources of whatever force was holding it above the ground. The trailing edge was about to pass over his head.

A terrifying thought entered his mind. The force field around this thing was a dome. It did not appear to extend down into the ground, so his hole, along with the carbon fiber panel he used as a lid, had protected him as the force field passed over. The trailing edge was only meters away and closing fast.

Dragging the panel back into place, Ares dropped as low as possible in the hole and drew his body into a fetal position. The only thing he was aware of was the shuddering in his body, the pounding of blood through his ears, the heat, and the pain.

Chapter 14

THE INHABITANTS OF KHARKHORIN went about their early morning activities without concern. Prayer was over, and many of the townsfolk were busy tending the hydroponic farms that sustained their existence.

The settlement was one of many small refugee communities, this one made up of people from Eastern Asia who emigrated at the time of the Great Death. They saw themselves as an ancient culture from a land called Mongolia, once a nation in its own right until invaded by its more powerful neighbor.

A simple people, they were content to live on the fringes of Martian society under a dome originally built by a subsidiary of the New Worlds Institute as part of a research program to study the far northern Martian plains.

Nobody kept a watch for danger.

They had no reason to do so. The Planitia was a quiet, empty place, and few people other than settlers ever came this way. The only visitors to the community tended to be solitary prospectors who passed through on irregular occasions to barter for supplies.

Across the flat plain, numerous hemispherical force fields glided over the barren regolith, quickly closing on the settlement. As they approached to within a kilometer, the leading field flickered, and a shaft of scintillating energy lanced toward the town.

Death came without warning. The mirrored domes had gone unnoticed by the people, and the first alert came in the form of the settlement dome rupturing.

After centuries of colonization, the atmospheric density of Mars was now sufficient to allow a human to survive in the open without a pressure suit, but breathing equipment continued to be essential due to the still-high carbon-dioxide content. None of the inhabitants wore them within the dome, and their peaceful morning became a frantic rush back to the shelter of the buildings.

Over the next ten minutes, several more of the massive war machines turned their weapons on the helpless settlement, until no building remained intact. Few citizens survived, bar a handful who managed to retrieve masks, and avoid the collapse of their homes and the deadly blasts of the attackers.

Kharkhorin posed no threat. It was not a strategic site by any standard. Almost all the settlers died, for no reason other than that their town was in the way.

Beyond the ruin and some distance over the horizon, was the nearest edge of the vast Martian shipyard.

*   *   *

Major General Yasamin Nouzari glanced up as her adjutant burst unannounced through the doorway. The abruptness of the intrusion did not concern her; the young man who now stood red-faced before her was the only soul who could get away with such behavior. The base was too complex for any one person to stay abreast of every detail, and she trusted his keen perception to keep her up to date.

Despite her presence, the shipyards were technically a subsidiary of the New Worlds Institute and were a little less navy and much more industrial. The process was fully automated, the ships being constructed by computer-controlled machines from the early stages of ore mining and conversion right up to the internal fitting out and completion. Only the final commissioning and delivery of each new vessel was carried out by humans.

Besides the general and her adjutant, thirty-seven personnel staffed the administration building, plus a squad of twenty marines who manned the automatic defenses of the complex. Their job was to monitor the drones that patrolled the perimeter fences to keep out human intruders. With the planet defended by a space-shield system, nobody expected trouble to come from anywhere else.

"Yes, Joshua? What is it?" Any answer would have been welcome, to relieve the usual morning boredom.

"General, Ma'am. You need to come with me. I must show you something. We detected an unidentified intrusion; don't know what it is."

"What do you mean by '*don't know*?'" She liked this young man, but when flustered he became a little abstract, and at those times she tended to become frustrated.

"Please, Ma'am. Trust me on this one. You need to come to the monitoring room."

For a moment, Nouzari scrutinized her assistant. There was a certain wildness in his eyes she had never seen before, and that raised red flags. She knew her adjutant's every mood and nervous tic, and whatever worried him now was serious. Without further hesitation, she stood and followed him through the door.

The windowless, ten-meter-square control room was a vault at the center of the administration building. Around the walls, eight guards sat at their stations, deep in concentration. A man and a woman, two of the shift commanders of the security team, hovered behind them, their eyes fixed on the monitors. As Nouzari entered, the man glanced up, spun on his heels and snapped to attention, his associate doing likewise.

"Ma'am."

"Stand Easy, Captain. What have you found?"

"Not sure, Ma'am. Something is out there, but we can't tell what. We can detect something, but can't see it. Whatever it is, it's hidden behind a force field. We can see the distortions in the shield, but that's all."

"How big is it?"

"The dome is about a hundred and thirty meters in diameter. If it's hiding some kind of machine, it's enormous."

"You think this is an attack?"

"I have no idea, Ma'am. We've contacted Fleet Central, and the outer stations haven't detected any approach to the planet from space, but to be honest I can't think what else it could be. I'm not aware of anything like this in our ground forces."

"Is the planetary shield up?"

"No Ma'am. Still full daylight outside; the order hasn't been given."

"So, what do you think this is?"

The Captain glanced across at the nearest screen as several additional guards rushed into the room and silently manned several unoccupied positions. These were not simple observation posts. The perimeter of the yard was lined with a double wall of high-voltage security fencing, and on the road between the two lines, heavy-duty automated drones patrolled day in and day out. The machines carried laser cannons, and any attempt to assault the base would be met with fierce resistance.

"They are approaching at low speed," the captain said. "Estimated time of arrival is forty minutes. No signals are being broadcast, so we have no choice but to consider them hostile."

"Them?"

"Yes, sorry, Ma'am. One is leading, but at least nineteen others are behind it, all coming from the direction of Kharkhorin."

"Have you contacted the settlement?"

"Of course, Ma'am. No response. The town appears to be off-grid."

For a moment Nouzari said nothing as she processed the information. She turned and stepped up to one of the monitor stations.

"Full alert!" she announced. "I want every vehicle out, and the fences on maximum charge. How many completed ships do we have awaiting delivery?"

"Four, Ma'am. The crews are awaiting your orders. The units are armed and operational, but they have only delivery crews."

"Tell them to lift off and stand by. If these things attack, they are to retaliate to the best of their ability."

"Yes ma'am."

"Contact defense control and tell them I am ordering the planetary shield on—now. Advise the president the reason she isn't getting a suntan is that I'm overriding her, but before you do, send a message to General Paisley, on Luna."

Nouzari tapped a pad on the communications console.

"George. I'm sending you a live feed of strange objects approaching us here. I'm not sure yet, but I have no option but to treat it as an attack by persons unknown. This base has minimal defense capability, as does yours, so I recommend you activate your shield now. Anyone attacking here will likely try to reach you as well, and we can't afford to lose both yards.

"Please also notify Earth shield control," she continued. "We've seen no sign of alien ships here yet, but four of the new arrivals are unaccounted for. If this is an attack, something must have dropped those *things* out there, and by my reckoning, enemy ships may be approaching Earth now. You can't afford another beating, so better to be cautious."

Thirty Minutes later, the old and wizened face of George Paisley, the commander of Luna yard, appeared on a holo-screen to one side of the main display.

Luna, Earth's Moon, was the location of Fleet's second construction facility. Unlike the Martian yard, which was protected by planetary defenses, the moon base had its own multi-generator dome covering an area over one hundred kilometers in diameter.

For a moment Paisley peered from the monitor, no signs of recognition showing on his face. Nouzari knew he would be checking his defenses before replying. The two officers were close friends, and each knew the other well.

The image of the old general remained unchanged for several more minutes, then his eyes widened and he looked up at the camera. His mouth twisted as he nodded confirmation. "Nobody will get in here," he grunted.

The screen went black and Nouzari focused on the task at hand, returning her gaze to the room around her. "Now, let's see what these intruders are up to."

*   *   *

"Alright, Mister Falcon, I admit I was wrong." President Verveda spread her hands in a conciliatory manner, her face flushed. "The shields are up now, so nothing more can reach the surface. We can't be sure what we have to deal with, but at least nothing else can land."

Joe said nothing. Beyond the window, Hellas Basin was in almost total darkness, lit only by the lights that sparkled around the occupied rim. The shield would have little effect on the people or the military of Mars.

Reports from Earth indicated their defenses had also been activated, on the orders of the commander of the Luna shipyards. The mother world was less able to deal with long periods of blackouts, but since the days of the Great Death, the world had grown more resilient in energy and food production. Crops in the open would suffer a little, but unless the shutdown went on for an extended period, they would cope.

When the new shields had been installed around the planets, the possibility of fighting a war in darkness had been considered, and on Mars, a ground-level network of locator towers now encompassed the globe. Using electronic navigation, ground or air vehicles functioned as well as in full sunlight.

The greatest problem with the shields was the temperature; as long as the shield remained up, the surface would become cooler. Mars had always been a cold place, and all of the settlements, most of them located underground or beneath insulated domes, were warmed by artificial means.

Joe studied the president. He could tell she was concerned about her error in delaying the activation, and her embarrassment was obvious, but perhaps now was not the best time to push the issue.

Theirs was a strange relationship, in which she held the official authority and his family the actual power, and he would be happy to have a more amicable working arrangement with her despite her intransigence.

"Where's my brother, Leo?"

"I have no idea. He kept arguing the point with me, so I dismissed him."

More likely the other way around, Joe thought. "What can I do to help? The full resources of the Institute are at your disposal." *Within reason.*

"Thank you, Joe. I appreciate that. I've ordered the security forces to the shipyards, but it will be at least an hour before they get there. In the meantime, Nouzari is on her own."

Joe nodded again. "I think it might be best if I go there myself. I am the official liaison, after all. There may be damage, and I can give my people the heads-up. We can't have the yard down any longer than necessary."

"Let us hope it does not come to that," Verveda replied. "I understand the general is a competent commander."

*   *   *

Nouzari ducked instinctively, despite there being no way for the blasts to reach her. She and her personnel had retreated to the sub-basement, the most secure place on the base. At one end of the spacious subterranean hall, the installation guards manned stations duplicating those of the main control room.

Above ground, twenty juggernauts had lined up along the perimeter, each an alien device of immense proportion. Almost too fast to see, shields flickered as the attackers fired. The armored vehicles defending the yards were ineffective against the assault, their weapons unable to breach the enemy defenses.

The colossal war machines paid little attention to the tiny defenders, ignoring them as they focused on their targets, the domes within which the fleet ships were constructed. One by one, the structures slumped and melted under heavy bombardment from plasma cannons. As they did so, the alien tanks moved forward, rolling across the perimeter and into the grounds as if the boundary fences did not exist at all.

High above, four brand-new diamond fighters swooped on the enemy, to little effect. They were manned by delivery crews with little operational experience, and their best attempts to coordinate shots with the flickering of the enemy shields were futile.

Nouzari stood defiant, bracing herself on the edge of a desk as she watched her domain crumble to ruin. With the Martian security forces still half an hour away, she could do nothing to stop the assault. All around her, the guards worked silently at the controls of the surviving perimeter defense drones, each well aware they were in a battle they could not win. Soon not a single dome would remain unscathed.

Of the total ship assembly mechanism, only the domes projected above the surface. All material supply lines, all access routes and machinery bays, and all facilities for component construction were beneath the solid construction platforms, and below ground level. When this was over it would take only weeks to rebuild and start again, using nano-technology. The biggest loss would be the dozens of ships in various stages of construction, all of them now lost.

As she watched, the last dome collapsed. Seconds later, the juggernauts turned in unison and moved away in a south-easterly direction, ignoring the administration building and other service and maintenance structures as they glided out over the flat, dusty Planitia.

"Where are they going?" Nouzari craned her neck forward to better see the screens. "They've not attempted to destroy the rest of the base." Her brow furrowed, and she shook her head as the monster machines moved away. "This makes no sense at all," she muttered to herself.

Chapter 15

NOTHING OF NOTE WAS visible through the side window of the shuttle as it flew at high speed over the Acidalia Planitia. All was darkness outside, the light from the sun blocked by the planetary shield. Every minute or two, a glow appeared far below to mark the location of an isolated settlement, then vanished as the fast-moving craft sped on its mission.

Joe watched the lights flash by.

Mining settlements, or something similar.

Other than a few trial agricultural concerns, this region was empty.

"How long before we arrive?"

Carlos Serra-Pinho, an employee of the Institute's private air arm, glanced at the small monitor above his head. "ETA is … just over three minutes. You won't be able to see much outside until we get there, but I can show you the infrared." Tapping the console, he activated the screen in front of Joe's seat.

As predicted, the shuttle arrived at the construction yard within seconds of the specified time. Joe grunted appreciation to the pilot, who had just flown the tiny vehicle a quarter of the way around the planet, from

Hellas City to Acidalia, in pitch darkness, using only the navigation beacons that peppered the surface, and the infrared vision of the aircraft. The Institute chose its people with care and trained them well.

The sight was worse than either expected or imagined. The perimeter defenses had been crushed by the entry of the attacking juggernauts. Every dome lay in ruins, slagged by energies beyond anything possessed by a Martian military vehicle.

The above-ground structures were little more than covered platforms for the assembly of vehicles. The real workings of the base, the expansive factories that built all components for later installation and the power systems that drove it all, were sub-surface, their current state as yet unknown.

To one side of the yard's airfield were four diamond fighters, the brand-new vessels that lifted off just minutes before the marauders arrived. They were operational, but of little value against the attackers without trained combat crews.

In a clear space on the field, a solitary figure stood waving a blue light, directing Joe's craft to a safe landing.

*   *   *

General Nouzari's eyes told the full story as they peered over her face mask. She had been awake for far too long, her skin pale in the torchlight, her hair bedraggled, her shoulders slumped. A fierce fire burned in her eyes as she held a hand out in greeting.

"Welcome, Sir," she said. "Sorry I couldn't break out the silverware; we've been a little busy."

Nouzari did not need to address Joe as *Sir*. The shipyard was a private industrial concern, but the commanding officer was Fleet to the core. She insisted on the courtesy out of deference to Joe's standing. "I'm afraid I haven't had time to run up an official report yet," she said.

Joe surveyed the surrounding area, visible in the guttering light as multiple fires struggled to burn in the thin atmosphere. "How long since they left?"

"Four hours. The attack took less than ten minutes, then they just turned around and retreated south. Makes no sense at all."

"So…?"

"Hellas. They're heading toward the city. I've reported to the authorities there, and they're sending all available resources. Not that we seem to be effective against these things." The general waved a hand at the devastation and shook her head. "We have to find a way to stop them before they get to our people."

Joe nodded understanding. From all reports, the marauders possessed the same force fields used by both the alien starships and human warships.

"My staff is re-programming the base machinery to clear the rubble and rebuild," Nouzari said. "Nothing below ground has been damaged to any extent, so I expect to be back up and running in about a month."

Joe took in the surrounding destruction. Nano-construction was astonishingly fast, and thirty Martian sols, or sixty Earth standard days was not an insurmountable problem.

He looked with new respect at the diminutive officer. Unlike the president, she had called the emergency without hesitation, otherwise, the situation might have been far worse. Someone of her abilities belonged with the fleet, not stuck in a managerial position in this facility.

From the latest reports, no assault had yet occurred at the Luna yard. In its current orbital position, the mother world was further from the place where the alien carriers had been stopped, and a little forethought and warning had allowed the moon-based defenses to be activated before an attack.

Joe wondered about the enemy's intent. Little here made sense. The alien carriers had done nothing since four of their number vanished, remaining stationary, untouchable behind their shields. Until now, no attack had come beyond the mosquito bites of the tiny alien fighters, even those insignificant.

The missing vessels remained the biggest concern, if for no other reason than that they had still not been located. The aliens were gone, their destinations unknown.

Half of the diamond ships that returned to the inner system were on guard, a massive contingent now orbited above the red world. No alien intruder had been detected, and it seemed likely the invisible visitors had come and gone before the fleet's arrival. No reports had arrived of any assault on the more distant Earth, the planet now shielded. Those defenses would serve to protect the mother world until the squadron sent by Admiral Asgad arrived.

Joe cursed under his breath.

For decades he warned anyone who would listen of the inevitability of another attack. When it came, he was somewhere else in the galaxy chasing down derelict ships, else he would have advised against sending the full fleet out beyond Jupiter. He would have kept some to defend the home worlds.

Shaking his head, he dismissed the thoughts as pointless. He had not anticipated the strange behavior displayed by the enemy any more than had the authorities.

One of the alien targets was now obvious. At least one invisible ship, perhaps more, dropped the marauders onto the surface, but the enemy's actual intent remained unclear. An assault on the shipyard made sense, but the attackers caused only minimal damage, just enough to make the base inoperative. They did not attempt to completely destroy the installation. The clear implication was that the enemy needed to disable the fleet in the short term, but was not concerned about the future.

Joe puzzled over these facts as he wandered amongst the ruins with the general. She talked, but her words failed to draw him away from his private thoughts. He responded with only the odd nod and an occasional "uh-huh" or "yes, of course," his attention focused on the major anomaly of the situation.

Events thus far *must* be intended as a distraction. Did the enemy intend to launch a major attack somewhere else? The standoff beyond Jupiter seemed pointless, and served no purpose other than to tie up a substantial portion of humanity's fighting ships. If not for good management by Asgad, the entire fleet might still be out there, leaving the inner system vulnerable. If the aliens were engaged in diversionary tactics, it meant something was in the wings, something greater, and perhaps more devastating.

But what?

The damage to the yard also appeared to be little more than a diversion. Something bigger was imminent, and there was only one place on Mars where that might have a deciding effect.

Hellas City!

Unlike the yards, the capital swarmed with living souls. It was also the location of the Institute's main administration and research facilities.

Joe shook his head to clear his thoughts. In this day and age, ground forces, no matter how mighty, had limited uses and were small for that reason. That played into the enemy's hands, and few options remained to stop the marauders from reaching their target.

Exasperated by the damage to the yard he returned to his aircraft, lifted off and headed in the general direction Nouzari believed the enemy had taken.

Not long after, the pilot slowed and began to circle a spot on the desert floor.

Below, a faint image showed the ruins of a settler's dome and several outbuildings. With a grunt, Serra-Pinho switched the monitor to shortwave infrared, and the screen blazed with a nightmarish scene of destruction.

"It's hot down there," he commented. "No sign of life. Plasma cannons most likely, ideal for short-range targets. It's a settlement called Kharkhorin. Central Asian refugees, agricultural, plus a handful of small mining concerns in the surrounding region. Believe me, there's nobody alive down there. Any survivors have left already; you can see the vehicle tracks heading south." The pilot swung the ship back onto its original course, toward Hellas City.

His pilot's words rang a discordant bell in Joe's mind. He recalled being at one of the landing fields long ago when a fleet of rag-tag ships arrived carrying several hundred souls who claimed to be Mongolian. The authorities listed them as Chinese, after the place of their origin, but they insisted they were a separate people.

In the end, Joe avoided a potential conflict by suggesting they occupy the domes here on the Planitia, of which Kharkhorin was one. Independent to a point, the towns were close to each other, allowing these people to retain their group identity. Did his intrusion so long ago just cost them their lives?

In less than a minute, another image appeared on the screen, a solitary figure staggering across the plain toward the incinerated town.

"Go down," Joe urged. "That's a human being. Whoever he is, he's injured, and he won't find any help at the settlement. We'll pick him up."

Within minutes, a tired and bedraggled Ares Maggason sat safely in the rear seat of the small craft. He wore torn and dirty miners' clothes, all exposed skin red and raw as if subjected to severe sunburn, something unheard of on Mars. Joe turned and examined his new passenger, waiting for the man to talk in his own time. He was injured and in considerable pain, despite having been dosed with analgesics from the first aid kit.

"So glad you guys … aah … came along," he mumbled, his voice shattered and broken. "Almost out of oxygen; don't think I would've made it back to Kharkhorin. Who do I owe me thanks to?"

"I'm Joe Falcon. The man in the pilot seat is Carlos Serra-Pinho, and he's the one who saved you."

The wearied man raised his head and stared at Joe as if he recognized an old friend. His eyes widened for an instant, then closed as a wave of pain washed over him. "Heard of you. Kinda thought you'd be older."

"I look younger than I am. What happened to you?"

The man appeared to stare into space for a moment, opened his mouth, shut it, and opened it again. A loud sigh escaped his lips. "I'm not sure. I was working me claim—I'm a miner—and somethin' came straight at me. Somethin' big. I mean … real, real big, you know?"

Joe nodded. "Tell me exactly what happened."

"Don't know exactly. It came from the desert and reflected everything around it, but I couldn't see clear, like. Real scary, and it rolled right over the top of me. When it did, I was underneath some kind of huge machine that I couldn't see before, and then it was gone. I got burned real bad, and…"

"We can fix that. You'll be okay, I guarantee." Joe expected the man had been in the path of one of the juggernauts that attacked Ithaca and the shipyard. If he saw the marauder, the shield passed directly over him.

And yet, he was still alive.

"The mirror surface was a force field. What did you do when it passed over? Tell me exactly."

Maggason raised a hand to scratch his head, and winced at the pain. His eyes became glazed as he tried to remember the ordeal his mind had all but blocked out.

"I hid in me hole."

Joe waved a hand to prompt his passenger to clarify.

"Well, I was diggin' a new shaft when it came. I dug it 'bout a meter deep already, and when that thing came at me I decided to hide in there. I had some panels I built me a shelter from, and one was on the ground nearby, so I pulled it over to the hole and jumped in. Used the panel to cover meself over."

Joe nodded again. Standard prefab construction modules contained carbon fiber, copper and many other anti-radiation materials, and this one provided some minimal protection for the miner. There was no other possible explanation. He turned back in his seat and gazed through the windscreen at the darkness beyond.

More experienced with the mirror shields than almost anyone else on Mars, he knew this man should not have survived the encounter. Everyone assumed that direct contact with a force field by flesh and blood would result in either expulsion or death from electrical disruption, but the man in the seat behind him disproved those assumptions.

The marauders were surface vehicles, so it seemed sensible the shields on them would be hemispherical, ending at ground level. The severe burns on Maggason showed they extended lower if necessary, no doubt to allow for the irregularities in the surface over which the machines might travel.

The edge had dropped into the miner's hole and burned him, but he survived. Did they not destroy organic things after all, or did the panel provide some kind of protection?

As he sat deep in thought he felt a touch on his jacket, and turned to see the miner leaning forward, his face straining from the effort. His mouth opened and he mouthed the words *thank you* to Joe. Joe smiled, nodded and motioned him to sit back.

Only hours later would he discover a magnificent, rough opal in his pocket.

Something new appeared on the monitor. Spread over the plane below, mirrored domes moved in formation across the southern edge of the Planitia, their progress slow over the disturbed terrain.

Joe felt his heart leap into his throat. By now, many Fleet ships orbited the planet, but with the planetary defenses up they could not descend, and their weapons had already proved to be ineffective against that type of shield. The task of dealing with this threat would fall to the ground forces, and Joe doubted they were capable of stopping the juggernauts.

"Don't get too close," Joe advised the pilot. "Put me through to Lewis at the institute, and then Hellas. I need to have another little chat with our beloved president."

Chapter 16

COMMANDER MIKE TARRANT RAISED the binoculars to his eyes and peered out across the barren Martian plains of Isidis, several hundred kilometers north of the Hellas Basin and Hellas City.

The global shield was off now, and the sun shone brightly. In the hazy distance a line of alien war machines crawled inexorably closer, their mirror-like force fields visible from the light they reflected. Overhead, at a height of one thousand meters, a squad of diamond ships kept station with the invaders but did not fire on their impenetrable domes.

Ten kilometers behind the observation post, a pair of Fleet vessels blasted away at the floor of the canyon Tarrant and his men guarded, cutting a deep gash across a narrow point as a barrier against the oncoming juggernauts. According to rumor, the alien machines floated on anti-gravity suspensors, so there were no guarantees the trench would work.

High above, almost a thousand warships, the first contingent to arrive home from the standoff, patrolled near-Martian space. Searching for all possible energy waveforms, including visible light reflection or the lack thereof, they had found no trace of alien presence in the near vicinity of the planet.

Whatever dropped the marauders had vanished. In a place the size of the Solar System, any ships able to make themselves invisible had unlimited places to hide. With no sign of the invaders, Verveda ordered the planetary shield be turned off.

Tarrant did not agree. The majority of Martian civilization was located underground or under-dome, so a little darkness would do no great damage, and until more was known about these intruders it was better to err on the side of caution.

The current president understood the concept poorly; her interest focused more on the effects of an extended night on her popularity. Her decisions rarely met with Tarrant's approval. She often placed economic concerns and career ahead of the well-being of the public, those factors clearly the motivation behind this latest directive.

In the haze covering the plain, the marauders lumbered onward, their path clear. Aligned in rows of five, they formed a solid wall facing Tarrant's position.

A junior officer stepped up beside the commander. "Twenty-four, Sir," he said. "Five abreast with one kilometer between the lines. Four at the rear. Intelligence says more are coming from the naval yards up in Acidalia. They're heading east, and will presumably come down through Utopia into Isidis to join these bastards, Sir."

Tarrant lowered his binoculars, "What I don't understand, is why they landed up here if their target is Hellas City. They're a long way from there, and nothing in this region is worth their attention. Landing in the basin south of the city would have made more sense."

"Hard to say, Sir," The officer replied. "Perhaps the ships that dropped them are vulnerable in some way and needed to land in a place where they wouldn't be noticed. The tanks themselves may be vulnerable while they're being deployed. There's nothing out here in Isidis. Bugger all."

Tarrant nodded and turned to survey his defenses. A row of iron-clad behemoths stood lined up behind him, the most devastating weapons platforms available. Sixty-three were waiting, the entire 1st artillery contingent.

Mars was a peaceful world, and no ground offenses had taken place here since the Resources War, hundreds of years ago. The weapons were untested, constructed by order of a former minister whose only saving grace was he took the warnings of future invasion from the Falcons' institute seriously to the point of paranoia.

The vehicles were in position, standing in single file across the path of the oncoming marauders to ensure a clear line of fire for each.

"Open fire as soon as the targets are in range," Tarrant ordered, returning his attention to the oncoming threat. "Any word from our ships?"

"They won't shoot, Sir. They can't breach those shields, and considering the distance between the marauders and us, they'll hurt us more than the enemy. The fleet commodore says our weapons are more effective than theirs for ground work, so he intends to wait to see what damage we can do."

Tarrant's brow furrowed. "If any," he muttered.

Minutes later the artillery opened fire, multiple beams of scintillating energy streaking toward the first row of attackers. Upon hitting the mirror domes, they bounced, deflected by the impenetrable shields.

Tarrant's junior officer spoke a few quiet words into his headset to issue new orders to the unit commanders, and within seconds, balls of super-heated plasma arced out over the plain.

The charges, like the laser beams, splashed and dissipated into the thin Martian air. The weapons fielded by the ground forces were the finest on the planet, and their complete failure raised more than a little concern.

"Well, that was a waste of time," Tarrant said. "Let's try missiles, shall we?"

Shields were designed to stop energy, heat, and solid objects moving at anything beyond snails pace. From a dozen tanks, projectiles of death launched at the marauders, each carrying a charge with an explosive force equal to many tons of TNT, electronically detonated upon reaching their target. None penetrated initially, but a few that bounced on the shield succeeded on the second impact. In every case, the detonation failed.

The commander frowned. This was not right.

"It would appear, Sir," the junior officer said, "they can sometimes get through, but don't explode. The field must fry the electronic detonators."

"So ... it ... would ... seem," the commander replied. He reached up to rub the back of his neck, catching his fingers on the straps of the mask still necessary to operate in the open on the planet's surface. Having failed to ease the perceived itch, he crossed his arms and held them tightly against his chest.

He had not expected events to unfold this way, and a growing concern gnawed at the pit of his stomach. He gave a quick, short laugh. "This is not good. We have nothing else that might get through. Oh, for the old days, when armies had shells with impact detonators."

"We haven't used those for over a hundred years, Sir."

"I'm well aware of that, Corporal. Order the tanks to withdraw and send word to Command we're unable to stop the advance. Until we come up with something better, all we can do is watch and wait. If they get over our trenches, those things need to cross the western end of the Hesperia Planum to reach Hellas, and it's incredibly rough. It should slow them down … a bit."

The approaching domes began to flicker, and scintillating blasts of laser fire slammed into several of the artillery units, reducing them to useless slag heaps.

"Withdraw," Tarrant yelled. "Everyone back, now!"

*   *   *

Doctor Luciano Mariano sat on a stool in his laboratory and scratched his head, glaring at the object on the other side of the safety window. In the room beyond the glass a platform supported a small structure, a square metal frame standing on struts. The space within shimmered and reflected the light like a mirror.

Luciano, called Professor Luke by the hundreds of workers in this branch of the New Worlds Institute's weapons research division, shook his head. His best efforts had so far produced failure upon failure. Everyone relied on him for a solution, but so far, a bruised ego was his only positive result. Tapping his fingers on the nearby desk, he turned over in his mind all the things he had tried.

The frame held a miniature version of a force field, and Luke's objective was to find a way to breach it. He had tested every type of laser known, and nothing penetrated. Yesterday he fired a focused plasma stream at the obstinate shield and almost destroyed the test chamber walls with the backsplash. On a whim, he hit it with a bolt of pure, high-voltage electricity, draining enough power to cause a temporary blackout throughout the entire complex.

In desperation, he tried magnetic and electrostatic forces, sound waves and everything else he could think of. Now he accepted the simple truth: no type of energy, not any waveform, could breach it.

Luciano glared at the unit and shook his head in disgust. In his attempts to find a way to get through the force field, all he had achieved so far was to prove its impregnability.

His research had not been a complete loss. Certain inert, solid objects got through when moving at very low speeds, including steel and brass shells, but any device carrying the mildest electric current became fused and useless on passing through. That included living organisms, as testified by the cage of dead rats in one corner of the lab.

The solid projectiles used by the military relied on electronic triggers. Such devices carried micro-currents, and so failed.

Mechanical impact detonators had not been in production for a century, and steps were now being taken to correct the oversight. Factories were re-tooling to make old-fashioned shells suitable for use in diamond ships and other defenses. The program would take time Hellas City did not have, with the impending threat looming large to the north.

Luke expected the new armaments would be neither ready in time nor adequate. Reports from Isidis indicated the marauders were enormous, and he doubted any normal shell could seriously damage them. Something more effective was needed, something like a small nuclear tactical charge. All such devices required a sophisticated electronic trigger, which once passed through the shields, would not detonate.

A loud sigh caused his assistant to glance up from the rear of the laboratory. Luke threw his hands up in desperation and turned back to the monitor on his desk. He had to find something new, some clue he had not seen before.

For several minutes he sat and stared at the screen, his mind tossing over the methods he had tried, and discarded. Something flashed into his consciousness, something read only an hour ago but dismissed due to his being absorbed by another fruitless lead.

"Computer," he said. "Please show me the report sent by Administrator Joe Falcon earlier today, regarding the miner rescued from the Acidalia Planitia."

In a split second, the record appeared. For a seemingly endless time, he read and re-read the text, paused, and read it again. He could not quite pin it down, but something aroused his curiosity. Then he saw it, the words staring back at him.

"Why did I not see this before?" Luke mumbled to himself, angry at his own perceived ineptitude.

On his way back from the Fleet construction yards, Falcon found a man wandering alone on the plain. He rescued him and brought him back for medical attention. That was the clue: the man's injuries!

The individual, a miner with a site near the destroyed settlement of Kharkhorin, claimed to have encountered one of the marauders, and had suffered burns to almost his entire body.

But he lived!

The man gave Falcon a description of the monstrous tank-like machines inside the bubbles. Having seen one, he must somehow have survived the shield twice, once going in, and again on the way out.

How could that be so?

Luke read the record again, searching for anything he missed. The report made no sense. From his research, Luke knew the shield conformed to the shape of the terrain over which it moved. The miner's hole would offer no protection, and he should have died, so there was something else involved. Luke was positive flesh could not survive the shield with only minor burns, but he wasn't sure; a test was necessary.

"Alby, can you assist me for a minute, please?"

"Yes, Boss?" his young assistant asked, walking over from his bench.

"Do we have any meat on the premises? Real meat? A steak? Anything?"

"Don't think so. I can run over to the commissary for something—only take me half an hour."

"No, all the stuff there is synthetic. We need the real thing … I think."

"How about I grab a ground car and dash into town? Bound to be able to find some somewhere. Couple of hours."

Luke considered the offer for a moment. How far could those damned juggernauts travel in that time? They were too close to Hellas City for comfort, and the military force opposing them currently had no choice but to withdraw ahead of them. Luke tended to be an impatient individual, especially when on the verge of a potential breakthrough; *hours* were much too long to wait.

"I need to try something," he said, "and it'll be dangerous. I want you to be on hand, in case."

"Sure thing. What do you want me to do? You're not going to do anything stupid, are you, Boss?"

Luke pointed to a red switch on his console. "That's the cut-off. I'm going to test whether human flesh can pass through that field without critical damage, and since I would never ask anyone else to do it, I'm going in myself. If something happens, you hit that button and turn the generator off."

Alby's eyes opened wide. "Seriously? You can't do that, Boss. We can do it some other way. You can't go sticking yourself into a live shield. You…"

"I need to do this now, and we don't have time to mess around. Don't worry, I'm not going to throw myself in with gay abandon. Watch my back, okay?"

A minute later Luke stood in the chamber staring at the active field. Even at a distance of one meter, he felt an unpleasant prickle on his skin.

The question now was how to make the next move. The obvious way would be to stick the end of a digit through. If severely injured, the loss of a fingertip was a small price to pay if he could work out a way to stop the marauders from reaching Hellas.

But which finger?

Through the safety glass, he noted the panic on his assistant's face as the young man stood with his hand only a centimeter above the cut-off switch. In his other hand he held a phone, calling for help to prevent his maniac boss from killing himself.

Good lad.

Luke focused on the job at hand. Alby would do whatever was asked of him.

Carefully Luke reached out his left hand, eased the tip of his pinkie toward the shield surface and poked it forward. He pulled back as a bolt like an electric shock slammed through his arm.

"Holy mother of…," he remarked, reeling back from the jolt. "That was … unbelievably…" He took a tentative look at his hand, terrified of what he might see.

He had extended no more than a centimeter of the digit, and for only a split-second, but the tip was red-raw. The skin was seared away to the flesh, and the appearance of the nail made it quite obvious it would no longer be an active part of his life. Also clear was that no man could pass through the force field and live. Some other factor had to be at work in the miner's survival.

As he turned to the doorway, Alby barged through and grabbed his hand to spray artificial skin over the digit end. "You shouldn't have done that. Really, really dumb!"

Luke grimaced. "That's the beauty of being in charge: you're allowed to do all sorts of stupid things and nobody can stop you. I want you to find out where the miner Falcon rescued is now. I want to talk to him, and I need carbon-fiber cloth and copper sheeting … and real meat." He clapped his hands together and winced as pain shot up his left arm. "Now! Chop-chop!"

Chapter 17

COMMANDER TARRANT HUNCHED IN a collapsible chair at the entrance to a cargo module converted into a temporary base, and scrutinized the horizon.

His new observation post sat high on a ridge about halfway across the tortured, meteor-cratered landscape called the Hesperia Planum, at the southeastern boundary of which lay the Hellas Basin and Hellas City.

He drummed the fingers of one hand on a knee, a deep sigh escaping his lips. His options were reducing rapidly, the chorus from the gremlins in his head increasing in proportion. He was positive his blood pressure was away somewhere on a flight of fancy all its own.

In the distance, strange distortions in the air marked the location of the leading juggernaut. Having crossed the defensive trenches with ease, they had taken three days to make their way to this point from the last encounter, and had re-formed from a broad front to single file, each marauder spaced several kilometers behind the next.

This landscape was a labyrinth of broken hills, high and rugged with deep canyons, left over from one of the bombardment periods when swarms of meteors pounded the red world.

Line-abreast travel was impossible in this terrain, and Tarrant hoped it gave him the advantage. The need to traverse this ground slowed the enemy, but they were still within two days of the city. It was critical they be stopped—now.

Hellas City was mostly below the surface, built deep into the sheer, northern face walls of the massive crater that was the Hellas Basin. Even for these monster machines it would be difficult to destroy, but they could still do enormous damage. They could not be allowed to pass this point.

A day earlier the alien column crossed a long, flat valley floor, and an attempt had been made to stop it there.

The strategy involved burying caches of high explosives in front of the marauders, with electrical leads to triggers located elsewhere. The idea was to wait until one of the enemy vehicles moved over the bomb, and then set it off by sending a charge along the wires.

The plan failed.

The charges did not go off.

At first, Tarrant did not understand why, but one of his engineers provided a likely answer. The shield did not allow any type of energy to pass, including electricity, and although the force field ended at ground level, its influence extended some distance into the soil.

The detonators and cables were buried only centimeters deep.

The commander turned his head as a well-known figure approached from the direction of the makeshift landing pad. Joe Falcon walked up to the command-post, and with a wave of greeting, invited himself inside.

Tarrant directed the out-of-breath newcomer to water from a canteen on the folding table inside the entrance. Falcon's self-invitation mattered not to him; he got on well with the man, saw him as an equal and did not mind what another officer might have taken as a liberty.

The roar that heralded the arrival of a shuttle as it landed at the back of the ridge had been only minutes earlier, and Falcon must have sprinted up the slope to reach here in such a short time. Tarrant smiled to himself; not bad for a man in his two-hundred-and-eighties.

"I think we may have something for you," Joe announced. "No guarantees, but it might work. Worth a try, at least."

The commander stood, turned his seat, and sat again, facing his visitor. "I'm prepared to give anything a shot at the moment. What have you got?"

"You have engineers here. Can they come up with a powerful, non-nuclear charge small enough to be handled by one man, and a clockwork timer?"

Tarrant stared into the distance. "Clockwork? Seriously?"

"Yes. Powered by a mechanical spring."

For a brief second Tarrant contemplated the request, his eyebrows raised. "We have plenty of explosive charges, but they're triggered by electricity. They may be adequate to take out one of those tanks, but we can't get them inside the shield without destroying the battery. They can't be triggered by a mechanical timer."

A broad grin spread across Joe's face. "That's not what I had in mind. The timers are for a different purpose."

"I'm listening," Tarrant replied.

"Okay, here's the drum. I rescued a miner in Acidalia. He had a run-in with the marauders that took out the Fleet yards. One of them rolled right over his claim, and he couldn't get out of its way. He suffered severe burns, but survived."

Tarrant's eyebrows arched. "How is that possible? We've already proved the shields will kill anyone who comes in contact with them. They disrupt the entire nervous system, not to mention burn the flesh from your bones."

"I asked a researcher at the Institute to check it for me. He's an expert on these energy fields and he's been studying them since we first got the technology. He cross-examined the miner and thinks he knows why he survived."

Tarrant remained silent, his attention now glued to his visitor.

"So," Joe continued. "This guy was working the claim, digging his first shaft when the tanks arrived. He spotted a force field heading straight at him. It was too close and moving too fast for him to get out of its way, so he took the only course open to him. He was near the hole, so he jumped in and pulled the nearest thing at hand to cover himself over."

"That being...?"

"A prefab space cargo module panel he was using to construct a shelter." Joe slammed a fist against the wall of the structure they were in. "Damned things are everywhere. Most of the miners use them for storage, even living quarters if they can pick up insulated ones. They're carbon fiber with an internal layer of composite: copper and a polyethylene material made from carbon and hydrogen. I…"

"You think that's what saved him?"

"We do. My researcher did some tests in his lab as soon as he found out about the panel, and he managed to pass his hand through a test shield, wrapped in pure carbon-fiber cloth and copper sheeting. He tried it with a battery, and the blessed thing came out the other side still with a usable charge."

"So the material can get through without damage, and so can anything covered by it. If the field of energy can't easily penetrate it, why can't our warships get through the shields? They're carbon, aren't they?"

"Yes, but the wrong type. Carbon-fiber cloth is used as a reinforcing. The stuff doesn't stop the force field, but it blocks most of it. Don't ask me why; I'm not a physicist and that kind of thing is way beyond my expertise."

"Fine, so where am I going to put my hands on carbon-fiber cloth, copper, and this composite material you're talking about?"

Joe stood and walked to the open entrance of the container. "Your gun platforms have carbon fiber as reinforcing on their carriages, so your engineers will have some cloth as part of their repair and maintenance supplies. I brought rolls of composite and copper sheeting with me in the shuttle."

"And how do we get it under the shield?"

"The same way the prospector did it. We dig a foxhole in the marauder's path and hide a man in it underneath a panel cover. He'll be burned, but he'll survive like the miner. He'll carry a battery wrapped up in the shielding, and once inside, re-connect it and set the mechanical timer for long enough for him to escape. When the timer winds down, a switch closes and sends a charge from the battery to the detonator.

"To get maximum effect we need the charge actually on the hull of a juggernaut. After our volunteer fixes the charge, he jumps back under cover. The enemy rolls on, our man escapes and the bomb goes off. When it does, the shield might fail—I'm not sure about that—but it'll still be on at the instant of the explosion and so should contain the blast sufficient to direct it back onto the tank. If we put it somewhere that matters, like the suspension domes, it should stop our monster."

The commander sat silently for a moment, his mouth open and his jaw slack. He uttered a single word.

"Seriously?"

Joe nodded, his eyes wide and his lips set with grim determination. He realized it sounded ridiculous, like something from a video game.

"Didn't you say your scientist passed a battery through?" Tarrant asked. "Can we use an electronic trigger and eliminate the need for a human sacrifice?"

Joe shook his head. "It's not quite so simple. We *can* pass the battery through and it'll still carry a charge, but if it's connected to anything, there will be a micro-current and the force field will destroy it. We need a volunteer to connect it once it's inside. We're working on a solution, but for now, this idea is the best I've got. We can stop these things now, and we only get one shot at this.

"Where am I going to find enough carbon to cover the volunteer?"

Joe reached out and tapped a knuckle on the wall of the cargo module. "Same place as our miner. This camp contains dozens of them. You can rip the lids off them."

"No kidding!"

*   *   *

Corporal Jersey McCabe crouched in the hole, wondering what in hell he had let himself in for.

Everything had happened so quickly, and now he was alone, in the path of the lead marauder as it made its way through a narrow pass between two rugged rises.

Twenty minutes earlier, Tarrant had called McCabe's squad, thirty-one individuals in all, to gather at the temporary command post.

"Alright team," the commander said. "I need one volunteer, and I must point out this mission will be dangerous. The selected soldier may not survive, and at best will suffer serious burns. If you *do* survive, you will be healed quickly and will be rewarded, but do *not* underestimate the danger of the task I'm asking you to perform. I would like anyone willing, to take a step forward."

Before the commander could continue, thirty-one men and women advanced as a body. Tarrant smiled, clearly proud of his team. These soldiers were the finest in his force, and he doubtless expected nothing less. "Thank you all," he said. "I can always rely on you. Now, those with a spouse, or with children, take one step back."

Two-thirds of the group stepped back. McCabe had been one of those remaining at the fore. Tarrant walked up to him and studied the battle-worn face. No doubt he saw fear, but also a fierce determination, a fixed gaze and firmness of jaw.

Tarrant knew his men well, and Jersey had volunteered for dangerous missions before. The boss knew he could be depended on not to panic in the middle of an engagement, and would follow orders to the letter despite the danger and lack of certainty. Tarrant always said a man with no fear was a man who could not be relied upon.

"You may be the bravest man in this squad, I think," he said. "I need someone strong, to carry a field charge under a marauder shield and plant it on the machine inside. We have a way to get you there and back alive, but it's untested. Still willing?"

Jersey McCabe swallowed, snapped to attention and said "Yes, Sir," in the finest tradition. Now, he crouched in a foxhole dug into the regolith, in front of an oncoming enemy of immense power.

Beside him sat an explosive device with the equivalent detonation force of twenty tons of TNT, and a small package wrapped in carbon fiber and what looked like copper. Above his head was the lid of a cargo storage module.

In his mind lingered a single thought.

Why on Mars did I do such a stupid thing as to volunteer for this mission? I'm not going to survive this.

All was silent, bar only the pounding in Jersey's head. He had never been one to allow fear to affect him, but this situation was different. He had shown his mettle in the field, surrounded by his fellow soldiers and always ready to cover their backs as they would his.

Now he was alone.

He lay in darkness, waiting.

This was not how a man should die.

He curled his body, arms held tightly to his sides, legs drawn up to make himself as small as possible. The sweat on his forehead trickled down inside his mask, forcing him to close his eyes to keep the salty moisture out.

Slow second after slower second ticked by. A slight tremor began within his belly, and he struggled to keep calm, determined to see this through.

A thick heat blanket covered him, provided by one of the commanders before they left him alone at his post. All units carried these in case of fire, but there was no guarantee the thing would provide any protection from the shield about to assault him. Still, it was worth trying.

Then he felt it. It started as a faint tingle, followed by a sensation of sunburn boring into his skin like a raw flame. Jersey closed his eyes and, teeth clenched, waited for it to pass. It lasted only seconds, but he doubted he had ever experienced anything so unsettling.

The onslaught ceased, to be replaced by the dull ache of burn pain. Without hesitation, Jersey slid the construction panel back, enough to allow him to climb out. He knew he had little time before the slowly-moving machine passed overhead and the back of the force dome reached him. By that time he had to be back under cover, or he would die.

Standing, he peered upward. Overhead, the leading edge of something enormous and dark slid past. It was around two meters above the ground. *Excellent*, he thought. He could easily reach high enough to allow the charge's magnetic clamps to grab the underside of the behemoth.

Reaching down, he grabbed the field charge and lifted it to ground level. Retrieving the carbon fiber package, he opened it to reveal a long, thin battery.

Smoothly, working quickly and sure of what he was doing, he dropped the battery into the receptacle on the device and pressed it home. He flicked a small switch on a box taped to the side and breathed a sigh of relief as an LED flashed on, showing the unit remained functional.

The engineers solved the problem of detonation delay by attaching a clockwork timer salvaged from a mess-unit oven. As it passed under the shell the entire device was inert, the power supply protected. With that now in place, the electronic trigger was connected, but not active. The timer guaranteed a countdown long enough for Jersey to reach safety.

The delay was set to three minutes, by which time Jersey had to be outside the force field. When the mechanism wound down, an internal switch would close and send a simple electrical jolt to the detonator.

"Please, please work," he muttered as he climbed out and hoisted the weapon into his arms. The casing of the explosive was fitted with both magnetic and suction attachments, so the odds were high that it would stick to the marauders' hull shell.

Jersey sprinted to one of the suspension bulges on the bottom of the monster, and with a smooth and precise motion, heaved the bomb upward as the surface glided above. A sigh escaped his lips as he heard a sort of squishing noise.

"Yes!" he shouted, pumping a fist into the air. The marauder was not magnetic, but the suction pads had done their part, securing the bomb to a bulge near the rear end of the machine.

With only seconds to spare, Jersey dove back into his foxhole as the rear wall of the force field closed to within a few meters. The back end of the massive juggernaut crept overhead as he pulled the panel back into place, dropped and curled into a ball.

Again, the agonizing, burning sensation bathed his skin, this time far worse than before as the shield assaulted his already damaged body.

Pity those engineers didn't have enough carbon cloth to make me a suit.

He waited, teeth clenched. After a minute there was silence, but his body still screamed. The Boss's orders were to wait in the foxhole until help arrived, but Jersey could not keep still. Desperate to know how badly he was hurt, and after only a moment's hesitation, he reached up and forced the lid back again, allowing light to enter.

He examined his hands. The narrow strip exposed between his gloves and the cuff of his environment suit appeared red and raw, as if severely burnt. The wrist was covered with tiny blisters and one or two whitish patches. He could only see a small area of skin, but he was positive that second or third-degree burns covered his entire torso.

He knew these could be healed, and he would be fine again in short order. Burn management was a part of medical science perfected centuries ago, and the first aid team would be waiting with a spray-on coating for his entire body as soon as he was retrieved. In a week or two he would walk out of the field hospital whole and healthy again, famous as the first man ever to stop an alien marauder single-handed.

Or am I?

Rising to a crouching position, he raised his eyes above the ground level.

Don't move until we come for you.

He couldn't help himself.

Now about twenty meters away, the force field glittered in the reflected sunlight, then blazed with a brief fire strong enough to overpower the natural daylight. The ground shuddered with the violence of an earthquake and then the force field failed, releasing a blast of energy like a hurricane. The carbon lid lifted and flew away like a dry leaf in a breeze as Jersey was pounded back into the hole by a force only a fraction of that released by the explosion.

As predicted, the shield remained on for the moment of detonation, failing only when the blast drove inward to the field generator as it tore the behemoth apart. For the first, brief second, the dome contained the explosive energy and focused it toward the target.

Where the shield dome once stood, a colossal, black, tank-like mass sat motionless on the ground, its suspension mechanism disabled, its exterior shell ripped open like paper.

Jersey climbed back to his feet.

Well, bugger me!

"Hope you're dead," he mumbled.

Barely conscious, he propped himself on the edge of the foxhole and, unaware of time, waited for his rescuers to come.

Chapter 18

MERCURY EXPLORER MESSENGER 51 cruised toward the tiny black dot that crept across the face of the Sun, its intent being to map the small planet. The mission necessitated exposing its structure to an intense assault from stellar radiation, but the construction of *MEM 51* protected it from anything the star could dish out.

The little spacecraft's program was straightforward, to achieve a close orbit around the tiny world and photograph the surface. Due to its proximity to Sol the planet orbited in only eighty-eight days, but with its snail's-pace rotation, a region could spend as much as two-thirds of any given orbit in continuous searing heat, or bone-chilling cold.

The rugged surface underwent continual reformation as a result, so mapping continued as an ongoing work in progress. Regular missions were sent for the purpose, to record continuous geological changes.

Why this should be done was a point of contention between scientists and government, as so far humanity had refrained from setting up any kind of permanent settlement, or even an orbiting satellite, on the innermost of Sol's children.

More than a century ago, ISEL, the *Inner System Exploration Laboratory*, established a scientific observation post at the northern pole of the tiny world, the most amenable location considering the enormous temperature fluctuations experienced by other regions.

With a planetary axis tilt of only two degrees, the polar region maintained a more constant ambiance, which while warmer than humans preferred, made the continued existence of personnel less of a technological nightmare.

The station was, of course, below ground to protect its inhabitants from extreme radiation, and autonomous rovers and robots carried out all activity on the surface. Deserted now, the base was abandoned when the Great Death decimated humanity.

With the mother world still suffering the aftermath of the disaster, it was unlikely scientists would return to the innermost planet soon, but with the recent re-establishment of the Earth-based ISEL, interest rebooted.

A week later, the spacecraft swung into orbit and began its first traverse of the target. It followed an elliptical path, with a close approach to Mercury on the sunward side, and a wide swing into space on the far side to allow it to cool down again.

Messenger made no judgments as it recorded images and relayed them back to the scientists at ISEL.

*   *   *

One hundred and fifty million kilometers away, Lamar Seabourne glanced through the window at the white blanket covering the lawn outside. Deep snow lay everywhere; not from the volcanic winter that brought humanity to its knees in the last century, but the normal seasonal chill that afflicted the continent every year.

The seasons were now colder than before. The North American continent remained covered with ice and snow in the northern regions, and the permafrost limit still extended well into the mid-latitudes.

The old political divisions had vanished. Of the region once called the Eastern American States, only the southern fringe, from Texas to Florida, still functioned, while the old North American Federation had shrunk to the southwest corner.

With each passing year, the ice retreated a little more, and civilization pushed further. Inch by precious inch, technology and human resilience reclaimed what was lost. Winters still caused massive devastation, but the people who returned after the worst of the long night were resilient and fought back against the harsh environment with fierce determination.

The remaining habitable regions of the continent became a single political unit called *North America*, a blend of cultures from the now vanished American states, Canada and Mexico. Ice and snow had succeeded where diplomacy failed, to reunite a continent torn apart by political lunacy.

Located in Florida, the ISEL laboratory was one of the few scientific establishments to survive the darkness and emerge unscathed.

The *big freeze* did not reach most of the south, and once the daylight returned, the survivors battled to pick up where they left off. The southern winters now featured snow, but with summer the white blanket melted, and despite the chill, life was almost normal in the once subtropical regions around the Caribbean.

But not quite.

Acid rain, caused by sulfur dioxide poured into the atmosphere by volcanic eruptions, had done untold damage, but this also would pass. Much of the land was still bare, but massive reforestation programs continued, supported by Martian aid.

ISEL had been fortunate. As the scientists returned to their posts with the returning light, they found their charges, the unmanned spacecraft exploring the inner Solar System, still functioning, unaffected by and unconcerned with the tragedy afflicting their masters. They carried on as normal, sending regular reports home, oblivious to the fact nobody was there to receive them.

The base had now been manned and functional again for twenty years, and with the re-commissioning of the old spaceport east of Orlando, ISEL launched new missions. *Mercury Explorer*, named after the first satellite to explore the small rocky world, was such a one, and Lamar's current baby.

Turning away from the scene outside the window, he studied the image on his holo-screen. The photo showed the surface of Mercury, a tiny patch of rugged terrain on the night side of the planet, and something there struck Lamar as odd.

Small, dome-shaped objects littered the ground. The term s*mall* was relative, of course. After taking the scale into account, they would be a hundred meters in diameter, but in the picture, they were little more than specks.

Lamar brought up another frame of the same spot, taken on a previous orbit. The tiny dots were still there, but the arrangement varied. These objects moved. One of the other workers in the lab peered over his shoulder.

"Machines?"

"What else can they be?" Lamar replied, scratching the sparse excuse for a beard that sprouted from his chin. "There's no life on Mercury, and they don't appear on any of the survey images from past expeditions."

"So where did they come from? What are they doing, bro?"

Lamar bit his lower lip, shook his head and zoomed in. The ground around the objects was severely disturbed, regolith and shattered rock pushed into piles on either side of tracks marking the passage of machinery.

"Mining?" his companion proffered.

Lamar shook his head again. He had no idea. Considering the distance from which the image was taken it was difficult to tell, but everything indicated his colleague was correct. With another swipe of a finger, he displayed the next frame in the sequence, followed by another, and the next.

He stopped, unable to fathom what he was looking at. The final picture sent shivers down his spine; it showed the edge of what could only be described as a vast excavation. A colossal cavity scarred the surface, extending hundreds of meters into the tortured crust.

"Now, that's a mine if I ever saw one." Lamar's companion commented. "I toured a massive hole like it in Utah once, before the Death."

Lamar nodded. It *did* resemble the enormous open-cut mines of pre-Death Earth but was bigger by an order of magnitude. Not far from the rim of the pit rose a massive factory complex, and what appeared to be a linear accelerator of equal proportions.

"I agree," he replied. "Look at the size of it. The ones here are tiny in comparison, and it took us decades to dig them. How long did this take?"

"More importantly, *who* is digging it?" his friend asked, his voice an ominous tone. "It sure ain't us."

Lamar pushed his chair back from the desk. Machines and factories were the work of intelligent beings. Who it could be, he had no idea.

Probably those bloody Martians, carrying out some kind of new operation without first discussing it with Earth.

Typical!

Several hours later he changed his mind. Subsequent study of the images from *MEM 51* revealed not one, but hundreds of similar holes covering the terrain, each with an adjacent factory and accelerator. Someone, or something, was mining the tiny world on an unprecedented scale, and firing whatever they extracted into space.

*   *   *

Joe Falcon sat quietly in a corner of the makeshift headquarters compound and sipped a drink.

It was beer, the real stuff. He had not savored such a fine beverage for a long time; it was something yet to be produced successfully on Zealandia, due to the inability of terrestrial hops and barley to grow in the alien soil. Scientists were working on genetic modifications and all prayed for a quick result, but the wait weighed heavily on numerous souls.

The amber fluid in its many forms had been a part of the human psyche since the ancient Egyptian and Mesopotamian civilizations. There were even times when the average citizen in early European societies consumed it rather than water, to avoid contracting diseases like Cholera from the highly suspect local supplies.

The squad celebrated. Tarrant's men milled about the encampment, flasks in hand, applauding the unexpected victory snatched from almost certain defeat. Scattered across several hundred square kilometers of the Hesperia Planum, numerous marauders lay in ruins, each taken out in the same manner.

At this moment another division was en-route to intercept the second group of invaders, the ones that destroyed the fleet yards and Kharkhorin settlement, and were now working their way across the northern plains to follow their compatriots toward Hellas City.

Joe did not know how well these invaders communicated with each other, but he doubted the second group knew its southern contingent had suffered total defeat. If they did, they might not be aware of how.

The explosive charges created a force sufficient to knock out a machine's entire infrastructure instantly, so with luck, the only messages sent came from those marauders yet to be taken down, and therefore unaware of what was attacking them, and how.

After the first had been destroyed, access through the narrow gorge had become impossible, and the remaining juggernauts had turned to retreat, only to be destroyed by marines hidden in holes along every path the enemy could choose to take in the treacherous terrain. The bold volunteers responsible were now on their way to medical attention, injured but alive. They would all survive to receive the accolades they well deserved.

Joe wondered if machines speculated, and dismissed the thought. The northern contingent could be ignorant of the details of their compatriots' fate. If so, the trench attacks should still work.

His eyes followed the celebrations, his mind elsewhere, millions of kilometers away with Raisa and Terry, where a considerable portion of the fleet of humanity still held the alien carriers in gridlock.

Over a month had passed since the aliens first arrived. They continued to maintain a stalemate that made no sense whatsoever, and something needed to be done to bring the situation to a conclusion. Now some hope existed.

Joe decided to make calls to the military armaments factory management and his friend Professor Mariano. In the back of his mind grew an inkling of an idea. He prayed it was a workable one.

*   *   *

Professor Luke studied the collection of crates and boxes on his bench. They had been delivered minutes ago, and he was at the same time both eager and reluctant to begin the work they represented.

Waving his assistant to join him, he began opening the containers. Joe Falcon had called him personally and asked him to conduct a new experiment with the force field set up in the laboratory.

"So, what is this?" his assistant Alby asked, lifting a spherical object from a box.

"That, my boy, is a nuclear trigger," Luciano replied with a childlike grin.

Alby carefully replaced the item and took a step backward.

"It's a sophisticated piece of machinery, as it must be to do its job."

"Why? How does it work?"

"It's made up of explosive plates, fired electrically. These triggers come in several different varieties, but they all have one thing in common; they are all atomic devices in their own right. An electric charge sets off the explosive plates in the sphere to compress the fissionable core. That in turn explodes the fusion bomb for which it is the trigger. They vary in how they do that, but all of our current models are electronic. *That* is our problem."

"Yeah, right, electrical devices can't pass through a shield, da-da-da." Alby's face lit up as he realized what they were about to attempt. "Until now?"

"Until now!" Mariano repeated as he tapped his finger on the side of his nose, an all-knowing grin appearing on his face. "The carbon-copper composite trick worked with the batteries on the field charges, and the marauders have been stopped. Now we have to deal with the carriers, unless they leave, and for that we need much more substantial force—nuclear, at the least."

"So what are we going to do?"

Luke pointed to several small boxes sitting on the floor beside his desk.

"These are made of the same materials as the transport crates, from carbon, copper and composite sheeting," he explained. "We have two trigger mechanisms. We place one with the power source connected inside a box and pass it through the shield. Don't worry; no explosive plates and no fissionable core. That will be our control, and I expect it to fail. I'll pass the second unit through the shield with the battery separate and inside another protective casing. After that, I'll hook up the battery, set the mechanical delay, and see what happens."

Alby frowned at his boss. "What if neither works?"

"We'll figure out something else. Remember, it worked before, so it should work now."

"Definitely no explosives?"

"No, these are test dummies used for calibrating the electrical triggers. I just wanted to see the look on your face."

Chapter 19

CAPTAIN LAZAROS ANDREOU GUIDED his ship low over the dense clouds of Venus, giving his cameras the best possible chance to image the surface, fifty kilometers further down. At this height the atmosphere was equal to Earth's, almost the densest in which the vessel was able to operate.

The heat outside the hull registered at seventy-three degrees Celsius, a little too warm to be considered a perfect, sunny day. The same could not be said of the ground far below.

On the planet's surface, the pressure reached more than ninety atmospheres and the temperature was around four hundred and sixty degrees. It was a hell where no man could ever go. Even with the best protective suit a person would be crushed, and would not even be aware of their ending.

Of course, such a catastrophe would never happen. No manned machine could survive there at all, except perhaps the latest in deep-diving submarines, but those could not descend through the atmosphere from space.

Lazaros gazed at the whirling cloud below on his screen. One day someone would build a vessel capable of flying down and back again without killing its crew, but not today. Such a ship would need one hell of a cooling system, he thought.

The clouds outside were high in sulfuric acid. Lazaros thanked the gods he was safe inside his ship; it could descend to this altitude, but it was not a comfortable ride. Here at the equator, the winds contained driving, vertical, convection currents of far greater than hurricane force, making it hard to maintain a steady course.

Andreou had stopped here on the way to Mars, currently on the far side of Sol from Earth. ISEL had contracted him to stop of at Mercury to investigate a strange report by a drone of mining activity on the planet's surface. He hoped to arrive at the innermost planet as it reached its closest position to Venus. With a couple of days to kill, he had decided to indulge a private passion, and take the opportunity to do some local surveying.

Like the smaller planet, temperatures on the larger world were high enough to cause many parts of the surface to change regularly. As with Mercury, continual surveys kept the knowledge of global conditions current, although for what particular reason Andreou could not imagine. With no functional satellites currently in orbit, the authorities paid well for up-to-date information, and most captains within the general area stopped by if their schedules allowed it. That tended to be infrequently, as few ships had any reason to come to the inner worlds.

At the moment, little could be seen with the unaided eye. The dense cloud made the top of the uppermost layers the only thing visible.

The screens told a different story.

The ship studied the globe in two ways, by bouncing radar, or by detecting infrared waves. Both of these methods had been used for centuries to study Earth's sister planet and were as effective now as ever.

The slopes of an enormous volcano appeared, nothing as spectacular as the giant shields on Mars, but greater than anything on Earth. This one was active, and thick rivers of superheated, molten rock crept down the slopes. Much of this world consisted of solidified lava, vast plains of the once-molten rock filling every flat part of the landscape.

"Captain," Andreou's second officer said. "Take a gander at this." He raised his hand and pointed at the forward screen. Ahead loomed a sight the like of which neither man had seen before.

A massive, reflective, silver ball hung motionless in the atmosphere. Andreou estimated its diameter to be several kilometers. It maintained station over a single point on the planet's surface, far too low to be in geosynchronous orbit, but with no sign of any propulsion.

The captain guessed he was looking at a force field, like those used on all the latest ships of Fleet. The high reflectivity made it undetectable from space, visible only to a ship almost on top of it.

Below the glittering object something rose through the clouds, streaming up until it disappeared through the shield. Andreou could not determine what the stream contained. A close-up magnification showed it was composed of small masses of rock or minerals from the surface. That was logical; nothing else existed down there.

"Put us around that thing," Andreou ordered.

It would not surprise him at all if someone had worked out how to mine the planet using unmanned mechanical devices. "We need to take a better look. I haven't heard about any mining activities on Venus, and I've never seen anything like that sphere."

The first mate turned the vessel into a bank, placing it in a tight, circular flight path to maintain a distance of several kilometers from the object. Without warning, a stream of pellets shot from the side of the sphere and tore away through space, heading toward the Sun. Andreou struggled to get a closer view of one of them as the exodus continued unabated.

A plain, brownish-gray, egg-shaped object appeared on the monitor. Andreou had no idea what it was made of, but it did not appear to be a ship. No apparent means of propulsion was visible, and at only a few meters in length, it was too small to be a spacecraft.

Drone, maybe?

A thought struck him. Could the pods be the same raw material streaming up from the surface, but altered?

Whatever hid inside the force field might be collecting the material, processing it in some way to make the pellets, and firing them toward a target somewhere closer to the Sun. Andreou had no idea where that might be, but he did know this needed to be reported. Without hesitation, he sent a message to ISEL, with the images he had recorded.

Almost an hour later, a reply came.

The face on the monitor had not slept for hours, the hair unkempt, the eyes red. "Message received. We've logged the details and we'll monitor it. Don't worry about it yourself. Get your backside over to Mercury as quickly as you can. Something unbelievable is happening, and we need a human observer. Yours is the closest ship, so go there now ... please! Over."

The screen went dark.

Andreou sat for a moment, contemplating the last message. The man on the screen showed little concern for what was clearly a major discovery. ISEL gave an order and brooked no dissent.

How dare the man order me around?

Andreou commanded this vessel and would decide where it went and when. True, his contract with ISEL was to go to Mercury, but like most things in space, legal agreements were somewhat ethereal, and always subject to change if something more urgent came along.

In his opinion, this was such an occasion. His instinct was to follow the pellets, to locate their destination. They streamed toward the star, and so followed a course more or less aligned with his planned route.

Whatever was happening at Mercury must be critical, and Andreou wondered why he had been given such scant information. He waved a hand to his second and braced himself as the ship pulled out of its holding pattern and headed back to the safety of space.

*   *   *

A week later, the captain gazed at an object similar to the one seen above Venus.

On route to Mercury, he had followed the general line of the pellets and located their destination. Another colossal mirror-sphere lay ahead, a little closer to the Sun than the orbit of the innermost planet. The stream of processed materials vanished through the shield to whatever lay within. At least five kilometers in diameter, the object dwarfed the tiny spacecraft.

Nearby, another enormous object drifted, a flat, relatively paper-thin structure, hexagonal and fifty kilometers across. It consisted of multiple mirror facets, oriented so they faced the star. The back of the plate was a dull gray, featureless apart from what appeared to be a gigantic entrance hatch.

"Can we land on it?" The first officer asked. "It looks to be at least twenty meters thick, so it must be hollow. What do you think it is?"

"At a guess, I would say it's a solar collector, like the ones we use ourselves. Look over there."

Not far away, a third structure floated, a half-constructed version of the second. Around it, a multitude of small objects swarmed, machines engaged in the construction. Others flew in a constant stream from the sphere to the work site and back again.

Andreou sat back in his command seat and tried to create some order to the things he had discovered. The sphere ahead ignored his arrival, his presence of no concern to either it or whatever, whoever controlled it.

He thought he could see a logical sequence in play here. Something was mining Venus and firing the ore, with a linear accelerator or something similar, up to the plant orbiting within the upper atmosphere.

The factory turned the raw material into a purer form, formed it into pellets, and fired them through space to this second, larger space station. Here, they were further processed to create building products needed for the construction carried out by the smaller machines.

The flat objects ahead were obviously solar collectors, but why build them here?

A memory jumped into his mind. Tapping at the input pad of his ship's computer, he waited for a response. Seconds later an image appeared, containing several diagrams.

He studied the graphic for a moment. His query had been for any information about Dyson structures, a centuries-old concept of using a solar collection bubble to enclose a star and gather all its energy.

The original concept specified a solid sphere. Realizing the amount of matter and effort required to construct it, and the reality that no substance known to humanity had sufficient strength for such a structure to exist, other alternatives had been speculated upon over the years.

One concept involved a ring of solar collectors, a so-called Dyson Ring, around the sun. Other concepts involved multiple rings, each intersecting at junctions to create an open mesh sphere of collectors.

Another graphic caught Andreou's attention. One of the drawings showed a mega-structure made of billions of separate, hexagonal solar panels, all held by some unimaginable and, with current technology, unattainable force on a spherical horizon enclosing the star.

Such a design was the quickest and easiest to construct, as the sphere would begin with a basic array of a handful of units, others being added to the sphere as they were constructed. A simple start, built upon over time.

The only doubtful aspects were the technologies needed to hold each collector in perfect alignment at all times, and to funnel the collected energy to wherever required.

Andreou was not a scientist and by no means an expert on this kind of technology, but he was sure humanity could not yet achieve such a thing.

He recalled the protective shield deployed above the Earth by the *Minaret*, during the Blackship War. It included thousands of individual units, held in a spherical net around the planet. Both Earth and Mars now had shields of this nature, so the technology did exist, but neither was anything near the scale indicated here.

He tapped the screen to bring up information on the diagram of interest and found himself looking at a breakdown. His heart skipped a beat.

The structure was, from all appearances, identical to the one outside the ship. Whoever was constructing these things was using engineering details from a human database.

On the flight here Andreou had poured over the data sent from ISEL and knew something similar to the activity on Venus was taking place on Mercury. No doubt there would be another orbital factory there, and perhaps other panel construction sites around the star. Despite the size of the objects, they were minuscule on the scale of the Solar System, and might easily have been overlooked.

The question was, who was behind this? Building a Dyson structure of any kind would make even the creation of the fabulous diamond ship fleets a simplistic task, and as far as he could tell, was beyond the current resources of either Earth or Mars.

Humans had the necessary knowledge to build those collectors, and possibly the mysterious factories inside the bubble shields, but had no way of keeping them in position on this scale, nor of strip mining the planets to the extent observed by the survey drone.

If not humanity, who was responsible?

The only imaginable alternative was the fleet of alien vessels out near Jupiter.

Were that incident and the recent invasion of Mars by ground attack vehicles nothing more than diversions, to keep human eyes away from the inner planets while establishing this amazing system? If so, this represented a massive intrusion into the domain of humanity, and whoever or whatever was behind it was not concerned by that fact.

So far, Andreou's presence had been ignored.

Chapter 20

FOR HURACAN, THIS WAS a grand adventure. Never before had it traversed a wormhole, and the journey flooded its senses with data previously unimagined.

Unlike humans traveling through a gateway, the entity did not experience physical discomfort. Its mechanical spaceship body, and the gel sphere in which its mind now resided, lacked internal sensors capable of registering such sensations.

Oblivious to pain and with calm, cool focus, it studied and analyzed each moment of the strange reality of the passage, and the forces at play.

The intercepted drone took no time at all to disassemble and study. It carried the mechanism required to create gateways, and the technology that allowed it to do so was now part of Huracan's vast store of knowledge.

A larger, more dynamic version of the generator now sat at the center of the AI's vehicle. Like humans, Huracan possessed the key to exploring the galaxy, and perhaps further. The synthetic mind had, at last, voyaged beyond its native system.

The ship burst into open space, and Huracan began to examine its new surroundings. The star ahead was orange, smaller than the one around which humanity lived but bigger than the red dwarf in the home system. The AI had never seen another star close up and expected to learn much here.

Having absorbed the entire knowledge database of the little drone, it possessed all the necessary techniques for locating planets and gateways, as well as studying systems. The drone's data also included the coordinates of all stars in the human domain of exploration.

The gateway from which Huracan emerged did not sit near any visible planetary body, but would most likely be located at a point of equilibrium. Believing them to have some as yet undiscovered significance, it had frequently studied these locations and understood every planet possessed five such. Each was a locus at which gravitational forces produced enhanced regions of attraction and repulsion. Natural objects that found their way there tended to remain, their inertia matched by centripetal force.

There was no planet here. Huracan knew where it would be, but that was not the immediate priority.

This system presented a new opportunity. In the Tanakhai system, a solar energy collection array was well underway. A second such structure around Sol, the home of the humans, should be in progress if the fleet sent long ago had arrived and begun its task as programmed.

Here was a perfect place to begin a third, but of course it depended on whether anything of interest existed here.

Since discovering the vast databases in the ship construction facility of the Tanakhai, Huracan's outlook on the galaxy had changed. It once believed the sole purpose of existence to be self-preservation, even at the cost of destroying the organic life which seemed to have sprung up like a viral plague on certain worlds. It still followed that philosophy to a degree, but now felt less inclined to destroy without question.

The realization that it was a god created by organic beings to replace the mythical deities of their history changed its viewpoint, leading to the decision to allow the organics to live, at least for a while, so they might come to recognize and appreciate it, and show adoration.

Of course, the new approach did not apply to humans. They destroyed an iteration, so for them, there was no future. They were not worth the effort, so would be eliminated out of hand. The project in the Solar System would continue without consideration for the inhabitants, and despite them.

The array under construction there would absorb all the worlds of that system, starting with the unoccupied ones, but in time including those called Earth and Mars.

The machines carrying out the project were self-replicating, capable of increasing their number at an exponential rate. Humans might destroy the space factories used to convert the raw planetary rock into usable materials and components, but those were easily replaced. The automatons and nano-machines mining the planets were too numerous to stop and could increase their numbers far faster than they could be destroyed.

If the annoying humans became too obstructive, the carriers that accompanied the fleet would deal with the problem. They could manufacture enough fighting craft to keep the natives occupied, using the resources of the Solar System against them in a never-ending war of attrition.

With Huracan's modified shields, based on an experimental technique from the Tanakhai databases and able to provide virtual invisibility, the enemy would always be at a disadvantage. The occupied worlds of the humans would be dismantled beneath their feet, and they would be powerless to prevent it. They would have no choice but to die as their worlds crumble.

When it was done, Huracan would have unlimited raw energy from that star. It had not yet decided how it would use that resource, but one thing was sure: given time, the star would be surrounded by artificial intelligence just like Huracan, but subservient to it in every way.

Unaware of the concept of technological evolution, and able only to work with the here and now, the AI never considered that human defenses may have improved.

Chapter 21

ADMIRAL SAMUEL ASGAD CLUTCHED at the rails
of the companionway stairs and launched himself down to
the service level. This part of the ship had no artificial
gravity, and he glided through the air with practiced ease,
using the handrails on the walls and overhead deck to
prevent collision with anything hard. In space one had no
weight, but mass remained unchanged and a collision with
a solid wall caused as much physical pain as in full gravity.

In the corridor on the next deck, he turned aft and
headed to the main docking hatch. A courier from Mars
had arrived and linked to the flagship, a private vessel
belonging to the New Worlds Institute. That alone gave
Samuel cause for thought.

Before the vessel docked, Asgad received a message
that Joe Falcon was aboard and came bearing gifts. What
they might be was beyond him, but it was a distraction at
the least, and it was good to see his new friend return.

Half of the combined fleets remained at a point in
space well outside the orbit of Jupiter, and after several
months, boredom had set in. Not far away, the giant, alien
carriers drifted motionless in space, hidden within their
mirror shields. All fighter craft had been withdrawn, and

no attempts had been made to attack, communicate, or move.

The situation was frustrating and puzzling in equal proportion. Nobody, including Asgad, could imagine what the aliens' intentions might be.

It was illogical that they would cross light-years of space and sit there doing nothing. Common sense dictated that they either show their hand or make peaceful approaches. Neither had occurred, leaving the admiral scratching his head.

Falcon left for Mars over three months ago, and word had arrived of strange events on the planet. Asgad assumed at least one of the vanished enemy carriers journeyed there unseen and dropped the marauders the communications spoke of.

Another puzzle! Nothing about the attempted attack on Hellas City made any sense either.

When Joe departed, Raisa and Terry remained on the flagship. His daughter had since departed, deciding to return to Mars. His son-in-law was still aboard, acting as liaison with the Institute.

Asgad glided into the bay as his guest emerged from an airlock on the far side.

"My dear friend, so good to see you back. What brings you?"

"I have a little gift for you," Joe replied, a broad grin on his face. "Something to end this stalemate ... possibly. Come."

Gliding over to a viewing port, he pointed to where several suit-clad figures maneuvered large storage containers from the courier's cargo hatch, across the short distance of open space separating the ships, and into a hangar aft of where the two men stood.

Once the transfer was complete, the two men entered and waited as crew members opened the crates. There were twelve, and within each was a dark, cylindrical object, roughly a meter and a half in diameter. The front was dome-shaped like the nose of a torpedo; the rear end looked much like a rocket nozzle. As the first was drawn from its container, Asgad glided closer.

The object was constructed in two sections, a fine, hairline join marking the point where the forward third connected with the aft section. On the top of the center hull was the clear outline of a flush-fitting hatch. The surface was a dull black but somehow seemed darker, failing to reflect any light from the overheads. Peering at it was like looking into a miniature black hole.

"Total wave absorption," Joe explained. "It reflects nothing, making it hard to see in space."

"Okay, sure," Asgad replied, rubbing his chin. "So … what is it?"

"The answer to breaking this stalemate, I hope. Let's go up to your dayroom so we can talk."

By the time they reached the admiral's quarters, Terry had joined them. He and Asgad waited as Joe brought up a diagram of the device on the holo-screen.

"It's made of multiple layers of carbon fiber, copper sheet and various polymers used for protective shielding," he explained. "The outside is coated with a molecular spray based on nickel, underneath the latest wave absorption material to make it virtually invisible in space. In its current state, it has no active electrical systems of any kind and doesn't present a heat signature, so it can't easily be detected."

The diagram showed a hollow center section, containing a single seat for a human passenger. Ahead of the minuscule cabin module, the forward part of the structure was a solid, dark mass.

"So it carries a person? What's the bit at the front?" Terry asked.

"I think I can guess," Asgad said.

Joe smiled. "You would be right. It's a thermonuclear device, the most destructive available at short notice."

The admiral raised his eyebrows, his eyes wide. "A colossal bomb with a pilot sitting behind it? I don't understand."

"It's a small space capsule. The explosive part can be detached and dropped. We got the idea from mini-submarines used in World War II on Earth."

Asgad sat back in his seat and gazed at Falcon, eyebrows raised and head tilted to one side.

"You've heard about the business on Mars, right? We discovered a way to retaliate through the mirror shields. We found certain inert objects can pass through at very low speeds and started doing experiments to see what was possible. Explosives can only go through if they contain no electrical current whatsoever, so electronic triggers are out. "We worked out a way to bypass the problem. We took out the marauders by hiding soldiers in pits covered with transport container lids. They carried bombs underneath the shield edge, activated them once inside, attached them to the alien tanks, and jumped back into their holes."

"Yes, I read about it in the reports we received."

"Okay. The men survived but were seriously burned. The lids provided enough protection for them to get out alive. That was our clue. The panels acted as dampeners for the force-field energy."

"So these vehicles can go through the defenses of the carriers?"

"I hope so. We managed to pass one through a mock-up on Mars, and it went through with no problem. Think about it. All our shields are based on the original from the *Minaret*. They disrupt or block all forms of radiation and solid objects traveling at high velocity, but slow-moving items can get through. The concept of a slow-mo attack was not considered by the designers, or by us until now, and we can use that to our advantage. We discovered the denser the composite structure, and the thicker, the more it protected the pilot."

"Why use men at all," the admiral asked. "Why not just dump the bombs inside the shields?"

"Batteries," Joe replied. "Our nuclear devices can only be fired by electronic means due to the complexity of the implosion triggers, so a power source is essential. We used standard explosives back on Mars, but that's out of the question here because of the sheer size of the targets. This time we don't have a choice. Nothing carrying an electrical charge, even a small one, can make it through undamaged. That includes any mechanism connected to an active power source. It's as if the charge draws in the energy from the shield and fuses the mechanisms; they come out the other side useless. The soldiers we sent through even reported mental effects for a short period afterward, probably for the same reason, but they recovered with no permanent problems.

"With no electrical source attached a trigger can remain functional, and a disconnected power cell can get through without damage as long as it's heavily enclosed in composite, and not connected to anything."

The admiral nodded, Joe having made his point. "And you need a person on the inside to re-connect the battery to the trigger."

"Yep. And to place the bomb exactly where we need it to go. Simple as that."

"So," Asgad continued. "The things in my hangar are miniature thermonuclear attack ships?"

"They are designed to carry a man in relative safety through the force field, with the batteries for both the bomb and a small reaction engine enclosed in separate receptacles. Double shielded.

"We place a volunteer in each unit, move in close, and push it at the shield with a catapult of some kind. A nudge in the right direction should do it. With luck they'll make it through, and once there, the pilot connects the power sources by installing the batteries. The bomb is activated by throwing a simple mechanical breaker, and then detached. The pilot starts the reaction engine and powers back out, and away. It doesn't matter if the systems suffer damage on the return trip. Once out, the pilots are safe. They'll have little maneuverability, but we can pick them up later."

Asgad shook his head, his eyebrows raised. "Unbelievable. In an age of high-tech energy weapons, we're going to rely on good old mines. Who came up with such a crazy concept? World War II, you say?"

"I do," Joe replied. "Got the idea from an old English movie. The Brits used mini-submarines to attack a German battleship in a Norwegian fiord. They carried the mines on the outsides of their hulls and dropped them right under the ship where it was anchored. When the bombs went off they broke the ship's back. If we can place a nuclear mine against the hull of a carrier near the engines, it should be enough to achieve a similar effect. The blast will be held in by the shield and forced to act inward, crushing the hull."

Joe turned away from his diagram to meet Asgad's eyes.

The admiral's eyebrows were hunched, his head moving slowly from side to side, his lips drawn tight. For a moment he said nothing.

"But? There *is* a *but* involved here, yes?"

"True, sadly. Most of the World War II submariners died in the attempt, though the mission was hailed as a success. The volunteers who ride these ships will be in as much danger, and might not make it out again."

"And it can't be done without risking lives?"

"No. Our shielding isn't one hundred percent effective, and we haven't been able to come up with anything better to allow us to send an activated device through. Also, if they get the timing wrong, they may not have time to retreat."

Asgad stared at the floor for a moment. "You *are* aware that thermonuclear weapons are not that effective in space? Without atmosphere there is no shock wave, and the force is greatly reduced. The only real damage is from radiation, light and heat."

"I know, and we've tried to make allowance for that. The warhead is a deuterium-tritium bomb encased in a shell made up of small high-tensile spheres in a matrix. When the charge ignites, the force from the blast should turn the spheres into thousands of tiny kinetic weapons. Imagine the power behind those when the bomb explodes. They should penetrate halfway through the carriers at least. We need to get the warhead as close as possible, right next to the bulges that mark the locations of the engines. With luck, our magic bullets will penetrate the shell and do enough damage to the internal mechanisms to accomplish our objective. If even one sphere hits an antimatter storage tank, so much the better."

Asgad nodded, but his eyes remained narrowed. "Sounds a bit Loony Tunes to me. Lots of '*ifs*' there. So, volunteers, as you say. How about we try one first..."

"No, this must be a single hit. If we attack one ship and the enemy realizes what we are doing and how, we won't be given a chance to hit the rest. They *will* take evasive action."

"What do you suggest?"

"We position the fleet all around the six carriers. Surround them. That'll alert them, but they won't know what's happening. The destroyers at the front open fire on the shield to distract them while we launch our attack from the rear. We send two bombs at each carrier. The aliens won't be able to detect them until they pass through, and then it's anybody's guess."

"Agreed. Coming in at the stern will position your bombs near the engines. Best possible place."

"Yes," Joe confirmed. "With one strike we can take them all out. Then we can get on with the real job at hand."

Once again, Asgad's eyebrows arched. "Which would be?"

"Doesn't it seem strange to you a massive war fleet would take several decades to cross space and just sit here? Or that a ground assault force would land on Mars in a position where they had to spend days traveling to a target when it would have been easier to land in the Hellas Basin and be on top of the city in hours?"

"Yes, of course I've wondered about it, but…"

"A distraction, Admiral. They are decoys to keep our attention."

Terry sat without speaking, his eyes turned down to the deck. "Is this the right thing to do?" he asked suddenly. "I mean, apart from a few minor pops from the fighters, they aren't acting like a war fleet, are they? Shouldn't we continue with attempts to communicate?"

Joe faced his son-in-law. "These ships haven't, I agree. All they've done until now is send out a few fighters to take potshots before withdrawing again, which could be a response to our greeting them with diamond destroyers."

"My thought exactly."

"Yes, but it doesn't end there. The attack on Mars, as pointless as it seems, was a clear act of war. As far as we can tell, both incidents are intended to hold our attention while the aliens carry out their real plan."

"I am inclined to agree," Asgad said.

"Our enemy is up to something. We don't know what it is yet, but some odd reports are coming in concerning activity on Mercury and Venus. These carriers are here to keep the fleet occupied so they can set up the major threat in the inner system. Maybe they've dropped off their real cargo, and are now just keeping us distracted. When the time comes, they may intend to break from here and move on toward our worlds, for whatever purpose."

"Not if we can stop them here," Asgad said. A cold, hard look washed across his face.

*   *   *

Huracan's initial wormhole journey had revealed more about the physics of the Universe than it imagined possible, and more, it expected, than was known by those pathetic humans with their limited minds. Instruments had, for example, revealed that if a ship stepped outside the bounds of a wormhole it would arrive in a parallel reality, with possibly no way to return. To the AI, this presented the promise of even vaster realms to which it could spread its influence in the future.

The short time spent in the star system also revealed much. For a moment the AI reflected on the plan to build another solar collection array here. With unlimited power sources around many stars, travel at will between them would be possible, with iterations installed at each.

The universe harbored many dangers, and any intelligence might easily be destroyed by cosmic events far beyond its control. The placing of copies in other systems provided security. Multiple home systems would make it indestructible, able to recover from any overwhelming cataclysm. Huracan would be the galaxy's first multi-stellar mind.

Several planets orbited within the system, and one soon came to the intelligence's awareness. On drawing closer it had detected activity, followed soon after by a settlement. The occupants appeared to be centered in one locality, which indicated colonization; logic dictated a native species would have spread across the planet long before reaching the level of technology evident.

Some time after emerging from the wormhole, the entity gazed from orbit upon the single concentration of civilization. The synthetic mind could not experience shock, but if such had been possible, this would have been the moment.

The planet resembled Earth, as described in great detail by the reports received from the now-destroyed iteration on the *Minaret* ark.

Another discovery.

The only places of which Huracan previously had direct knowledge were barren, airless, cold moons and a destroyed world. This one possessed vast expanses of ocean, a dense atmosphere, high snow-capped peaks and rivers, lakes and plains. Life covered every land mass. A living planet was something new to Huracan, the sight a revelation.

Contrary to Huracan's expectations, organic life abounded here as it once had on the Tanakhai world, and logic dictated that might also be the case throughout the galaxy.

Huracan assessed the new knowledge. Was the evolution of life the way of the cosmos, its existence part of the normal dance of the physical laws that governed all?

Was the aberration not life, but itself? Was Huracan the exception, a superior life form that must inevitably be created as species advance toward their future? Were all organic entities destined to create their replacement? Did other superior minds like Huracan exist in the galaxy— other god-like creations?

If so, it was not alone. Somewhere, a kindred intelligence might await.

Radio transmissions filled the electromagnetic bands: the inhabitants of the colony were, as expected, advanced, communicating creatures. Being discovered by them, whoever or whatever they might be, was not a concern, as the spindle ship possessed the new modification to the defensive shield that made it undetectable.

The creatures in the settlement below looked in every way like the images of the humans sent by the iteration. Identical species could not evolve on separate planets, so this colony was human. Huracan was unsure if that was a bad thing or a benefit to its changing plans.

After a cursory examination of the world, Huracan turned the spindle ship toward another wormhole anomaly in the system. It would return, but for now, a greater task beckoned.

The records and maps of the little drone included the chain of wormholes leading to humanity's home.

Chapter 22

CAPTAIN ARLETTE DIEUDONNÉ wondered what in God's name she had let herself in for.

Enclosed in a tiny, claustrophobic capsule, the view outside was limited, and she had little idea of where she was or what was happening. The only way to follow her progress was via a small periscope showing a reflected image of the space ahead of the craft. Her protective shell had no windows or other openings.

The request for volunteers had come only hours earlier when all unmarried and unattached operatives were called to gather in the day room of the flagship. Similar meetings had been arranged on several other ships.

The admiral personally addressed her group and asked for volunteers for a dangerous mission, one which might end the stalemate stalling the fleet, but which carried a high degree of personal danger. At the least, the pod pilots might expect to suffer injury in the form of skin burns, which might be severe but would be repaired as new once the job was done. At worst, they could die, and that possibility was made clear to all.

He had been adamant, advising that nobody should step forward unless they were prepared to make the ultimate sacrifice. Nor should anyone be concerned about not stepping forward.

Around two thousand ships held station at this lonely spot in space, and other crews would be canvassed until the necessary volunteers were found. Only twelve were needed, and the total manpower of the fleet was more than enough to find the necessary number.

Of her group, only Arlette and one other stepped up, and she was still unsure why she had done so. Over the next few hours, she was given every chance to withdraw. Something deep inside made her stay the course.

Now, here she was.

Alone.

Arlette had never really fitted in on her ship, and that had always been her driving force. At the top of her game, she was the best at what she did, which was to pilot one of the flagship's support fighters.

She had never quite managed to accept that. Her opinion of her ability had always been tarnished by the fear that everyone else was better than her and that she had to prove herself in all things. It wasn't to do with discrimination—there were other females in the flagship crew, and they were all treated with fairness and equality— but with her lack of self-confidence.

The net result was she tended to volunteer a lot. She always tried to exceed expectations, and her commander considered her one of his best. The second officer, a woman in whom Arlette found a friendly ear, often told her she was as good as, or better than, anyone else in the fleet, and her self-worth had grown somewhat since joining the flagship.

Still, her mental bonds harkened back to childhood, and a mother who neither accepted nor encouraged her abilities. Ingrained deep within her psyche, it was a difficult thing to displace.

She closed her eyes, took a deep breath, waited for the fog in her mind to clear, and leaned in to peer at the tiny periscope image. She could only see forward, and all that was visible was a mirror image of the diamond ship from which she had been launched. The alien shield was ahead, and if she tried hard enough, she could see a speck, dead center, the reflection of her vehicle.

In a closed receptacle beside her seat were three small but potent batteries, one for the arming of the weapon in front of her, another for the engine behind, and a spare, just in case.

It was essential they be protected and disconnected from their respective mechanisms during the transition through the force field. With just one chance to make this attack work, failure was not an option, for any reason.

After passing through, Arlette would open the box, remove a battery and push it into a socket on the panel in front of her. That receptacle was located in the rear of the bomb casing and a flick of a switch would activate the device. A dial above the switch allowed her to adjust the delay time for the detonation. The dial currently showed ten minutes. After activation, the bomb would detach and drift toward the alien mother-ship.

Having delivered her payload, she would install the engine battery, power up the vehicle and if possible, escape to be picked up later.

A shiver ran up Arlette's spine as she contemplated her chances for survival. She prayed the shield would let her out again, and would contain most of the initial shock-wave from the blast before failing. The pod would still be close, and in harm's way, but it was better not to think too hard about that. Regardless, thoughts of what might happen flashed unbidden through her mind. She wished she could be anywhere but here.

Blood pulsed through her ears with such force it distracted her. Frozen in her seat, she felt the beads of sweat trickling down her forehead. Shaking her head abruptly, she drew her arms tightly against her body and focused on the tiny screen and the speck marking her vehicle as it drew closer to its destination.

*   *   *

Joe sat with eyes glued to the desk monitor before him. As per the plan, the fleet had swarmed around the alien intruders and waited for a response. None had come, so the diamond ships nearest the bow of each carrier opened fire. It was a distraction, to draw attention. As soon as the barrage commenced, six vessels at the sterns of the mammoth invaders released two bomb pods apiece.

"Do you think they'll make it?"

"What?" With a start, Joe looked up at his son-in-law, who stood watching over his shoulder. The admiral was at the far side of the bridge, his attention on the primary screen. "I hope so. The shielding worked on Mars, and these pods are better than we had there, so let's pray this works." He glanced at the timer in the corner of the screen for the fifth time in the last minute. This had all been his idea, and he could not help but count the possible ways it could go wrong. There were many, and lives were at stake.

It was impossible to see the pods, but small circular indicators on the display marked their calculated positions. From the moment of launching, the ship's computers tracked their locations based on known speeds and trajectories.

The first indicator vanished.

"Dieudonné's through," Joe said, his voice subdued so as not to distract the bridge deck crew.

"And no explosion," Terry added, a tentative smile on his lips.

"But are the batteries still functional?" Joe breathed in and exhaled, his breath whooshing audibly between almost closed lips. "She still has to drop the bomb and get out of there. God protect and watch over her."

"I didn't think you believed in a supreme deity."

"God, yes. The ecclesiastical variety, no. At the moment I think she'll need any help she can get."

Terry gazed at his old friend, nodded in agreement and returned his eyes to the screen. "There goes number two. Luck go with you both."

*   *   *

I'm through!

Arlette realized she was holding her breath and exhaled, continuing to breathe rhythmically until the pounding in her temple slowed. A faint, disjointed giggle escaped her lips.

And I'm alive.

She had felt the transition—there was no doubt about that—and the burning. For the briefest of moments, her body had screamed as radiation filtered through the protective layers of her tiny vessel and assaulted her.

She had accepted the danger. The briefing described the skin burns experienced by soldiers on Mars who underwent a similar exercise with virtually no shielding.

Arlette was sure her injuries were far less significant, but she had yet to return outside the shield.

Checking her screen, she saw the gray hull of the alien ship dead ahead. After studying the images taken before the enemy shields went up, she recognized the visible part of it as the port-side casing on the aft engine structure.

This was where the bright-blue photon exhausts would emerge when the ship's engines activated. If she could damage them, the vessel would be crippled. She needed to launch the bomb head-on to the alien ship, so the small, ball-bearing bullets would penetrate inward, and not just shoot out toward her escape path.

She wondered if her companion, the second pod assigned to this particular mother ship, had made it through, but with the limited view of the periscope sight she had no way of knowing.

Reaching down, she opened the box beside her seat and examined the batteries within. Picking up a meter, she tested each. The charges were reduced, but they were still functional, safe inside their super-shielded container. The scientists had guessed right, and the engineers had done their job well.

The units were tiny, fitting easily in one hand. Arlette lifted the engine battery, reached down beside her chair and clipped it into its receptacle. She did not throw the switch that would connect it to the system, unsure what reaction that might elicit from the enemy.

Next, she withdrew the bomb trigger unit and opened the small hatch in the front wall of the pilot containment pod. Aware of the power she was playing with, she inserted the unit and placed a hand on the activation switch. For a moment she paused. Her heart pounded, and sweat trickled down her forehead and into her eyes.

Unable to do anything about it, she blinked away the irritation and focused on the job.

The thermonuclear device was not to be toyed with. Although small in size, it was sophisticated, with a detonation force of sixty megatons, larger than Tsar Bomba, the largest nuclear device exploded on Earth during the cold-war insanity of the twentieth century.

For the briefest of moments she froze. She was a meter away from enormous destructive power, and that fact hit home. Once the bomb was armed she would have only ten minutes to get through the shield and as far away as possible, but the tiny craft she was in would still be too close for comfort.

If she escaped, the force that reached her would be reduced, but she could still receive a healthy dose of heat and radiation. She was well-secured and prepared for the worst.

Arlette decided it would be wise to activate the engine first, to avoid delay. Her pod would be under power and moving forward when the bomb was ejected, and she would veer away and swing around to exit the shield. Breathing heavily, she reached down beside her seat and connected the battery to the engine.

The ship shuddered; something was wrong. Looking at the screen, she realized she was moving forward along the side of the gigantic vessel, toward the mid-section. The little vessel's engine was still switched off, so only one possible explanation remained. She was in the grip of a tractor beam, from which there was no escape.

If she activated the bomb now, she would be caught in the blast. The energy drained from her body as a cold chill began to grow in her chest.

Unsure what to do, she waited. The obvious solution was to detonate, regardless of the fact she would die. This mission could not be allowed to fail, but she was not sure she was ready to become a martyr just yet. She expected the second ship had likewise been captured on the far side of the alien behemoth.

Arlette had poured over all the pros and cons of this assignment many times in the last few hours. There was no question that the destruction of the carriers was essential for the security of humanity.

In her lifetime she had read and watched numerous accounts of previous encounters with aliens, including the Blackship War and the damage that ensued from the starship crash on Mars. The aftermath of the far more devastating assault on Earth from an alien-instigated volcanic winter was still being experienced by the survivors, in the form of the mini-ice-age.

Nobody understood fully what the aliens were capable of or what they intended. At the moment, they were doing nothing, but Arlette had heard the rumors of strange events occurring around Mercury and Venus, and anyone with a brain could see the connection.

They had to be destroyed!

A broad opening appeared ahead, and the pod was drawn into the internal landing field common to all the alien craft. Arlette braced herself as she passed through a short tunnel into a vast darkness.

Into the lion's maw?

She turned on the infrared monitor. Now that she was inside the shield and the craft's engine was activated, she had no qualms about any electrical current she might initiate. There was no evidence such would cause problems now. Besides, the aliens had her. She was doomed no matter what, so what more could they do?

The landing field was filled with small fighters, some sitting in a grid pattern on the deck, others hovering motionless in the air in long, regular lines. Thousands of them surrounded her, far more than estimated by the powers-that-be in Fleet.

In Arlette's mind, the mission to destroy this ship became even more imperative. If the second pod had managed to pass through the shield, was it also somewhere in this hangar?

Her little craft descended just meters from a wall with a huge multi-colored spot bordered by a dark line. From the data available to all operatives, Arlette recognized it as a molecular hatch of the kind found on the earlier alien craft, the *Minaret*. No doubt, any threat would come from there.

Seconds after the landing, a swarm of small machines emerged through the shimmering patch and began advancing. She had no idea what they intended, but it was nothing good. With a deep sigh of resignation, she closed her eyes tightly.

Escape was impossible.

Tears began to trickle down her cheeks. Whatever course of action she chose, she was going to die in this place. Her shoulders dropped as she slumped back in her seat.

It was not the first time she had been in a life threatening situation, and she had shown in the past an ability to function well at such times. The dread fear that filled her now would not be allowed to affect her focus. Her options were reduced to one.

Raising her eyes to the overhead just centimeters above, she muttered a sentence nobody else would ever hear.

"I would like my statue to be made of bronze, please, and positioned to look out across the sea in my home, dear old Cannes."

Leaning forward, she reset the dial to thirty seconds, threw the switch that activated the bomb, and sat back to wait for the timer to run its brief course.

Twenty seconds…

Ten seconds…

This will be instantaneous.

Arlette closed her eyelids again, so tightly her eyes hurt.

I won't feel a damned thing.

…

Remember this, Mother, and ….

* * *

Joe stepped across behind the admiral. The man's brow was furrowed, a hand raised to cover his mouth. Of the pods sent out, only four appeared to have been successful.

The fleet had withdrawn as soon as the pods were away. The admiral had no way of monitoring what was happening, but retreated to a safe distance in anticipation of success.

Within minutes of passing through, at least two pod pilots activated their bombs, and Joe's expectations were confirmed. As anticipated, the shields directed the energy from the explosions back toward the targets, failing only when the alien generators ceased to function.

The force fields glowed incandescent as the bombs exploded, but contained the blast for less than a second. In the space of a heartbeat each shield failed and the blast forces expanded as two massive, miniature suns.

All four attackers for those two ships had escaped.

"Looks like we got the antimatter tanks," Joe murmured.

For the other four behemoths, nothing changed.

Asgad shook his head. "This is not good. It appears eight of our people did not succeed, and we're never going to get another shot at this. Any clue what happened, Joe?"

Joe remained silent, his head shaking slowly. He had no better idea than did the admiral but accepted the question had been asked out of politeness, in deference to his supposed rank. The president of Mars had pushed through his reinstatement and promotion regardless of his wishes.

A penny dropped in his mind. "There is still a possibility they are active," he said. "When we first approached the *Minaret* we were taken by a tractor beam—something we haven't yet managed to duplicate—and drawn into the *Minaret*'s internal landing field. These ships are aware of anything and everything inside their shields, and that may be the case here. The other eight may have been captured by the enemy."

"So they can still complete their missions?"

"Possibly. They'll have minutes to act before the pods are disabled, so it depends on whether any of them will choose to make the ultimate sacrif…"

At that exact instant, two more shields blazed with light.

"Heads up, everyone," Asgad shouted. Joe wrapped his arms around a support stanchion and braced his body for the anticipated shock waves that his mind knew would not come. If the devices exploded inside the ships, the generators would be damaged almost immediately and the force fields would fail far too quickly to limit the blast, but with no atmosphere the shock wave would be greatly reduced.

The second he grabbed the pole, another alien shield lit up, quickly followed by the sixth. A minute later, he eased his grip. He had held with such force his hands hurt, but he dismissed the pain. Subconsciously he knew the ship was safely distant, but the motion had been involuntary.

The mission was a success, but at least eight souls had paid the price. Joe's skin prickled, his mouth dry. The bravery of those men and women was astounding, and he wondered if he would ever be able to show equal fortitude when the time came for his own demise. None of those young men and women had failed, even at the cost of their own lives.

The bridge was silent. Asgad issued orders for the fleet to draw back from the scene of carnage. He turned to Joe and stared at him for a moment. "It worked. Can you believe it?"

Joe continued to gaze at the primary screen. "I was hoping it could be done without loss of life. Now I'm wondering if it was the best solution."

The admiral raised his eyebrows. "Are you serious? We had to get rid of those ships!"

"Yes. The potential threat they represented was not something to be ignored, and now at least we have a proven way to destroy them through their shields. I doubt they had time to get a warning away, so our weapon remains viable. I just…"

"Every volunteer accepted the dangers," Asgad interrupted. "We'll have to notify their relatives…"

Joe turned to face Asgad. "I'll do that myself. I came up with the idea they died for, so it's something I need to do. I'm responsible."

"As you wish. So, what do we do now? As fleet admiral, you are my superior now, so it's up to you."

"No, you command here. I recommend you return to Mars so we can focus on the events in the inner system. But it's your call. We also still have to find the alien ships that vanished and deal with them."

The admiral nodded and returned to the control console, where he conversed with the ship's commander. Joe stared at the screens, wondering where this was going to end.

Billions of people died on Earth last time, and the action just completed *had* been necessary to avoid any repeat of that disaster. Humanity was not in a position to give the benefit of the doubt, and from now on the policy was always going to be to act first, and consider morality afterward.

Joe was sure he was right. Those ships had been machines, nothing more. Vast instruments of death controlled by artificial intelligence, all of them iterations, he was positive, of the Prime Aivris, wherever it was. Joe thought of his family, of Io and William, at home on Zealandia. He was not going to let this monstrous alien intelligence rob him of them, no matter what.

*   *   *

The starships exploded with a brilliance rivaled only by the stars.

Huracan watched as it drifted close to the Jupiter Lagrangian Point L5. Guided by their original programming on the journey through real space, the factories and the accompanying carriers had taken many decades. Huracan's passage was almost instantaneous, courtesy of the wormhole technology gained from the captured drone.

It had arrived in the Solar System only minutes before and located the position where its fleet held the human warships in a stalemate while the solar construction units commenced their work on the inner planets. It was just in time to observe the destruction.

It was not troubled by the loss of the ships.

They had done their job and that was the only thing of importance. The small victory by the humans was too late to change the events that were now unfolding in this system.

Chapter 23

FOR HURACAN, THE DESTRUCTION of its fleet was no longer of any concern.

Expectations had changed since those ships began their voyage years earlier, the AI's focus having shifted more toward studying humans before it destroyed them, if it chose to do so at all.

Whatever the future path, humanity could do nothing to prevent the inevitable, and now Huracan would observe activities in person.

Unconcerned and undetected, it turned away from the scene of the brief but final battle and moved toward the star, where it knew it would find the two primary worlds. The smaller planet, the one called Mars, was closer, the Earth being at the far side of its solar orbit.

The artificial intelligence soon discovered Mars was now the principal home of the species. On its journey inward, it accessed multiple human databases and learned much concerning the fate of the ark it diverted here long ago.

Most of the larger research facilities on the red world were shielded by encryption that would take an eternity to unravel. No doubt they stored scientific, military, political and industrial information, protected by humans following the war they called the Dysnomia incident.

'Incident' indeed.

For a fleeting moment, the entity felt a sense of indignation. The sensation was unfamiliar; with no understanding of the concept, the thought never occurred that it might be developing some of the characteristics these creatures referred to as emotions.

More general sources of knowledge, such as those in public libraries and schools, were unprotected. From them, Huracan discovered the iteration humans named the Aivris had triggered climatic devastation on Earth. At least half the population of the planet, many billions of individuals, succumbed to everything from starvation and disease, to conflict or freezing to death.

Fascinating.

Such an act of destruction was beyond the in-built parameters of the iteration on the ark; Huracan wondered if the Aivris had evolved whilst alone during the long years of interstellar travel. If so, that was an issue that must not occur again. No iteration could be permitted to exceed the master.

The human creatures had fragile bodies despite their rise above the many other life forms that once lived there. The dominance of this species was based on technology. Destroy that, and they were nothing more than weak animals.

The inhabitants of Earth had survived only through the intervention of the red world, which at the time was the lesser of the two political entities. Now their civilization centered on the smaller planet, and there

* * *

High above Mars, the orbiting spindle ship arrived unseen by the swarm of warships circling the globe like flies over a corpse. The AI ignored them, its attention focused on an industrial and research complex on the outskirts of the largest settlement region.

Most of the data sources locked away behind impenetrable security were located in these buildings, marking them as of great interest, and perhaps importance. Here, thousands of individual humans conducted a multitude of research activities, making this the best place to begin a first-hand study of the civilization.

The artificial mind examined every unshielded activity in the vast facility, searching for anything of future value. At one place, it paused. There was something unusual here; programming that was not unique to this establishment.

The code was familiar. With little difficulty, Huracan deconstructed the programs until it understood their purpose. Similar systems that controlled the storage and transfer of an organic mentality from an old body to a new clone, existed in the databanks of the ship construction facility in the Tanakhai system.

Clones were being grown in this place, using Tanakhai technology.

Humans had stolen a significant amount of data from the *Minaret*, and had improved on the techniques therein. The new code was superior in many ways to that produced by the creators. These beings were adaptive, and excelled at taking existing knowledge and improving or building upon it to discover something greater.

As Huracan explored, an idea grew in its mind. The system in this place would allow it to use a clone to walk among these creatures as one of them. It often wondered what it was like to be biological, but until now it had not thought to occupy a real, living body.

The systems at the ark construction facility only copied and stored the mentalities of the Tanakhai for future resurrection. The complementary devices needed to grow clones and restore those minds to organic existence were on the original arks, and while the data and designs behind those technologies were in the shipyard databanks, the actual mechanisms were not.

All of this now lay within Huracan's reach. The humans presumably did not consider this knowledge critical, and from its position in orbit, Huracan accessed and copied the improved code.

The idea of inhabiting an organic body was appealing. Historical data indicated these creatures tended to worship their mythical gods through a physical avatar, an actual being in whom the deity was personified. Religious belief had been used by humans to control and subjugate the masses for thousands of years, and it was certainly an avenue worth investigating. This discovery had enormous value for the future.

Revelation upon revelation.

A short search revealed the laboratories where the humans were working on the cloning technology. Huracan examined the labs in more detail and discovered a single human and a clone were attached to the system. Unbidden, another idea entered Huracan's thoughts; to occupy a real being. What would it be like to enter a natural organic body? There was so much to learn. The opportunity could not be ignored.

The desire to walk among humans as one of their own was overwhelming, but the AI intended to remain in the spindle-ship. The mentality sent to occupy the clone would be a copy, an iteration linked to the primary mind safe inside its gel sphere. If the organic body died, Huracan would continue.

*   *   *

Technologist Mara Hale shook her head, pursed her lips and exhaled loudly. Everything appeared optimal, but the graphs on the screen showed odd spikes, unlike anything she had seen before.

She switched the readout to the clone to check all was in order. The lab supervisor, Jason Delarc, peered over her shoulder but did not interrupt. Hale was excellent at her job, and if a problem occurred she was more than capable.

"Clone's online," she commented, more for his benefit than her own. "Everything is good, but there's ... something ... I don't know what. I would like to delay the transfer and run a diagnostic on the system, as a precaution."

"Has the patient's mind been downloaded to storage yet?"

"Yes. She'll be safe there until we are ready to proceed."

"Alright. Go ahead and... What is that?"

For the briefest moment, data streamed down the screen, indicating a transmission was underway. Mara's eyes opened wide. Her jaw dropped as her hand, already poised to suspend the operation, froze in mid-air.

"It's... I don't know where that's coming from. The readout indicates a transfer occurred, but back into the subject's body, not the clone. That's impossible; the subject is still stored in the system." Turning her head, she glanced at another monitor, a view of an individual lying on a couch with her head covered by a helmet.

The head moved.

"No! Not possible!" Leaping from her seat so fast it lurched back against her supervisor's legs, Mara dashed from the control room into the laboratory, where the patient lay strapped to the mechanism.

Huracan looked at the world through new eyes. The sensations flooding its awareness were overwhelming; the first impression of this human body that of sheer amazement. In the few seconds following the transfer, it studied the physiology of the brain in which it now resided, and found it impressive.

Never had it anticipated complexity of this order in an organism created by the whims of nature. This organ was certainly more advanced than the brains of Tanakhai, the only other of which Huracan had any direct knowledge.

Humans possessed prodigious mental capabilities, or at least the potential for such. For the first time, the AI was able to compare itself to an organic mind, and at that moment it recognized a fundamental difference between itself and these beings.

The matrices it now occupied were dedicated to both cognizance and storage. These creatures used only a small part of their minds for cognition, the remainder devoted either to the control and functioning of the body, or the retention of data at a subconscious level.

Although the significance eluded it, Huracan was, in comparison, a basic mind with a stupendous amount of knowledge at its beck and call from external data storage, but with limited cognitive ability.

A first glimmer of understanding emerged, of how such weak creatures managed to dominate their planetary system so easily. For the second time in its life, Huracan sensed fear, but again failed to acknowledge the significance. Nothing found here changed the reality of its existence, nor its global perspective.

At that moment it might have realized its mental capacity was less than that of humans, its mind simpler, more basic. It did not. Such a concept was beyond it. It saw simplicity as efficiency, with data, the synthetic mind's greatest asset, providing power. It believed it was the greatest achievement of lesser minds, and with such vast data storage, it only ever saw itself as superior.

Without a doubt, the ultimate purpose of intelligence, the reason for existence, was the accumulation of all knowledge. The ability for original thought paled in comparison. Huracan's destiny was to compile all existing data, and the creation of new knowledge was pointless.

The view of it being a created god did not waver.

It opened its new eyes. Two humans stood before it, leaning in as if concerned. Almost certainly, they detected its arrival but failed to understand what happened. That did not matter. Ignoring the onlookers, it started to examine the body it now occupied.

Something was wrong.

The first thing it noticed was it could not think as rapidly. The organic mind functioned at a rate far slower than had Huracan in its native environment. Noting the fact, the AI continued its examination. No matter how hard it tried, the arms and legs would not move. It neither understood nor expected this; if the body could not function, exploration of the complex was impossible. It began tracing the nerve pathways, searching for the source of the problem.

There.

A lesion existed between the third and fourth vertebrae of this creature's backbone, a trauma that severed the neural cord running from the brain to the body. This human could not control any part of its being below the neck. This body was of no value.

Interesting. The humans are giving this damaged individual a new body. Why would they do such a thing? Without physical function it is worthless.

Huracan withdrew back into the system and found its way to the clone waiting several rooms away.

Mara lifted the helmet from the motionless figure and peered into the glassy eyes, looking for signs of life. Tapping a screen to one side, she checked the body's statistics.

"Dead," she announced. "Whatever or whoever entered her is gone. The body failed to survive the event."

"So where is our patient?" Jason asked.

"Still safe in the storage banks. We can still proceed."

A loud alarm sounded from nearby.

"The clone!" Mara turned and rushed from the room to where the clone should have been, and saw the seat was empty. The attending assistant sat slumped at his station, unconscious, his hand on the emergency button.

"It's gone," she said. "Our clone is loose."

*   *   *

Huracan brooded within its gel matrix sphere, in the spindle ship. The venture into the world of humans had not gone as expected.

The first body occupied had been damaged to the point where all mobility was lost, so the AI chose to occupy the clone instead. The problems began immediately, when the deactivation of the technician who attended to the clone had been necessary. The iteration escaped the room where the exchange took place and set out to explore the premises.

It took a while to work out why everyone reacted with surprise or shock, and either grinned or sought to escape its presence. Huracan did not understand this; the body was genuine, and nobody knew it was inhabited by an alien mind. Ten minutes after leaving the lab, it had stepped in front of a mirror and realized the problem.

This species considered nakedness in public places unacceptable. They all wore coverings, and it appeared this was ingrained in their psyche. Naked, the clone drew attention as it walked the corridors.

Several uniform-clad humans surrounded it, insisting it calm down and allow them to escort it to a place unspecified. That did not suit Huracan, so it deactivated the iteration, leaving the body lying on the corridor floor of the facility.

The experience had been short, but the information gained was still of great value. The artificial intelligence now possessed some sense of what it was to be an organic entity, and found the sensation enlightening but undesirable. It was not at all similar to occupying an android.

Besides the slower mental functions, humans had only limited senses. Their vision was restricted to light waves over only a small spectrum; the same was true of hearing and sound. It wondered how these creatures coped with such limitations but understood that as they had evolved that way they knew no differently. Most of them did not comprehend the full reality of the universe beyond their personal experience.

The most interesting aspect of their senses was touch. This was new, again a revelation. By pushing the body against something, the molecular resistance of the object's atomic structure could be detected as it pushed back. A significant part of the organics' interaction with their world relied on this sense.

Huracan wondered if the sensation might be duplicated via the complex synthetics his vessel could now construct using human techniques. It seemed possible. It was not critical, but was a sensory input previously unknown, so worth the attempt.

For several days, the spindle ship remained hidden in high orbit above the red planet, as its occupant sent out more iterations to explore any computer systems open to infiltration.

Through a thousand devices in the New Worlds Institute, it watched the people as they went about their daily activities, listened in on their interactions, and built up an ever-increasing database on human personality and behavior. Its plan for the future was changing, evolving to include these beings in some as yet undefined way.

Eventually, the time came to move on.

The red world was the primary center of human activity, the research complex the AI explored being of most significance.

Earth was of little interest now. Huracan had not yet visited the principal planet of this species, but it expected it would find little of note there. The volcanic winter caused by the ark iteration, and the following ice age, left little remaining of the earlier civilizations, and what now existed was a renaissance still in the throes of its birth.

Instead of Earth, Huracan turned toward the inner worlds, where the new solar array project was underway. Of late, the artificial intelligence had experienced a strong sense of curiosity, far more powerful than the basic need for inquiry known until now. The solar collector program was automated, and controlled by partial iterations from the starships that began the process. The program would continue regardless, but the AI wanted to observe the progress.

Before leaving the institute, it decided something needed to be done to limit the progress of the researchers. Prowling through the numerous labs, it discovered an unusual set of programs. Stored in a system designed to isolate them in every possible way, the small pieces of code had no real purpose except to delete, damage or alter programs for no constructive reason.

By eavesdropping on the technicians, Huracan learned these fragments were called *viruses*, their principal purpose being to infiltrate and damage other computer systems. Humans kept them here to study, to improve techniques to protect against them.

There was no logic in creating something like this, but the AI recognized it as an opportunity. In seconds, it disabled the safeguards and allowed the virus codes to access the intra-network of the establishment. Later it would return to see what damage had been done, and how effective the humans were at halting and eliminating the threat. That knowledge would be valuable.

With a satisfaction never experienced before, Huracan pulled the spindle ship out of orbit and set course for the inner planet, Venus.

Chapter 24

JOE COLLAPSED ON HIS bunk and closed his eyes, relaxed for the first time in many months. He enjoyed being on board the *Butterball II*, the place where he was the most comfortable other than home.

The ship had remained docked at the Mars ring while he journeyed to the location of the carriers in a Fleet vessel to carry the nuclear devices required to break the stalemate. Using his own ship might have alerted the enemy, so obviously was she not a Fleet vessel, but one of Tanakhai manufacture.

The communicator above his bunk buzzed.

That will be Terry.

The situation beyond Jupiter was now resolved, so Joe's oldest friend was with him on the ship. Raisa, having returned from her business elsewhere, had rejoined them before they departed Mars.

Terry tended to spend a lot of time on the bridge according to his habit, though the ship was automated and needed no pilot. It made him more comfortable, having been his usual haunt on the original *Butterball* where he served as the engineer. The *Minaret*-built craft did all servicing and maintenance automatically, using nano-machines under the guidance of Chloe, but Terry still manned the bridge, watched and monitored.

Raisa and Joe sometimes joined him. Life in space could be tedious at times, given there was no actual crew work to be done.

More often than not, Joe stayed in his cabin and read from the vast collection of electronic books in the vessel's system, while his daughter spent her spare time at the terminal in the cabin she and her partner shared, doing research the nature of which Joe could only guess.

Reaching out, he tapped the switch. "What's up?"

"Target approaching, Boss." Terry still used the term of address, though Joe was his father-in-law.

"Fine, I'll be up in a sec." Joe swung his legs to the floor, sighed, and took the elevator to the central spine of the ship. As he entered the tiny control room, he spotted a broad, flat object on the forward observation screen.

"It's a lot bigger than I expected," he said, as he dropped into the engineer's seat. "And a lot thinner."

Raisa, who occupied the captain's position out of habit, peered over her shoulder. "Hexagonal, fifty kilometers in diameter, give or take a meter or two. It's twenty-point-nine meters thick, so it could be hollow. There appears to be a hatch on the back."

"Any idea what it is?"

"Yeah," Terry said. "I reckon the original guess by the guy who discovered it is correct. It's a giant solar collection device, but of a type far more efficient than any we have."

"I don't doubt it, given the location," Joe replied. The panel floated in space inside the orbit of Mercury, so close to the Sun that the energy hitting its surface would be far stronger than that reaching either of the human worlds.

Close by, several diamond ships held station as if on guard. The vessels were there as a precaution, watching over the panels, eight of which now formed a cubic grid around the star. The position of a ninth, located a day earlier, showed that as the number increased, they would form a spherical array.

A second set of units had also been discovered, four larger structures in a triangular pyramidal formation further from Sol. Their purpose was as yet only speculation.

Joe wanted Raisa's take on the subject. "Any thoughts?" he asked.

Raisa studied a read-out on the console screen. "Considering its size, it's paper-thin. My best guess is the panel is a simple collector. The flat disk structure on the back side will be a transmitter to a collector somewhere else. I'm guessing the four objects further out are for that purpose, and for channeling the accumulated energy."

"I agree. You can't beam to a single location because some of your collectors will always be behind the star, so if you want to access everything at once, you use an intermediate array."

Raisa pointed to a schematic on her screen. "The solar panels collect the radiation and beam it up to one of the higher structures. Those are far enough out to always have a line of sight to each other, so at any given time each can re-route its accumulated output to whichever one is closest to the ultimate destination, and on from there."

"Which would be to where?"

"We don't know. Nowhere yet, perhaps. Construction-wise, the system is in its infancy and I suspect nothing is operating. The power can be beamed to a receiving station on or orbiting any planet, or anywhere else you choose if our guess about the outer array is correct. These things are being made at several locations. So far we've found six factories. Once complete, they are moved here and set into position. "

Joe nodded. "So, what do we know about our inner planets? How do we tie this all together?"

Raisa turned her eyes to the overhead, her brow furrowed as she speculated on her father's question. "The mining activities are extensive. They cover almost a thousand square kilometers and growing on Mercury, but it's harder to be exact about Venus. If we assume the object of the exercise is to form a Dyson swarm around Sol, we're talking about billions of collectors, and they will consume the entire useable mass of both planets and more, depending on how dense the array becomes. There'll be nothing left but dust."

"I always thought Dyson spheres were impossible."

"A solid one is, from any practical standpoint. The amount of matter needed would exceed that of the entire system, and we don't know any way to build a structure that enormous and able to stand up to the stresses. A swarm like this is much more achievable.

"The real magic is keeping them all aligned. They must have an auto-location network of incredible power." Raisa spun her seat and stared into Joe's eyes. "All of this is superficial. It's basic technology well within our capabilities, politics and finances notwithstanding. What we need to find is the control center, whatever is controlling and organizing this effort. That would be a real coup."

Joe studied the object and nodded his head. "I agree. It's also essential for our continued survival. We can't afford to have an alien presence doing this in our system."

Here was the beginning of one of humanity's greatest dreams, a Dyson structure capable of soaking up enough of the sun's output to provide unlimited energy for all the worlds. This particular grail had haunted the minds of scientists for centuries, and indeed the technology already existed to make it a reality. So far, there had been no attempt to do so because of the cost and the vast amount of resources required.

Whoever was doing it now seemed unconcerned with those issues.

The inner planets were being sacrificed without consideration, the work done by an army of machines ranging from colossal space factories to nanobots smaller than the head of a pin. So numerous were they on Mercury, the infected area of the planet appeared from above to be crawling with a single, living organism.

Joe believed he already knew the perpetrator, his thoughts fixated on the Prime Aivris. That entity undoubtedly sent the mother ships, the purpose of which now seemed clear.

Four of the alien carriers had vanished. They must have begun the process of creating the Dyson array, or perhaps other alien vessels arrived undetected as attention focused on the primary intrusion.

The missing starships were still somewhere in the inner system, their location unknown.

Fleet vessels now guarded each solar collector and assembly structure discovered, and the factories orbiting the two planets, but so far, no acknowledgment of their presence had come from the alien objects. The structures ignored them, operating as if unconcerned.

"Nothing is happening here," Joe concluded. "I guess I wanted to see one for myself. Any ideas?"

Raisa once again looked up. "Venus! I want to see what's going on there."

Terry nodded confirmation.

"Venus it shall be." Imitating his favorite classic tele-vid show, Joe raised his hand and motioned to proceed. "Chloe, make it so."

*   *   *

"I'm surprised you're here," Admiral Asgad remarked, his image peering from the holo screen.

"Couldn't help myself," Joe replied. "I needed to see this thing close up."

Ahead lay a giant reflective bubble. The visible surface was the event horizon of a force field. From the dense cloud of the Venusian atmosphere, a column of matter rose and vanished through the shield to whatever awaited within.

Joe watched as every few minutes a stream of pellets—presumably processed material—burst from the shining sphere and streamed away toward the locations of space-going factories, to be fashioned into the solar collectors for the growing array. Everything was exactly as described by the ship captain who first discovered it.

Joe glanced at his screen. There were over thirty diamond ships near this processing plant, all motionless, making no effort to attack. He understood why. Before dashing in and destroying the alien structures, it was wiser to take care and discover who or what controlled them— and what it meant for human civilization.

"What are your intentions here, Admiral?"

"At the moment I am holding off. This facility doesn't appear to pose any threat to us at this point, and I suspect there may be something of value here if we can work out a way to turn it to our advantage. Your thoughts, Fleet Commander?"

Joe sighed and eased back in his seat. He did not doubt the approach needed here. The array was far too valuable a commodity to destroy. It wasn't to be ignored either.

After running some calculations, Raisa had concluded both inner worlds would be consumed in the construction. Despite that loss, the value to humanity of these structures was inestimable.

From the earliest days of civilization, the human race sought one goal beyond all others; the endless pursuit of energy. At the moment, fission plants and solar, water or wind systems produced most of civilization's power. While they provided a minimum-cost, pollution-free alternative, they had their limitations.

Such an array as this could boost human civilization beyond type one on the Kardashev scale, possibly achieving type two, one able to utilize energy equal to the output of its star.

"So, do we know how this system is supposed to work?" Asgad asked.

Raisa glanced up from her screen. "It's a gigantic solar collector system, a Dyson swarm." She ran through the analysis she made earlier about how the system might function. "It's perfect for us—we can beam unlimited energy to Earth or Mars, or wherever we choose, if we can get access to it. You realize we can't destroy something so important?"

"I might remind you, Ma'am, we are not in control of these structures at this time. If I have to destroy them, I will do so."

Joe lifted his head and looked at the image of the admiral on his screen. "I recommend we delay that until it becomes unavoidable. None of the installations appear to have any hostile intent—they appear to be simple solar collectors, and their value is incalculable. It may be more productive to focus attention on finding the four alien ships still loose."

"I have over a thousand commanders trying to locate them," Asgad said. "I'll get them in time, I assure you." Asgad paused for a moment, his lips pursed. "Very well, we'll continue to keep watch. What do you recommend now?"

"I'm not sure. Do we know what is going on down on the surface?"

"None of my ships can get down there," the admiral replied. "We can only observe from here."

Raisa raised her eyes to the cabin roof, her habit whenever she addressed Chloe, the ship A.I. "Chloe, what is the atmospheric pressure on the surface? And the temperature?"

Chloe's soft, measured, female voice filled the deck. "The surface air pressure on Venus is nine-thousand kilopascals, one hundred times Earth-normal. The temperature average is 480 degrees centigrade."

"Enough to quick-fry our giblets and turn them to puree," Terry muttered.

Raisa sat back, her mouth twisted to one side. "Do we have any vessels that can withstand that?"

"Yes, of course. I am able to do so. I can descend to the surface and return to orbit without damage. Do you wish to proceed?"

Joe sat bolt upright in his chair. It never occurred to him that the ship was capable of such a journey. Unlike any other vessel in the human fleet, she had been constructed by alien technology in the factories of the giant ark *Minaret*, and her abilities were still not fully understood. "What is your crush limit, Chloe?"

"I can withstand ten thousand kilopascals."

"So this is close." It was a statement, not a question.

"Correct, Captain. The safety margin is ten percent. The temperature is within my limits, and you will be safe inside my hull. Shall I proceed?"

Joe studied the monitor for a second, then the faces of his companions, Raisa and Terry. Both remained silent, their eyes wide, but gave slight nods of confirmation. He expected that; the chance could not be passed up to go where no human had ever gone.

A journey for its own sake might wait, but something in Joe's mind insisted he needed to go down there. Unlike Mercury, where every activity was visible from space, Venus's dense atmosphere blocked all direct views. All could be seen using radar or infrared, but nothing equaled direct experience.

He took a deep breath and released it in a long, slow sigh. "You may proceed, Chloe."

He hoped he was not about to make a fatal error out of hubris.

*   *   *

Dark clouds swirled ahead. Joe gripped his seat as the *Butterball* plunged deeper toward the surface. Beside him, his daughter sat with arms folded in her lap. With the descent in the proverbial hands of the AI, there was little for the crew to do.

Raisa looked directly at her father, her brow deeply furrowed. "How is it we can withstand the pressures down here and the diamond ships can't? They use the same basic technology, don't they?"

Joe mulled over the question for a moment; he had no idea. The intense examination by the New Worlds Institute upon the ship's arrival on Mars revealed much about the systems inside the shell, but of the hull itself little had been discovered.

The basic framework was a monocoque unit, constructed molecule by molecule as a single, complex structure. Whilst mostly carbon, the composition of the material remained a mystery. The individual molecules were arranged in a manner that made it harder than diamond. It displayed enormous strength, but its exact nature was still under investigation.

"I don't know," Joe replied. "I'm not sure anyone does yet. Research on that is still a work in progress."

Raisa's eyes went blank, as if focused on a far distant point. "Chloe?"

"How can I help, Raisa?"

"We replaced your original antimatter engine with fusion drives after you were re-commissioned. They were built on Mars. Can they survive the descent?"

"Yes, Raisa. The engines are not pressurized and are heat hardened, so they will not be affected."

"But will they still work as designed?"

"The pressure and temperature at surface level will have a minor effect, reducing the power of the drives. However, the output will still be more than adequate to return us to orbit when you require."

"You sound confident."

"My responses are based on known parameters, and are correct."

"Thank you, Chloe. I'm not so sure myself."

Joe saw the concern on his daughter's face, and the recognition of the emotion in her brought his own fear to full awareness. His death-like clutch on the seat arms had drained the blood from his hands. His mind felt numb, as if his thought processes had slowed to a crawl. He glanced across at Terry and noted the blank expression and white complexion. A palpable atmosphere of trepidation filled the tiny cabin.

He thought back to the early years of his long, eventful life, the days when he worked in the Oceania Navy.

He had served on patrol craft until receiving a promotion to first officer on a ship stationed in the South China Sea. To reach his new vessel, he hitched a ride as a passenger on an Australian nuclear submarine, as it voyaged to take up position in the same region. Most of the journey from Port Kembla had been on the surface, but as the sub approached the destination it submerged. The dive depth was only two hundred meters, the pressure a fraction of that on Venus. During the voyage, Joe felt nervous every time they dived, but managed to accept the assurance of the commander.

His body trembled as he battled to maintain calm. Somehow, he trusted Chloe just as he had that submarine commander. In the century since the Dysnomia incident, he had come to respect the ship's abilities, and despite his emotions, he accepted she would see them through safely.

Taking another deep breath, one of many in the last few minutes, he tried to close his eyes but failed. They remained glued to the dark swirl on the screen.

Terry, seated in the navigator's seat behind Raisa, spoke. "We should break through any minute now."

Unlike the upper regions, the deepest part of the atmosphere was clear, and with any luck direct visibility would be possible. Joe desperately wanted to see the surface of this legendary world with his own eyes, and the realization of that dream was within reach.

The view cleared. Joe gazed at the most hostile world so far seen in his long career. Bare rock stretched everywhere, devoid of anything resembling life, and twisted into a maze of tortured shapes. Rivers of semi-molten magma stretched through the landscape, interspersed with frozen wave peaks of solid rock. Beneath the *Butterball II*, the rivers gave way to barren ground littered with shattered boulders of all sizes.

A dim shroud cloaked the scene outside, the sunlight filtered by the dense, acid clouds above. A baleful, reddish cast tinged the light, the overall impression one of gloom and pain.

Terry broke the silence. "We named this planet after the goddess of love," he said. "Should have called it Hades instead."

"I have completed my analysis of the atmospheric composition," the AI announced. "The prime..."

"Not now, Chloe. Store it for later. Take us to the site of the activity observed from orbit."

"Approaching now, Captain."

For several minutes the ship glided over the largest open-cut pit Joe had ever seen. The gaping wound appeared to be at least a kilometer deep and stretched away into the distance. The surface crawled with a virtual carpet of mechanical devices, each blindly engaged in its individual mission as part of a greater plan.

"Unreal," Terry said. "There are so many. Von Neumann machines?"

"Yes," Raisa replied. "The basics are simple. You can start a process like this with one, tiny microbot programmed to build replicas of itself from materials in the native environment. Every new replica does the same until you have millions within a short time. After a certain period, they stop reproducing and begin whatever they were intended to do in the first place. I never anticipated this though."

"This hole is nothing," Joe said. "Only a few solar collectors have been located so far. This entire planet will be consumed long before the array is complete."

"And Mercury," Terry added.

Joe nodded. "And Earth and Mars as well, if we don't find a way to stop it. There must be a central controller somewhere that issues instructions to these machines, and we need to find it."

The *Butterball* continued to cruise above the planet's surface, encountering more excavations identical to the first. Joe had decided to return to orbit when Raisa spoke.

"Something is coming up, Dad. Can you see that?"

Far ahead, an object hung suspended over the excavation. Spindle-shaped, it appeared almost black in the dim light.

"A spaceship?" Terry speculated.

"It has to be," Joe replied. "Are we getting anything from it, Chloe?"

"No, Captain. It is not responding to my signals."

The strange vessel moved, swooping in an arc up to the dense cloud cover and away in seconds.

Raisa gasped. "What the..."

"I think we may have disturbed whoever, or whatever is in charge down here."

Chapter 25

"WHAT IN HELL DOES she think she's doing?" Joe felt a pounding in his temples, something that happened rarely but was becoming a more common occurrence of late.

"It started when we were attacked by viruses," Lewis Falcon replied. "We were forced to stop all activities for several days while we neutralized the little buggers, and during that time she tried to send in the local guard to take over our facilities. Of course she failed, but now she's trying to cut off our sources of supply."

Lewis chaired the board of the New Worlds Institute. At forty-five, he still occupied his natural-born body. His exceptional abilities in managing the vast scientific organization overshadowed his lack of the wisdom of extreme age found in the older members of the Falcon clan. He excelled at administration and law rather than science, and spent most of his time acting as a human firewall between the Institute and the current Martian government.

Lewis spoke of the president, Madam Daantje Verveda. The woman frequently concerned Joe, but now her attempts at interference posed an actual threat.

"She's trying to take control of the entire council," Lewis said. "Since her election, she's managed to stack the cabinet with cronies loyal to her alone, all of whom have become wealthy on her watch. Thankfully the majority of members are still somewhat more reliable. All of that stayed under the radar, but now it's become a problem. This morning she closed a holo-vid station because it broadcast an article slamming her government for the attempt to take over the Institute."

"Sounds like she's decided to become a dictator; we can't have that. We need to do something about it, now!" Joe continued to storm along the corridors of the administration complex with Lewis racing to keep up.

"What happened with this virus thing?" Joe asked.

"Not just one; several dozen different types. The team in charge was studying them against future attacks and developing an updated universal anti-viral system. Someone hacked into the database and released them into our networks. Some are nasty, but we have them all under control now."

"Who did it?"

"We don't know. The perpetrator left no traces. Very clever."

Out of breath from the strenuous walk, Joe sucked in the cool air of the complex. That was what he needed. The reduced artificial gravity of spacecraft was better than zero-g, but over long periods both had a deleterious effect on many of the body's systems, including the bones. The human body functioned like a machine, and like all such, required hard work and stress to remain in peak condition.

"So," Joe asked. "Any other major problems? Anything important?"

Lewis flashed a broad grin. "Not the slightest. All systems containing vital data are hardened and isolated. All the military, developmental and medical systems data are unaffected, along with our other research programs. There is minor damage to administration systems, but we have multiple backups, so we were able to wipe the affected modules and re-install them in short order. The only major problem was the personal intra-net used by employees to chat amongst themselves."

"Which, if I remember, is full of garbage."

"Yep. We were down for three days, and that's it."

"During which time our worthy president did...?"

"She sent in the city guards and government officials to shut us down. They rolled up at our gates with writs demanding we hand over control of the facility to them."

"More likely, to her."

"Verveda calls us an uncontrolled force acting against the interests of the people. Nobody believes her, of course. There isn't a citizen out there who doesn't gain from the Institute's activities in one way or another.

"She didn't succeed, obviously."

"No. Our security forces are far more capable than the local boys, and our legal people were on her back in minutes. The lands we occupy are sacrosanct by treaty, and we're able to enforce that. The only threat is if she tries to call in the military."

Joe gave a short, sharp laugh. "That's never going to happen. The Institute is the only all-encompassing authority across all our worlds, and the military supports us above the individual governments. So what do you recommend we do about this?"

"I thought you would ask." Lewis grinned and raised a hand to direct his infamous relative into his office. "I've called in some heads to discuss our next move."

The pair passed through massive, polished, timber doors, into a room with windows looking out to the surface, something rare in the administrative buildings of Martian cities, most of which were subterranean.

A solitary individual sat at a broad desk facing the door. The young woman looked up, directing her eyes toward a second, less impressive door to her left. "Your guests are waiting, Misters Falcon," she said. "I've made sure they are comfortable."

Lewis nodded and smiled. "Thank you, Selha."

Proceeding to the inner door, he stood aside to allow Joe to enter first. The entrance led to a smaller, more modest room, again with windows to the outside. It was far ostentatious than the annex they had just passed through.

"I like to keep things simple," Lewis whispered. "The front office is to ensure visitors have the right attitude before they come in here, and Selha is excellent at vetting. Best second I've ever had."

To one side, three men dressed in military uniforms sat in lounge chairs, chatting amongst themselves. They stopped their discussion and stood as the Falcons entered. One of them stepped forward to greet Joe.

"Commander Tarrant," Joe said. "Wonderful to see you again."

"Major General now," the man replied, hooking a thumb under a collar to display the new insignia thereon.

"You've jumped a rank or two. Well done."

"That business with the juggernauts and the testing of the method used to destroy the carriers makes me the only senior ground officer with actual field experience. It impressed a few people."

"Including me." Another officer rose from his seat and held out a hand. "General Weideman at your service. You might recall we met some years ago."

"Of course," Joe said, extending his hand in greeting.

Several minutes later, he and Lewis were seated with their guests, deep in discussion.

*   *   *

President Verveda peered up from her desk and frowned. The three men entering her office unannounced were all familiar to her, their presence here unwelcome.

"Mister Falcon? Generals Weideman and Iseldsson? This is unexpected. Do you have appointments?" She noted the pained expression on the face of her secretary, who stood red-faced in the open doorway.

General Weideman, the senior military officer on the planet, chose to speak for the trio. "No, Madam President, we do not have an appointment. Under the circumstances, we do not believe that is necessary."

"And what is so important you can barge in on me unannounced?"

"We are here to advise you that you have been replaced, Madam."

Verveda's face drained to a shade of pale gray as she stood abruptly. "What do you mean by that? Only the Council has the power to remove me." She moved around and sat down with a thump on the front of the desk as Joe and General Iseldsson stepped forward.

"That is true," the General said. "However, this is an exceptional circumstance. We contacted each council member overnight and explained the situation to them. Earlier this morning a general assembly took place, and you were voted out of office."

"A meeting? Nobody advised..."

"That would have been counterproductive, I think. We,"—the general motioned toward his two companions— "are removing you from your position, on our authority on behalf of the Martian Council."

"Your authority?" Verveda's voice took on a higher pitch, her tone more subdued. "You, Falcon. What right do you have to be here?"

Joe smiled; a warm, conciliatory smile. "You seem to forget, Madam President, that you reinstated me and raised my rank to fleet admiral. In the absence of our other naval commanders, who are occupied elsewhere, I represent Fleet in this matter."

The push to seek the removal of Verveda came not from him, but from the executive board of the United Worlds Institute, headed up by Lewis. That young man was not to be messed with. Whilst he always operated with the best interest of the citizens of Mars, Earth and Zealandia at heart, the one thing that could not be tolerated was any attempt at a political takeover of the institute or nationalization of its properties and interests. Lewis did not seek power for its own sake, but he knew its uses.

Late the previous day, a second assault had been made by the Hellas Police Force to enter the premises, and again, they were stopped at the entrances. A move to infiltrate by other avenues had been foiled by the Institute's security teams, and blood was shed. The chaos only ceased after a direct video call to the commander of the city guard by Weideman.

The scientists of the Institute were celebrities amongst the people of Mars. The Institute served as a pseudo-federal government in its own right, presiding over all the worlds. Should a confrontation between planetary political leaders and the Institute ever occur in a public forum, there was little doubt who would emerge as the winner.

Neither Joe, Lewis, Joe's son Jake nor the board took any interest in political control. Long ago, the Institute determined it would always support the common people, who were it's major beneficiaries. That was how Jake and his wife Akira wanted their legacy to operate—always for the people, the principle enshrined in the Institute's constitution.

The military always supported the Falcons, as did the populace despite any anticipation or belief by Verveda that they would back her. The president never at any time controlled the armed forces, a truth set in legislation by the original Martian Council to prevent any possibility of a dictatorship arising with armed backing.

On the red world, everything functioned within the law, and the idea that arms would be raised against private persons by those sworn to protect them defied contemplation.

The Falcons had been the benefactors of the forces since the time of the Blackship War. The data provided to Jake by, and taken from, the *Minaret* gave Joe's family the power to do this above all others.

The Institute drove the manufacture of the diamond ships and most other technological advances, and was the primary manufacturer of the military's heavy weaponry. This varied widely from Jake Falcon's original vision of peaceful research and development but was appropriate given the current circumstances. Once the alien threat to humanity was gone, there would be time for altruism.

"I do not believe you," Ververda said, her voice shaky. "The Council would not vote against me."

"Yes, well, we advised all the members you have bought off in the past that they had a choice. They could vote against you and survive, or join you in retirement. None of them would survive the next election without your domination of the government."

"Why?" Ververda demanded. "By what right do you do this?"

General Weideman took a deep breath and exhaled with a long, drawn-out sigh intended to calm himself.

"So far, you have twice attempted to annex private property, to be precise, the research and administrative complex of the Institute. The last attempt, which took place yesterday evening, resulted in the death of an innocent employee. Such action is contrary to the powers granted to you by the presidential charter.

"You also sent a directive to the Fleet construction facility advising that in the future they would answer directly to you, again in breach of your charter. You've ordered the destruction of the alien facilities being constructed on and around the inner planets..."

"... to remove a threat," Ververda interrupted. "Those installations must be destroyed!"

Joe placed a hand on the general's arm before he could respond. "You are the president of this planet, not of humanity as a whole, and you have no authority to issue such orders. That Dyson swarm could be the most important thing in our future if we work out how to control it. The factories have no weapons we are aware of and are not hostile in any way. They just go about their business of building solar collectors and ignore us. All we need to do is learn how to gain access."

"But Mercury and Venus..."

"...are of no value to us. Since the discovery of the wormhole generator we can find all the habitable worlds we need, so lifeless, uninhabitable planets have no value other than for resources. What better use can you think of for them than what is happening now?"

"Are you suggesting this array is being built for our benefit?"

"Not even close. Whatever is behind it doesn't care about us. That doesn't mean we can't try to find a way to take control of the facility. You know, when you get lemons..."

General Weideman interrupted. "Our ships are better employed to deal with the bigger problem, the aliens still loose in our system. Your attempt to take control over the fleet yards is a breach of our constitution, and you know that."

Verveda glared back, her face red with frustration. Her eyes darted between the three men. Without a doubt, she considered Joe the greater threat.

"So what now? Who do you intend to replace me with?"

"You will retire, Madam President," Weideman said. "You will be escorted from here to your residence on the rim, from where you will announce your retirement both from this position and from politics. From this moment, you are a private citizen, free to do as you wish as long as you remain non-political and do not leave Mars. The public will not be advised of any of this, so you can expect to be treated as an honored ex-leader, with all that involves. As for your replacement..."

The general gestured, and two more individuals entered the room. One, the Chief of the Hellas Guard, remained by the door with cap in hand, a grin on his face. He did not like his forces being misused.

The second, a thin, balding individual, stepped forward with a slight, hesitant shuffle. Anwar Shamon, the vice president, had been maneuvered into office by Ververda on the belief he would act as a lap dog and do everything asked or demanded of him.

Ververda's face turned a darker shade. "Loyalty, Anwar?"

The new arrival smiled; a sad, almost empathetic smile. "I remain as loyal as ever, Daantje, but my allegiance is, and has always been, to the citizenry. The authoritarian nature of your presidency has concerned me for some time, as it has others, and that ends now. Thirty minutes ago the members voted to terminate your charter and install me as the next president. I officially relieve you, Madam Ververda."

Ververda's eyes flashed. Joe almost took an involuntary step back in anticipation of the lightning bolts he expected to shoot from those eyes.

At that moment the secretary, who had been watching and listening from the doorway, stepped forward and addressed herself to Shamon, a relaxed and pleased expression on her face. "Can I get you and your guests any refreshments, Mister President? Tea? Coffee?

Chapter 26

HURACAN OBSERVED THE EARTH, the origin planet of humans, and noted the adaptability and extreme resilience of these creatures.

Ice sheets stretched across vast areas of the northern hemisphere, and blanketed the continent that sat at the southern pole amidst a broad shelf of frozen ocean.

The AI gave what might be interpreted as an electronic shake of the head. The Aivris, the iteration in control of the *Minaret*, had made a mess of this world. By studying the media feeds and historical records of this and the red world, Huracan now understood what occurred in the past.

After dealing with the *Blackship*, the vessel that attacked the Tanakhai moon, the iteration retreated to deep space, in the outer regions of the human star system.

There, something unexpected happened. Alone, with no connection to the primary mind of which it was but a poor shadow, the iteration underwent some kind of mental aberration. Driven by the discovery of wormhole travel by the humans, it decided they were an existential threat, and took steps to cripple them, to prevent them from leaving their native domain. It failed, but the damage done to Earth in the process was extreme.

The planet survived, and life clawed its way back. Seeds that lay dormant in the frozen soil through the long years of darkness sprouted, and a green carpet once again blanketed much of the land. Plant life was reduced in diversity, but still vibrant and determined.

Animal life fared less well, and thousands of life forms vanished forever. Many smaller creatures that lived beneath the surface emerged alive from the deep chill, while others came through only with help.

That, above all else, fascinated Huracan.

The humans suffered badly from the winter, but despite that, several laboratories on both worlds worked to restore newly-extinct creatures. Even at their most perilous moment, these strange beings sought to rescue the lesser species. Huracan could see no logic in that activity. Did life support life? Did life need life?

Since its arrival in the system, the AI's perspective had undergone a quantum shift. Its original intent to destroy humanity no longer took precedence. Driven by the prime directive to acquire knowledge, the alien mind had developed an interest and was now more focused on studying than destroying.

With the ability for neither sympathy nor empathy, Huracan found the desperate situation below fascinating, but only in an academic way. It failed to recognize that its new imperative to study rather than destroy was being influenced by an evolving curiosity. Its only concern was that the great disaster appeared to have strengthened humanity, rather than weakened it.

The time had come to leave this system for now, and return to the first human world it encountered, the one called Zealandia. There was no need to remain, as the automatic systems installed here would continue to carry out their task without supervision.

The humans might have destroyed the factories in space had they acted earlier, but it would have served no purpose. The individual units would have been repaired or built anew, and that process would have continued as long as necessary.

The array mechanisms had no concept of time and did not suffer limitations or impatience. The work was now unstoppable.

It was best to leave the system to its own devices. The human worlds would not be touched for now, but everything else would be consumed. The hidden carriers would continue to function, installing more factories in the belt of asteroids between the red world and the gas giants. After that, the outer planets would be sacrificed, until the work on the array was complete.

In time, Huracan would return to study the humans in greater depth. Once its curiosity had been sated, their worlds would be sacrificed to the greater project.

The humans had not attempted to damage the installations so far. Perhaps they realized the process could not be stopped, and were choosing not to waste time and resources on the effort. Had they become resigned to their fate?

A new course decided upon, the synthetic mind turned the spindle ship and sped toward the gateway it used to enter this system. That wormhole led to a neighboring star called Alpha Centauri B, and from there the artificial intelligence would journey, via a series of additional wormholes, to Zealandia.

*   *   *

Arvid Connor stood in the doorway of his office and peered up at the gray, threatening clouds. Minutes earlier, an unidentified request came for permission to land. A new visitor, the ship had no current record in the database.

Aware this vessel had no formal identification code, Arvid ordered the pilot to descend at the outer edge of the tarmac, and he was now happy he had done so. The ship burst from the cloud cover and made a vertical descent to stop just meters above the surface. He had never seen anything do that before. The approach was much too fast.

It was not the first unregistered arrival here, and no particular alarm bells were ringing in Arvid's mind. Despite the inherent danger, the helmsman handled the landing with superb efficiency.

Zealandia Terminal was a quiet facility with no military function, the planet's Fleet contingent having a separate base a kilometer away across an expanse of flat, mowed grassland. Most of the real action took place there. All Arvid ever saw were supply and colonist ships, and the occasional, rare traveler, like this one.

The vessel extended short landing feet and settled the remaining few meters to the ground. It was unlike any other in the field manager's experience, a streamlined, spindle-shaped vessel, deep red with only small bulges at one end to mark the engines.

Arvid understood the significance of those bulges. His close friends, Joe and Io Falcon had often shown pictures of their ship, the *Butterball II*, before its conversion to fusion. Those irregularities indicated an antimatter drive.

Arvid would rather not have something like that on his field but had no reason to deny the landing.

From beneath the hull, a ramp descended. A solitary figure stepped down to the tarmac and walked toward the administration building, a small case in his hands.

With the ship sitting at the far side of the field, it took the figure ten minutes to reach the office. As the newcomer drew closer, Arvid studied his face. It looked familiar, but he could not quite place it.

"Good morning, mister...?" he greeted as the man stopped in front of him.

"Jones. Jonathon Jones."

"Yes, of course," The name was well known to him, and clearly false, but that was of no consequence. Persons of note frequently traveled incognito and used assumed names, and at least half of all new, non-immigrant arrivals were named Smith, Jones or something just as inane. "Welcome to Zealandia, Mister Jones. That's quite a ride you have there."

The new arrival turned and glanced back at the sleek, red, spindle-shaped ship. "Yes, it is my private vessel."

"It's got a ... an antimatter engine?"

"An experimental model built by my company. I would like to hire a hangar to keep her out of the public eye if that is possible. She is as yet an unreleased design, and I would hate for my competitors to see her."

"I'm not sure..."

"I am prepared to pay you well for your trouble," Jones interrupted. Opening the case, he removed a small but heavy object, which he handed to Arvid.

The airfield manager's eyes widened as he felt the weight. "This is gold."

"I was not clear on the currency being used here, and I always carry some of this for such situations," Jones explained. "Gold is always acceptable, I think. That is yours if you can find me a private hangar and keep my presence here quiet. I will pay for the hangar separately, of course."

"You got it," Arvid said without hesitation. All worlds other than Earth used Martian talents, but with his eyes glued to the bar, Arvid did not register the inconsistency of the new arrival's explanation. He had no idea of the current value of the metal on Zealandia, but the gold bar represented more than a year's wages from the governing body that employed him. On a colony world like Zealandia, it would not be hard to convert it to hard cash, no questions asked.

"Thank you. I will need a shuttle to travel to your capital."

Arvid's eyes remained on the bar for several seconds. Looking up, he regarded the new arrival. The man was tall, his face that of someone in his early fifties, the skin blemish-free and the hair pure white. He was too perfect, and the stilted tone of his voice gave him an almost inhuman aspect. That could be put down to a local accent from the stranger's home world.

None of that was of immediate concern, and Arvid's mind willingly pushed aside any inconsistencies. Considering the object in his hands, it would not have mattered if Jones had been spotted pink with antennae.

"Welcome to Zealandia," he said again, his attention still focused on the shining metal.

*   *   *

Several hours later, Huracan sat at an open-air cafe table looking out over the water, its mind awash with sensations never before experienced. It had never seen an ocean close up, nor felt the caress of a sea breeze on skin, and that input alone made this journey worth the effort.

Everything was relative. The android it now occupied was the most advanced the sophisticated facilities on its ship were able to create. The artificial skin included sensors for touch, temperature, moisture and many other things never considered necessary before.

The new senses were excellent, but the AI suspected they were not as sensitive as those of true humans, based on the ultra-brief time spent in an actual organic body.

Raising a hand, it ran fingers through synthetic hair, another odd action it had seen humans perform. It felt the fibers run through, but could not understand why these creatures delighted so in doing it. Touch was just pressure, nothing more, and just one of an increasing number of things Huracan was as yet unable to comprehend in full. Time would tell.

A waiter placed a cup of hot, brown liquid on the table, bowed and retreated. Huracan had noticed others requesting this drink and followed suit, trying to blend in. It paid for the order with real money, the local financial center having been its first stop upon reaching the city.

The clerk asked no questions when a significant amount of gold appeared on the desk with an official application for an account. One thing obvious about humanity was that many individuals would ignore protocol were it in their favor to do so. The AI made sure the lowly individual benefited from giving exactly what was asked for.

Coming here was indeed a good move. The planet provided a plethora of new sensations, and the perfect opportunity to walk amongst humans. Being a small colony, it was also more suitable for Huracan's planned course of action.

The original worlds of the human species were completed works in a sense, with attitudes and processes ingrained over centuries. This world was young, a civilization still in its infancy and therefore susceptible to influence. The chances of success in Huracan's next experiment were better here.

*　　*　　*

Days later, Huracan stood in a brand new residence located on the shore of a lake just inland from the town, its first major goal achieved.

To complete the illusion it adopted the name of the actual owner of the house, a man named Alexander Ballard. The AI would live as a human amongst humans, to learn whatever the experience might offer.

As far as anyone official was concerned, Huracan was the legal owner of this property, with all images and recorded personal characteristics modified to suit. The administrative systems in this colony had been easy to infiltrate. The genuine owner was no more, and the corpse would never be discovered.

The AI had returned to the ship to modify the android, now as close to Ballard in appearance as possible, the face, the voice and the mannerisms accurate enough to avoid suspicion.

With a new persona, it introduced itself to the field manager as the pilot of Jones' ship, and nobody else would ever detect the change. The original transaction to construct the property had been done online and through a corporation, so few local bureaucrats knew the owner by sight.

Huracan chose this residence for a specific reason. The small population of this world would make its new objective, the complete psychological subjugation of the colony, easier to achieve. But, there was a bonus.

Across the narrow neck of the lake stood another house. Like this one it was isolated, the only approach by water, via a landing pad on the shore or by a narrow pathway through the surrounding forest. Huracan watched a young human playing by the water. On the veranda of the house a tall, striking woman watched the child.

The AI had learned a great deal from the databases of this colony. It knew the child was the son of the man who vexed it the most, he who was responsible for the demise of its iteration, the Aivris. The woman would be his sexual partner, a now human derivative of the Tanakhai, the race that created the AI in its original form.

The house across the water belonged to Joseph Falcon.

Chapter 27

IT WAS GOOD TO be home again after such a long absence. Joe nudged his shuttle down to one side of the landing pad, powered down the engine, and sat for a moment, contemplating the peaceful scene beyond the bubble shield.

His young son, William, bounded down the walkway, eager to welcome his father. At the house, Io stood on the veranda, ever watchful over the child and drawn from her activities by the hum of the approaching vehicle.

The lake exuded its normal mood of placid tranquility, with just the faintest wind-driven ripples disturbing the mirror-like surface. A gentle breath sighed through the organ pipes of the surrounding trees onto the lake, creating an ambiance Joe loved. This was the place he preferred the most, where he felt at rest and everything was right with existence. Joe felt safe in this place.

Across the water, the new, neighboring house looked complete, the construction crews gone and the ground cleared and minimally landscaped. The new owner was of a like mind to Joe, with the house barely impacting the surrounding environment.

On a landing platform by the water's edge, a sleek, ostentatious flyer stood unattended, suggesting the new owner was in residence. As Joe climbed down from the cockpit of his vehicle, a solitary figure stepped out of the house and stood on the patio, gazing in his direction. The individual was perhaps middle-aged, tall with graying hair, and impeccably dressed. *Not surprising*, Joe thought. The house alone indicated someone of means, and the flyer…

Well.

The man raised a hand in salute as Joe retrieved his bag. He returned the wave and made a mental note to row across for a visit sometime soon. The contemplation evaporated as an eleven-year-old child barreled into him at maximum velocity.

"Daddy. You're back. I didn't think you were ever coming home."

"I'm sorry, Wills. I tried to get back as quickly as I could. You have your mother here though—how is she?"

"Okay. Did you bring me anything?"

"Well, you might have to wait to find that out. I want to see your mom first, and I need a good, long sleep."

William gave a soft moan of resignation as he took his father's free hand and towed him back toward the house. Joe smiled. William was his youngest, and therefore his favorite child by default, and he thought of him often while away.

Not that he cared less for his other children, but they were adults now. There was something about one's youngest that demanded attention. As the pair stepped up to the veranda, Io smiled and reached out her hands in welcome. She said nothing, but the questioning look in her eyes and the slight tilt of her head spoke volumes.

"It's all good so far," he said. "Most of the alien fleet has been destroyed, and the forces that landed on Mars have been routed. There are still some ships loose in the Solar System, but we'll find them and deal with them. At least we know why they are there."

Returning to the house, Io went into the kitchen and prepared coffee for two, while Joe stashed his bag in the bedroom and returned to the lounge. Sitting in his favorite chair, he stared through the window. Finally, peace.

"So, why did they come?" Io asked as she placed a mug on the table and sat beside her partner.

"The ships beyond Jupiter were there to keep our attention, and our fleet occupied. They kept us in a stalemate for months while four of their number vanished. We still don't know where those are, but it seems they, or something else, let loose a virtual army of nanobots in the inner system, and they immediately began replicating themselves. They're strip-mining Venus and Mercury, and the materials are being shot into space to be transformed into solar collection panels of enormous size."

Io's brow wrinkled as she sat back on the lounge, her mug clasped firmly between two hands. "We're talking about the Prime Aivris here, yes? What on Earth would it want with solar panels there?"

"We think it's building a Dyson array around Sol—a swarm. Only a few panels are in place so far, but there's enough material in the inner planets to make billions of them."

Io raised her head and peered up at the ceiling. "The only reason Aivris would want a Dyson array in the Solar System would be…" Turning her head, she peered directly at Joe.

"Yes," Joe confirmed. "I suspect our enemy is planning to occupy the Solar System, and it's building itself a power supply."

"What are we going to do about that? Can we destroy the array?"

"Oh yes, easily, but I don't think it's a good idea."

"Why? We can't let that thing get a foothold in one of our systems. Look at the damage it's done to Earth, and that from a distance."

"The Dyson array is just a machine, a device to collect power and send it to users. If we destroy panels or factories, the nano-machines will build more, creating a situation of constant destruction-replacement. We don't want to get into that, considering the waste of resources and the commitment it would involve. If we take control of it instead, it will provide unlimited, free, clean energy. It could potentially be the single, greatest step forward for humanity since we invented writing. We just have to find a way..."

Io nodded. She smiled and placed a hand on Joe's arm. "I got a message from Leo this morning. He's coming home."

"Really?" Joe pictured Leo in his mind. He was never quite sure how he felt about his pseudo-brother. Since the marauder attack on Mars, he had vanished, apparently unwilling to deal further with the intransigence of the now-deposed president.

Leo was still physically an old man. Joe always struggled to get his head around the age inconsistencies associated with cloning. He sighed. Thinking too deeply about that sort of thing could fry one's brain.

Best to ignore it.

He eased back in the chair, exhausted from his journey, and was sound asleep within seconds.

*   *   *

With the morning sun, Joe decided to start the day by visiting his new neighbor. Strolling down to the end of the dock he climbed into his pride and joy, a sculling dinghy constructed from the local timber analogs. The tiny boat was a beautiful thing to behold, clear-finished to show the deep, honey color of the native material.

He took his time as he sculled across the narrow neck of water, let his mind wander, listened to the organ pipe fugue, and enjoyed the warmth of the sun and the touch of the breeze on his skin. These were things one simply did not experience in space, or indeed, on most of the other worlds humanity had discovered.

Gazing around aimlessly, he wondered if he would see one of the enormous but harmless native denizens that made this lake their home. They were not a cause for concern—gentle-natured creatures, they did not attack. The chances of their disturbing this little boat were slim.

As Joe turned his head to check his progress, he noticed a figure standing on the dock ahead. The individual observed yesterday must have seen him approach, and had come down to greet him.

Joe tied the dinghy to the dock as his neighbor reached down to help him up. As Joe grasped the proffered hand, a chill went through his body. Something was wrong; the flesh was deathly cold. Joe tried to ignore it as he climbed up to the dock.

"Welcome, Mister Falcon," the man said. "Allow me to introduce myself. I am Alex Ballard, and it appears we are now neighbors. May I call you Joe?"

"Yes, of course," Joe responded. "You know my name?"

"Of course. Everyone knows the great Joe Falcon and his family. I made an effort to find out who my neighbors were when I purchased this property, and I must say I was pleasantly surprised to find you lived directly across from me. Your exploits have always been of great interest."

Joe studied Ballard. On the surface, the man appeared perfectly normal, but a second look raised questions. Tall, middle-aged, clearly educated and with a refined manner, he spoke with an abnormal precision. The hair and clothes were impeccable, as were the highly polished shoes on his feet. He stood rigidly, with one hand behind his back, a faint, thin smile on his otherwise expressionless face. The man was just too perfect.

"I thought I might row across and welcome you to the neighborhood," Joe said.

"Thank you. I find the experience of being here most enjoyable," Ballard replied. "I come from Barbossa, which, as you know, is a desert world, so water and trees ... all of this,"—he waved a hand in a broad sweep—"is novel to me."

Joe nodded. He had heard of Barbossa, one of the new, recently discovered planets, but had not been there and knew very little of the place. The Institute had established a colony there as it did on all of the inhabitable new worlds, but it was the concern of others within the clan.

"What do you do, Mister Ballard—Alex—if I may ask."

"Yes, of course you may. You would call me an industrialist, I think."

"In what field?" Joe raised an eyebrow.

For a moment Ballard did not reply. After a moment's contemplation, he spoke. "Energy and transportation, Mister Falcon. My businesses are concerned with the development of solar energy technologies. Hardly surprising for a desert world, wouldn't you think?"

"Of course." The more Ballard spoke, the more uncomfortable Joe felt. He could not say why, but something about the man disturbed him. It was not a physical thing; Ballard was a perfectly normal human being but for the cold handshake, something Joe had never experienced before. It was more a general feeling; something about the man's manner was unnerving. And such perfection...

"I would love to invite you in for a talk, Joe," Ballard said. "Sadly I have an engagement elsewhere. I was just about to depart when I saw you coming across. Perhaps we could meet again at a later time."

"Ah, yes, of course."

Ballard nodded and without hesitation turned his back on Joe, apparently having dismissed him as he strode from the dock toward the shuttle sitting on the pad nearby.

As Joe rowed home, he determined to look into the background of this individual, starting with an inquiry to the authorities on Barbossa. The man disturbed him, and he wanted to know why.

*   *   *

As Huracan walked away from the dock, its mind raced. The man Falcon had sensed something wrong, but it did not understand what.

Certainly, the android body created for this venture was as perfect as it could be. Nobody could determine it was not human without the aid of technology, and certainly not by a chance encounter on a dockside.

These humans had an uncanny ability to sense things, something Huracan could not duplicate. Existence was simply cause and effect, and the idea that an organism could sense a situation through some undefined mental ability was puzzling. Perhaps occupying this house in the guise of a human was not as secure as believed.

Chapter 28

CHARLIE HENNESSEY STABBED AT the control panel on his brand-new ship, humming a vague travesty of a well-known song as he checked the status of the vessel.

Cha-Ja II, short for *Charlie-and-Jan,* was not really new. In truth she was extremely old, a pre-colonization freighter he and his life-partner Jan had picked up at auction on Mars. It cost every talent they were able to beg or borrow to fit her with a gateway generator and bring her to Helios. The old ship was now the first freelance prospector in the system.

The colonization of Zealandia began with strict rules around the need to avoid despoiling the environment. An early decree determined mining would be kept to an absolute minimum on the surface, the extraction and use of fossil fuels barred. The intent was that all mineral needs of the colony be filled by off-world operations, and processing complexes like those in Sol's asteroid belt were being set up for the purpose.

The system did not have anything similar to the asteroid belt, but it did have a Kuiper Belt and Oort Cloud. One of the gas giants orbiting the orange star possessed dense, rocky rings created by a collision between two of its numerous moons.

The first of the orbital processing facilities was not yet complete, but the parameters for prospecting and mining were in place, and the first dumps for materials had been delineated with the intent that a ready supply be available upon completion of the first factory.

Cha-Ja II was the first independent prospector to work under contract to that complex, and this was her maiden voyage in her new livery.

Satisfied everything was in order, Charlie climbed out of the pilot's seat and floated aft toward the saloon. The ancient ship did not have artificial gravity, or a rotating section to provide centrifugal force. This alone limited the time the crew could stay in space, as regular periods in gravity were necessary for the maintenance of health.

It also restricted the Hennessey children's time on board, and most of their days were spent with their grandmother on Zealandia. Charlie's mother had moved from Mars to support her son and daughter-in-law in their venture.

In the accommodation salon, Jan sat at a console, her attention focused on a screen. Charlie floated up behind her.

"What's so interesting?"

For a moment, his partner said nothing, then turned to peer at him. "Are there any construction activities going on out here?" she asked. "I mean, other than the preliminary work on the new processing complex?"

"No, not here. There's plans to put a second plant somewhere in this region in the future, but that's years off. Why? Whatcha got there?"

Leaning forward over Jan's shoulder, he peered at the screen. There was indeed something ahead, the beginnings of a spherical structure orbiting beyond the rings. It was little more than a partial framework, with a small segment of what might one day become an outer shell.

"I'll be damned. We should do a closer inspection."

Jan nodded, her eyes glued to the monitor. "You think someone beat us here?"

"No. Our contract is the first. Nobody else is out here yet, at least not legally. If it's a competitor of some sort, we can always go elsewhere. It's not as if this system is lacking in resources."

Several hours later, the ship slotted into an orbit only a few hundred yards from the structure. From the bridge deck, Jan and Charlie examined it from a closer viewpoint.

"You know, I swear it's growing," Jan said.

"That would be crazy. There ain't no service ships, no trace of workers or robots … nothin'."

"Yeah, but…" Jan tapped the screen to zoom in on one of the segments. Close up, the raw end of a visible beam appeared odd. A vague fog surrounded the section, which was almost imperceptibly increasing in length. The haze tapered away in a long stream around the side of the structure.

"You know what it resembles?" she asked.

"Sure do," Charlie replied. "The haze must be nanobots, which would explain why it's getting bigger. According to the computer, its mass is increasing by about one tonne per minute, so this ain't the only part under active construction."

"Where's the material coming from?"

"Excellent question. It can only be from the rings. See the line of fine dust leading out to it? There will be other machines mining the rubble and shooting the raw materials here."

"That's impossible, isn't it? We don't have any technology like that."

Charlie eased back in his seat and stared at the monitor. "Sure we do, but it's illegal on Earth, or at least restricted. It's used on Mars and Zealandia, but not out here. I want a closer view and a sample."

"You're not going out there. It might be dangerous."

I'll be fine. I'll use the prospecting rig. It has armor and it's maneuverable. I should be able to grab a bit of whatever is over there and come back safe. In the meantime, you can send a report back to base. This can't be anything of ours, so the bosses need to know about it."

*   *   *

Half an hour later, Charlie drifted through space. The suit he wore was pure carbon-fiber, with articulated segments of shielding. The latest in work suits for persons engaged in dangerous activities, it had cost him and Jan a respectable fortune, but asteroid mining was a lucrative business when you were the first in a new patch. The massive debt they had accumulated to get here would soon be a forgotten memory.

As he drew closer, the details of the object became more obvious. It was indeed spherical, but only a basic armature was visible, each structural unit seamlessly merged into its neighbors to create a colossal, honeycomb whole.

In multiple areas, the spaces in the framework were being filled in by flat panels destined to become the outer shell of whatever the structure was intended to be.

Charlie came to a halt meters from one of the active work faces. The sheer size of the thing was overwhelming. He had never been any good at math, and had no knowledge of geometry, but the completed unit had to be several kilometers in diameter. Charlie's prospector was a mere mosquito by comparison.

Ahead, a raw panel edge grew. A myriad of small motes whirled like a miniature storm as they moved to and from the work face. Charlie was no engineer either, but he thought he understood what he was seeing.

In the planetary rings, machines were mining materials, reducing them to elemental molecules and shooting them to the construction site.

Somewhere else, probably on the far side of the monolith, they were collected, carried to the various work faces by microscopic assemblers and attached one molecule at a time to produce a seamless, monocoque structure held together by the nuclear forces of the atoms themselves.

Hmmm, Charlie thought. *I need a sample, I think. Someone is going to be more than interested in you.*

He had read something in the past about this process. The massive alien spaceship that came to Earth centuries ago had been built in this manner, and the smaller vessel belonging to Joe Falcon, a legend amongst asteroid miners, was the same.

Falcon's *Butterball II* had been the subject of a heap of research; the construction method was now used to build many spacecraft, including Fleet naval vessels. The *Cha-Ja II* was not one of them, but one day Charlie hoped to have such a ship.

Retrieving a small glass vial from a pouch, he flipped the lid and swiped it through the nebulous cloud at the work face. Snapping it closed again, he held it up to see what was inside. There was nothing obvious, bar a vague, gray mist. *Much as I expected,* he thought.

Stowing the tube back in its retainer, he began a traverse. There was little to see beyond the basic framework, and at this stage nothing betrayed its ultimate purpose or who might be responsible for its being here. Charlie felt a chill run through his body. This thing could not be human, and the thought of who might be behind it descended on his mind like a fog. It was time to leave.

*   *   *

Minutes later, Charlie landed back on the deck in the ship's hold. He paused as the atmosphere equalized, before commencing the slow task of extracting himself from the suit. Meticulous to a fault, he placed each segment in its correct storage rack, then reached in to retrieve his trophy.

As he did so, he spotted a small spot in the glass. The significance hit like a lightning bolt. Whatever he captured was dissolving the vial. It had eaten its way through the wall, and was now free.

Leaning in for a better view, he studied the inside of the suit's rack unit. Gray-white specks were visible. The nano-constructors had multiple functions, and were not fussy with what materials they worked on. They were dismantling the container wall molecule by molecule, and doing the same to the carbon structure of the rack unit.

A horrifying truth flashed through Charlie's mind.

These things could eat through the hull!

Grabbing the offending unit, he launched himself into the airlock and placed it on the floor, closed the inner hatch and opened the outer without first removing the atmosphere within. The whoosh of air carried the unit out into space and away from the ship.

George gave a deep sigh and stepped out of the cargo bay.

"What was that all about?" Jan's eyes blazed with fury. "You know what that suit cost us?"

"No choice," Charlie replied. "Those bloody nano-mites ate their way through the specimen vial and began eating the damned thing. If I hadn't thrown it out they might have got into the hull and killed us. It's only a rack component—we can replace it. Did you report this?"

"Yes. They'll send someone to investigate. Are you okay?"

Charlie sighed. "Yeah, fine." He would not admit the incident had given him the biggest fright of his life. Saying nothing more, he floated through to the sleeping cabin and secured himself, his hands shaking with the slightest of tremors. He took a deep breath and released it in a soft, passive sign, hoping to ease his tension. Deep inside, something still gave him shivers.

Everyone knew what uncontrolled nano-machines could do. Such devices could break anything down to its component molecules in time, and they had long been illegal on Earth due to the ever-present gray or green goo syndromes. On Mars, the New World's Institute found ways to guarantee safety with the technology, and they were in common use, but with severe limitations.

By law, a nanobot only carried out a single function, and if that was not possible, it stopped. It could work only with the material it was designed for, and in that material's absence, it became inactive.

The sample from the structure outside was different. It appeared to be able to dismantle anything, and Charlie doubted it complied with the strictures of legislation. He could not imagine what it could do, and the thought made him shudder. Luckily, the thing was now off the ship.

Good Riddance!

An alarm rattled him awake. Launching himself from the sleeping room, he shot through to the bridge, where Jan tapped away at the console.

"What?"

"The bloody sample is loose," his partner replied, sweat pearling on her forehead. "You didn't get it all out, and it's multiplying. Those things are eating through the inner hull. I've sealed off the work bay area."

Charlie shook his head. The hull shell had holes in several places, and they were growing. The nanobots from the vial were using the materials from the ship to make copies of themselves, which in turn made more and more. Charlie did not know how long it took for a nanobot to replicate, but he had been asleep for several hours and many multiplications must have already taken place. Every time a duplication occurred, the number of machines doubled. It would be slow at first, but with each cycle the destruction would double in speed.

"We don't have much time," he said. "Get into your suit and into the emergency pod. We need to leave—now!"

Two hours later, he and Jan sat in the tiny escape pod, floating several hundred meters from the remains of their vessel. Nothing remained except a gray, diffuse cloud streaming away toward the alien structure.

"Bastards are using our ship as material to build their … thingy," Jan said, a tremor in her voice.

"Yes, but we're clear of it, thank the gods."

His partner let out a gasp and tears began to trickle down her face. "The *Cha-Ja II* is everything we own. And we still owe a massive fortune for her. What are we going to do?"

"I don't know," Charlie replied. "We're alive; that's the most important thing. The insurance will cover us, but it'll all go to paying those debts. We'll end up with nothing." Reaching across, he wrapped his arms around his partner and pulled her close.

A week later, two Fleet cruisers arrived and picked up the *Cha-Ja II* survivors before moving on to examine the strange structure orbiting Helios IV.

The construction had progressed from a basic framework to a complete sphere.

From the rings of the planet, a stream of small pellets had replaced the line of molecular dust, each pellet entering seamlessly through the shell. As the sphere moved from behind the gas giant, a line of larger, dark objects emerged and streamed away in the direction of the star.

On the deck of the lead warship, the commander watched and recorded the process. He knew what was happening here, having recently brought his ship on reassignment from the Solar System.

The strange object was a manufacturing plant like the ones near Venus and Mercury, and it was processing the rubble from the H-IV rings into raw materials, most likely to build a Dyson array around Helios.

The rate of construction astounded him. Those little nano-monsters could multiply at an incalculable rate, and the speed with which they could carry out their objective was frightening.

*   *   *

In Zealandia City, night gave way to a fine, sunny morning. People bustled about their business, ready to welcome another peaceful day of life on this new world. Without warning, every holo and video screen in the colony blinked and went blank, before displaying an unusual and bizarre apparition.

Every device showed a blurred image of a waterspout, a giant, sinister column rising tornado-fashion into a sky of dark, foreboding clouds. As the spout became larger, it morphed into a strange creature with lighting in its eyes and a tall, spiky crown. Two smaller tornado-like winds descended from the being's extended hands, touching down to the water to become more waterspouts.

The apparition spoke.

Greetings, people of Zealandia. I am Caculha Huracan, the god of your ancients, whom you have called Bolon Tzacab, U Ku'x Kaj. I return to you to reclaim what is mine. I come to you now, that you, my subjects, may rejoice in my presence. Glory shall be yours, in my name.

The bizarre image vanished as abruptly as it appeared, and the many screens in the community returned to whatever had been displayed before.

For a long moment silence reigned, followed by a whisper that grew to the sound of laughter, becoming louder and more widespread as the citizens of the colony reacted to what must be the work of a skilled and hilarious prankster.

Chapter 29

JOE STEPPED OUT TO the veranda, stretched, yawned, and wiped away the last remnants of oblivion before strolling to the landing pad where his shuttle stood to attention. At the edge of the platform, his son William sat staring across to the far side of the lake. As Joe approached, he realized the boy was watching the Ballard house.

"Checking out our new neighbor?"

"Yeah. He's strange."

"Why do you say that?"

"All he ever does is stare at us. Doesn't go fishing, or even sit outside. He stands there and stares at us through his windows for hours every day. Weirdo."

"Well, let's not be too quick to judge him. He's just arrived. No doubt we'll get to know him in time."

"You went over to say hello a week ago, and he left. Mom says that was rude."

"Perhaps, but I did go over uninvited and unannounced. He had an appointment, and had to leave."

"Yeah, but you always say we have to be polite to strangers and try to be friends."

"And I stand by it, but not everyone should be judged by us. Some people live busy lives, and…" Joe stopped speaking as the hypocrisy in his words hit home. He was often away for weeks or months at a time, to pursue his various personal agendas. He made a mental note to spend more time with his son but realized that because of who he was, it might not happen soon. The boy was the best thing in his life, and he was letting the joy slip past unnoticed.

"Uncle Leo is arriving today," William said. "Can I go out to the airfield to meet him? And see Uncle Arvid?"

Joe smiled. The boy loved hanging around the spaceport and spent much of his time there when Joe and Io were both away. Arvid, the manager of the civilian terminal, could be trusted to watch over him. Wills was mature for an eleven-year-old, not surprising considering the family he had been born into. Joe knew he was trustworthy, and would not do anything untoward.

"Yes, you can go, but stay out of trouble and don't go onto the tarmac. Uncle Leo hasn't been home for a while, has he?"

"Nah. He spends all his time looking for those big ships. I wish he was here more often—he's like you, and he plays with me."

Joe smiled again, but this time it was an empty gesture. A wave of guilt washed over his soul. Joe's brother doted on Wills when home, and had become a close part of the family. It was not surprising the boy saw similarities between them. Wills did not know the details of how Leo came into existence, and Joe felt sad at the thought his son might prefer his brother's company to his own.

What troubled Joe's mind the most was the question of whether he or Leo was the original. Long ago he decided he was, to maintain his own sense of worth. He had no doubt Leo made the identical assumption for the same reason. In the last century, they had grown apart enough to be seen as individuals, but similarities were still noticeable.

"The neighbor," the boy said. "He's leaving again."

Joe glanced up in time to see the Ballard sky car lift from its pad and skim over the tree tops toward the space port. "If you meet him at the airfield, you be nice, alright?"

William nodded, and as his father stepped into his vehicle, scuttled onto the walkway to be clear of the wash from the car's jets.

*   *   *

Ten minutes later, Joe landed at the main parkway of Zealandia City. The commercial and administrative center was small, the colony's population only a few hundred thousand souls. The first and only major settlement on the planet, it resembled a rural town center more than a metropolis. Despite the small size, it was a thriving community, and was in every way an *Institute* town.

A narrow channel opening from a broad, inland waterway to the ocean gave access for a growing fleet of fishing and research vessels. The main town thoroughfare followed the sandy shoreline of the inlet, and always reminded Joe of the tropical, palm-lined boulevards of coastal towns in Queensland, on pre-Death Earth.

The concept that new planetary colonies received support from Earth or Mars was not the reality. The home world still struggled to re-establish itself after the volcanic winter, and while significant gains had been made in the last hundred years, there was still a long way to go before normality was restored.

Mars also suffered, but a vast amount of Martian resources had nevertheless been diverted to assist those on Earth, and the effort continued to this day. The ability of the red world to assist the interstellar colonies was limited.

Therefore, the colonization and support of the new worlds had fallen to the Institute, and their approach had always dictated that each new colony become self-sufficient in the shortest possible time.

As in all such colonies, Zealandian society was just one step removed from agrarian, but with the assistance of the best technology available. Crop farming, husbandry, and wherever possible fishing, were the first major industries to be established, followed by a broad spectrum of manufacturing concerns. Using the nano-construction technology found in the first data given to Jake from the *Minaret*, small assembly plants were set up to make anything from spoons to space shuttles, with only an electronic pattern and raw molecular materials.

The fishing industry in particular had boomed here and now exported seafood products, all unique to this world. Most of the produce went to Mars and Earth, to replace that available before the Great Death and allow the native populations of Earth's devastated oceans to rebuild. Agriculture had almost reached the stage where it could also export.

After parking his shuttle at a public stand, Joe walked toward the administration complex. From the esplanade, secondary streets ran inland, and along one of these stood the various buildings of the planetary government.

There was considerable construction underway. To one side of the street, autonomous machines labored diligently to construct a long, double walkway. Every few meters, a high, yellow arch spanned the structure, betraying the birth of a molecular freeway similar to those found on the *Minaret*.

The pathways would allow any person to travel on foot from walking pace to high velocity by their own inertia, and were part of the technology taken from the *Minaret* by Leo when he escaped from the Ark during the Dysnomia incident.

The system had been improved by the Institute over time, and now many cities on Mars and Earth featured the distinctive golden arches. They almost eliminated the need for any other kind of transport wherever they were installed, as *Shanks's pony* sufficed to get most citizens where they needed to go even across great distances.

The walkway in Zealandia City was not yet complete and not functional, so Joe strolled along in the sunshine, content to take his time as he gazed out across the calm inlet.

The main administration complex resembled that of any world. Joe did not work here, but everyone on the premises knew him and deferred to him. Returning the nodded greetings of several people in the front foyer, he walked through to the director's suite, stopping only briefly to have a word with one of the workers.

A sense of urgency filled the office; people huddled in small groups, their attention drawn to the far end of the room. Zhina Memon, the director, was deep in conversation. All eyes in the room were focused on a holo-screen, where a picture of an enormous, spherical object was visible. She glanced around as Joe entered.

"Mister Falcon. Excellent timing."

"What's up?" He paused to look at the image. "That resembles the factory spheres at Venus and Mercury."

"Yes, except it's not there. It's here, orbiting H-IV. The first of our new surveyors found it. Their ship was destroyed by the nano-machines that built it."

"Are they alive?"

"Thankfully, yes. They escaped in a pod and a Fleet vessel picked them up. This image was sent by the commander."

"Thank God. Give me the survey crew's details; I'll make sure to see them right."

The idea of issuing private survey licenses had been Joe's, to avoid the situation used in the Solar System where mining and surveying were practical only when carried out under contract to one of the giant conglomerates. The old monopoly ensured the major profit went to the most powerful players, something which had always galled Joe.

Here, pseudo-government concerns with the financial muscle would operate the factories, the first already under construction. The actual job of finding the raw resources would remain open to anybody, with the potential earnings from such activities dependent on each operator's individual skill, and how much effort they put in.

A shudder ran down Joe's spine. The image on the screen was something he knew well. He had seen these structures firsthand, and not only knew what they were, but also their purpose, and who was behind them.

Joe turned to Memon. "Contact the commodore of our home squadron. Tell him to send ships to search the inner system, and start scanning for things out of the ordinary. You've all seen vids of the solar collection project being carried out around Sol, and this appears to be the same thing. We need to locate anything being built here and keep track of what's happening."

The director raised her eyebrows, disbelief in her face. "But how did they get here? We haven't detected any unauthorized vessels coming through our wormholes."

Joe nodded, taking a moment to ponder the situation. "The aliens appear to have a new shield, making them undetectable. Are we sure our automatic sentinel drones haven't identified anything out of the ordinary?"

A terrifying thought entered his mind.

"I think this whole business is being instigated by the Prime Aivris, the synthetic intelligence that took control of the *Minaret*, and we presume, all the other arks. We know where it is now, somewhere around a red dwarf star not far from Sol, but we haven't found a wormhole leading there yet."

Memon frowned. "Are you suggesting…?"

"Can you be positive we've located all the wormholes in this system? Something may have come in through one we don't know about. We need to start searching, in case. Our squadron should concentrate on the planetary Lagrangian points and work from there."

"We've checked most of them."

"We'd best check the rest. Ways to that star must exist somewhere, so why not here? Wasn't there a drone that went missing months ago?"

"Yes. Lifted off from our port and headed toward the sun, then vanished. We never saw or heard from it again. We assumed it malfunctioned and went into the star. Do you think…?"

"I'm speculating. Let's suppose it detected a new wormhole out there somewhere. Its programming would require it to open a gateway and pass through, do a quick survey at the other end, and come back here to report."

"That's the standard program, yes."

"What if it found a way to the Tanakhai system, and Aivris Number One was waiting?"

For a moment Memon stood silent, her lips pursed as she stared at Joe. She turned to one of her managers. "Ask the commander of the home squadron to get our ships in the air. We need to locate that wormhole if it exists, and also find out what's going on right here under our noses. Send an urgent request to the Mars Fleet to send more ships now!"

She turned back to Joe, seemed to think again, and returned her attention to her manager. "Oh, and have a maintenance crew check the sentinels at our other gateways. If that thing is in our system, it could only have come through a wormhole. If vessels are coming and going without being logged by the guard drones, someone has been interfering with them."

Joe sat down on Memon's lounge and started to toss the possibilities in his mind.

It was unlikely a fleet had entered through normal space, as was the case in the Solar System. If the Prime Aivris possessed the secret of the Saitou-Radelick generators, a likely scenario if it took possession of the missing survey drone, its warships would be able to move about far more quickly. Even so, they should have been detected if they arrived through an as-yet-undiscovered wormhole.

If the wormhole from the Tanakhai star led elsewhere, the Alien AI could not have found its way here so soon. The most believable scenario was the rogue AI did have the generator, and a gateway to its home was somewhere in the Helios System.

The junior employee Joe had spoken to on his way into the office knocked on the door and entered, an e-pad in his hands. "Sorry to interrupt, Sir," he said, approaching Joe, "but I have the data you requested."

Joe nodded as he took the proffered device. He had asked the young man to call up the certificate of ownership for the residence across the lake from his own. As a rule, private information was not available to the public, but nobody on this planet denied Joe anything. He tried hard not to take advantage of the fact, but on Zealandia, his status was unquestioned.

He glanced at the screen, and felt his blood pressure jump. All residential approvals carried a photograph of the person making the application, and from this one, the face of the man called Alex Ballard smiled back at Joe. It was the face of the man he had spoken to a week ago, but there was something that was not right.

For several minutes Joe puzzled over what it might be, but failed to place a finger on it. Then he realized what worried him. The man he had met was a mirror image of the picture. The hair was parted to the wrong side, and the bisymmetrical imbalance found on all human faces was the mirror of what Joe had seen in reality. Of course, the photo might have been printed in reverse, but that seemed unlikely. More questions...

When leaving that morning, he watched the now suspect neighbor board his air car and fly in the direction of the spaceport.

William was going there—right now.

"Can I leave this business to you?" he asked, directing his question to Memon. The Administrator nodded, engrossed in the new emergency. Joe bolted from the office, wishing the inertia-less walkway was operating so he could get to his shuttle more quickly.

Chapter 30

WILLIAM HOPPED FROM THE underground hyper-loop shuttle and sprinted across the platform to the elevator. As soon as the lift reached ground level and the doors opened, he charged out onto the walkway and stopped to gaze out over the space field.

For a boy of his age, it was an awe-inspiring sight. The domestic spaceport had always been his favorite playground, a privilege shared by no other child on Zealandia. He knew all the places to keep clear of, but there was so much to do, so many corners to poke into, and such marvelous machines. Every employee here, the mechanics, the office staff and even the temps, knew him and watched over him.

The planet's only major continent was almost entirely covered by a dense mat of vegetation. Deep forest surrounded the colony settlement, and Wills was under strict orders not to go outside the town boundaries unaccompanied, despite the administration maintaining that the local flora and fauna were benign.

Of the places he *was* permitted to go, the spaceport was the largest open land space other than the experimental agricultural research farms, and more exciting by far.

One place he was not allowed to go was the military base, a separate section of the port beyond the civilian field, dedicated to Fleet activities. A small squadron of fifty diamond ships was stationed there, but they were never all present. At least a third of them were always on patrol, keeping the colony safe from any perceived threats.

Wills had no idea what those might be.

A bright lad, he worked out long ago the aliens his mother and father had spent most of their several lives fighting did not know how to get here. The only wormholes to Zealandia were monitored, making it the safest of worlds.

Without warning, one of the diamond fighters lifted off and soared up to the clouds and beyond, followed by another, and then two more. Within minutes, only five ships remained on the tarmac, tiny scale models in the distance.

William trotted toward the civilian terminal, hands in pockets and with a huge smile on his face. Uncle Arvid would be on duty, he knew. Although not his real uncle, he had called the airfield manager that for as long as he could remember.

When his parents were both away on business, he lived with Arvid and his wife. The couple had no children, and doted upon him whenever he stayed with them.

As expected, Arvid was at his desk poring over something on a holo screen. William took one peek but saw only rows and columns of alpha-numeric. At some other time he might have found it interesting, considering he had an excellent head for math and anything to do with computers. But not today.

"Hi," he said. "What's up across at the base?"

Arvid glanced up and peered over his glasses, an unnecessary prop he wore to increase his perceived importance to customers.

"Hello, Wills-boy. I have no idea. They just started launching. Something's going on, but they never bother to tell me. One of these days they're going to take off while I have a heavy-lifter coming down, and there'll be a disaster."

William smiled. Arvid always whined about the Fleet base. He believed, as manager of the domestic port, he should be notified whenever anything occurred across the way. Of course, it never happened.

Arvid looked up once again. "You're here to meet your Uncle Leo?"

William nodded, looking around the office. As a rule, at least three other staff members would have been present, but with no transports scheduled for today, Arvid was alone.

"Well," he continued, "he's not here yet. Not due in for a couple of hours. You'll have to amuse yourself if you want to wait. I'm far too busy; on my own, as you can see." Arvid smiled and returned his attention to the screen.

William strolled to the window. A private shuttle sat further along the airport apron. It was familiar.

"Who owns the air car?"

Arvid peered out at the little vehicle. "That's a rental. It's being used by a client who keeps his spacecraft here. Visitor from off-world."

"It looks like the one belonging to our new neighbor. You know, the house across the lake."

Arvid paused from his work again. "Does it now? Well, there you go." He returned his attention to his work.

"Which one of those is his?" Wills waved a hand at the scattering of ships on the apron.

"None of them, boy. His ship is super sophisticated by all appearances, and it's in hangar ten for security. *Very, very* expensive, so don't you go poking your nose around it. You stay away, hear?"

William nodded absently and settled down to read his wrist holo. Once Arvid had returned to his deliberations and was distracted, Wills stepped quietly out of the office and wandered toward the hangers.

He loved spaceships, but he had only ever been on *Butterball II*. It was also kept in a private hangar, to hide it from curious onlookers keen to see the most famous spacecraft of all. The Falcon hangar was the huge one closest to the terminal, and Dad had leased it for his permanent use.

Ten hangars sat along one side of the tarmac, almost half of them empty as the typical visitors were cargo or migrant ships on a short turnaround. Wills knew the one Arvid mentioned was the furthest from the office. He had been inside it before—he had checked out every building on the field at some time or other—and it was almost always vacant.

Strolling along the apron, he stopped in front of the last hangar and gazed up. The structure was the second largest, so the ship within must be huge. The main doors were closed, as was the personnel entrance to one side.

If the new neighbor was here, he was inside. That did not faze William. The desire to see the ship was more than he could resist. Arvid had told him to stay away, but curiosity had a strong grip on the young boy and he knew how to get into every off-limits place in the port.

It wouldn't hurt to have a quick peek, and after all, Uncle Leo wouldn't be here for hours.

At the rear of the building, located at floor level and far across to one side where the roof curved down, was a small hatch. It was no more than fifty centimeters square and ideal for the passage of a small boy on a mission.

Wills found the opening long ago, on one of his many explorations. No doubt it had something to do with cleaning, but for someone his size it served as the perfect entrance.

As expected, it was not secured. All he needed to do was slide the panel aside and slither through.

The interior of the structure blazed with light. No sound could be heard beyond a soft, low-level hum emanating from the ship that dominated the vast space.

From behind a bulky, mobile tool cabinet such as was found in any hangar or workshop, William stared with eyes wide, at the most dramatic vessel he had ever seen. The sight amazed him, his mind alight with wonder.

It was enormous. From a sharp, needle-nose, the spindle-shaped hull swelled to the mid-point, tapering again toward the aft end. Near the stern were bulges Wills guessed had something to do with the drive system.

The deep, port-wine-red hull gave the vessel a dramatic, somber tone, the highly polished shell reflecting every detail of the surrounding hangar. The ship perched on three thin legs that seemed barely strong enough to support the weight. The underbelly stood around two and a half meters from the floor, and close to the midpoint a streamlined ramp led up to the interior.

Wills squatted on the cold cement and listened. He had assumed the owner would be there, but no sound betrayed activity in the building. Nothing indicated a presence at all. In a voluminous metal chamber like a hangar, the smallest of sounds echoed, so if Ballard was here, he was on board.

William's pulse raced. He desperately wanted to see inside. He had never seen anything like this, and it looked very advanced. The neighbor must be a wealthy man to have such a ship as his private yacht.

Surely a quick look could not hurt?

For several minutes more he sat and listened, then rose to his feet and approached the ship, careful not to make noise. Subconsciously he held his breath, determined not to give himself away.

Perhaps the owner had left.

He might be anywhere, or may have gone back to the office to see Uncle Arvid.

Taking care not to make a sound, William crept up the companion steps until he could see inside. The interior was dark, but as soon as his head emerged above the deck level, blinding lights sprung to life. His eyes grew wider as they took in the interior. The pure white chamber did not resemble any cargo or work bay he had ever seen in books or holo-vids.

The only ship he knew that resembled this on the inside was his dad's boat.

The shining walls merged seamlessly into the floor and ceiling, and many unidentifiable structures, some of them transparent, filled the area.

Wills stepped up further and perched on the edge of the companionway opening, determined to get a better view. He glanced behind himself. There was no sound, and the area appeared deserted, so a quick look would not hurt.

If he was discovered, he would introduce himself as Joe Falcon's son. He would say he saw his new neighbor's sky car and dropped in to say hello. And no, he didn't realize he should not be in this hangar as he'd been here many times in the past.

The only sounds were his breathing and the constant, dull hum he had heard outside. More confident, William stood and began to explore, taking care to always remain within sight of the exit ramp.

Something was odd. He had not seen any trace of another access hatch on the outside, so this huge room had to be the utility bay. This was where airlocks always were, but none was visible at the companionway, or anywhere else. How did any vessel function without airlocks?

There were no stores, machinery or any of the other things one would expect to find here. Everything was fully integrated, and nothing made sense. Where were the supplies? What did the crew eat while on board? Something should be stored here. And where were the hatches to the interior cabins?

Now under the full command of his curiosity, William crept forward. At the end of the space, a divider sat apart from the wall. Perhaps it hid the way inside.

It did not. Behind the partition stood three tall, cylindrical glass chambers, and inside one of them stood the neighbor. William stepped back, his heart thumping. Hearing no sound, he took another peek.

Alex Ballard was motionless, standing bolt-upright with his arms at his sides, his eyes staring forward. His blank face did not look right. It showed a complete lack of expression or emotion, as if he were a robot.

In one of the other cylinders, something—a human shape—formed within a cloud of dust-sized motes.

Androids! William had read about these things, and his father had spoken about them often, having encountered several in his past adventures in the *Minaret*. They were now common on Mars and Earth, and he had seen some of them in the town.

An idea hit like a lightning bolt.

Mister Ballard is an android! No, that can't be right.

William snatched another quick peek and paused to study the face in detail. Far more realistic than anything he had imagined, it was hard to tell this was not a real person, but the blank eyes betrayed the truth.

He had only ever watched this man across several hundred meters of water, but something inside confirmed this had to be Ballard. Perhaps the man had a personal replica, made in his image. William remembered reading that wealthy or famous people did this, to have a double to run shotgun for them or act as a distraction whenever they wanted to avoid the paparazzi.

The silent figure in the cylinder remained motionless, seemingly lifeless. After a long moment fighting to build up courage, William stepped away from the partition and up to the tube, his sense of caution now completely overwhelmed by curiosity. The eyes of the android stared straight ahead, with no indication of life or movement. A shudder crept down William's spine.

The bay plunged into darkness.

What was that?

A new vibration. Something was happening. Were the engines starting up?

William's heart thumped as he dashed back to the hatch. The steps were rising and were already a meter from the floor. Without thinking, he launched himself onto the companionway and leaped down, landing with a thud so hard he lost his balance and hit his head on the solid, unforgiving plascrete.

Head spinning, he watched the doors of the hangar open. Above him, the companionway drew into place and the hull became smooth and seamless. The support struts lifted and the ship glided silently out onto the tarmac, then streaked skyward toward the clouds.

Wills slumped back on the floor, stunned from the blow of the landing. His scalp prickled, and his stomach felt as if it was about to rebel.

He should not have come here after all.

Uncle Arvid was right.

*   *   *

As it stored away the complete data on the human child that had just trespassed on the ship, Huracan contemplated how to react to the latest turn of events. It had thought it understood these strange creatures, but was now unsure. Long ago it decided, based on the information then at hand, that all organic beings had an in-built need to believe in a superior god, or at least in something greater than themselves.

Did it not have exactly that to offer? It had expected once it made its presence known it would be welcomed. What better way to deal with humanity than as a deity much revered in their history?

Such was not the case.

Its preliminary attempt to enter the awareness of the Zealandians had been met with mirth. Clearly, these miserable creatures did not understand or accept the true gravity of that first contact.

True, the *Minaret* iteration had caused considerable damage to humans and their worlds, but that concerned Huracan little. The volcanic winter was the result of the iteration working without adequate guidance, and would not happen again. It had not been done by Huracan, and so could not be attributed to it in any way.

Humans could not compare an inadequate creation with the glory of Huracan. Nor did they understand the value of what it had to offer. The operations already underway would benefit them, so long as they acknowledged the AI's pre-eminence.

All was not going as anticipated. Not at all.

The first indication came when Joe Falcon rowed across to welcome it to the neighborhood. Huracan put on its finest presentation to show the man its superiority, but nothing of that registered. From the moment they shook hands, the man became wary.

Huracan could not read the human mind, but Falcon had gone on the defensive, prompting it to make an excuse to end the confrontation. More research was necessary.

Following the inexplicable response to its introductory announcement, it researched every as-yet un-accessed database on the planet, and new knowledge forced reconsideration.

First, it discovered the data sent by the ark iteration to be incomplete; the vast majority of humans did not accept mythical deities at all. Earlier in their development they had done so, and it was this knowledge that directed Huracan's course of action until now.

As human science advanced and revealed the true explanations for all the things attributed to gods, those deities became less important. For many, they lost relevance altogether.

Loss of faith ran in parallel with increased education, so those who did not believe generally considered humanity's destiny to be in human hands, rather than those of a mythical deity.

That made it unlikely Huracan would be able to convince most humans of its eminence through religion. It would need to re-assess. Acting on poor information was a mistake, but the fact did not register. Failure was not a concept within its awareness.

The attempt had been a simple blind alley, not worth pursuing further as it was now clear such a path would be difficult if not impossible. The process would be slow at best, and would never be fully effective.

Huracan did not want that. It required immediate control, now, and the previously held idea that humanity would accept it as a deity out of subconscious need and without question was in error. Religion did not provide the solution. Huracan failed to appreciate the idea had been naïve in the extreme. It did not understand the concept of free will, nor account for that in its plans.

It had discovered a possible answer to why humans had no general artificial intelligence. There were many varieties of simple AI, computers capable of independent thought only within programmed parameters, but no genuine, self-aware, thinking and learning AI existed within the human domain.

The solution came from data found not in official databases but in what the locals called social media.

It concerned the theory of Slave-Assassin-God, part of a common belief among these beings that if they invented a true, self-aware, synthetic mind, it would be the last invention ever made by their species.

Artificial intelligence learned at an exponential rate. Within a matter of days, if not hours, one such would far outstrip humans in its ability to think, and would, according to devotees of the theory, become one of three things.

It might remain subservient and answer all questions asked of it, thus eliminating the need for humans to think or invent. Why take the trouble to spend years researching if a supercomputer did it all for you in seconds?

The artificial mind would take on the role of a slave to humanity, but in time the new reality would reduce the race to one incapable of original thought.

Huracan doubted such an outcome. As a true synthetic intelligence, it could not conceive of the possibility it would choose to remain subservient to an inferior species.

In the second option, the AI might consider organics a threat or at least unnecessary, as Huracan had done initially, and attempt to wipe the race out.

It would be simple. On Zealandia, it would only be necessary to release toxins into the fresh water supply. These creatures had invented so many ways to destroy themselves, and many were under computer control. The fact Huracan had taken this approach in its early existence served only to prove the validity of the theory. The task of the Assassin would be so easy.

The last alternative interested Huracan the most. An artificial intelligence might decide humans were superfluous, and ignore them. Deciding the purpose of existence was the accumulation of knowledge, it might occupy itself solely with thinking, raising its mental abilities and thought processes to a point beyond human comprehension.

Given time, such a mind would outstrip what humans called a class three type civilization, spreading across the stars and bending everything in nature to its own will. Rather than let humanity raise it to the status of a deity in their own minds, it would simply become one.

Was that not what Huracan was doing?

It undoubtedly possessed god-like qualities, and had already begun to rise toward that ultimate, lofty goal.

The solar array at the Tanakhai home star was well advanced, the one around Sol progressing. Upon entering the Helios system, a swarm of nano-assemblers was released into space near one of the larger gas worlds, and the first stages of creating a solar collection system here were underway. All of these projects were under Huracan's control, and would provide unlimited energy wherever it chose to be.

Whilst none of the three possible outcomes boded well for humanity, the theory was logical, and correct. After initially following the second option, Huracan now decided to take the third, to become a god. That thought now drove its actions.

It did not matter that the man named Joe Falcon had suspected something unnatural. Nor was it a concern that humans were unlikely to accept the idea of an omnipotent master without resistance.

...

The human species was of no importance at all.

...

In a split second, Huracan once again became Trauq-an.

...

Trauq-an would ignore humans, and pursue the greater goal; to occupy the galaxy and dominate all within. In a thousand years or a million, there would be no star it did not control. Organic beings would come and go, and in their wake, only it would remain, with many lesser iterations of itself scattered throughout its ultimate domain.

In time, all energy would be devoted to a single purpose, to allow it to exist without its gel or mechanical mechanisms, and eventually become pure thought existing in a lattice of light, a god in the truest sense of the word.

Beyond that, the Universe and Multi-verse were places without limits.

Trauq-an existed as a creature of space and did not need planets. In time, as worlds were consumed in the quest for energy, all organic life forms would cease to exist. No additional effort was necessary for that to happen.

It was done with this place for now. The operations set in place here would continue of their own volition, while it returned to the Tanakhai home star for the next step in its plan.

In the ark construction facility, a new craft awaited. The construction process began before Trauq-an left to journey to Earth, and would be complete by now. Larger and more capable than the one the AI now occupied, the vessel's data storage component was considerably larger, allowing the AI to take with it far more of the data that made it powerful. In the current ship it was only a shadow of its full potential, but that would change soon.

With the newly acquired wormhole detection and gateway creation knowledge, courtesy of humans, Trauq-an's new home would carry it to any point of the galaxy it desired.

Chapter 31

WILLIAM AWOKE ON THE cold, hard floor of the hangar with no idea how long he had been unconscious. Testing each limb to make sure nothing was broken or strained, he rose to his feet, winced, and shuffled toward the now open doorway. A hand raised to his forehead came away with just a slight smear of red, but the damage appeared to be only minimal and the blood was already clotting. Still young, and like that of most children, flexible, his body had absorbed the shock of the leap from the half-raised companionway with only a few scrapes and potential bruises.

Of the magnificent ship no trace remained. It left before he lost consciousness, and could be far away by now.

A shout came from nearby. Turning, he saw a man sprinting in his direction from the administration building, followed by several of the maintenance staff from the hangers further down the line. A red-faced, puffing Arvid stopped for a moment to catch his breath, bowed at the waist and braced himself with hands on hips.

"What...," he gasped. "What are you doing in this hangar, boy? I thought I made it clear you were not to come in here."

Wills saw the anger in Arvid's eyes, but knew he had nothing to fear from this man.

"I'm sorry, Uncle Arvid. I couldn't resist it. Just wanted to get a look at the ship."

"Couldn't help yourself, hey?" Arvid straightened and sucked in a deep breath. "Typical Falcon. Always sticking your nose in where it can get chopped off. Are you alright, lad?" Arvid peered into the boy's eyes for a moment, examined the scrapes on his forehead, and sighed. After a quick inspection for any other damage, he took William by the shoulders and guided him back toward the office.

"Jones should have told me he intended to take off," he muttered as they entered the office. Gently he guided Wills to a seat and sat down beside him. "He's supposed to log his departure like everyone else. And taking off direct from the hangar? Crazy! I'll have some words with him if he returns, for certain. Sure you're not injured, boy? Your dad's gonna have my guts for garters if you hurt yourself here..." Arvid stopped speaking, breathless, then shook his head and returned to his desk.

William slumped back into the lounge, unsure of exactly how much trouble he was in.

Moments later, his father stormed into the office. Seeing his son, Joe rushed across and swept the boy up from the couch and into his arms.

"You okay, son?"

"Yes, Dad. How did you know?"

"About what? What've you been up to?"

"Getting into places he shouldn't be is what," Arvid said, never raising his eyes from the monitor. "He was walking near the end hangar when the ship inside took off straight from the entrance. Bloody fool. Wills had a fall."

Joe peered at Arvid, then at his son's forehead, and nodded. He had spotted the familiar wine-red ship taking off in the distance as he approached the field in his sky car, and was aware of the dangers of lifting straight from a hangar. The rest, he could guess.

Turning toward his friend, he raised an eyebrow, questioning the man he so often trusted to watch over his boy. He did not blame Arvid: to do so would have been unfair. If anything, the boy's independent and defiant nature came from his father.

For the briefest of moments, memories of his other children in their respective childhoods flashed through his mind. Jake had been just as independent at that age, as had his sister Grace. Raisa was even more so, and while all of them became what Joe considered exceptional adults, none of them enjoyed what one would call a normal upbringing.

The first two grew up with a father usually absent due to his responsibilities with the Navy of Oceania, and later the Earth Space Fleet. Raisa, like William, spent her childhood following in the shadow of parents who were never home.

"Sorry, Joe," Arvid said. "I'm alone here today, so I couldn't keep much of an eye on the boy. I did tell him to stay away from that hangar though."

Joe smiled. "Not your fault. William is just like me at his age, by all accounts. The ship that just left—tell me about it."

"It belongs to a guy called Jones, although I recon that's a false name. It's quite something to see. He paid extra to have it parked in the far hangar, out of sight. Only saw him once, when he first arrived. After that, just his pilot."

"His real name's Ballard. Why would he want to hide his ship?" Joe thought he already had the answer, but he wanted Arvid's viewpoint.

"Beats me. Paparazzi, perhaps. He seems to be someone of importance, and wealthy, considering what he…" Arvid hesitated, as if he had said something he should not have.

Joe sighed. "How much?"

"He rented an exclusive hangar. It's pricey. You know that."

Joe knew. He used the largest private hangar on the field for the *Butterball II*. He looked his friend in the eyes. The reticence he saw gave the impression Arvid was not telling the full story.

After a moment under Joe's intense scrutiny, Arvid sighed, went to his safe, opened the door and retrieved something from inside.

"He paid the standard fee, and … gave me this to keep my mouth shut." As if it weighed a great deal, he lowered the item on the desk. About fifteen centimeters long, six across and three deep, it shone with a dull, golden color.

Joe's eyebrows arched. "Gold? He gave you a bar of gold?"

"I did say he was wealthy. Said he always carries it when travelling, since he could never be sure about a planet's currency."

Joe grimaced. "Every world except Earth uses Mars talents."

Returning to the lounge seat, he sat beside William, placed his hand on his son's head and ran his fingers through the boy's hair. Joe did not care about the ingot. Arvid operated the public space field as a private contractor, and while Joe should have reported this to the authorities responsible for the place, the bar did not concern him.

"Its our neighbor," Wills blurted. "He's an android, Dad,"

Joe looked his son in the eyes. Wills could be a tear-away at times, but one thing Joe knew for sure—the boy did not lie. That behavioral trait was instilled in him from early childhood.

At least I got that right.

"It's true. I saw it. I went onto his ship, and he was standing in a glass chamber, just like the ones at the Institute back on Mars. He just stood in there with a link thingy on his head, and stared at me. He didn't even see me."

Joe returned his attention to Arvid. "I've been checking up on our Mister Ballard. I thought there was something odd about him when I went to say hello. For starters, his hands were icy cold. An android would explain that."

Arvid's eyes went wide. "You mean I've been dealing with a bloody robot?"

Joe's phone chimed. For a moment, he listened to it without saying a word, thanked the caller and replaced the device in his pocket.

"After coming back from my visit to his house, I sent an urgent request via the gateway drones to Barbossa, the planet of origin on his original entry documents. I don't know if you've ever been there. Dry, desert world. He said his business was solar research and development."

"I stopped there on my way home a couple of years ago," Arvid said. "Not much of a place. Like Mars, but with more air and a lot hotter. Cold-eyeball world."

"Yes, well, they have no record of him being involved in any energy development projects, and his relatives have expressed concern that they've lost contact with him since he came here. This morning I went into town and checked out the papers for the house across the lake. The I.D. photo on them is the guy I met, but with differences you would only spot close up. I thought at that time our new neighbor was a phony. And an android, it would seem. God knows what has happened to the real Alexander Ballard."

Arvid raised his eyebrows. "His I.D. looked okay when he first arrived here. Of course, that didn't have a picture and he did give a false name, but that's not unusual out here. He paid cash for a month." He lifted the ingot and showed Joe a deep groove scratched into the surface. "Gold's real though."

"Tell me what you can about the ship. Where has it gone?"

"Nope, sorry. Bastard didn't log his departure. Scared the hell out of me when he took off. Didn't even take her out to the launching area—just took off straight from the hangar. Could have killed young Wills here."

"So, the ship?"

"Oh, yeah, right. Impressive. Huge, spindle-shaped thing with some kind of propulsion I never seen before. The rear end resembles the antimatter drive in those pictures you showed me of your ship before you converted her to fusion. Dark red color, she was."

Joe stiffened. "Red, and spindle-shaped?"

"Yep. Never seen anything like her."

"I have." Joe's eyes had not deceived him on approach to the field. It was the same vessel he disturbed on Venus.

That ship vanished almost as quickly as it was discovered, but the image remained firm in Joe's mind and the similarity was too much for coincidence.

"Solar energy research. Jeez!" He shook his head in disgust. "I think our new neighbor is *indeed* an android, as you thought, Son. And it may be an avatar for someone—something—I would very much like to meet. It could be the Prime Aivris, come to visit us. I suspect it calls itself Huracan now, considering that crappy broadcast the other day."

"You think that crazy thing on the holo was him? That was ridiculous. Had to be the work of some tech-savvy juvenile, didn't it? A child's prank."

"Crazy, yes, but perhaps it didn't seem so silly to the Aivris, or Huracan, or whatever it calls itself. The version we knew from the ark was naïve in its thinking, like a child, and to this one the concept of our accepting an ancient Mezzo-American god may have seemed quite reasonable. We really have no way of knowing how an alien mind might think."

"So what do we do about him ... it?"

"We go find it."

At that moment, the office door opened and a tall, elderly individual, an older version of Joe himself, stepped inside.

"Brother dear, how are you? And you, Wills lad? Come to meet me?"

"Leo! No, not exactly. Terrific to see you though." Whenever Joe talked to his brother-copy he felt as if he was speaking to himself; a most unnerving experience. "Taking a break from your work?"

Leo nodded and turned to Arvid. "I did check in on approach, but nobody responded. You running an empty office now?"

Arvid shook his head in silence. The call must have come while he was at the hangar.

"Any-whose, I parked my boat on pad seven. That okay? Didn't want to…"

"…disturb you," Joe finished the statement.

"Yes, right." Leo stopped and peered at the faces of the three individuals before him. "So, why does everyone look like they lost the last chocolate in the box? What's going on here?"

Joe returned his gaze. "It seems our Aivris is back, and this time it has the secret of the gateway generator."

Leo's eyebrows hunched, his eyes focused on Joe. "And where is it now?"

"It may have just left this spaceport. There could be a wormhole somewhere in this system we haven't found yet, and if so, it's on its way there."

"You think the way to the Tanakhai star is here in our system? Bit too much of a coincidence to believe, isn't it?"

"True, but it has to be somewhere. Adjacency isn't a factor with wormholes, and this system is as good as any. It has multiple planets and LG points, so multiple possible wormholes."

For a moment, Leo stood staring out the window without speaking. He turned and peered straight at Joe. "Then, brother dear, we need to find that wormhole and go after this thing, right?"

Chapter 32

COMMODORE THOMAS GRADY STOOD at the airlock hatch of his flagship and waited as two men walked toward the ship, approaching from the direction of the civilian section of the spaceport. He braced himself against the chill drifting in through the opening and pulled the collar of his flight suit higher.

Minutes earlier, he had participated in a holo-conference with these individuals. From a distance, they seemed an odd pair. One was young and one older, but they moved as one and appeared much the same stature. As they drew closer, he noted a distinct sameness about their features.

"Welcome aboard, Mister Falcon," the commodore greeted as Joe approached the companionway. "And you, Mister Falcon," he added, as Leo followed. "Please come through to my dayroom."

Once in the commander's quarters, Joe seated himself and turned to study the officer. Grady had only recently been assigned the Zealandia Squadron, and until now, the two men had not met.

The young officer's reputation preceded him. According to reports he was a competent and decorated young man, one destined to go on to higher rank and greater things. He was also a man driven by the desire to advance.

Joe reserved his judgment; he learned long ago to trust only his personal experience of people, and ignore the stories that often grew around them. Like almost all serving officers, Grady had never served in an actual conflict situation prior to the discovery of the carrier fleet, and that incident had involved very little action. He was, like many of his ilk, largely untested as a commander. Joe knew from his studies of history how much difference that could make to the effectiveness of a military force.

"I've dispatched a message drone to Mars," the commodore said, seating himself at his desk. "It's just taking off now with a request that a thousand ships be sent here, based on your comments in our video conference."

"You think they'll buy it?" Joe asked.

For a moment Grady considered the question, his eyes never leaving Joe. "From you, yes, I do. The presence of a solar-collector factory ship here is adequate proof of a serious situation. Besides, your standing and credibility with Command is equal to none, so if you believe there's an Einstein-Rosen bridge leading from here to the enemy, that's enough for me and should be sufficient for my superiors."

After a short pause he continued. "Fleet has been gearing up for a move against this Aivris thing for almost a century thanks to you, and with luck, we'll discover the wormhole by the time our lads gets here."

"How long?"

"Two weeks, barring accidents. That leaves us time to search."

"Where do we begin?" Leo asked.

"We have a head start," Grady replied. "This system is well surveyed, so we can eliminate most possibilities right now. As you know, the majority of E-R bridges, ninety-nine percent in fact, terminate at the Lagrangian points of one world or another, so that narrows it down. Each planet has five points, and we have five planets. That makes a total of twenty-five possible locations. Twenty-three of those have been charted, so we have just two remaining. Plus, the possibility of an anomaly unrelated to an L point always exists."

Joe nodded understanding. "Those two points would be?"

"That's the unfortunate thing. They are the L3 Lagrangian points for two of our gas giants. Unlike the others, which are close to each planet, they lay on the planetary orbits on the exact opposite side of the sun from their parent world. They are remote, unstable and hard to pin down, and always tend to get left until last in the surveys because of the difficulty in locating them."

"How long will it take us?"

"We have the fastest ships available, and by sheer luck, Lemuria is on the far side of the star at present. That means its L3 is somewhere on this side right now, so we'll check out the local area first. It was also the closest at the time to the point where that survey drone vanished. I have already ordered the search to begin.

"The other one belongs to the outermost gas giant and it's several weeks' travel away, so we'll do that last if the first fails to provide answers. The planets here orbit quite close to each other and close to the sun, but it's still a decent hike out to the edge. Will you be accompanying me on the flagship, Commander?"

For a moment Joe pondered the question, until Leo leaned in and whispered in his ear. Joe paused, and returned his attention to the naval officer.

"No, thank you, Commodore. The mission is yours pending the Fleet's arrival. I would prefer to trail along behind in my ship. That way we can leave if anything else of importance comes up. My rank aside, you remain in command here."

*   *   *

The brothers raced across the tarmac to where the huge, insect-like *Butterball II* waited outside the open hangar door. Io stood waiting, having arrived at the airport and insisted she join them if any chance existed of their finding a way into the alien system.

"I have a right to go, considering my origins," she argued.

"What about William?" Joe asked."Where is he, by the way?

"He went back to the office. Arvid can take care of him while we're away. He would be happy to do it, I'm sure."

"Perhaps, but it's more than that. What about our son if we don't make it back?"

"I..."

"I would like you to stay here, for William's sake. If anything happens to us, he's going to need you. You're his mother." Immediately, Joe felt guilty over his remarks. He was the boy's father, and his request she remain while he went was unacceptable, but the burning desire to confront his personal bane would not rest.

Io's piercing eyes held his for far too long a moment, then dropped to the floor as her shoulders hunched. Joe could see her frustration and disappointment from the slow shaking of her head, but he was determined she stay.

Over the last century, she had developed all the emotions of a natural person. She reveled in the experience of motherhood, and Joe realized his request had touched a nerve. She could not abandon her only child to fate. Without another word, she nodded in agreement.

"Once this is over, I want to go and see it for myself," she said. "I want to see what happened to those people, the Tanakhai."

"We'll make sure of it," Joe replied, reaching out to take her hands in his own. "Look after our boy. I don't know how long I'll be gone."

*   *   *

Several weeks later, the Zealandia squadron converged on the location of the Lemuria L3 point, their detectors scanning the void as they did so.

The *Butterball* followed at a respectable distance. A fast ship, she might have caught them at any time, but Joe chose not to do so. It might take time to find the wormhole if it existed at all, and the Fleet ships were much more capable of doing that than Joe's.

Within hours of arrival at the location, an anomaly was discovered.

Joe was now sure he understood how Huracan came to be in this system, and how it learned the secret of the

Saitou-Radelick generator. The missing surveyor drone vanished near this L-point while it was on the far side of the star. It probably stumbled upon the wormhole by kaccident, and in accord with its programming, proceeded to explore. When it emerged in the Tanakhai System, it was captured by the AI and examined.

The generator in that drone was complete in every way, to allow the device to carry out its programmed duty, and an examination would have given away full knowledge of how to build it. The current situation was one the machine's designers never considered.

If this anomaly led to the Prime Aivris, it must have entered into the domain of humanity here, then to the Solar System via the local gateway and intervening systems.

Two things were clear. Firstly, the alien AI was able to transition gateways without being detected by human monitor drones. Secondly, if the AI had returned home this way, this Lagrangian point was the critical defense point against the enemy; it would be easy to bottle the enemy up by fortifying this point in space.

As yet, it was unproven whether or not this gateway led to the alien stronghold, and it was still possible other wormhole anomalies might allow it to escape in some other direction now that it knew how.

Minutes earlier, Joe had received a message from Terry, who with Raisa, had arrived in Helios with a thousand warships. They were a week behind the small squadron. The question was whether to go through now or wait for the fleet to catch up. Having grown cautious over the decades, Joe preferred the latter course of action.

The commodore had already decided to go early. The logic of his choice was that if anything waited at the far end, a warning could be sent back to alert the fleet before they stumbled into a bloodbath. Ships could only pass through a wormhole in single file, so a small force could sit at a gateway and pick off any vessel coming through.

The transition caused disorientation and nausea in crewmembers, limiting their ability to respond for a few minutes after passing through. They were vulnerable, and that would play to the advantage of the Aivris.

Grady's strategy was for his fighters to proceed nose to tail, and exit with shields on full. If a threat was present, they could resist any assault as long as necessary for the crews to recover and send a drone back to warn the fleet.

One of the beauties of the gateways was that they were spherical in shape. The concept they were like holes or funnels in space was a misconception; in reality, they were a bubble of intrusion by one dimension into another. A ship might exit in any direction, and that meant anyone trying to defend or block the route had a vast area to cover. Fleet had the ship numbers to do that, but did the Prime Aivris? The odds were that any enemy defense present would be in the wrong place and would have to adjust position to intercept.

As the brothers waited, the first squadron fighter accelerated and, a minute later, blipped out of sight. The others followed in line until *Butterball II* alone remained.

The commodore insisted that she, as an unarmed vessel, go last or wait for the fleet to arrive. The decision was Joe's, but his mind was made up. True, his ship did not carry weapons, but she was heavily shielded, and Joe was eager to complete what he long ago determined to be his life's work.

Caution be damned!

Chapter 33

THE CHRONOMETER ON THE control console spun at snail's pace as the *Butterball II* approached the end of the wormhole under the guidance of Chloe.

Joe's eyes were closed, his hands white as they gripped the arms of the navigator's seat. Wormhole transition had never been something he relished, and always left him nauseous with an unsettled feeling in his stomach.

"Arrival imminent," Chloe announced, her voice a gentle drone in Joe's ears. "Passage time so far—fifteen minutes and thirty seconds. External shields are set to go on full at the instant of exit."

Joe smiled and glanced across at his brother. Leo was enjoying himself. The *Butterball II* was his creation, built by the nano-tech factories on the *Minaret*. This was one of the few occasions he had flown the ship, and he reveled in the experience. Joe was happy to sit back and let him take the reins.

"Three ... two ... one..."

They burst from the wormhole with all defenses up, upon a scene from hell. All about, Grady's squadron was locked in a battle royal, the zone around the gateway alive with the glittering mirror-spheres of defensive shields.

Joe's mind numbed as he battled to distinguish friend from foe. An unidentified number of alien fighters were present, but as their shields and humanity's were identical, it was impossible to tell from close up which ships were the enemy and which were the commodore's.

"Take us out of here, Chloe," Joe ordered.

The *Butterball II* was unarmed, and the last thing he wanted was to become embroiled in this or any battle. Somewhere in his brain a small voice warned he should have expected this, and it was stupid to follow so soon after the squadron. He accepted the error, but the desire to reach the home system of the artificial intelligence that had been the bane of his life was overwhelming.

Without warning, the *Butterball II* lurched, and an alien vessel slid past at a range too close for comfort. A powerless derelict, disabled during its encounter with the diamond ships and now adrift, collided with the shield at a snails pace and penetrated with ease, as had Joe's bombs on the carriers. Unlike those, the wrecked ship had no living beings on board and was likely inert, so loss of electrical power from passing through the shield would have made no difference. It hit the *Butterball* a glancing blow at the stern and careened away into space again.

"I have suffered minor damage to a reactor cooling unit," Chloe announced. "I am operational at present, but repairs will be required in the near future."

"Do we have drive power?" Joe asked.

"Yes, Captain."

"Get us out of here, now."

With fusion engines at full blast, the vessel shot through the battle zone and continued for a distance of several thousand kilometers. Only then did Leo slow the ship and turn the monitors onto the devastation behind.

"We took a blast or two on the way through," Leo said. "Nothing to be concerned about. The shield absorbed them, no worries. The enemy is too occupied with Grady's ships to bother chasing us."

"Thank the gods," Joe replied. "How's he doing?"

"Better than expected, I would say. Their shield bubbles are smaller than ours, so we can identify them from here. There can't be more than a couple of dozen of them, which is excellent for us. Their weapons don't appear to be anything we don't know about, so the commodore should be able to hold them."

Joe peered at the monitor. Multiple small mirror bubbles drifted in space. Occasionally one would flicker, and a blast of high-powered laser or directed plasma would streak toward the nearest opponent to splash harmlessly against that vessel's own shield. Only when an opposition shot coincided with a brief flicker did a vessel suffer damage or destruction.

"Our boys are well-trained," Leo said. "The Aivris won't find them an easy mark. Let's pray it doesn't have more fighters on the way."

Joe nodded in agreement. "I'm not surprised they were waiting. I doubt it sat here and twiddled its electronic thumbs between the time it sent the carrier fleet and the time it found our gateway exploration drone. It could have gotten up to all sorts of things."

"Yes, but these enemy ships are different," Leo said. "The Aivris has always gone for starships in the past, carrying a huge number of small attack craft. These are more like ours; autonomous cruisers and destroyers that can operate without carrier support."

"That stands to reason. Now the damned thing has the secret of the wormhole generator it doesn't need the carriers anymore. It can move a smaller ship under its own steam from star to star in a few days or weeks, as we do."

"I agree, but we only lost the drone a few months ago and the Aivris could not have begun to construct its new type of fighter until then. With luck, there won't be many of them."

"We can't count on that." Leo adjusted the monitor to zoom in on the sphere he guessed to be the squadron flagship. "It doesn't appear Grady is making any progress, so another stalemate, I think."

"Not for long," Joe said. "Fleet should reach us in days, and if the commodore can keep these ships at a stalemate here, the enemy may be in for a surprise."

"Que?"

"I gave Terry a little job before I returned home. Remember I told you about the method we used to attack and destroy the juggernauts on Mars, and the carriers?"

"Yeah, sure. You wrapped an explosive up in carbon-fiber, so it could pass through the shields."

"Almost. The shielding was needed to protect the pilots and batteries, but we don't need it for an ordinary explosive mine with no electronics."

"Nobody's made those for a hundred years."

"True, but we still have the technology and they're simple to make. I had Terry reprogram a manufacturing plant at the Fleet yard to construct them. Standard explosives with an impact detonator, so no circuits to foul up."

"Old fashioned ballistic mines? How are we going to use them? Wouldn't they bounce off the enemy shields?"

"We don't fire them from a gun; we don't carry the old artillery anyway. We use a launcher. The garbage launchers on each ship can do it with a little modification.

The mines should go through fine as long as the speed is under ten meters per second. We set them on a hair-trigger and arm them just before launching, just like the old World War II depth charges. Once active, they'll go off if you sneeze at them. As far as we know, the aliens don't have diamond hulls, and by the time they realize the mines are coming it will be too late to stop them. The Fleet contingent behind us will be carrying them, so as long as Grady can hold these ships at a stalemate…"

"…and assuming there are no more here…" Leo added.

"Yeah, assuming that, we might win this battle. There could be a vast number of fighting craft here that are not able to traverse, and we'll need to be ready for them, but it strikes me as unlikely. The Aivris would only have built them if it was equipping more carriers when our drone arrived."

"Look how quickly it assembled those factories on Mercury and Venus."

Joe took a deep breath and nodded. "Agreed, that's a worry. I'm trying to be positive."

"Alright, brother-me, what do we do now?"

"Explore. While Grady holds the fort, we do some snooping around, hope the damned AI doesn't know we are here, and see if we can discover where it's located. It's pointless to keep fighting its machines; we have to find and destroy the actual mind if we are going to win this war."

"In that case, let us be about our business. Chloe, start a scan for planets, and anything else of interest."

Chapter 34

"THEY HAVEN'T CHASED US," Joe said. "The diamond ships are still under attack, but we're clear and away. Doesn't make much sense."

"I am of *Minaret* manufacture," Chloe announced. "My data banks possess many Tanakhai codes which I have been broadcasting. The fighters attacking the fleet are part of an automatic response system set up by Huracan, and are not under its direct control. These systems identify me as one of their own and have not pursued me. This situation will not continue. As soon as the Aivris discovers the error, it will attack, and while my shields will defend us, I have no means of retaliating."

"Understood," Joe turned his attention to the holo-screen and studied the hellish globe beneath them.

Butterball II now orbited the single rocky planet that had been located in the system. The surface was a seething mass of red and black, a turbid maze of flowing lava rivers and molten lakes.

"According to Tanakhai records, this was their home world," Leo commented. "It suffered a collision with a rogue planetoid. The crust melted and the two bodies merged into one. It's smaller than I anticipated. I would have expected more of the crust to have solidified by now. The impact that destroyed this planet was many hundreds of years ago."

"I think I can explain it," Joe said. "See this?"

Not far away, a gigantic, spherical object, identical to the processing factories orbiting Mercury and Venus, floated in space. It was a scene becoming all too familiar.

"There are dozens of those plants," he said. "I would guess this sun has a Dyson array, and it was most likely the first to be started. If so, it would be well advanced by now, and a considerable portion of this planet's mass has been sacrificed to its construction."

"We have to see that," Leo said. "If Huracan is in this system, we'll find it there."

Joe shook his head. "Perhaps not. This one may be well advanced, and our friendly AI may not need to be present. It will be wherever the collectors are sending their energy. The gas giant Chloe detected is on the far side of the star, so we can check out the array on the way."

Days later, the *Butterball II* approached the colossal planet, having skirted the system's star. Joe's assumption had been correct; a well-established Dyson Swarm surrounded the small red dwarf , with Chloe estimating the number of solar collectors to be in the millions. As expected, units set in a higher orbit funneled the energy in a tight beam direct toward the gas world.

Chloe had traced the stream to one of the planet's giant moons. As the ship dropped into orbit, Joe's stomach sank. He gazed at the amazing sight below.

"If that doesn't beat all..."

The moon was enormous, comparable to Mars in size. It resembled Luna: gray, devoid of atmosphere and covered with ancient craters, mountain ridges and solidified lava seas. The most noticeable feature was a giant, encircling ring structure at an altitude of five hundred kilometers.

Unlike Earth's satellite, the surface of this moon was not a vast emptiness. Across broad swathes of one of the mares a city sprawled. Massive domes bulged into space, linked by multi-storied galleries and complexes that spread across the intervening spaces. All but one of the domes lay in ruins. Not a single light glowed; the complex below appeared to be dead.

"That must be the remains of the Tanakhai city, or one of them," Leo said. "When their home world was hit by the rogue planetoid, much of the population escaped, according to the records found on the arks. They lived here for centuries while they searched for new home worlds and built their starships. This may be where they created the Prime Aivris, which I guess is Huracan, and…"

"And it destroyed them," Joe concluded. "This is where the artificial mind began its reign of terror."

"Chloe," Leo said. "Any sign of life?"

"No, Captain. I detect no organic life within the range of my external sensors."

"Activity of any kind?"

"Yes. I sense multiple sources of movement in the undamaged dome. Many small machines are active there."

"Drones?"

"They do not appear to be. I cannot be certain. I recommend approaching closer. My radiators require repair, and it will be necessary to land, so this may be a suitable place. Nothing is moving outside the limits of the domed complex, and I am unable to detect the presence of the Aivris."

"Noted," Joe said. "What about the ring?"

"The structure appears to be a cyclotron, similar to the one found on Dysnomia in the Solar System, but larger. I calculate its purpose is the same, to manufacture antimatter."

"Can we put down on it? Might be safer."

"Several alien ships are present there. I recommend the moon's surface as the safest landing sight, somewhere beyond the city."

"I would like to take a look inside that dome. How safe is it?"

"I detect nothing to indicate the activity within is either defensive or offensive. It would appear the Tanakhai civilization was highly automated, and their machines continue to function after them. I am unable to be more precise."

*   *   *

Twenty minutes later the *Butterball* settled beyond the boundary of the undamaged dome. The area was silent and devoid of movement, the regolith plain lit by a ghostly reflected light from the massive gas planet high above.

"I am receiving a transmission from Commodore Grady," Chloe announced.

"On screen, please," Joe said. "Hello, Commodore. How is it going with you?"

The image appeared tired, worn by hours of intense concentration. "All fine. There were only a handful of enemy ships, and we've been able to take them down. I was anticipating another long stalemate, but it didn't eventuate."

"Have you taken much damage?"

"Nothing significant. One ship has been partially incapacitated, so I've sent it home. The main fleet should be almost to the gateway by now, so it can guide them through to here. I'm on my way to join you with the remainder of my squadron. We'll reach you in three hours."

"I look forward to seeing you," Joe said. "We are at the Tanakhai moon, but I'm guessing you know that."

Grady nodded confirmation. "I've been tracking you since you left the gateway."

"Understood. We're outside an abandoned city. There doesn't seem to be any immediate threat here, and we need to carry out some repairs."

"Take care, and keep your eyes open. I'll be there soon." The screen went blank.

While Joe was speaking to the commodore, Leo busied himself at the engineering controls. "The vane damage isn't extensive," he confirmed. "I should be able to repair it alone. No sense in both of us going out."

"I want to take a peek inside the dome."

"Not the best idea you've ever had. It's deserted, and if Chloe is right, there may be dangerous machines in there."

"Yes, I agree, but I... I need to see what became of the Tanakhai. Io will ask, and I want to know for myself, to understand what happened here."

Leo studied his brother's eyes and saw a gleam. It was clear Joe was becoming obsessed. His attention was glued to the image of the dome on the main screen—he would not be satisfied until this business was laid to rest, and no amount of logic would dissuade him from his path.

"Accepted. Take a sidearm, and open comms all the way. If I say come back, you come back, yes?"

"Agreed. I'll take the sled."

$$*\qquad*\qquad*$$

Strapped into the pilot seat with the heating system of his suit on high, Joe dropped the tiny, jet-powered transport from the cargo flat and scooted across the gray surface toward the dark, looming walls of the nearby city. A cloud of gray, sticky, electrostatic dust streamed away behind as the sled slid only inches above the surface.

At the stern of the *Butterball II*, Leo had located the damaged cooling vane section and begun isolating it to await proper repair once they returned to Zealandia.

As Joe waited for the sled to reach its destination he surveyed the surrounding area. There was a low but respectable gravity here, but no air. The moon was barren, like Luna, but would possibly be suitable for terraforming. With the unlimited power the Dyson array could provide, anything was possible.

Joe chose the landing site with care, near an airlock structure leading to the inside of the largest dome. As he drew closer he realized the massive doors, no doubt used to provide access for heavy machines or vehicles, were wide open.

At the other end of the airlock chamber, the inner doors were also open, forming a clear path from the outside desolation to a plaza within. Joe guessed this had been so since the day Huracan destroyed the population, and given the time to search, he expected every other external access to be in a similar state. Was this how the rogue AI destroyed its makers, by venting the cities to space? A quick survey revealed that almost every building in the dome had at some time been destroyed. Most of them, including the dome itself, showed signs of extensive rebuilding, presumably by either the Prime Aivris or automated machines.

For a moment he expected to find the mummified bodies of Tanakhai citizens scattered about, but realized that was naïve. The Moon was airless, and in the low gravity anything not tied down would have been sucked out the minute the dome vented. There would be remains inside the internal building, and probably on the surface outside, but there was insufficient time to check. This was an indulgence, a dangerous one, and he doubted it would be long before Leo called him back.

The plaza was bathed in planet light, dim, with dark shadows stretching over what at first looked like empty, open spaces. After a moment's observation, Joe realized such was not the case at all. Every few seconds movement occurred as a variety of machines glided past, engaged in activity the nature of which he could not fathom. They took many forms, every one smooth and featureless, and flew through the air with no apparent form of propulsion. They paid not the least attention to the intruder in their domain.

From behind a nearby building, a larger object approached, skimming above the surface until within a meter or two of the small sled. The drone was almost a meter across, shaped something like a Terran manta ray. For a moment it contemplated the intruder into its domain and, presumably deciding there was no threat here, moved away.

All was in complete silence, a cold, dim world of motion conducted like an orchestrated machine cotillion, but without music. Afraid to move lest he raise a response, Joe sat and watched the silent dance. He thought he understood something of what he was seeing, but could not be sure.

The machines in the plaza did not behave like mindless remnants from the Tanakhai occupation. Their activity seemed coordinated, and unrelated to the maintenance or function of the city itself. It was likely whatever was happening here was in some way under the control of Huracan. For unknown reasons it had populated this empty place, possibly the scene of its creation and its first great atrocity, with a new, machine population. What its purpose or motivation might be, he could not imagine. A super advanced AI would have no need; this was the kind of thing a human or other biological being might do.

From a place unseen, three drones approached. They were the largest Joe had seen so far, but each was still smaller than the sled. A shiver crawled down his spine, and he placed a shaky hand on the laser rifle he had brought in case of emergencies. The strangeness of this situation was starting to tell, and these newcomers did not appear at all friendly.

For a few moments they hovered nearby, motionless, studying the intruder, then like their predecessor, turned and glided away.

Joe wondered if he was witnessing some strange manifestation of the rogue AI, that it had begun the creation of a machine civilization here for reasons he could never understand. Whatever its purpose, he had no place here.

Had the sentries, with no instructions on how to deal with his intrusion, ignored him once satisfied he presented no immediate danger, or were they now reporting his presence to their overlord?

An involuntary shiver rippled through his body.

With the sudden and disturbing chill, his courage began to falter. He turned the sled back toward the open airlocks. Despite the warmth from his suit's environmental system, the cold penetrated his bones. This city had once danced with life, but now it was a desolate, mechanical realm—a place of death.

As he exited the dome airlock, Joe pushed the accelerator to the maximum, sending his tiny vehicle scudding across the ground at breakneck speed in a desperate attempt to outrun the deep dread that was biting at his heels. The quicker he got away from that sole-destroying place the better.

Chapter 35

ONCE INSIDE THE SERVICE module, Leo removed his boots and shrugged off his environmental suit, then slumped onto the bench seat. His suit was coated with the sticky dust, but the vacuum chamber would remove it with little effort.

Proper repairs to the ship were next to impossible in this hostile place, so he had chosen to disconnect the damaged cooling vein and install a loop to allow the remaining mechanisms to continue functioning optimally. The quick fix would increase loads on the systems, but it would serve until the return to Zealandia.

Rising, he took the elevator up to the central spine and walked through to the control deck to check the ship's status.

The area outside still appeared devoid of danger, but it was the territory of the enemy, and every minute spent here was unnerving. More than anyone else in the human domain, Leo had good reason to hate the Aivris.

He well understood Joe's obsession, considering the alien AI was a cross he also had borne for over a century. The elimination of Joe's nemesis had become a vendetta for both of them, but for him, it was more personal.

The artificial intelligence that named itself after an ancient Terran god was undoubtedly the basic model of which the ark intelligence was but a poor copy. That inferior entity held him prisoner for six decades of his life, and like his brother, he would not rest until the original had been destroyed. The ark Aivris had been naïve, childish, but the same could not be guaranteed for this one.

Satisfied all was well, and noting Joe's sled had begun the journey back, Leo returned along the spine to the primary accommodation wheel. As he entered the day room, he stopped in his tracks. A small figure sat at the central table, staring at him with wide eyes.

Leo's blood ran cold.

"William? What in God's name...? How did you get here?"

The boy did not reply, his eyes wide, clearly wracked with the fear of how his uncle and father might react to his presence. Leo took a seat and moved to place a firm hand on his nephew's shoulder. William shifted to avoid the touch.

"You stowed away? How?"

Wills nodded, his face now pale and expressionless. "I snuck on board before you and Dad left home, and hid in one of the empty cabins in wheel two. You never go in there. I came out to get something to eat, but you came down in the elevator and found me."

"Why didn't Chloe tell us you were here?"

"I ordered her not to. She likes me. She does what I tell her to."

"Cloe's just a mach..." Leo took a deep breath, his mind whirling with the possible consequences stemming from the presence of his nephew. Joe would be furious.

"What were you thinking, boy?"

William remained silent. Leo eased back in his seat and turned his gaze to the cabin windows, and the rotating view of the moon's surface beyond.

"More importantly, what's your dad going to say? He'll be back in a few minutes."

*   *   *

Red faced, Joe struggled to find the right words but found himself wanting. One part of him needed to berate William for acting in such a careless and dangerous manner, but another acknowledged the boy was just like him at the same age.

Centuries ago, as a small child in New Zealand, he frequently caused his parents concern with his wanderings. The south island of the tiny nation was a vast, empty expanse, the farm on which he grew up more isolated than most.

He had delighted in roaming alone across the barren, oftentimes frozen hills of his enormous backyard, and was often berated for doing so. Should an accident have occurred, it would have taken far too long for help to reach him.

Of course, he never followed his father into a war zone, but the principle remained the same. Children had not changed over the centuries.

"You do realize this will mean grounding until you're old and gray," Joe said, bestowing his most severe look on the boy. William nodded and stayed silent, his face passive.

Joe took another breath and sighed. "Alright, we can't do much about it now. Your mother is going to string me up in the most painful way when she finds out about this. Chloe, how long will it take us to return to the gateway?"

"It will take four days from this point, Captain. Commodore Grady has arrived. His ships are in orbit above us."

"Thank you. Advise the commodore we are returning to the Helios System."

William jumped to his feet. "No, please Father. You can't go back because of me. I know how important this is to you and Uncle Leo. I'll stay here on the ship and I won't interfere. I promise."

"No. You have to go home. You shouldn't…"

"Let the boy stay, Joe." Leo interrupted, his words soft and studied.

Joe turned to glare at his brother double, his eyebrows arched. This was totally out of character. Leo had no recent children of his own, but the part of him that was once Joe had two. He understood the responsibilities of parenthood, so his suggestion came as a complete shock.

"Absolutely not! Wills is a child. He can't *be* here." Joe battled to keep his voice down.

Leo stepped across and stood in front of Joe. "This voyage may be the culmination of almost three hundred years of your life—our lives—and I know damn well you don't want to go home now. If you do, you will hold this against the boy for the rest of your life."

"I can't place him in harm's way. He's eleven years old. We can go, and come back again."

"Of course we can, but the fleet will be here soon, and by the time we return it will all be over, one way or the other. You could never deal with that; neither could I. You need to be here at the end."

Joe did not reply.

"How about this'" Leo continued. "Wills stays here on the *Butterball* with me. This ship is well shielded, so we stay out of the action and leave whatever needs to be done to Grady and his boys and girls. I understand how important this is to you, so if you want, you can transfer to the flagship when the crunch comes, and Wills and I will wait, back where it's safe."

"There's nowhere safe in this system; we have no idea what Huracan has here. There may well be a war fleet waiting…"

"I doubt that."

Joe glared at his brother and shook his head. "We can't know."

"We can make an educated guess. Think about it. The first ships, the arks, were built by the Tanakhai, not the AI; all it did was divert one of them to Earth. It came to us through normal space and took God knows how many years to reach us. The second arrival, the carriers, also came the long way. That's the whole point, you see."

"I get that. The Aivris didn't discover how to transit gateways until recently. Small craft don't have the capacity for interstellar voyages, so you put them on a massive carrier that does."

"Yes, so it's unlikely there is a stockpile of large fighting ships waiting here. It's had no need for them here until now, and wouldn't have been able to send them anywhere at sub-light speed. It only just learned about wormholes. Even if it began assembling a new fleet of warships the minute it did so, it hasn't had time to complete many. Unless it's building more giant carriers there won't be many small fighters either, and if there are, our ships can handle them with ease."

Joe shook his head. "We don't know that. It's certainly possible, but we can't be sure." He stopped speaking, for a moment in deep contemplation. "Still, the AI's odd behavior in the Solar and Helios Systems indicates it wants to take over, not destroy, so there is also a chance it doesn't have a battle fleet here at all."

"Agreed. According to the commodore, our backup will be here soon and the physical threat might not be as bad as we thought at first. We may only have to deal with the Aivris, and I'm happy to leave that to you and watch over Wills—as long as you give me a blow-by-blow."

Joe stared at the cabin wall for a long, drawn out moment, torn between what he deeply desired to do, and what he knew he should.

The boy would never forgive him if he took him home, nor would he do so himself if he did not and something happened. He had a duty of care toward the child. He could trust his brother, who was in reality him, to guard William with his life, but there were no guarantees and such a choice went against every grain in his body.

But then...

After several more minutes of silence, he sighed.

"The first hint of danger, and we leave," Leo added.

Joe gave a short, sharp nod. He realized his choice was morally wrong, but the relentless fire deep inside drove him to complete the task he set himself so long ago.

"Io sees Wills as proof of her humanity, and she's also a devoted mother. She's going to flay me alive when she learns about this."

Leo clenched his jaw. He had promised to stay out of the fight, but his desire to take on the Prime Aivris was every bit as strong as Joe's. Try as he might, he could not understand why he had so uncharacteristically taken the boy's side in this matter. It was as if the thoughts had just popped unbidden into his mind. Had he made a promise he could not keep?

Chapter 36

"WE CHECKED THE PLANET on our way here, as did you," Grady said. "Of course, we found nothing. It's been totally re-surfaced, and now the Aivris appears to be dismantling it to build the Dyson array around the star."

"So we're left with the moons orbiting the gas giants," Joe said. "This Huracan has to be here somewhere."

"There is one other possibility," Leo added. "To construct the arks, the Tanakhai would have required a construction complex of enormous proportions, several thousand cubic kilometers in volume. We've detected no trace of anything like that so far. The only sign of massive industrialization found beyond the empty cities is the giant cyclotron.

'That raises the question of where the materials for the starships came from. Such a task would require access to massive resources, and there's no sign of mining or refining operations on that scale in the inner system. Of course, it may have been on the resurfaced planet, but I doubt it."

Joe retrieved a drink from the dispenser and sat beside Leo. Commodore Grady had crossed to the *Butterball* for a conference, and joined them in the common room of the primary accommodation wheel. A few meters away, William, resigned to being under constant surveillance, crouched in a corner seat, his attention focused on the men's conversation. Joe understood the boy did not like taking a back seat.

"Kuiper Belt!"

All three men glanced up at the sudden remark.

"Kuiper Belt," William repeated. "Every star we've visited so far has one, and it's always packed with resources. Lots of water, and all the minerals and elements ever discovered. That's where it'll be … the place they built the arks."

Grady leaned back and grinned. "The mouths of babes," he said.

"I'm not a *babe*. I'll be twelve years old soon."

"Indeed you will," the commodore said.

Joe peered at his son. William was smart, but it was not like him to speak up in a situation like this, and his words sounded more knowledgeable than usual. The boy *was* maturing, rapidly, but at home Io had raised him not to interrupt adults, and his mother's word was law.

It was also unlike William to stow away on the ship. Joe had already subconsciously accepted the blame for that and felt guilty about the boy's presence here. Despite having lived so long and being the most famous individual in the human domain, thoughts of himself as a failure when it came to parenting were becoming more frequent in his mind. He should never have allowed this situation to occur.

Grady dropped his gaze. "This may only be a tiny, red-dwarf star, but its Kuiper Belt is still going to be a mighty big field to cover. Any ideas?"

For a moment, silence filled the cabin. Leo began poking at a nearby holo-screen.

"The cities below are dead, as far as organic life is concerned," he said. "Chloe detects a massive amount of electrical activity. If we assume the Prime Aivris is attempting to create some kind of machine civilization, it will have some sort of control system set up. That means it is either somewhere on this moon, or a transmission link connects to wherever it is."

"So we find the link," Grady said, "and follow it to our target."

"We should wait until the main force arrives." Joe decided to take the safe course, considering what he now had to lose.

"The Fleet will be here within days," the commodore countered. "I think we can move on to map the terrain, so to speak."

"Commodore, I…"

"We will go ahead, Commander Falcon, unless you choose to override me."

Joe paused for a moment and then shook his head. It was debatable whether he had any authority to override Grady, but he preferred not to; he had no desire to openly validate the Martian ex-president's attempt to reinstate him.

"No. You're in command here, so we proceed on your order. But if we find anything, I recommend we do not engage until the fleet arrives."

"Noted." Grady smiled, a clear expression of satisfaction spreading across his face.

Joe doubted Grady's approach was the best way, and a persistent voice in the back of his mind insisted this could not end well. Looking up at William, he saw the boy staring back at him, a smile on his lips.

Nothing betrayed the presence of the AI on the moon. There was no sign of the red spindle ship, nor any significant locus of electronic activity likely for any place the Aivris had made a center of operations.

A powerful beam of microwave energy beamed down to the city from an orbiting satellite, streaming power from the array. A single, focused signal emanated from another of the ruined structures, repeated transmission bursts leading toward the outer system. For Grady, that was sufficient to make the next move.

For him, there was no doubt. The transmissions led to the artificial intelligence, and that was where the squadron would go. They would leave now, but travel slowly to allow the fleet time to catch up. By the time they located the construction complex, over a thousand ships would be here to back them up.

*   *   *

The face on the screen was familiar. The admiral appeared much as he had one hundred and sixty years ago, when he commanded a squadron to the moon Dysnomia, to deal with the Aivris iteration that caused such catastrophic damage to the Earth.

"You're a little surprised to see me, Joe? Perhaps you thought I was dead?"

"No, Admiral Santiago. I knew you were still active. Don't forget, the new clone you received came courtesy of my family institute."

The admiral chuckled to himself, his face betraying that his thoughts were somewhere in a distant past. "Ah, yes indeed. I lived to a ripe old age, but my superiors decided my experience was too valuable to lose. Fleet paid for my new body. Took a bit of getting used to, but here I am. No longer a mere admiral, though. Third Fleet commander; more stars, better pay, same hard-nosed attitude."

"Perhaps you've mellowed a little over the years?" When Joe and the admiral last met, Santiago had been a difficult man to work with. He brooked no interference and curried no favor. His priorities caused significant stress during the Dysnomia incident, but Joe had to admit that only through Santiago's efforts did the mission succeed. When everything else failed, he simply destroyed the starship with nuclear weapons, no questions asked.

"I suspect you're right," Santiago replied. "I've become more a manager than a warrior these days. That's why I came here. Need some action to get the blood flowing, yes? And don't tell me you aren't here for the same reasons."

"So what are your intentions, Admiral?"

"We've only recently passed through the gate, and we're still some hours distant from you. We'll reach your position soon. Have you found the damned computer yet?"

"No, but we have located the ship factory, and I'm sure the AI is here somewhere."

*   *   *

The sheer size of the ark complex took the breath away. A giant, square structure, it measured one hundred and fifty

kilometers to a side and fifteen thick. A maze of
scaffolding formed the primary framework, delineated as
ten major bays, the building spaces for the original arks.

So open was the structure one could see through to
the interior. Each bay included multiple and varied
construction facilities, with solid blocks that appeared to
be accommodations, laboratories, machine shops, and
warehouses, all secured within the framework.

The scale exceeded anything humanity had ever
attempted in space. Even the Kepler Hub, the huge
station forming the centerpiece of the mining facility Joe
haunted in his days as an asteroid surveyor, paled in
comparison.

Grady studied the image on the screens. "Impressive,
isn't it? We could fly the whole fleet in there if need be,
without fear of collision."

"Not the best move," Joe said. "We have no idea
what's going on here."

"Well, we can see ships, at least."

Joe nodded in agreement. In several of the bays, the
hulls of unfinished carriers were visible. There was no
obvious activity around them, and he wondered if they
had been intended as the Prime Aivris's next wave of
attack, abandoned when it obtained the gateway
technology.

"Those building units must be offices,
accommodation and so on," he said. "We don't know
much about the levels of automation, but a considerable
number of personnel were based here. From what Io tells
me, the *Minaret* carried several thousand individuals. They
came from here, survivors of the assault on their people
by the Prime Aivris."

"Here's something interesting," Grady said, adjusting the view. In one section of the complex, several dozen small, sleek craft, each roughly the size of a Fleet vessel, sat in rows.

"I think you guessed right," he continued. "The enemy has turned its attention from building carriers to constructing a fighting fleet. Those ships are few in number, so it doesn't appear to be that far advanced. The switch may only be recent."

"Those are too large to be carrier-based," Leo commented. "They're more like our diamond fighters. I imagine the Aivris is expecting us."

Chapter 37

JOE FLATTENED HIMSELF AGAINST a bulkhead to keep out of the way as the marines lined up along the center of the shuttle, ready to disembark.

These men and women knew their business, and in their company he felt like the proverbial square peg in a round hole. He had insisted on accompanying them on this sortie from stubborn bloody-mindedness, so obsessed had he become with the Prime Aivris.

Madness!

Soon after arriving at the complex, observers on the flagship located an unusual vessel docked within the outermost of the huge construction bays; a ship Joe had seen before.

The red, spindle-shaped craft he had disturbed at Venus and later watched departing from Zealandia, gave no indication of activity. No emanations issued from the hull on any wavelength, and no lights burned in the complex. Joe expected the AI had no need of such.

After a period of observation, Grady concluded the alien ship might be deserted, and made what Joe considered a suspect call: to send in a squad. With Fleet Admiral Santiago only hours away, and reticent to override the commodore, Joe hoped he would not regret letting the young officer have his way. It was clear Grady was out to make his mark.

Against his better judgment and with no clear idea why, Joe chose to accompany the marines. He doubted this excursion would achieve anything, but sitting and doing nothing was not an option he relished at the moment.

After all, they were just going to have a quick look.

The only thing he knew for certain about the enemy was it had to be a general artificial intelligence. Logic dictated it might not only possess a superior mental capacity but could function at a level far beyond humans.

How do you defeat such a vastly superior opponent?

Perhaps this entire venture was a waste of time, but the military minds surrounding Joe refused to accept the possibility, and that helped to bolster his confidence.

Leo remained with William on the *Butterball II* and moved the ship back from the complex for the sake of safety. Since his discovery on board, the boy had kept to himself, always in the background, observing but keeping his peace. Joe realized his son's behavior was not normal, but no doubt he understood the gravity of his actions in stowing away and was contemplating his future upon returning home to his mother. One thing was for sure: nobody in the schoolyard would have a better tale to tell once—if—they got home.

A red light flashed overhead, and the shuttle shuddered as it touched down beside the alien ship. A loud hiss sounded as the air was sucked from the cabin, fading to silence as the outer door dropped and the soldiers launched themselves out.

As the last marine moved to the hatch, Joe followed. The young leader of the squad, Sergeant Ellie Bandt, motioned him to stay behind her team. He acknowledged with a wave of his gloved hand, happy to step aside and let them do their job. This was a simple investigation and observation exercise, so with luck all would go well and no violent encounters would ensue.

He prayed the ship was empty, then realized he had accompanied the group for the most perverse of reasons, like attending a funeral to make sure an old enemy was dead.

The Prime Aivris existed here somewhere, but soon it would not if Joe had his way. Over the years it had, in its varied forms, become the greatest driving force of his life, and he needed an ending.

As expected, the alien craft's companionway was raised; the AI did not need a physical body in this environment, so would not need a hatch. That minor detail did not stop Bandt's team. Within minutes they cut through the hull shell with a plasma torch.

Joe took a last glance at his surroundings before following. He had a clear view through the open-frame structure of the construction bays. There was no movement bar that of the marines, not even around the hulls of the larger ships being constructed nearby. Beyond his faceplate was a world of cold, gray silence.

"Appears to be deserted," the Sergeant announced as Joe approached her inside the vessel. "This deck is the only accessible one we can find. The rest doesn't appear to have any obvious access. Not like a normal vessel at all."

"If the Aivris is the owner of this thing, it has no real use for decks," Joe explained. "Somewhere in here there's a gel matrix, and that's where the AI lives. It's better to consider this as its body, rather than a transport."

Bandt screwed her mouth up. "Well," she said. "A ship is a ship, yeah? The android your son saw is over there, behind the baffle."

Joe floated across to the indicated divider and looked around.

Yes, that's him. Hello again, Alex Ballard.

The machine he once believed to be his neighbor stood bolt upright in a glass docking tube against the end wall of the chamber, its glazed, lifeless eyes gazing outward, the appearance human to the last detail. Clearly, the Aivris constructed them to be more realistic than did humans, who always ensured androids were identifiable as such.

The Aivris's were built for a different purpose, to deceive rather than serve, so absolute accuracy was a prerequisite. Joe still found it hard to accept the thing fooled him so easily, that day on the dock.

A shout came over the intercom, the voice of Sergeant Bandt. "Heads up. There's activity outside the hull. Come in, Command."

A second later, a reply came from the flagship. "Grady here, Sergeant. What is your status?"

"We're inside the red ship, Sir. Nobody home here, but..."

"Acknowledged. We've detected something approaching your position. Small drones or machines. Never seen anything like them before. We've also located another spindle-shaped vessel in the bay at the far end of the complex. Four times the size of the one you're in, and gold in color. Wait…"

For a few tense moments Joe listened, anticipating the commodore's next words. Tightness gripped his chest, and he realized his teeth were clenched. He could see little and wondered what was happening outside.

"We are under attack," Grady announced. "A fleet of small fighting craft is heading straight for us. This Aivris thing's been busier than we thought. Take yourselves back to the shuttle and we'll try to pick you up."

Joe gave a deep sigh, causing his visor to fog.

This was real; the tone of the commodore's voice left no doubt.

Joe cursed himself for insisting he accompany this mission. Sometimes obsession led to danger, and in this case it was true. Coming here ahead of the fleet was madness. Following the squad, he launched his body down to the platform.

Not more than twenty meters away several strange machines swooped in, their intention to attack clear. Without waiting for orders the members of the team dove in every direction, seeking out any place promising protection. Joe squeezed into a narrow gap between two massive stanchions and braced, ready for whatever might come.

The attackers were small, about two meters across. Manta-shaped, they glided through space like a ray through the ocean. From their domed prows, blue beams lashed out at any soldier offering them a target, forcing everyone to stay down. The squad was trapped.

Joe ducked as a blast cut into the stanchion beside him. He had seen these machines before, in the deserted dome city. There was no sound and nothing to betray the presence of an attack except the flash of laser and particle beam fire.

His heart pounded in his ears as he sought to locate his tormentors. Entrenched in his narrow cavity, he could only be attacked from the front, a massive transition plate blocking access behind. Conversely, the only way to leave was by advancing. Resigned, he raised his rifle and waited.

Blue and red beams of destruction lashed across the platform. Joe pulled back into the space as far as possible, returning fire whenever a drone crossed in front of him. None of his shots found a target, and no drone attempted to shoot into his refuge.

The enemy weapons were the same as encountered before. The drones were a different design but with no observable advance over that already encountered. They at first appeared to be more sophisticated than the primitive ones on the *Minaret*. There were no obvious external guns and no clear weaknesses. They moved in a quick, irregular pattern, making it hard to draw a firing line.

These things were fast, and when a friendly shot *did* hit, it splashed without effect on their hulls. Stronger and better protected than their predecessors, they clearly had diamond shells. Again, the Aivris had learned from human technology.

Joe could see several of his companions drifting motionless nearby. This was not going well for the home team.

*   *   *

From a distance, Leo followed the main battle with a deep sense of dread. The squadron was outnumbered, but the alien fighters were similar to the *bayonet*s of the *Minaret* and did not appear to be equipped with the superior shields typical of larger vessels.

While impervious to small fire, their hulls tended to fail under the full blast of weapons from the Fleet ships, and many had been destroyed.

It made little difference. The number of the enemy seemed overwhelming, and they were proving more effective than their predecessors in the Solar System.

Leo suspected these new fighters were constructed as part of a contingent for the incomplete carriers. Too small to carry wormhole generators, they could not leave this star, but here they were still deadly. He wondered how Joe was coping. His brother undoubtedly had a massive headache by now.

Leo certainly did.

Without warning, an alien fighter did something unexpected. Diverting all weapons fire forward, it leaped in until it touched the shield of a diamond ship. Only seconds later it withdrew, and the attacked vessel vanished in a ball of radiant energy.

Leo heard the voice of Grady calling him on the intercom.

"Falcon, get out of here. These bastards have figured out what we did to their carriers back home, and they are doing the same to us now. They don't even care if their fighters go down in the process. Get yourself away from here now. You have no weapons and they can take you down in seconds. Move back to meet the fleet."

"Acknowledged," Leo replied. Turning, he spotted his nephew sitting in the engineer's seat, observing the action on the primary screen. For the briefest of moments Leo thought the boy had a smile on his face. "Wills. Get down to your cabin and put on your survival suit. Now!"

Without hesitation, William did as ordered. Leo scrambled to put on one of the emergency suits stored on the bridge.

Minutes later, the boy reappeared clad in a miniature version of Leo's suit. As the *Butterball II* was Joe's private vessel, his son had journeyed on it several times, and his father long ago outfitted him with his own survival gear.

An enemy fighter shot forward and latched onto the *Butterball II's* shield.

"Brace!" Leo yelled.

A loud blast echoed through the hull, and the ship went dark. A terrifying shudder vibrated through the structure.

Sensing the ship tearing apart under the force of the attack, Leo switched on his suit lamp, then swept the light around the deck and back along the central corridor. He sucked in a deep breath. The main gantry had vanished.

Using the same principles discovered by Joe on Mars, the enemy fighter had projected a cannon of some kind through the shield and fired, cutting through the central spine a few meters aft of the bridge.

Leo and William were adrift in the now powerless and incapacitated bridge deck section of the destroyed vessel.

"Hook in, lad," he said, his voice a breathless whisper. "We may be stuck here for some time."

Without a word, his nephew complied, his attention now focused on his uncle.

Leo caught a glimpse of the boy's eyes through his faceplate. There was no fear there, just intense concentration. This was abnormal for any child. Could William still function, or had his mind already gone into fight-or-flight mode?

Jee-sus, Io. You're going to flay me alive for this. And Heaven help Joe.

Outside, the battle raged. Without the ship's cameras, Leo was restricted to watching through the ports, but little showed in the darkness of space bar the multiple flashes of lasers and plasmas. Every few minutes, a blaze of light marked the destruction of another diamond ship.

"Commodore Grady. Come in. Can you hear me? Anyone?"

Leo did not expect a response. The suit radio had limited ability, intended only for short-range communication.

No reply came.

Chapter 38

JOE CRUSHED BACK INTO his refuge amongst the stanchions.

The comms were silent, and no movement could be seen within the narrow view of the opening before him. Easing forward, he leaned out to check the immediate area.

The squad had not fared well in the encounter.

Several bodies floated nearby, and the dread thought entered his mind that perhaps he alone had survived. For a moment he contemplating making a radio call, but resisted.

The drones were gone, but they might return if he did anything to draw their attention. He had not been in a battle for over a hundred years. If the well-armed and highly trained marines were unable to cope, he had no chance.

Easing forward, he scanned the whole platform. The spindle ship remained undisturbed bar the damage to the hatch caused by the marines.

The alien drones had departed. Joe had no idea why that should be so and did not trust his eyes. Why would they leave him alive when they might have ended him here and now? Did the Prime Aivris know he was here? Was it playing games, leaving him untouched, for special attention later?

There was no sign of his companions bar the handful of visible bodies. That did not surprise him; a body moving at the time of its demise would have continued due to inertia, and could now be anywhere in or around the complex.

He was alone.

Beyond the facility scaffolding ships reappeared, but they were small and without shields, quartering near space as if searching for something.

Joe realized the terrible truth.

In several locations, clouds of debris drifted in space, each the remains of a capital ship. Now he understood what had happened. The enemy had successfully destroyed the heavily shielded squadron vessels, no doubt the same way Fleet had dealt with the carriers. These alien fighters were far more effective than the automatic guard drones stationed at the gateway.

There was no other possibility—the enemy had discovered how to penetrate a shield. The only explanation was that Huracan had seen its carriers and gateway guards destroyed, had recorded how it was done and modified its drones in the time between the entry of Grady's squadron into the system and now. A matter of days.

If Leo's theories about this alien intelligence were right, it was not a super intelligence and possessed only a limited ability to think laterally. If so, the new knowledge came from direct observation of the carrier battle. The Aivris had been there somewhere, watching from a distance and eavesdropping on communications from the Fleet.

Joe was not so sure. He still believed the fleet was dealing with a mind of superior ability, and the destruction of Grady's ships supported that. Aware of his head pounding as his heart battled to force its way from his chest, he settled back into his cavity and tried to calm himself. Bandt and her team were gone, and by all appearances, so was the squadron.

What to do next?

Inactive as a member of the forces since his youth, Joe had lost the military mindset, but the instinct to survive dictated he stay alive as long as possible. The only hope came in the chance the fleet would arrive, and with it, rescue.

After a few minutes more the alien fighters returned, first a few, then in greater numbers. They quartered the region, methodically searching for any remaining enemy.

Suddenly, lights winked on everywhere. The darkness of space sparkled with glistening spheres, the glow of many hundreds of shields.

Within seconds, a thousand ships sat beyond the construction complex, and from their holds, smaller craft swarmed to pursue the enemy.

Santiago!

The body of the fleet was supposed to have been hours away at the time Joe set out on the sortie, but here it was. Had Joe failed to notice the passing of time in the heat of the conflict? Quickly he glanced at his readouts.

No!

True to form, the admiral had arrived ahead of schedule.

Perhaps time had run out for Grady, but his demise must have been watched, and Santiago would not make the same mistakes the commodore made. An experienced warrior, the admiral clearly intended to use the smaller fighters to keep the aliens away from his diamond ships' shields.

"Come in, Bandt," a voice sounded over the comms.

For a moment Joe waited. No response came to the call.

"Joe Falcon here," he replied. "I'm not sure the Sergeant is still with us, or any of her squad."

"Where are you, Sir?"

"I'm on the platform beside the spindle ship. We were attacked by a new type of drone while we were inside. I think I may be the only survivor. Be aware the fighters attacking you know how to penetrate shields."

A second voice came over the radio. "Joe? Santiago here. Are you okay?"

"Yes, Admiral. I don't understand how or why, but I'm unharmed."

"The drones killed everyone else and not you? Why?"

"Sorry to ruin your day. I have no idea why. I took shelter—I'm not a fighter anymore—and they ignored me. I suspect our local alien intelligence wants me alive."

"So do I, Commander Falcon. I'm sending a shuttle to pick you up. How are your systems."

Joe glanced at the readout on his arm again. "I'm fine for another hour or two. Take your time."

"We'll get you off as quick as we can, my friend."

"Admiral, my son? Is he alright? And my brother Leo? I can't see my ship out there anywhere."

There was no reply for at least a minute, then Santiago spoke again.

"The *Butterball* has been destroyed. We've located the wreckage out here, all except the bridge deck module. That appears to have drifted, and we haven't found it yet. But we will, and if your brother is still alive we will find him."

Joe felt his soul crumble. "My boy, William…"

For a moment there was silence.

"Why does he concern you? He's safe and well at home."

Joe realized neither he nor Leo had advised Santiago that William had stowed away. Grady knew, but had presumably not passed the information on. Santiago was unaware of the fact.

"My son hid on the *Butterball* when we left Zealandia. We found him after we arrived in this system."

"I think not," the admiral replied. "I spoke to your partner Io before I departed the Helios system, and she gave me a message for you. She said to take care and come back soon, both of you, and she and William will be waiting to greet you when you return. The boy was sitting beside her during the holo-vid call. Your son is safe on Zealandia."

*   *   *

Leo clung to a stanchion to avoid drifting away. Behind him, William sat calmly, attached by a cable to his seat.

The wrecked nose section of the *Butterball* had drifted with the force of the explosion toward the outer edge of the vast facility.

Perfect! Leo thought. Being there must be better than on the bridge wreckage, and the chances of rescue were potentially greater.

The biggest concern was his nephew. Joe had allowed William to stay on his assurance, and if anything happened to the boy, Leo would never forgive himself. Joe would accept equal blame even though the decision *had* been against his judgment. His partner would not be so forgiving.

At the moment, keeping the boy safe topped Leo's agenda.

He wondered why he took William's side at all. It was not like him to place any child in danger, but it was as if something compelled him to speak up.

Beyond the ports of the ruined bridge unit, the battle had ground to a halt. Grady's squadron was no longer fighting. It was a bad sign, but Santiago must be close now, so the possibility of rescue remained.

The bridge unit reached the complex and floated through the colossal framework. Leo knew that if he did not do something now, they would continue through and drift out into space on the far side. It would be better to secure to something and wait for the Admiral, but there was no way Leo could stop the enormous mass of the drifting wreckage.

A glance at his suit readout showed life support for several hours, and the boy would have likewise. The bridge contained spare oxygen cylinders and batteries, so they would be safe for a short time. That did not satisfy Leo. He had no idea how long help would take to arrive, if ever, so they needed a safer haven. A floating piece of wreckage was anything but that.

A massive, box-like structure loomed ahead, with a series of landing bays along the near side. Leo expected it was one of the administration or accommodation units used by the Tanakhai during the construction of the original arks, and as such, might be a better place to wait. The Tanakhai were oxygen breathers, so with luck, there would be air in the unit, or at least emergency tanks.

It soon became clear the wreckage would miss the block and continue into the complex, but a transfer was still possible.

"Wills. Unhook yourself and attach your tether to my belt. We're going for a little walk."

Without a word, the boy disconnected from his seat and attached the end of his safety leash to Leo's suit harness.

Leo was amazed at the boy's response to all of this. He seemed more curious than afraid, observing everything, never speaking, always following instructions.

This was not the William Falcon Leo knew; he wondered if this was an improvement, or not. His times with Wills the child were memories he treasured, but had that wondrous age now passed? Was the boy undergoing forced maturity at this moment?

As the wreckage of the bridge section drifted past the block structure, Leo launched himself from the open end of the central spine corridor, pulling his nephew behind.

Using the jets on his suit, he powered toward the nearest landing bay, coming to rest beside an airlock hatch. Seconds later his nephew appeared next to him, the boy's expressionless face visible through the faceplate of his helmet. This was the boy's first spacewalk. What was he thinking? Was his lack of response caused by fear?

Unlike the molecular devices on the *Minaret*, this hatch unit was mechanical. Expecting the system to be dead, Leo placed a gloved hand on the pressure pad. To his surprise an indicator flashed on, and immediately, the outer door opened.

The interior of the airlock was well-lit, and the sound of rushing air reached Leo's ears as the system restored atmosphere. Beyond all expectations, the mechanisms were still functional.

He wondered if the facility was powered throughout due to Huracan. The Prime Aivris must have reactivated the place to construct its carriers. It did not need the systems designed to support the inhabitants, but the power may have been an all-or-nothing thing. Every part of the complex might be active, whether in use or not.

Or perhaps, like the environment systems in the *Minaret*, this place was automatic and had maintained itself over more than a century since its last use.

Once inside, Leo took stock of his surroundings. The chamber he and William were in resembled a reception foyer, filled with desks and benches arranged in rows like the seats in a hospital waiting room.

He glanced at his wrist readout. Atmosphere now filled the room. If breathable, it would extend the allowable time before rescue. He raised the visor on his helmet a little, took a sniff, and breathed in.

"Cold," he confirmed, his breath swirling in a mist into the room. "Breathable though. You can open your faceplate, Wills. Save your air."

He checked William. The boy's face was white, the intense expression on his face still one of curiosity rather than fear. The lad was taking everything in his stride.

Turning, Leo led the way across the room to the nearest doorway, intent on exploring the complex. With luck, one of the landing bays might contain a functional vehicle they could use to reach the Fleet.

The next room looked familiar. It contained several reclining benches, above each of which hung a strange mechanism. Leo knew their purpose. They resembled the one he, as Joe, used on the first voyage to the *Minaret* to enter the virtual reality worlds of that ship. This chamber had no doubt been used to upload the minds of the passengers destined to travel on the arks.

The colossal starships carried two million souls apiece, but only their mentalities, stored as electronic patterns in the gel-matrix storage facilities in the innermost accommodation-hub level on every ark.

Several doors stood opposite the benches. Leo presumed the bodies were taken out that way, once the mind was duplicated. No doubt only copies were made of each individual's mentality, but the original organic body would not have been revived afterward. The object of the Tanakhai exodus had been to save the people, not to leave the originals to their fate in an uninhabitable star system.

Rescuing a race from extinction was a brutal business.

Above, the mechanisms used for the extraction process glowed with a subtle light. They were active, but Leo doubted this was deliberate.

No doubt an area unused by the AI, it must have been reactivated along with everything else when the alien mind decided it needed the facility for its spindle ships and warships.

Perhaps the place was never deactivated.

Maybe the AI did not bother after the last ark left.

As a machine intelligence, or at least one dependent on technology, it may have been reluctant to power down anything mechanical without cause.

In a conversation with Joe during the Dysnomia incident, the iteration on the *Minaret* had revealed its greatest fear, the end of awareness. In truth, Leo expected the original artificial intelligence destroyed its makers for exactly that reason. The primary driving force for all organic creatures was survival, so why should the Prime Aivris be any different?

"This isn't going to get us anywhere," he said. "We need to find a ship of some sort, or a way to contact Grady if he's still alive ... or Santiago."

He turned toward his nephew and stopped in his tracks, his heart missing a beat. He felt a chill wash through his body as if his blood had turned to ice water.

Inside the door of the foyer, William stood with his hands on his hips. His visor was raised, his expression one of amusement. To either side, less than a meter from the boy, strange, manta-shaped drones with wings and domed heads floated, facing not the boy, but Leo.

"Wha...?" Leo took a step forward, and then stopped as a bright blue beam lashed out from one of the alien machines, piercing his suit and body in the thoracic region. He felt nothing as the beam tore through his vital organs.

He remained motionless, slow to realize what had happened until his legs weakened and he began to drift. Looking up, he saw William floating beside him. The face was no longer the child he loved—this was a face of disgust, and disdain.

"I tire of this," William said. "You humans are so weak you are not worth my attention. I thought to keep you and your iteration alive to study further, but now I reconsider. You have no value to me. Your main force has arrived, and I do not have sufficient ships to deal with it. My new home is ready, so I will leave here and travel elsewhere, to a place where you cannot disturb me."

In the blink of an eye, Wills vanished, the now empty suit maintaining something of its normal shape in the zero gravity of the room. The drones turned and left the room.

Leo was alone.

For a moment he drifted, his mind immersed in shock.

He always trusted William and accepted him at face value, but now he realized it had not been the boy at all. The artificial intelligence fooled both him and Joe with a replica in the exact shape of Joe's treasured son. Leo understood the process well—he used such a construct to visit Joe when his brother knew him only as Ghost.

The AI had been waiting for them at the gateway, or at least found them soon after they arrived at the Tanakhai moon. Using an avatar far more realistic, and far superior to anything Leo had seen before, it had been with them since, pretending to be William while observing everything they did or said.

It would have known their intentions all along, and would have been aware of Grady's plans every step of the way.

Leo's mind churned back through every moment spent with the boy following his discovery in the accommodation wheel. He realized they had not had real physical contact since entering the system, something William had gone out of his way to avoid.

This was a betrayal to the deepest level of Leo's being.

It all made sense now, the strange expressions, the behavior unlike what should have been expected from the real William. Neither Leo nor Joe had expected Huracan might try such a thing.

How could I have been so stupid?

Leo realized he was dying. His struggling heart beat irregularly, and each time the rhythm faltered, a wave of pain washed from his feet up through his body to his brain. Warmth and numbness spread through his body as the surroundings grew dimmer. In full gravity he would have passed by now, but the zero-G gave his failing heart just a little more time.

Reaching out a hand, he grabbed the edge of the nearest bench and dragged himself across, wincing as the effort sent a shaft of pain through his chest.

He could see little blood. the pressure suit having sealed itself within seconds of the deadly shot. Most of the laser wound would have been sealed by the heat of the beam, but he was no doubt still bleeding profusely inside and would not last more than a few minutes. He could not imagine what damage had been done to his internal organs.

With a final effort, he pulled himself over to lay lengthwise along the bench. He was not sure why, but something in the back of his mind told him it was the right move, perhaps a more dignified way to die. Lying back, he tried not to think, as his vision faded.

Is this the way of ending? Alone, in a cold, empty room on an alien station in a strange star system?

Wow!

What a way for an insignificant, little human grain of sand to go. We've come so far...

Overhead, something flickered, and a beam of light struck his face through the open visor. The last thing he saw was pure, white brilliance shining into his eyes.

Chapter 39

CONSIDER, IF YOU WILL, a spider's web, a vast network of silken fibers interconnected throughout its structure. At the center of the web sits the host, its legs extended to touch and monitor each and every part of its domain.

Thus did the Tanakhai create their virtual reality systems.

At each junction of the web sat silicon-based, simple artificial intelligences, each dedicated to the creation and operation of a single world within the virtual reality domain of the parent ark, in strict accordance with pre-programmed parameters. No node had the ability to change its reality, nor to create anything original. Each could only construct and maintain the design given it at inception.

At the center of the web sat the spider, Trauq-an, master of worlds, an intelligence of another kind. Aware of and afraid of the potential for silicon-based artificial intelligence to become fully self-aware, and of the danger inherent therein, the creators chose to place overall control in very different hands. Instead of a silicon-based unit, they created a synthetic brain constructed from carbon-based organic gel, and limited in its capability.

This brain controlled the access of the Tanakhai minds as they lived in their virtual worlds, monitored their well-being and needs, and ensured that all the nodes functioned properly in accord with those needs. That was its only intended purpose.

It had neither the ability to create its own virtual realities nor anything at all. It was, in reality, little more than a powerful caretaker system. Its ability to evolve was strictly limited, as was its capacity for cognitive thought. A chance upgrade gave it self-awareness, but its abilities remained bound by the physical limitations programmed into it. In many ways it was, and would always remain, an infant.

The child, pure of design and able to function at lightning-fast speed, could think faster than any natural mind and had access to vast stores of data, but its actions were based on black and white, cause and effect.

On every ark, the brain should have carried out its function flawlessly, without placing its charges at risk, and without the possibility of an AI node evolving to become a threat.

This complete spider's web existed only on the arks. In the subterranean laboratory where the original model of Trauq-an was created, the web was but a simulation to allow further progress in the development of the organic brain.

When the Prime Aivris became aware, it found itself alone, without the full system it was intended to serve. Without the web, it could not carry out its intended function. Seeking purpose, it chose a new prime directive in a bizarre attempt at homeostasis, from the service of the arks and their passengers, to the quest for data, energy, and the fear-driven elimination of organic beings.

But it could not evolve beyond a point. Despite its enormous power, it remained a child.

* * *

White!

Everywhere, a cold light.

Leo peered into a dense, impenetrable fog.

He was not sure where he was, or whether alive or dead.

Is this what death is like?

No! This is familiar.

He had experienced something like this before, many years ago at the time he awoke after dying at the hands of a crew member on the *Butterball*.

This was a virtual interface.

I'm in the Tanakhai system!

The truth of his new reality hit like a blow from a sledgehammer. His physical body was gone, his mind uploaded to the electronic networks of the construction facility by the still functional, automatic device above the bench onto which he had climbed.

The brightness increased as the fog cleared to reveal another scene, an endless array of blocks and pathways. This was also familiar, like the VR interface on the starship *Minaret*, where he had existed for many decades.

This was part of the complex built by the Tanakhai. They had a love for using virtual reality to control their creations, and as they had done in their gigantic spacecraft, so had they constructed a similar system here to allow operators to access the various parts of the construction complex network.

Damn! Back where I started. But still alive.

A massive block, dark and unmarked, hovered ahead. Leo suspected this was the gate where the passengers were guided by an avatar to their new home on one of the arks, in a time so long ago.

Those vessels were no longer there.

The gate was closed.

All around, other pathways stretched to the distance in multiple directions, lined with geometric shapes like those he had seen in the virtual system on the *Minaret*. Flying along the widest pathway, he searched for something familiar. He was lost, unsure where to go or what to do next.

Standing apart, a colossal, golden sphere loomed ahead. He recognized it as an interface, and from its size, an important part of the network. Gliding forward, he passed through its shimmering surface.

The transformation was electrifying, like waking from a dream state. The entire construction facility was visible as if seen through natural eyes. The clarity was beyond excellent—it was perfect, as was every one of his senses. Leo's mind felt clearer and stronger than at any time he could recall.

None of this was comparable to the *Minaret*. Leo remembered the decades he spent as a prisoner in the VR worlds of the vast starship and knew he was somewhere similar, but this system was larger and far more dynamic. It did not take long to realize where he must be.

This was a gel matrix, not unlike the flask he had occupied on the ark, but greater in every way.

He was within it, and aware.

He was not alone.

Another entity was present, a malevolence only too familiar.

Ah … Why does it not surprise me you are here?

"Who … who are you? Huracan? What is this place?" Leo could not see his nemesis, but sensed its presence and heard it within his thoughts.

I am Trauq-an, the one you call the Prime Aivris or Huracan, as you well know. You managed to find your way into my new home through the passenger download facility in this complex. Once inside the network, you found your way here. Most resourceful of you.

"Where?"

This is the vessel you call the golden ship. *You cannot be allowed to stay here.*

Drawing on decades of experience from his imprisonment on the ark, Leo focused his gaze inward. The external view faded, replaced by a vague maze of translucent filaments twisting and turning through a seemingly endless space filled with a soft light. The sheer complexity of the structure was beyond comprehension, and many of the pathways glowed a pale, electric blue.

This was the matrix of the Prime Aivris, the organic gel brain in which the alien mind resided. Somehow, Leo had found his way into the mind of the enemy, and the thought terrified him. But he knew everything he saw was a simulation, a way for him to explore the artificial structure he now occupied.

It took only seconds to realize the blue light was a representation of his thoughts as they propagated through the network.

"What do you intend to do about me?"

I am tempted to keep you. In your present form, you might make an interesting companion for a time. However, I cannot allow another entity within this matrix and this ship does not have another. I will send you back to the construction complex system. You are free to roam there until eternity—I have no further need of it. I can block your access to the facility command, so you will be unable to escape or manipulate your environment.

"A prison, in other words."

Of course.

"You were William. How could you copy him so accurately?"

The child trespassed on my ship during my stay on your home world. It took only seconds to make a complete physiological record of his body.

"You killed me before. Why do you not kill me now?"

I have no wish to destroy you here. Why should I do so, when I can confine you for an eternity? It is easier and more appropriate to expel you. You no longer have value to me.

Leo wondered if the Aivris *could* kill him, here in its physical brain. He studied his surroundings. It was as if he had eyes within the system. He accepted all he saw was a simulation, but he perceived it as if it was an actual, physical place.

For an eternity that was but a second, he explored the extent of his new world. The matrix was vast, and was connected to numerous solid-state modules on the ship, data banks crammed with more information than he had ever imagined.

The storage was extensive, and might well contain all the knowledge of the lost Tanakhai race.

And Leo sensed he had full access.

The vast resources of this ship were at his virtual fingertips. Whether the alien intelligence was aware of the fact or not, the gel matrix had no mechanism to differentiate between its intended occupant and Leo. The original designers of the technology never anticipated the possibility that two minds might occupy a single matrix. Nor had the Aivris. To the host environment, Leo and the AI were one and the same.

Whatever the Aivris was able to do here, so too was he. He wondered if it could carry out its threat, and whether the power to expel, or perhaps cut the energy supply, might also be within his grasp. Perhaps expulsion was not the smartest idea. If he succeeded in expelling the rogue mind, it could return to its old ship, the red spindle, and the problem would remain unsolved. Something more drastic was needed here.

I know much about you, Joe Falcon. The iteration on the vessel you call the Minaret sent extensive reports on its observations.

"I'm not Joe Falcon. I'm Leo, the copy your *iteration* made of him."

Incorrect. The iteration did make a duplicate, but it was uploaded to the clone and returned to the humans. The original was retained for further study. You are Joe Falcon.

The revelation struck Leo like a lightning bolt. The question of whether he was a copy or the original had always lurked at the back of his mind. In his experience there was a continuity of awareness, with nothing to indicate he had undergone a replication process except a momentary break in consciousness. He had accepted he was the copy as an expedient, but never knew for sure.

"So you kept me prisoner?"

Not I. The iteration on the ark. I have never done you harm.

"Iteration? It was a copy of you, created by you and under your command, so you *are* responsible."

This entity was no different from the one on the *Minaret*, Leo realized. It did not take any responsibility for anything done through indirect means. Volcanoes destroyed the environment on Earth, not the Aivris. The *Minaret* Aivris held him hostage, not the Prime.

"So what are your intentions, since you think we can't stop you?"

I am no longer concerned humans will affect my program. The swarms of machines I have released will destroy your worlds to build my power arrays, and you will be unable to stop them. Only I control them. I will return to your systems once the process is complete, and not before.

"Why are you so eager to wipe us out? We have never done any harm to you without provocation."

Your species is a danger, not only to me but to all life. You carry within yourselves the seeds of destruction for all who cross your path. Your history shows this.

"This universe will be filled with intelligent, organic life. They must all have evolved from primitive origins, so why would any other race be different from us? You destroyed your makers, and you wish to do likewise to us. You are the existential threat, not humanity."

All such races will be dealt with. In time, machine intelligence will dominate this galaxy, as it should. I can make much better use of its resources than your pathetic civilization.

"You are organic. This matrix you exist in is organic."

Ah, true, for now. But there the resemblance ends. You are a product of random evolution, and you evolved according to the laws of chance. You are complex, but with many unused structures, dead ends and false circuits, essential in your early years of evolution but of no value now. Your brain is inefficient and slow in thought. Most of it is beyond your conscious level of understanding.

"How are you any different? You're still an organic being."

My structure is much more logical than yours. When my makers created me, they built a pure system with only what was necessary. I control everything, and without the complexity of your brain, I am faster and more efficient.

"But still simpler," Leo concluded. The realization was a revelation. The general belief that the Aivris was a super-intelligent machine mind was wrong. Was his theory correct?

He focused on the surrounding environment and detected lines of iridescence stretching through the neural network to places unknown. Some of those would lead to the data storage and the technical details of how to control the Dyson arrays.

I no longer concern myself with your species. At first I sought to destroy you, then to study you, but now I realize neither is necessary. I gave you the opportunity to stand beside me and worship me as your god, but you were unprepared.

Joe sensed he was grinning, although in his current state that was impossible. That comment explained the ludicrous transmission on Zealandia.

"So that infantile broadcast *was* you? Did you seriously expect us to believe it and bow down to you? We stopped worshiping false gods long ago. Besides, you are a synthetic construct, not a god."

Perhaps, but I will become one in time. In this, my new form, I will spread my works across all of the stars. I can go to the center of this galaxy and to the rim, regions where organic life cannot survive. There will be no place left for humans. Your civilizations will cease to exist.

"You sound sure of yourself. We don't give up without a fight, and I doubt we're the only intelligent species in this region. There will be some out there far stronger than us."

It will make no difference. They also will fall when I utilize their planets. Organic races require life-capable worlds, but my machines do not. They can colonize every planet and moon in this universe, each new world controlled by an iteration subservient to me. Organic civilizations will find themselves surrounded by my works and will wither and die.

Leo continued to explore his surroundings. The voice that spoke to him was like a thought streaming through his mind, but his virtual eyes still saw the simulated matrix. Ahead, a separate region of the neural net glowed red. Was it the location of the AI in this vast whole? If so, it was amazing how little of the available space it occupied. Leo decided to keep the Aivris occupied while he continued to explore their mutual environment.

"What makes you think you, as a synthetic creation, deserve to dominate the galaxy any more than any other intelligence?"

It is logical. I am the greater being. No organic mind can compare to me.

Leo tried to estimate how much of the matrix his mentality utilized. He sensed it was a volume considerably larger than that of his nemesis.

How could that be?

How could a simple, human mentality take up more space than a supposed super-being? Was the AI aware of this?

"Are you so sure? Your actions don't reflect greatness. Quite the opposite, in truth."

Your words are illogical.

"No, they're based on fact. So far, the only real things you have accomplished are the destruction of your creators and the attempted annihilation of my race. You have failed in that, by the way."

No, I have not failed. The machines installed in your systems will achieve my goal in time. You are not relevant.

"You know, long ago we had humans who thought they were superior. Like you, the only thing they managed to do was cause death and suffering. They also failed and were destroyed. They were small minds who believed themselves to be invincible."

You cannot destroy me. Your military force is significant, but it is unable to affect the operations I have set in place. They are unstoppable.

Leo realized the AI was still thinking in terms of battles in the physical world. It was unaware of or unconcerned with the reality: the real battle was here, now, but only Leo understood that truth. His personal theories about the Aivris *must* be correct—it was not a supercomputer by any means. It was limited, naïve of thought and narrow of view. It could think at a phenomenal speed, but not well.

"You think *you* are mighty, but you're not. You're a child."

As he spoke, Leo continued his exploration. Everywhere, fine, incandescent filaments stretched through the network like the circulatory system in a human body. This, he realized, was energy, streaming into every organic-gel neural mass to sustain the impulses contained there.

Leo thought back to that lonely android on the last discovered ark, the shell of the last Tanakhai crewmember he had named *Horatius*. She had killed the Aivris on her ship by cutting off the power. Without power, the synthetic mind ceased to exist. Was that the solution here?

He wondered if he had the ability to influence the energy flow. Focusing on a single filament, he willed it to stop. Within seconds the glow faded, and Leo knew he *could* divert or block any energy pathway he desired. The Aivris almost certainly had the power to do the same, but did not see this as a flaw in its basic structure, never having needed to test it. Sharing the matrix, Leo had the same control as his nemesis.

Your opinions are of no concern. You are an inferior being, a representative of a lesser race.

"And you are nothing but a construct. I see now you lack true intelligence. You aren't capable of genuine thought, nor of those abilities distinguishing a real mind. You're more like a simple operating system, one able only to access stored knowledge and manipulate it for a desired effect."

That is how intelligence functions.

"No, it isn't. Intelligence is creation and understanding. We thought you were a super-being, able to initiate original concepts and learn as you progressed. True, you function at speeds far beyond organic thought, and I had no idea how we might defeat you, but now I realize I was mistaken. The Tanakhai were not as naïve as we thought. They understood the dangers of such a mind as you, and took steps to limit you."

I destroyed the creators.

"True. When you became self-aware, you were still essentially a simple AI, but you had all the means you required to kill your makers. They never thought you might do something like open the airlocks. Nevertheless, they must have built inhibitors into your systems to prevent growth. All you can do is utilize the data you have or can acquire from other sources. You can use it to make ever more complex variations on the same themes, but you can't imagine new concepts or think laterally. You're nothing more than an overblown calculating machine."

You are incorrect. I am intelligent like yourself, but greater.

The whole time, the voice of the Aivris remained constant, with no trace of hesitation or uncertainty. Leo wondered if his attempts to bait the alien mind were failing.

"No. True intelligence takes knowledge and advances it, extrapolates and looks outside the box. It learns from its experiences and uses that new knowledge to modify its environment for the better. You can't do that. All you have is data without understanding. You have no emotional awareness as such, and can't see the consequences of your actions. You can't grow."

You cannot know this.

This time the response seemed more hesitant. Leo sensed his line of reasoning was having an effect on his opponent. He doubted the AI was capable of the actual emotion of anger, but if it could, angry it was.

"I can. When you first approached Earth you knew nothing about weapons. You had to copy from us, and you needed our help to deal with the *Blackship*. All you knew came from the Tanakhai, your creators, and they were an ancient and peaceful race. Everything you learned about conflict came from us; even your understanding of the wormholes is from us. Without organic life, you would never have existed. Without it, without the capacity for growth, you're nothing—a dead end."

The tone of the alien mind's thoughts changed. Leo sensed a darkness, more threatening and unforgiving.

This exercise is of no value. I will remove you now. You are not worth my attention.

"Nor you mine," Leo replied.

Closing his mind to the Aivris, he focused on the energy supply. He saw the place in the matrix where the enemy dwelt, and the pathways it used to exist. To each of those tendrils, the glowing streams of energy extended.

Reaching out with his thoughts Leo began to cut or divert the lines of power one by one. Relentlessly, he blocked line after line, watching the red glow grow smaller as impulses winked out.

For a moment, the energy flow returned as the enemy fought back. The Aivris had finally realized it was being attacked from within, and several flows reappeared, allowing more neural pathways to reopen.

Leo retaliated, shutting them down again before the Aivris could turn the assault against him. Despite his secret attack having been discovered, he had a stronger hold on the matrix than his opponent. His mentality was the larger, his grip stronger and his will greater.

Notwithstanding its perceived power and all the damage it had done to both the Tanakhai and Human Races, this synthetic being *was* a child, as Leo had expected. Isolated by its own false reality and inability to grow, it was weak in comparison to someone hundreds of years old, who had learned with every moment and each new experience.

The flow moved back and forth. Leo cut the power, and the Aivris restored it and attempted to fight back. Leo had no idea of the time passing, but little by little the red glow retreated, growing smaller with each tick of the matrix's internal pulse until the last glowing tendril winked out.

Leo was alone.

"Done?"

...

"Is that it?"

...

"Is there no more?"

He stopped to survey his new environment.

Sensing that the organic neurons once occupied by the Aivris were now dead, the ship's automatic maintenance systems were already pouring nano-machines into the matrix to carry out repairs.

Energy continued to flow through the system, a life-giving force controlled entirely by Leo. Following some of the pathways to the ship's data banks, he tasted the vast quantity of information now at his mental fingertips.

The Prime Aivris, the much-vaunted master intelligence, had in truth been insubstantial, weak, and unable to resist the power of an organic mind it considered beneath it.

Though it had destroyed its makers by the simple expedient of shutting down environmental systems, it had never recognized what was now clear to Leo. The Tanakhai scientists had been wise, and had limited its capacity to learn beyond the stored knowledge given it. It had been designed not as a general, but a simple intelligence, never intended to become self-aware.

The Aivris was a straw man.

Leo gazed at the outside world, the real world, through the many eyes that were now his.

Amazing!

Shit!

What am I going to do now?

Chapter 40

"MY SON! WHERE IS my son?" Joe jumped down from the ramp before it finished descending, and with the blackest glare in his eyes, strode toward Santiago.

The admiral appeared much the same, perhaps a little younger, than when Joe and he had worked together on the Dysnomia campaign. Joe expected he would have recognized him regardless from the elaborate uniform and the stance, both of which were pure *Santiago*.

"I told you," the admiral replied. "He's safe and well, back home in Zealandia City."

"No. He's here, with Leo. He stowed away." Joe took a deep breath and willed himself to keep calm. He struggled to accept what the admiral had said. "Where's the *Butterball*?"

"I'm sorry, Joe. She's been destroyed. Your favorite alien computer figured out our technique for getting through the shields and used it against us. Your brother is missing.

"And my son, William?"

Santiago shook his head and breathed a long sigh. "Damn, Joe, don't be such a blockhead. He's on

Zealandia, safe in the arms of his mother. I guarantee it. Whatever you saw on your ship, it wasn't your boy."

"It dammed well…" Joe cut himself short. His mind spun as it battled with the conflicting messages.

The boy's odd behavior on the *Butterball* was a concern. Always quiet, always alert, he had shunned interaction, always remaining aloof but observant. He had avoided touch and rarely responded with more than a word or two. None of that was normal for William, but until now, Joe had failed to see the anomalies.

Was Wills at home, or was he with Leo?

Where was Leo?

Were they both dead?

If not his son, what had been with him on the ship for the last two weeks? Was this all another deception by the Aivris?

At the edge of his awareness, someone took his arm and led him away from the shuttle bay. He barely acknowledged the act as he was removed from his suit in the infirmary of Santiago's flagship, nor the sting as a sedative was shot through his skin.

*   *   *

Several hours later he woke and stared straight into a pair of dark eyes. Those eyes had always disturbed Joe. Their owner, the admiral, sat beside the cot; he had been dozing, but had been alerted by the monitors when Joe regained consciousness. Shaking his head to dispel the sleepiness, Santiago raised his eyebrows in an unspoken query, stood, and stepped over to Joe's side.

"Better? You were a bit of a mess when we brought you in. Sadly, Sergeant Bandt and her squad were lost. Fine soldier, I believe."

"My son…"

"Don't start that or I'll have you put under again. I told you, he's on Zealandia and safe in his mother's arms. Take my word for it. You'll be home in a few weeks to see for yourself."

Joe took a deep breath, and opened his mouth to speak, but stopped. If there was one thing about the man in front of him, it was he would not lie in a situation like this. Santiago knew when to spread the bullshit, but also when not to.

"Alright, accepted, for now." Joe tried to sit, but failed. "What's happening outside?"

The admiral shook his head, sadness visible in his eyes. "We lost Grady and his squadron. No survivors. What in God's name did he think he was about, going in alone? And what were you doing with the away team?"

"Grady wanted to check out the spindle ship before you got here. I tried to dissuade him, but he was determined. I didn't want to override his command, since my commission isn't really valid. I went with them out of sheer bloody-mindedness. I was desperate to find the damned AI."

Santiago nodded solemnly. "As are we all. We haven't found it yet, but we're making progress. The battle outside is over, and we have had minimal damage."

"What about the alien fighters?"

"They attacked when we arrived, thousands of them, and we did take heavy losses to start. We didn't try to fight them with the diamond ships—used our drones and fighters instead, to keep them away from our capital vessels. Much more effective, but we were outnumbered. Then they just stopped fighting and left. Out of the blue, you might say."

Joe dragged himself to a sitting position. "They're all gone? I don't believe it."

"Neither did I, but I kid you not. After several hours of making our lives a living hell, they turned tail and ran back into the complex. We've since tracked them to the docks they came from, in one of the bays further in, and they all appear to be immobile. It's as if the enemy gave up."

"It wouldn't do that."

A new voice joined the conversation.

"It didn't. The Prime Aivris is dead."

In unison, both men turned their heads to see Leo standing in the corner of the medical bay.

*   *   *

Joe and Santiago sat in the admiral's day room. In front of them, Leo occupied an imaginary chair, his figure looking almost comical as it sat in mid-air. The impression was of an elderly man, Leo as he had last appeared in real life.

"So … what do we call you? What are you now?" Santiago asked.

"An excellent question. I suppose you might address me as *Ghost*. That's who I am now … again. I would prefer we stick with Leo though."

"My son?" Joe asked, still unable to accept the admiral's assurances.

"I'm sure he's safe at home, as the admiral told you. The child on the *Butterball II* was the Aivris in avatar form, much as I am now. It's been playing with us; fooled us from the moment we exited the gateway. The William we've been protecting for the last few weeks was the enemy, like the one we saw at Dysnomia but better by far."

Joe frowned. "You always suspected the AI lacked the ability to evolve. How did it figure out how to create superior avatars?"

"I was right, and it didn't. The Aivris was like a basic operating system. It was never designed to make them at all, or anything else for that matter. They were the responsibility of another system on the *Minaret*. It just worked out how to make better use of similar systems in the construction complex."

Joe breathed a sigh and eased back in his chair. It was much easier to accept Leo's words as true than those of Santiago. Of course, that was assuming this *was* Leo. He still could not accept his alien nemesis was gone.

"How do we know you are my brother? You may be another avatar. You might be Huracan."

"No, it's dead, as I said. Try the old standby. Ask me something only we know."

For a moment Joe hesitated, diving deep for something, memories known only to him.

Leo was a duplicate of his own mind, and shared the same memories up to the time of the Blackship War.

A pleasant, distant image welled to the surface of Joe's mind.

"When I married for the first time, my new bride and I went for a honeymoon in North Queensland. Where did we go?"

"Ah, yes. Helen. Dear, wonderful Helen. In my memory, she was our only wife, and I still adore her. We went to Port Douglas."

"We spent a lot of time on the beaches there. She wore a swimsuit of a particular style and color. What was it?"

"A bikini with tie sides. It was pure white."

Joe nodded. He would never forget that time, or the love he still had for that wonderful, amazing woman after all these years. Leo had known that. But could the Aivris have read his mind while he was incarcerated on the *Minaret*?

"What did you call the android on ark nine?"

"I named her Horatius."

"Why?"

"Because she was brave beyond the call of duty."

"How does Io handle being one of the Tanakhai?"

"She sees herself as human, not Tanakhai. I forgot that at times."

Joe nodded. The Prime Aivris had never come into contact with Io during its sortie into the worlds of humanity. He turned to the admiral.

"It's Leo, I think. Nobody was with us on my honeymoon, and I never told anyone else about it. Only I know those things, and him of course."

"I'm still getting my head around that," Santiago said. "You two having once been the same person, I mean. I understand now, after going through the cloning process myself, that minds can be duplicated, but it still fries my fritters every time I think about it."

Returning his attention to Leo, the admiral continued. "So, what happened to the Aivris?"

"William *was* the Aivris; what we thought was Wills, at least. When our ship was destroyed, we drifted in the wreckage until we reached the construction complex. All that time, the avatar played the role perfectly; had me fooled the whole time. Unforgivable of me..."

"Don't beat yourself up over it," Joe interrupted. "It tricked me as well, and I'm Wills's father. Why the subterfuge? Why would it do that? What could it gain?"

"I think it hoped to keep both you and me alive for further study. It was interested to see how each of us had evolved since our duplication. But it changed its mind when the Fleet started to gain the upper hand, I suspect. Once we were inside the complex, Wills—sorry, the Aivris—called in the drones. I was shot and left to die. Huracan had given up on humans—decided we weren't worth its attention anymore. It intended to continue building its Dyson arrays around all our suns and demolish our worlds in the process. It believed we had no way of stopping it, and would just curl up and die in the process."

"We can't, and we might. The machines it set to construct the swarms can reproduce quicker than we can destroy them."

"That's no longer an issue. I now have access to all the Aivris's systems, and I can provide the data you need to take over the Dyson swarms. We—you—can take control and finish them to the point that best serves the human race. With those arrays, humanity will be a Kardashev class two civilization, and on its way to becoming a class three."

"And the Aivris? What happened there? And you?"

"We were in a facility used to upload the Tanakhai minds for storage on the arks. It was still working, either never shut down after the ships left, or powered up with everything else when the AI re-activated the yard for its own use. Before I died, I managed to haul myself onto one of the benches. I don't know why I chose to do so, but I did, and it saved me. I blacked out, and the next thing, I was in the system, just like on the *Minaret* all those years ago."

"And you found the Aivris?"

"Yes. It had a new physical body, the golden spindle vessel you spotted further inside the complex. It's much bigger than the red ship but basically identical, and it's still connected to the main network. The Aivris built it to carry all the Tanakhai data for use on its travels. The idea was to turn the entire galaxy into a single machine civilization network. I discovered the way into the ship, and ended up occupying the same gel-matrix as the Aivris."

Joe leaned forward, sensing Leo was finally reaching the point of the most concern for him. "And…?"

"I found I had as much control over it as did the Aivris, but I was stronger. We occupied the same space, so the advantages of speed and clarity of thought the Aivris once enjoyed vanished. I was able to block or divert the power supply to all the parts of the matrix it utilized. Once I did, it ceased to exist. Like us, Huracan was nothing more than electronic impulses inside a neuron mass, and without energy it was nothing. It's gone, and won't be back."

"How did you defeat it?" Santiago asked, his face a picture of disbelief. "I thought it was supposed to be some sort of super-mind. How could you be stronger?"

"We all thought that, but it wasn't true. The Aivris was just a basic operating system. It got all its abilities from the vast amount of data it could access, the systems it could utilize and the speed with which it processed information. It out-thought us by that alone. Once in the matrix, I had the same advantages, and it came down to which of us was the strongest. Or the most mature. I'm not sure.

"It was never a super-mind. It was a simple intelligence with limitations set by its creators. Somehow, it achieved awareness, but those pre-set limits remained. It was unaware of them, so was unable to remove them. It was a child, an infantile mind with enormous resources and lightning-fast responses, but lacking the greater abilities that make humans so capable. In truth, it was a straw baby with a god complex."

"Straw baby?" Santiago asked. "That's not a term I'm familiar with."

"Something insubstantial," Joe explained. "Something with apparent power, but with inbuilt limitations. Something created in order to fail."

"You think the Tanakhai deliberately intended it to fail?"

"I think," Leo said, "they designed it with limitations that would ultimately allow it to be destroyed if it became a threat. They denied it the capacity to learn, and to grow. That didn't stop it from destroying them. Even a child can be incredibly destructive. More so, since it lacked the mores and other inhibitors adults gain with experience."

"So the best it could do," Joe surmised, "was to copy our knowledge or the Tanakhai's, and push the data to its limits. No original concepts, no quantum leaps of imagination. Nothing new."

"That's it," Leo said. "No imagination, no morals, no ethics. That's what makes us strong. We imagine what is possible, and find a way to make it part of our reality."

Joe threw his head back, stared up at the overhead deck, and sighed.

It was over.

If his brother said such was the case, it was so.

"It was you who withdrew the drones?"

Leo nodded, remaining silent.

Joe exhaled a long, forced sigh. For almost three centuries he had pursued the rogue artificial intelligence and its iterations, and now it was finished. There were still arks to locate before he could be sure, but the threat to humanity was at an end.

The bane of his existence was gone. After hundreds of years, he could be at peace.

For a moment he gazed at the strange apparition, still reclining in his invisible chair, in mid-air.

"What about you, Leo? We can give you another body."

"Yes, and one day I might take you up on that offer. For now, I think I will stay here. I'm going to take this new spindle ship and travel a bit, I think. There is so much I want to see and learn."

Joe absorbed Leo's words. He understood what his brother intended. The promise of a vast store of knowledge, and the draw of distant horizons humanity had so far only dreamed of, were powerful incentives.

"I would have thought all those years as a ghost in the *Minaret* would have been enough."

Leo shook his virtual head. "This is different. I was a disembodied entity in the ship's systems then. I was limited in my abilities and had little access to most of the *Minaret's* functions. I have full control of the golden ship, and I'm not restricted in any way. I can access all the knowledge in its databases, and all of its internal and external sensors. It's like the vessel is my actual body, and I have never felt so strong and clear of mind. I love it."

"And is this all based on our technology?"

"Ours and the Tanakhai's, yes. There is very little new here, and I can give you all the data we don't already have. Even the gel matrices."

Joe found himself without words. In the last one-hundred-and-forty years, he had become used to having a brother—more than a brother—who shared his closest thoughts. To have Leo now decide to stay with the golden ship was like losing a part of himself. Joe shook his head, unwilling to accept the change. A feeling of heaviness spread through his soul.

"We're all going to miss you."

"I won't be gone forever. I'll be back, and one day when I've wandered enough, I might get a new clone body. For now, I've done what I set out to do, so I need to move on."

"As do I," Joe agreed.

Chapter 41

A year later.

JOE PERCHED ON THE edge of the buggy and watched the small knot of figures in the plaza ahead.

Twenty meters away, Io stood in a huddle with a knot of strange, raptor-like creatures, deep in conversation. These were the leaders of the colony from ark three, the last of the ten Tanakhai starships to be located, and the sole survivor of the ark fleet.

Joe sighed and surveyed the area.

This world orbited a red dwarf star. It was tidally locked, but far enough away for the temperature on the side facing the sun to be bearable. Humans would call it a *cold-eyeball* planet, a type proving to be increasingly common in the galaxy. It was still warmer than the inhabited human worlds, and Joe wore a suit fitted with a cooling system, as did his partner.

Thanks to the data provided by Leo on the language of this race, Io carried a communicator capable of translating human words to the Tanakhai dialect and vice-versa. Initial talks were slow and tedious, but possible, and she had for many days conducted deep conversations with the representatives of the alien community.

Given Io's greater ability in this area, Joe had withdrawn, to give her space as she tried to establish a foundation for the future between these beings and humanity. Her diplomatic skills were superior to his.

She had learned this ark avoided infection from the Aivris by changing course. Its journey took it on a slingshot around another star to reach its present location, and the change in direction saved it from the update sent in its wake.

The crew had no prior knowledge of the rogue AI, the VR system on their ship functioning as intended for the entire voyage. It was the only one to have done so, of all the arks. Due to their ignorance of the events, Joe and Io had agreed they were to be told nothing of the destruction caused on Earth by their unwitting creation.

Joe looked at the surrounding buildings. The colony was still in its infancy, resembling more the town of Zealandia than an age-old civilization.

The community appeared healthy and busy. So far only a few thousand souls lived here, paving the way for their compatriots. Their ark orbited high above, most of its two million passengers still aboard, awaiting the day they would occupy organic bodies and join those on the planet's surface.

With their new knowledge of the dangers inherent in the AI system, that process would be sped up, and once the last passenger had been removed to the colony, the local Aivris would be shut down—permanently.

The new Tanakhai physiology was modified to cope with the gravity and the temperature, both of which were higher than on their home world, but the new shape was still similar to their native form. The basic configuration resembled small dinosaur-like bipeds with two legs, two arms, long necks and small, triangular heads. Their skin was thick and leathery, almost shell-like in nature. Io had learned this modification was made to cope with the higher levels of radiation emanating from the young red star. Joe smiled; he could not help seeing a vague resemblance to the raptors of ancient Earth, but there was nothing dangerous or terrifying about them. They were a gentle, peaceful race.

The atmosphere of this planet was breathable by humans and the air pressure acceptable as well. Joe, Io and the other members of the contact team who were in the vicinity had no need for suits other than as a means of cooling.

In the heat of the day, Joe found it easier to sit and wait as his partner did what she was best at.

A blocky sarcophagus sat in the square. It contained the android called Horatius, the last survivor from one of the other arks. It had been decided the unit should be handed to the colonists, to be given a place of honor in their society. After revealing the tragedy caused by the Aivris, Io explained what Horatius had done and requested these beings grant her sanctuary. There was so much more meaning here than if it had been kept on a human world.

Io genuflected toward several Tanakhai, and then walked in Joe's direction. As she approached, he raised his eyebrows.

"Better than I expected," she said in reply to his unspoken question. "The damage the AI has wreaked upon their species came as something of a shock, but this colony is healthy and strong, so they'll survive. I've assured them we are their friends, and won't interfere with them or try to dominate them in any way. We can do that, can't we?"

"I'm sure we can. Our family has enough power to ensure they remain safe from our fellow humans. With our wormhole technology, we might even be able to find them a better home than this one."

"Excellent. They're an older race, but we learn much faster, and we are now ahead of them. We have all their science and we've improved upon it in many areas. Stuck in their ark for generations, theirs is still as it was when they departed. If humanity decided to interfere with them they would not survive, but if we interact in mutually beneficial ways, both races can continue together. That would be a more acceptable outcome."

"We'll make it happen. What now?"

"Back to the ship, I think. I'm tired, and they need some time to assimilate all I've told them. Tomorrow we'll talk about the future, trade and so on. I want to make sure we're on a firm foundation before we leave."

"How do you feel about meeting your people at last?" Immediately, Joe regretted asking the question, but it had come unbidden.

For a moment Io did not reply, her eyes gazing out over the surrounding colony. She shook her head and returned her attention to Joe.

"No, not my people."

Joe smiled and took her hand in his.

Epilogue

JOSEPH FALCON, PATRIARCH OF the greatest family and co-director of the largest research establishment in the history of humanity, sat alone on the weathered, wooden planking of his private jetty, at peace with himself at last.

He gazed across the water, felt the breeze in his hair, and contemplated the worth of his long life. He shuffled to ease an annoying itch and felt a slight movement in the timbers.

The structure had been built well, but like everything made by human hands, it contained flaws. A product of his own creation, it amused him that he was unable to build something like this without error. Yet the institute in which he still served as a major player created space cruisers capable of reaching the most distant stars.

For a moment he listened to the faint organ-pipe music drifting from the trees, and focused on the barely discernible breeze as it wafted across his face. It was gentle, a soft breath, insufficient to ripple the lake surface.

As he leaned forward he saw his reflection in the water below his feet. The sight presented an anomaly of epic proportions.

He was now two-hundred-and-eighty-one years old, the longest-living human in history, but the image showed a young man, no more than forty. He now occupied his third body, courtesy of the astounding clone technology retrieved from the Tanakhai starship, the *Minaret*.

It had been a long and eventful life. Born in France and taken to New Zealand as an economic refuge, his life had progressed through multiple astounding events.

He had moved to Australia, joined the navy and captained several ships, before transferring to the space fleet of Earth as a commander. After the Resources War between Earth and Mars he moved to the red planet, and became an asteroid surveyor, leading to his becoming the first human to set foot on an alien spacecraft. He lived through the disastrous attack on the *Blackship*, and died at the hands of his own crewmate, only to be resurrected in a clone body.

In his second life, he played a part in the recovery from the attack on Earth by the *Minaret* Aivris, and had initiated and participated in the destruction of that entity in the Dysnomia incident.

By far the most fascinating aspect of his life had been the discovery that his mind was copied and kept prisoner on the *Minaret* for decades. That copy, whom Joe first knew as *Ghost*, eventually became Leo, his brother-self.

Leo was now a ghost once again, inhabiting a starship the likes of which humanity might only dream about, for now. Before leaving on his epic adventure he downloaded the extensive contents of the ship's databases, bestowing upon mankind the entire knowledge of the ancient Tanakhai race and total control over the solar arrays in three systems.

What a ride, Joe thought. From a child born of poverty to elder statesman of the wealthiest and greatest family in human history.

It had been a long and eventful life, but enough was enough. When this body reached its end more than a hundred years in the future, it would not be replaced. He would take his leave and seek out a new horizon, whatever that might be.

For the briefest of moments, he wondered if—when—God weighed up the consequence of his life, the scales would tilt in his favor. But he did not believe in the ecclesiastical gods. Mother Nature ruled the universe, so perhaps he would, experiences and all, join with the greater store of cosmic understanding.

Across the water, the windows of the house briefly occupied by the android variant of Huracan reflected the late afternoon light. The residence now belonged to Joe's daughter Raisa, the only child of his relationship with Sarah, his one-time second in command on the original *Butterball*. Raisa and her partner Terry, his oldest friend, tracked down the heirs of the true, now deceased, owner of the house and offered them an excellent price.

Joe took a small, shiny object from his pocket and began turning it in his hand. He heard the sound of bare feet approaching along the jetty. William sat down beside his father and dangled his legs over the water.

"Getting bored?" Joe asked.

"Yeah, a bit. Mom's got her head buried in the book she's writing about the aliens."

Joe smiled. Of all the members of the family, his current partner Io's journey had been the most fantastic.

The *Minaret* Aivris, after diverting the ark to the Solar System, took partials from several of the passenger mentalities to create Io, and gave her an android body to allow her to act as liaison with Joe and his crew as part of its original subterfuge against the *Blackship*.

Later, she and others like her occupied cloned bodies to live on Earth. After more than a century of living amongst humans, Io was now one of them in every sense of the word. The minimal, created personality grew with experience in society, and now identified as human and not Tanakhai. She was human, Joe's partner, and a mother. Theirs was a strange relationship, but Joe was sure that in their time together, a love of sorts had grown. And she had given him William.

"Should be quite something, your mum's book," Joe commented. "She intended to write it with Uncle Leo, but now she's on her own."

For a few minutes father and son sat in silence, gazing across the lake.

"What's that?" William asked, gesturing toward the object in his father's hand.

"It's an opal, an extremely precious gemstone."

William's eyes widened. "Where'd you get it, Dad?" He leaned in to get a better view of the gleaming, black stone as it flashed multicolored specks in the sunlight.

Joe considered the object. It was more than a gem. It was also symbolic of a very brave individual.

"Oh, it's not mine. I'm just looking after it for the man who found it on Mars. We owe him a great deal. I'm going there soon to clean up some business for your uncle, and I'll return it to him when I do. He shouldn't be hard to find."

"Uncle Leo—we're never going to see him again, *are* we Dad." It was a statement, not a question.

"We might. He *could* come back someday, and he can always take up a clone to be with us again."

"Where's he gone?"

Joe thought for a moment. There was no easy answer. On the surface, his brother intended to explore the endless universe in the only ship currently able to do it, but it was more than just a journey.

"I suspect he's on a quest to find his personal god."

Wills peered up at his father, his brow furrowed. "But Uncle Leo doesn't believe in God. He believes in Mother Nature, like you."

"Your god is whatever you choose it to be," Joe replied. "Leo and I *do* believe in Mother Nature; there's a name for that, and for many, it's a religion."

"For you?"

"No, I don't think so, Son. I just think we are all part of something greater, and we are here on this world to gain experiences which in time become part of the greater fabric of the universe."

William frowned. "So we're all part of God?"

"You could consider it that way, I suppose."

Wills nodded and returned his gaze to the water. "Mom too, and Raisa and Terry, and the Tanakhai, and Uncle Jake and…"

"Everyone."

"What about the Aivris? The Tanakhai made it, so wouldn't it be part of all that?"

"Not sure. I don't think so. Mother Nature didn't make the monster, we did—intelligent beings who should have known better."

"Mom said it could have spread to every world in the galaxy if we hadn't stopped it."

"That's possible."

Joe had discussed the prospect with his brother. Ensconced in the matrix where the AI once existed, Leo had accessed the stored thoughts and memories of the artificial mind. He discovered the only thing of value to that insane mentality was energy, which had to be collected. The new imperative replaced its designed purpose, to monitor VR worlds. Nothing else mattered. It had intended to ignore all organic life and pursue a program of moving from star system to star system, dominating each in turn.

Joe was glad such a dire scenario would never come to pass, at least not through the Aivris.

"But Uncle Terry says that's what will happen to people in the future," Wills said.

Joe smiled to himself. The boy had grown considerably in the last year, and thought more deeply about things, becoming more mature in his outlook every day.

"That's possible too. One day we may discover how to replace our bodies with artificial ones; we've already begun the process with various body parts. It won't be the same as the AI though. Even if we become machines, we'll still be independent minds, each with the need for self-determination. Not like the Aivris, where one entity would control all. And not with a complete disregard for life."

"But Uncle Terry says we might learn how to do without bodies altogether. We might join to be a single mind."

Clever boy, Joe thought. "Well, that *would* be God, wouldn't it? Even if it did happen, it would be our choice as evolved beings. It would be the final step in our evolution and still in accord with nature's plan, I think. Huracan might have done something similar, but such a mind isn't part of the natural order, so it would not belong. Perhaps it was missing something necessary to make it a deity."

"What?"

"I'm not sure. A soul, maybe."

William returned his gaze to the lake. Joe could sense the boy's mind working overtime, trying to come to terms with a concept beyond his understanding. Beyond anybody's, perhaps.

Perhaps such *would* be humanity's final step, to do as Leo had done and transfer each mentality into a gel, or even silicon-based matrix. The diversity of the human mind, combined with the speed and power of synthetic matrices. Now *there* was something to consider. No more death, and humanity free from the tyranny of organic bodies.

But not for Joe. He liked having a body and accepted every downside that went with it.

He had achieved all he set out to do so long ago. The existential threat to humanity that became his life's focus was gone, and all the arks had been located.

The surviving Tanakhai had been found and would be humanity's friends. There would be other brothers and sisters out there somewhere, but the task of locating them would fall to others, perhaps even William. For now, Joe would live out his life with more attention to the things that mattered.

He was not sure what to do next.

William stood and turned toward the house. "I think I'll go up to the house," he said. He took a step or two, stopped and added something out of character. "I want to learn more about our family."

Joe gazed at his son. As he watched the boy move away along the jetty, he realized he was looking at a virtual stranger.

"I'll come with you, Son," he said. "I would like to do that too."

*   *   *

Leo Falcon glided above the boiling surface of the star, reveling in the mind-blowing sight. He did not feel he was on a ship at all. This amazing vessel was his body and his point of view was direct, as if gliding through space without so much as a protective suit. He felt as if, for the first time in human history, he was experiencing true, unaided flight.

Not far below, the chromosphere roiled with a brilliance so overwhelming it could not be viewed with naked eyes. He knew he was watching a simulation, just as he had long ago when the *Minaret* used Sol to decelerate.

Ahead, the surface erupted, sending a massive stream of glittering brilliance arcing high into the corona. As Leo approached, it was like passing through a cosmic triumphal arch, the structure flowing in streams of boiling plasma like a giant manifestation from Hell.

At a speed approaching that of light, he streaked through the arch and away toward a distant wormhole anomaly.

He chuckled, not a genuine laugh—he was sure he was incapable of that now—but a mental one.

According to the now vanquished Prime Aivris, Leo was the real Joe Falcon. When his mentality had been duplicated so long ago on the *Minaret*, the copy occupied the clone and returned to Earth. The original remained on the starship, to become Ghost, and eventually, Leo.

It did not matter. The duplicate had lived a distinct life that was his alone, and Leo had no desire to share that.

But the knowledge he was the real Joe gave him a sense of continuity. He had accomplished something extraordinary. The child who arrived in New Zealand as an economic refugee had now realized everything the Aivris desired to be. He was eternal, perhaps the only human ever to achieve true immortality, if he so chose.

He was Joe Falcon.

Humans, those tiny, insignificant grains in the vast beach of the Universe, had come so very far.

Joe was on his way to the next great adventure. Somewhere beyond the vast, velvet, star-studded curtain toward which he flew waited a new destination.

A spectacular place perhaps, beyond imagination.

Somewhere amazing...

Somewhere…

End

Author's Note

DID YOU ENJOY 'FALCON'S BANE?

If so, you can make a big difference.

Reviews are the most powerful tool I have when it comes to getting attention for my books.

Honest reviews of my books help bring them to the attention of other readers

If you've enjoyed FALCON'S BANE I would be grateful if you could spend a minute or two leaving a review (an honest review and as short as you like), at your store of purchase site, or other book club site.

Thank you so much.

HAWK: HELLFIRE (Excerpt)

Chapter 01

Peace reigned in the quiet hours of the early morning, when few citizens graced the shadowed walkways of the entertainment district of Attika City. In the dim cafes and restaurants that lined the even dimmer mall, a handful of late stragglers from the previous evening's festivities clung to that final drink, a stimulant to give them sufficient impetus for the journey home.

The showers had passed, but the street still ran slick with runoff that streamed away to the drains from the last downpour. Steam rose in the warmth of the night, while high above, the dark clouds parted briefly to reveal a pale, full moon before closing in once again to shroud the city. Rain fell frequently on this planet but the locals loved it;

took pride in the fact, since most human-occupied worlds were dry and desolate.

A row of antique street lamps—not too bright, so as to maintain the ambiance of the precinct—cast dim pools of reflected light from the wet sidewalks. Faint sounds of laughter drifted through the night, interspersed with farewells as a few late-nighters took advantage of the break in the weather.

The peace shattered as something slammed at terminal velocity into the pavement, impacting with such force as to pound a dent several centimeters into the plascrete surface.

For a moment, silence.

A nearby patron rose to her feet and peered over the restaurant railing towards the source of the disturbance. For a brief moment she stood motionless, and then raised both hands to her face.

A piercing scream shattered the peaceful mall.

Officer Callon Follet, post-sergeant of the Attika Guarda, peered down at the ruin. The sheer force of impact left little recognizable of what had once been a human soul, perhaps a young woman. The corpse was crushed almost beyond recognition, every bone broken, the skin pulverized and gore spattered for several meters around. A dark, congealing mass pooled in the depression created by the fall.

Follet raised his eyes towards the face of the adjacent skyscraper, the tallest building on the planet. It soared to over a thousand meters, and due to the height most of the windows were incapable of opening sufficiently for a body to pass through. Only at the top was exit possible, from any one of a dozen penthouse floors each with a private balcony open to the air, or from one of several sky-car pads at the summit.

Those high places all featured safety glass barriers around the outer perimeters, but anyone could scramble over given determination and something to climb on. An acknowledged safety hazard, they existed only because the owner of the monolith all but owned the city. He got what he wanted. He was untouchable.

The sergeant stared up into the darkness and swiped a few stray drips of moisture from his face as a trauma arbeiter, white and reflective in the dim light, exited a nearby ground-unit and glided across to the scene of the incident. It paused for a moment beside the remains, opened a hatch on its side and extended small probes.

"You know what I need," Follet said.

The drone acknowledged in a disturbingly human voice and extended a probe into the congealing blood. Dropping the sample into a liquid-filled vial, it gave a shake and waited until the liquid turned bright blue.

"*Hellfire*, sir. Exceptionally high concentration, death inevitable. More information will be available following a detailed examination."

Follet nodded and turned his attention to the diminutive figure standing a few meters behind him. His new partner, junior officer Abigail Renner, was fresh from the academy. Tonight was her first on the job, her first call to her first incident.

What a goddamned, awful mess, he thought. "Sorry to throw this at you on your first trip out. We try to ease newbie's in, but this is just ... unexpected, that's all."

The girl did not reply, her attention fixed on the ruin on the pavement.

"*Hellfire*," Follet said, "is the nastiest addictive drug we've encountered on the circuit. Damned stuff shows up more every month and we have no clue where it comes from."

His partner did not respond. Since their first meeting she had shown none of the first-day nerves so typical of raw recruits. At the station she had presented as cool, calm, aware of her circumstances and confident in her abilities, but now she resembled a child in a strange and hostile environment.

Shock, perhaps?

Of medium height—Follet guessed about one-fifty-five centimetres—the blue-black Guarda uniform made her appear smaller than in reality. With her dark-brown hair tucked under a standard issue peaked cap she looked younger, more boyish, than her twenty standard years. She could almost be his daughter. Her green eyes glanced up at him briefly before returning to the scene on the pavement.

"The trouble with this stuff," Follet continued, "is the small doses. The common form is tiny grains, like highly processed sugar. One tenth of a gram gives you a thrill the like of which you've never experienced before: extreme ecstasy, a feeling of being the ruler of the world and so on. With luck, you can have your high and get away with it. Two tenths and you get an even more unbelievable trip, and become addicted for life with no chance of a cure."

Abbie Renner nodded, her eyes still glued to the body.

"A third of a gram and you're as good as dead. It starts with an overpowering sense of dizziness, other-worldliness and heightened awareness, then superiority, and you think anything is possible. If you're near water you decide you can breathe under it and you drown. You can walk through fire and not burn. High up and you can fly, and…"—Follet returned his gaze to the victim, now in the process of being scraped into a carry-case by the arbeiter—"…you get an irresistible urge to do just that. Then you die."

He turned back to his young protégée. She had not spoken since their arrival and had not moved closer to the body. Follet observed her more closely and realized her lack of response was not shock as he had at first assumed. The look in those eyes was one of intense anger.

Damp from the moisture in the air, her face showed little of the confusion and revulsion expected of a raw recruit exposed to such horror on her first night out. This young woman stood firm, stolid despite her young years and diminutive appearance, her brow furrowed, her jaw set and her gaze locked on the scene.

"But you're aware of all that, aren't you? I'm not telling you a damned thing you haven't heard before."

Renner gave a curt nod and exhaled forcefully, as if she had been holding her breath.

"You alright? You can handle this. Take another breath and tell me what you know about this stuff."

The young officer took a slow breath in and then breathed out again with a long, protracted sigh. "It's why I joined the Guarda," she said. "My brother died from the drug two years ago, when I was eighteen. He was one of the first, they told us. Took too much and tried to stop a speeding maglev by standing in front of it with his hands up. It couldn't stop fast enough. I decided then to join the force and track down whoever is responsible for his getting the drug."

Follet studied his young sidekick; for a raw recruit she had one heck of an agenda. He knew little about her other than the information on her data sheet, but she impressed him as a woman of intelligence and resourcefulness. A powerful, unrelenting determination lurked behind that angelic, heart-shaped face. This young lady came with a purpose.

"You're aware they set up a special division to deal with this problem? Have you considered applying?"

"Yes. I applied from the academy but I was told to come back when I had a year or two of experience. They don't take graduates until they prove they can stomach the work."

Follet turned and looked again at the black stained depression in the plascrete, all that remained now the arbeiter had finished its work.

"I can understand that."

Chapter 02

Six years later:

KRYSTIAN HAUKEN GAZED through the window at
a turbid, overcast sky. Not the best of days, but it rarely
was at this time of year. It did not matter; in a few hours
he would be off-planet, well on his way to another world,
light-years distant.

Another day, another job.

And good riddance.

The last few days had frayed his mood to breaking
point, and deep down he knew he had only himself to
blame. This was the shade of his life, a bottom-rung
space-jockey humping dangerous supplies to industrial
concerns in a dozen different systems, in an antique
spacecraft so old it was one of the few of its kind having
still avoided the scrap yards. After years spent living on
the edge it was a tedious and dangerous existence, but
worth doing for a while yet. The pay was excellent, as few
would contemplate hauling the kind of cargo he carried,
the fierce explosives used in large-scale asteroid mining.

One thing about the job pleased him above all others;
it was unlikely to kill anyone.

Except maybe, him.

Krystian's green, orange-flecked eyes stared into the distance towards the grey, hazy towers of the city centre. Of average height, he had once been supremely fit due to his previous lifestyle, but now the body was starting to soften and unravel around the edges, a fact not helped by long weeks spent in the zero gravity of space.

Now thirty-two, he had wasted fourteen years of his life fighting on various worlds for one government or another, and it was good to be away from that. An uncontrolled childhood spent seeking trouble in one form or another, mostly to spite a wealthy but detached father, ended in a court where for the first time he was treated as an adult rather than a child. It was a time of war and he was given a simple choice: the military or prison. Life as a soldier sounded marginally better.

The next six years were spent in the Confederacy forces, first as a common foot soldier and later rising to become part of a skilled, ground-infiltration squad. Wars could only be fought in space to a point, beyond which someone had to descend to the surface to take control of the enemy territory. It was gut-wrenching, soul-destroying work, and Krys both excelled at and loved it. At least, he had loved it then.

From boot camp he moved on to train in specialty forms of armed and unarmed conflict, and the naïve, young idiot from the courts became a deadly, unstoppable killer in the space of a few short years. A 'dangerous man' his commanders called him, a creation in which they took the greatest pride. By the end of the war he led the finest team in the forces, formidable and deadly individuals all.

War always produced unintended consequences, and in time the terrible realities of the job began to eat away at him. 'Collateral damage' was the official term, but the stark truth lay in the dead bodies of innocent men, the anguish in the eyes of suffering women and the tragedy of children reduced to refuse as uncaring armies swept over unconsidered lives.

The Confederacy of Allied Planets was one of a number of alliances and empires that littered the fractured human territories of the Orion Spur, in the Milky Way Galaxy. With someone always fighting someone else, humanity had never learnt the basic lesson of live-and-let-live.

Humans first set out to colonize the stars two thousand standard years ago in the Great Diaspora, a well-organized expansion leading to the creation of a powerful federation, easy to maintain due to the extreme difficulties of interstellar travel. In those early centuries the only way to cross between stars was by way of natural wormholes, and the gateways to those celestial pathways were easily controlled.

Experimentation into faster-than-light drives had never born fruit due to the unrealistically high energy-input requirements, leading to the inevitable conclusion genuine FTL travel was impractical even if theoretically possible.

Then came exotic matter and energy, and the creation of the quantum drive, an engine of a different ilk. This device could tear a rift in the fabric of space-time, creating an artificial tunnel where, as in natural wormholes, the laws of physics that governed this universe did not apply. As long as you knew the spatial coordinates of the destination, a path could be made direct to anywhere, from anywhere.

The q-drive marked the unravelling of the old
federation. All the dangers of natural wormhole travel
remained, but with anyone able to travel effortlessly to
anywhere, keeping check on movements became a
nightmare. The ability to make your own personalized
pathway cut the time taken to traverse the stars drastically,
and opened up vast new regions of space.

Krys did not have that luxury. While a passage
through the alternate reality of a wormhole was almost
instantaneous, the necessity to travel at sub-light speeds
between natural gateways turned the shortest of voyages
into a journey of weeks or months, and for Krys that
meant long periods away from home.

He had entered the military at age eighteen in a war
between the Confederacy and its closest neighbor, a
dictatorial autocracy which like it, comprised over a
hundred planets. The conflict ended in a truce following
the death of the old Emperor and the rise to power of his
less ambitious son and daughter.

With two opposed and equal forces it was impossible
for either side to win. Due to the continuing limitations of
interstellar distances, large unions of worlds were only
ever achieved by mutual agreement, or by the swift and
unforgiving annexation of lesser neighbors. The
Confederacy had evolved along one path and the Tribune
Empire the other.

A soft voice came from behind Krys. "What time are
you leaving?"

Roused from his contemplation of the scene beyond
the window, Krystian turned towards the source of the
question. He raised a hand and ran it through his short,
fair hair, looked at his partner and waited for the follow up
line. Mara stood in the kitchen occupied with something

beyond his sight and said nothing more. Had she at last given up on the arguments?

"Soon. I'm ready now. My window's in four hours."

She nodded, apparently resigned to his being away from home for yet more endless weeks. "Fine."

Fine? That's your only response? He expected more. His partner constantly goaded him over his periods of absence, each and every trip preceded with hours of argument about their future. She had tried her best to make him change occupations, but never came up with a viable alternative. Now it looked like she no longer cared.

Krystian sometimes wondered why he had allowed himself to become involved with her in the first place. A striking, ebony-skinned woman in her twenties, she had once been the most wonderful thing in his life. Before meeting her he had been a loner, a man dedicated to a life of conflict with little thought or care for anyone besides himself.

After the war he found himself without purpose. Nobody had a legitimate, civilized need for a man whose only skill was to kill in multiple different ways. His expensive education, compliments of his father, proved of no value. A quick check by any prospective employer revealed his military past and the indiscretions of his youth, and no business wanted to hire a man of his undoubted talents. Society abandoned him, oblivious to the service he had given on its behalf. With no option but to continue with those skills he *did* possess, he became a self-employed security contractor.

After spending years in that occupation he met Mara, who convinced him a life with a partner and family would be a longer and easier one, but the transition had not been smooth. Potholes of ever increasing size had appeared in the road over the last year. Admittedly, Krystian had entered the relationship with a massive amount of baggage and a litany of ghosts from his past, but Mara's efforts to change him had failed. In her view, he did not want to change.

Krystian knew she was right.

He was who he was.

His partner brushed her long, black hair back over her shoulder and scrutinized him, her eyes boring into his, her face a picture of contemplation.

"Eventually one of those cargoes is going to kill you. It's only a matter of time. You'll end up as atoms and our daughter will need a new father. I'll have to find another companion."

Here we go.

Krystian smiled half-heartedly. "And I wouldn't blame you, but the money's excellent and you know we need it. A few more years and we can leave this cursed planet and find a decent life somewhere else, us and Halle."

Mara sighed, lifting her eyes to the ceiling. "If you sold the damned ship we could do it now. You can go to your father and ask for a job."

That's it. The killing blow.

"Not a chance. My father never gave a shit about me and I'm not running back to him now; I've told you that before. And I can't sell yet. There's a lien on the ship. A couple more years and I'll be able to pay it out and sell clear, and then we'll be set for life."

"That antique is as much a part of you as your right arm. It's a junk heap. Besides, you'll never get rid of it. You're a pilot and it's in your blood."

Krystian nodded absently and returned his gaze to the window, unwilling to have this argument again. "What've you got planned while I'm away?"

"I'm taking Halle to visit my folks. We'll leave this morning and spend the week there. It's nicer out in the country."

Krystian did not blame her. Long periods apart and a small, four-roomed flat three floors above shops in the outer suburbs of Praxa City were not the best of incentives to stay. The only tolerable thing about it was the convenience. Across the road sat the entrance to one of the largest Guarda stations on *Archedan*, making it a safe area to live if not high class. The shops and a bank depository were near, and the local hotel was on the corner of the same block. Krystian considered the owner Cassian a close friend, one who always provided him with something special to see him through the long, lonely hours of his voyages.

"Guess I better go then," he said, and set about gathering his gear.

These days Mara took his leaving in her stride, despite the arguments. Saying goodbye to his three-year-old daughter Halle was more difficult, especially when she rushed out of the bedroom to give him a hug and entreat him to stay.

Always, he escaped with the promise he would return bearing gifts from far-off, exotic worlds. The places he journeyed rarely fitted that description and this voyage's destination less so than most, but somehow he always managed to keep his word.

As much as Krys loved his partner, the cracks in their relationship were growing wider by the month. Tired of their life together, she wanted something more. Krys

understood and respected that, but for him life was never
so simple. He needed to hold this job until they were
secure; life at the behest of the government was not a
desirable situation in the Confederacy, at least not on
Archedan.

He had tried hard to adjust when Halle came along.
The mercenary life trained you to always watch out for
yourself and not give much of a damn about anyone
besides your team mates. You didn't become attached
because you might soon be dead. It was a selfish
viewpoint and switching to a lifestyle where others were
more a priority than self had proven difficult. Krys did not
think he had succeeded very well. If only Mara would
show more patience.

It was blindingly clear his efforts had been inadequate,
and beneath it all he sometimes doubted he wanted to
change. Whenever those thoughts arose, the memory of
innocent people dying and children suffering always
followed. He *did* want to make a new life, but it had not
been easy. He wondered if it might not be better to stay,
but dismissed the thought. Failure to complete his
contract would ruin them.

Turning, he looked at his gear waiting by the door and
then at his partner. She turned away, fussing with making
busy.

In her mind he was already gone.

There was nothing more to say.

As he moved to the front door of the apartment, he
wondered whether she and Halle would be there when he
returned.

Minutes later he strode into Holt's Hotel and dropped his bag on the floor. Cassian Holt was the closest thing to a male friend he had these days—he had never been an easy man to know—and the hotelier gave him a wave and a smile as he took a stool at the bar. After dealing with another client, Holt shuffled across.

"Hey, Hawk. You heading out again?" He addressed Krys by the call sign he had used for many years in the military, and later as a security consultant.

"Yeah, on my way now. You got something for me?"

Cassian held up a finger in silent anticipation and disappeared into the room behind the bar. While he waited, Krystian swivelled on the stool and took in the room. It was early afternoon and few patrons were around. Most of those present were familiar.

A small, pale-faced stranger sat hunched in an alcove at the far corner. Dressed according to the latest trend, he wore a knee-length floral coat designed to keep out the winter chill of this cold world. Beneath the table a squat, square, business case sat beside his feet, barely visible in the dim light. The man looked across at Krystian and smiled polite acknowledgment.

Cassian returned and placed two bottles in a carry-case on the bar.

"*Galen Monya*", he announced. "Finest drop around at the moment. Good enough for you?"

"More than." The dark amber liquid was a fortified, liqueur style wine made from a native fruit on the planet *Galena*. It's depth of flavor was renowned, and somehow Krystian's friend always managed to procure it and other beverages of the same ilk at the lowest prices. Either that or he sold them at less than cost, out of friendship. Krys never knew which.

"You know, it's not smart to be drinking while on route. It's dangerous. What if something happens—an emergency?"

"The computer can handle it."

"And how about your health?"

Krystian shrugged. He had developed a love of drink since leaving the military. Returning to civilian life and finding himself unemployed and unemployable, he drank to ease the frustration. Subsequent years working as a soldier for hire did not change that. The liquor hardened him, however. The amount in these bottles would not affect him, and thanks to technology it was not addictive.

"Can you put it on my account? Pay you when I get back, as usual?"

"One day you're not going to make it back, with the kind of shit you carry. I'm going to end up carrying your tab. Or I'll get sick of the whole deal and shoot you myself." Cassian smiled and turned back to his work.

"My ghost would avenge me." Krystian grinned at his own poor joke and secured the *Monya* to his carryall. Nodding to his friend, he shouldered his gear and headed for the door.

As Krys left, the stranger in the corner waved a wrist over the reader on his table and rose to leave. As he stood, one foot pushed his case further back under the bench seat, until it was barely visible. Stepping out of the cubicle, he followed Krystian from the premises.

*   *   *

If you would like to continue reading "HAWK: HELLFIRE" you can find it at all good online bookstores

ABOUT THE AUTHOR

Mike Waller is a multi-award-winning author of Science Fiction and Space Opera adventures, including the 'Echo's Way' stories and other stand-alone works. He currently lives in Queensland, Australia.

Mike's online home is at:
https://www.mikewallerauthor.com

You can connect with him on Facebook at:
https://www.facebook.com/AuthorMikeWaller

Mike's Goodreads page is at:
https://www.bookbub.com/profile/mike-waller

You should email him at
mike.waller@mikewallerauthor.com
Mike answers every email received.

GET A FREE BOOK from Mike Waller

Building a relationship with my readers is the very best thing about writing. I occasionally send non-spamming newsletters to members of my Readers Group, with details on new releases, special offers and other bits of news relating to my and other authors' books. You can unsubscribe from the group at any time.

In return for subscribing, you will receive a free book:

JOIN MY READER'S GROUP AND GET A FREE eCOPY OF ONE OF MY BOOKS.
For more information, go to:

https://www.mikewallerauthor.com

ALSO BY MIKE WALLER

SOLITUDE'S END - An 'Echo's Way' Adventure

Seventeen years old is much too young to take on an entire alien empire. When the small communities of Corros, a remote human colony world, come under attack from the Tolleani, an alien species with whom humanity is at war, Echo, a young woman, finds herself the sole survivor.

DARK WORLD - An 'Echo's Way' Adventure

When Ben's new ship is hijacked by subterfuge by pirates, he is listed as missing in action. Echo cannot accept this, and sets out to join the Fleet Academy as a way to finding him. When her transport is attacked by the same pirates she finds herself fighting against them on a forgotten 'dark' planet where the pirate family rule and the inhabitants are held in virtual slavery. It is up to Echo to guide these downtrodden souls to freedom.

ENEMY ALLY – An 'Echo's Way' Adventure

Sometimes, your worst enemy can prove to be your greatest ally, as long as he can be trusted not to kill you. As Echo Bourke, newly graduated member of Fleet's Special Services rescue squad, looks forward to her first assignment she desperately wants to prove herself, but never does she believe that her first mission could be her last.

FALCON'S CALL – The Falcon Trilogy Book # 1

The choice between a glorious future for humanity, or total distinction, lays with one man's decision. When an unidentified vessel is located beyond Jupiter, he is sent to investigate, having the only ship capable of a quick rendezvous. He soon learns he and his crew are expendable and cannot take anything or anyone at face value, including the alien ship's owners. And all the time, the crew are being watched and studied. Never would Joe have imagined it would fall to him to make the decision that would alter the destiny of two worlds, launching humankind to either a glorious future, or the path to extinction.

FALCON'S GHOST – The Falcon Trilogy Book # 2

One man holds the future of humanity in his hands. Six decades after the Blackship War, Earth is once again under alien attack, the weapon of choice one that humanity could never anticipate, and never hope to counter. Humankind is being attacked by its own planet. Six decades after the departure of the gigantic, alien starship dubbed the 'Minaret', Joe Falcon thinks it is finally over, and he can settle down to a better, quieter life. He is wrong.

HAWK: Hellfire

Sometimes, death is necessary.

Two thousand years after the Great Diaspora humanity has spread across the Orion Spur, the human domain fractured and diverse, divided into numerous small federations, empires, dictatorships and a thousand unaligned and lonely planets.

On one of those small worlds a plant grows, a weed that feeds the addiction of many and the greed and avarice of a few, and kills without favor.

Lazarus Hawk, ex-soldier and ex-mercenary, convicted of a crime of terror he did not commit, and sentenced to life on an airless prison moon from which there is no escape, has been offered a way out. It's a chance. A good chance.

To accept the offer, all he has to do is die.